SWEET CAROLINE

LENNOX VALLEY CHRONICLES
BOOK 3

HANNAH BRIXTON

CONTENT WARNING

This work of fiction is intended for adults and describes mature situations that may be triggering or upsetting for certain readers.

Topics dealt with in **explicit** detail include: alcohol use, alcoholism/addiction (and the recovery/sobriety journey), grief, infidelity by an ex-partner, manipulative behavior by a secondary character, emotionally abusive behavior/bullying by a parent, physical injury (broken bones, blood), mental illness (depression/anxiety), classism, psychological trauma, internalized ableism, fire, and explicit language. Multiple scenes of explicit consensual sexual activity include toy play, cum play, anal play, squirting, oral sex during menstruation (without blood), a soft hand necklace (without choking/breath play), masturbation, sexual degradation, and bondage.

Topics dealt with in **moderate** detail include: vomit, panic attacks, medical/hospital content, and unexpected and traumatic parental death.

Topics dealt with in **minor** detail (including brief mentions and off-page events) include: motor vehicle accident, biphobia, war, societal racism, and interactions with law enforcement.

Please read at your own discretion.

For anyone who feels like screaming.
Fucking do it.
And do it fucking.

PROLOGUE
MILES

Ten months ago

Bent tones speed toward me and drone away, like some kind of fucked-up accordion. Blinding lights, angry voices, blaring horns—every jumbled sensation crescendos and whips past, like the Doppler effect or some shit.

Wait. I frown. *Isn't that a weather thing?*

With effort, I lift my head, blinking against flecks of cold that dot my heated cheeks.

It's snowing?

My feet seem to drag on the asphalt. Loose gravel skitters away from clumsy steps.

Fuck. Gotta piss.

I slop my attention to the left, blurred vision crawling to catch up with where I point my face. A grass median with a ditch. *Piss ditch.* Perfect.

Lights slice the dark to pieces as I lurch ditchward. *Pissditch-ward.* Even in my mind, the syllables slur.

Tires screech and swerve.

Someone shouts, "The fuck is wrong with you?"

I turn toward the voice.

Headlights sucker-punch my eyeballs. I wince and spin away, stumbling back. Slipping on the wet slope.

There's a sickening crack when I hit the ground.

White-hot pain shoots from my fingers to my shoulder. My face skids in slo-mo across icy grass and something sharp gashes my lip open at the corner of my mouth.

Fuuuuuck.

The taste of metal on my tongue. I spit out blood then roll onto my back, groaning when pain stabs through my now-fucked arm.

Above me, clouds drift past. The moon looks like a pierogi. Or maybe a fat banana? Pierogi-banana.

Get help.

I shift a bit, clawing for my phone. *Shit.* Can't reach my ass pocket like this.

Guess this is where I die. A drunk dumbass in a piss ditch.

I close my eyes.

Snow on my face. Cold and wet.

Blackness.

Blankness.

Then... beeping.

Head throbs.

Might throw up.

I try to move. Everything hurts. Face feels like it fought a cheese grater and lost. Arm weirdly heavy. I lift my head maybe an inch.

My arm's... in a cast?

Shit.

Pale blue blanket. White sheets.

Hands. A gentle voice. "Hey there."

"What happened?"

Fat, clumsy lips. Throat so dry it might crack, like I swallowed rocks. Mouth tastes like rocks, anyway. Rocks and blood and puke.

Buzzing inside my skull. Can't hear what she says. Her name? Then something, something, Harborview Medical Center.

I blink hard. Try to focus. The throbbing buzz lets up a bit.

"You had quite a night. Police picked you up on I-90."

The interstate? Jesus. How the fuck did I even get there on foot?

"You're lucky to be alive."

Fuck. This is bad.

"My phone?" I force a swallow.

A straw at my swollen lips. A sip of water. Better. Barely.

"You need to call someone?"

I nod. Regret stabs my brain.

The scraping of a drawer. My phone on my chest.

I manage to pry open an eyelid. Screen cracked. Battery at nine percent. Nearly fumble it. Nausea as I find my brother's name. Nausea while I wait for him to pick up.

Don't throw up.

"Miles?" Jude's groggy voice. "Miles, it's five in the fucking morning."

He's already disappointed in me.

Fair.

"It is?" *Shit.* I squint at the clock. Can't make out the numbers. "Sorry. I'm... I'm at the hospital."

"Fuck. What happened this time?" He sounds exhausted. Worried.

This is all my fault.

"You need me to drive out there?"

Another wave of nausea churns. My head pounds. Breathe.

Don't throw up. Don't throw up.

"Miles, you still there?" He sounds more awake now. Probably pissed. "Miles!"

Definitely pissed.

"I can't..." My voice is rough. Salty tears sting my lip. "I'm not..."

"Okay," he sighs. "I'm coming to the city. You at Harborview again?"

"Yeah."

He mumbles something to Olena. "Getting dressed now. Be there in an hour, okay?"

"Jude, I can't do this anymore." My voice breaks and my hand starts to shake. I go to switch hands, then remember. Squeeze harder. Will myself to steady.

For once in your life, get your shit together.

"I don't wanna feel like this anymore."

His end goes quiet. "Yeah?"

"I'm done. I need help, Jude."

1

CAROLINE

Dumping a cheating boyfriend should be like firing him from a job. But, instead of making him turn in his company ID and credit card, you should be within your rights to demand he returns what really matters: all mutual friends, the cute pet names he used to call you, and your dignity.

Fletcher clearly didn't get the memo.

I scowl down at my phone.

FLETCHER

Silent treatment still in effect? Fine babe. Suit yourself. But you're gonna have to play nice with me Saturday whether you like it or not.

Wear that Benedici dress I got you in Milan. Paid enough for it, so it might as well get some use.

Jesus. The audacity.

Can you have a tension headache in advance?

I pinch the bridge of my nose, making a mental note to burn that dress, then silence my phone as I tuck it behind the art gallery's front desk. Well, *desk* might be overstating things. It's more a glorified lectern than usable workspace.

Loud drilling starts up again across the street and I roll my shoulders, trying to ignore how the floorboards vibrate beneath my heels. I smooth down my linen blazer, then pull out my tablet.

Don't scream. Just focus on work.

I've been doing a lot of that lately: shoving down the urge to scream. I could really use a good scream. Or maybe a racking, sobbing cry. A tantrum.

An orgasm?

Something. Anything to get rid of this relentless dread.

Stop being dramatic, Caroline. I can practically hear my mother reminding me to stand up straight and smile.

If only I could remember how.

It's bad enough I have to go with Fletcher to this fundraiser. Worse still that I have to wear his engagement ring and pretend he didn't sleep with half of Washington state on the campaign trail.

My phone pings again and I close my eyes, knowing he's gonna keep after me until I give in. The same persistence that makes him a gifted campaign manager also makes him a huge pain in the butt.

Why did I agree to this again?

Right. My father.

I try to catch myself before I get too worked up and swallow past the restless feeling gripping my chest. It'll just be a few more weeks.

A month out from the election, Dad's really been pulling out all the stops to bolster his chances at winning the governor's seat; the *last* thing the Pete Brennan campaign needs right now is a PR nightmare—like a messy breakup between the candidate's daughter and his campaign manager. So I'd promised Dad I would keep up the charade—grit my teeth and pretend to still be with my cheating ex—until votes are cast in November.

Agreeing to the ruse had been one thing. Actually having to act like nothing's wrong at public functions, when all I want to do is stuff Fletcher's silk ties down his smarmy throat? Let's just say, it's been tense.

"They can't be drilling much longer, can they?" Julian asks no one in particular, catching me off guard. I'd almost forgotten he was in the room, perched silently near the front window like some kind of gray-haired sleeper agent. He aims his curatorial scrutiny across the street over lowered reading glasses.

"I hope not," I say, attempting an air of cheerful optimism.

That's when I see the painting beside him: that abstract piece he'd been eyeing—all mustard yellows and browns with little flecks of red. With all due respect for the artist, it's run-of-the-mill. Dated. Like something you could pick up at Ikea to decorate a low-budget hotel room. Twenty years ago.

Okay, maybe that's not my most respectful take.

The urge to scream is back in full force. What with all the hard surfaces in here, a good scream would probably get the gallery walls singing. Maybe I could achieve some kind of glass-shattering resonance with enough reverb to knock that thing off the wall.

I clench my jaw and close my eyes, reminding myself art is subjective.

"Quietest exhibition we've had in a long time," Julian mutters as he flips through a Portland artist's portfolio—the one I'd left on his desk after sorting through the mail yesterday. "The noise is driving all the foot traffic away."

"Whatever they're working on will wrap up soon, I'm sure," I offer, trying not to get too gloom and doom about the next several months.

In reality, the noise is only part of the reason the gallery's been quiet. I've peeked at the pieces Julian's considering; more abstract paintings and a few garish geometric sculptures. Nothing new. Nothing unique. A tiny piece of me dies inside; there's so much stunning, modern art out there and *this* is what he's thinking of bringing in?

"Maybe we just need to get creative," I say, forcing a bright, hopeful tone. "Get some new artists in, host some fun evening events, and drum up a bit more interest around town?"

Without raising his head, Julian looks up at me over his glasses.

"I have some ideas," I add, shooting my shot. "And some incredible artists I've been following online. We could try featuring a few young local creatives. Something a little more... edgy. I could give you their—" I cut myself off when Julian shakes his head, the almost-fatherly dismissal all too familiar.

"Leave the curation to me, Caroline." He shuts the portfolio, then stalks toward his office at the back of the gallery space.

I hurry to mask the way my chest deflates. "Sure. Yeah. Of course."

Returning to my calendar app as he passes me, I try to focus on adding the registration details to each of the events lined up for next month, but I'm not really seeing the dates in front of me.

Thanks to my father's career in the public eye, slapping on an approachable, pleasant facade has become virtually second-nature to me. But something about pretending everything's fine these last few weeks has felt different—almost suffocating.

A jarring, metallic crash rings out, and I startle.

Equally suffocating? The relentless banging and grinding coming from that construction site. But, when I realize it was only our sidewalk sign getting knocked over by the wind, I consciously relax my shoulders and head out to fix it. Bracing myself for the auditory onslaught, I clutch at my blazer and push outside.

A gust catches the door and hurls it wide, and I have to make a mad grab for my scarf to avoid losing it to the street. I snag it at the last moment, shivering as I wrap it back around my neck. It's cold, even for early October.

Lennox Valley is known for its fall windstorms and the weather is really giving it everything it's got today. I glance at the debris-littered road and sigh in defeat, knowing my morning run tomorrow will amount to nothing more than jumping hurdles over fallen branches. Guess it's finally time to take the plunge and check out that gym nearby.

Stooping, I right the fallen sign, then brush a wet leaf away from the edge of the lettering.

"The Gareth Mason Art Gallery: Unleash Your Imagination."

If only Julian would unleash his.

Or maybe I need to leash my own.

After all, it really isn't my place to make suggestions for the gallery's collection. My role is event planning, not curation, even if I do know a thing or two about business—and art. Julian had only agreed to hire me last year so his wife, Sunny, could start to step back from her managerial role. She'd convinced him the gallery needed fresh ideas that would appeal to younger patrons, but he was clear my job was limited to planning events, at least at first. He hasn't been as enthusiastic as Sunny about sharing the workload.

It's not that Julian doesn't trust me or my eye for art; he just doesn't like change.

Sunny's emerging from the back office when I crack open the door to duck back inside, and she flinches at the noise. I shoot her an apologetic look and hurry to pull the door closed behind me, grateful when the grinding and drilling muffles to a more tolerable volume.

"My God!" she says, her face a dramatic mask of frustration. "I'd rather swallow a razor blade than listen to this for one more day!"

I try to suppress a laugh; Sunny has the larger-than-life flair of a Disney villain contained in the body of a slight, semi-retired Korean woman: equal parts fabulous and terrifying.

"Caroline, I can't take it anymore!" Aiming a sparkling index finger my way, she adds, "I'm getting a coffee."

I smirk as I cross the room, returning to my lectern-desk. "But won't that mean going out into the noise?"

"Be that as it may, the show must go on, dear." Wide-eyed, she comes up beside me and grabs my arm. "And this show requires caffeine." She turns to snatch her vintage fur coat from the closet around the corner and slips the sleeves over her many rings and bracelets. I'm not sure how she does it; the amount of jewelry she wears should be gaudy but she somehow pulls off chic.

"Wait," I say suddenly, shutting off my tablet. "Let me go grab you a coffee."

She places a hand on her chest. "Are you sure?"

"Absolutely." I join her at the closet to grab my favorite wool peacoat. "I could use the fresh air and I need to make a phone call."

"Oh, you angel child!" Sunny drawls, shrugging off her fur and stowing it away once more.

With her coffee order stored safely in my phone, I push out into the cold. High-pitched drilling pierces the air, and traffic lights swing overhead, groaning in the wind. My hair whips against my face and I bunch my shoulders in a futile attempt to block out the latest auditory assault, unsure I'll even be able to hear Adrian over the noise. But, desperate enough for a pep talk from my best friend, I hit the call button next to his name as I pick my way through the scattered leaves and twigs already littering the sidewalk.

He answers and, just as I'm about to shout over the drilling, the universe throws me a bone and it quiets down—for now, at least.

I exhale.

Small mercies.

"Hey," I say, then pause. "Um, so, what's the normal amount of screaming to hear inside your head? Asking for a... me." I chuckle joylessly.

"Uh..." Adrian's baffled silence hangs for a moment on the other end of the line. "Caroline, the normal amount of screaming inside your head is zero."

I frown. "That can't be right."

"You okay?" he asks. "Like, how worried about you should I be right now?"

I scoff, though the caution in my best friend's voice takes the edge off my prickly tone. "I'm fine. Just... crawling out of my skin. Fletcher texted me about the fundraiser this weekend. He called me *babe* again. No big deal. Sorry. I'm probably overreacting."

"Uh, *hell no*," Adrian says, defensive bestie mode activated. "I reject that. I don't care if you're stuck playing happy couple with that dickhead; he shouldn't act like he didn't ask you to marry him and then fuck his way around the state."

I wince at the reminder. I'd found countless texts on his work phone—evidence of hookups in every upscale hotel room paid for by Dad's campaign. "Yeah, okay, you're right."

"At least the thing on Saturday means I get to see you," Adrian says. "Want me to be your human shield? With Fletch?" He comically gags on my ex's name in solidarity. "Because I will not hesitate to aggressively side-eye that piece of shit for you all night."

"Ugh, yes, please." Maybe if I stick close to Adrian, I won't have to spend the entire evening forcing myself not to recoil each time Fletcher touches me. "And feel free to invent any cooked-up scenario you can think of with Found Family that will just... keep me busy with charity stuff."

"On it. I mean, you cofounded it, so it would be believable enough."

"Oh, and if you catch wind of my dad lecturing me again about my life choices, can you, like, pull the fire alarm or something?"

Adrian laughs. "Well, I wouldn't say no to hot firefighters coming to our rescue."

I tilt my head, already a bit defeated about the likely need for rescue, and tuck my scarf tighter around my neck.

Thank God I have Adrian in my corner. His snark not only got me through our college political science program, but it was all that kept me going the last year or so working for my dad. After seeing firsthand what I was putting up with—the long hours, the unreasonable demands, never seeming to do enough to please my father—Adrian had completely understood when I decided to cut and run, even though it meant leaving him behind, along with the youth mentorship charity we'd started together.

Dad understood less.

Okay, *less* might be too generous.

"Wish I could just skip it, honestly." I grimace slightly, feeling guilty about the idea of bailing on Adrian; I'd promised myself I wouldn't miss a single event when I left Seattle.

"You could."

"Um, no, I absolutely could not." I pull open the door to Bean Bag Coffee and get in line.

Ditching this party is not an option. Dad's annual donations to Found Family are instrumental in running the charity. In the early days, his public support and political contacts were what got it off the ground. The least I can do is paint on a smile and fake it with Fletcher—help Dad out until the election. That's what a good daughter would do.

Plus, there will be press coverage. I have to show up—as both a devoted daughter *and* devoted cofounder. I will be positively oozing devotion in all directions.

"Uh, well," he deadpans, "after you quit on me last year, I never put anything past you."

"Well, technically, I quit on my dad," I correct him, though I can't deny his snarky tone lifts my spirits. "And you know I needed to move here for Grandpa."

Dad still rolls his eyes to this day about my decision to leave Seattle and move in with my grandfather, and not just because I quit working for him. With his sights permanently set on the fast-paced political scene, Dad has never grasped why Grandpa—or anyone, for that matter—would choose a small town over the big city. We had the money to pay for whatever level of care was necessary after Grandpa's fall, he'd argued. I didn't need to personally help out.

But it wasn't about that for me.

Grandpa is one of my favorite people and he's been more of a father figure to me than Dad has, in a lot of ways. We've always had a special bond, preferring the quiet, simple pleasures in life over the extravagance my parents enjoy. After Grandma died a few years ago, we've only gotten closer. And we make pretty good roomies, it turns out.

I put in the order for Sunny's coffee and pay the barista.

"Anyway," Adrian starts, changing the subject as if he can sense I need a distraction, "how's my hometown treating you?"

Having grown up here before moving to Seattle for college, he's effectively swapped places with me—upgrading to the big city while I've fled to small town Lennox Valley.

"Still loving it," I reply honestly. Lennox has had my heart since I was a little girl spending summers here with my grandparents; I'd never wanted to leave.

"Except for how much you miss me."

"Obviously." I step aside to let a mother with a stroller grab her enormous iced coffee. "I know my dad still doesn't get it. It's...

I dunno, I can't explain why, but Lennox feels more like home than Seattle ever did."

The truth is, even after a year, I'm still just as enamored with living here as always.

"And I know leaving you and Found Family was unfortunate collateral damage, but I'm still your cofounder for life. I'll still help out where I can. So you're stuck with me."

"Whatever. You left me and crushed my soul and I'll never recover."

I scoff. "Don't act like you hate being in charge of everything and everybody now that I'm gone."

Adrian laughs. "Touché, touché." He lets out a whooshing sigh. "And, hey, speaking of crushed souls, at least this soul-crushing shit with Fletch ends in a few more weeks."

"It can't come soon enough."

Once votes are cast, I can finally ditch my ex and never speak to that cheating bastard again. Or at least try. Because, unless my dad loses and kicks Fletcher to the curb, he isn't going anywhere. But a girl can dream.

Just the idea that I'd dream about Dad losing flings guilt through me like a handful of glitter. So much for being a good daughter. Pretty sure a *good* daughter wouldn't wish harm on her father's political career—especially one she helped build.

The barista slides me Sunny's coffee, and I mouth *thank you* before I turn to go. When I push outside once again, the construction noise kicks me square in the eardrums and Adrian says something I don't catch.

"What?" I turn away from the drilling and go to plug my other ear, but stop myself before I spill hot coffee down my neck. "It's loud out here, sorry."

"We should celebrate once it's over," Adrian shouts again into the phone.

"Oh, sure," I reply, my heart not really in it.

I'd probably feel better if I could go public about the breakup, but the polls have been neck and neck lately. I can't ask Dad to risk the election just to let my breakup with Fletcher out of the bag. Between Dad's singular focus on votes and Mom pleading with me to hang on a little longer, the pressure is on to suck it up. There's no turning back now; I made a promise to my father. As much as Dad can frustrate me, and as much as I may regret signing up for self-inflicted purgatory at Fletcher's side, there's too much at stake with so many eyes on my family.

So, for now, celebration feels too far off. For the next month, I'll have to keep my emotions in check, stuffed down under every fake smile for the cameras.

Pleasant. I'll be vaguely pleasant.

And vaguely dying on the inside.

2

MILES

I swear to God: some people shouldn't be let out of the house. Especially this fuckstick doing lat pulldowns beside me.

We've all let out a grunt or two at the gym, but this guy's sounds are... I mean, I'm no pearl clutcher, but let's just say there's a time and a place for sex noises and a busy gym on a Tuesday morning ain't it. Not even the music in my headphones can drown this dude out.

A glance at the clock on the wall reveals it's a few minutes past six.

For fuck's sake.

When I catch Gus' eye across the gym, he grimaces—and not just from the pair of eighty-pound dumbbells he's shoulder pressing. He sets them down and gives the moaner a long side-eye, then mouths *what the fuck* my way.

I shrug and shake my head, then set up for my next set of squats at the rack.

It's not only me and my best friend who've noticed this morning's human train wreck; everyone within a twenty-foot radius has the same awkward look on their face. I can't tell if the guy's doing it on purpose or if he's straight up oblivious but, either way, it's uncomfortable as fuck—like making eye contact with a dog while it's shitting.

But I try not to judge. It's not like I've always been on my best behavior in public.

I know what it's like to be stared at. Whispered about. Hell, probably pitied.

But, even at my messiest, I never pulled this kind of shit.

At least, I fucking hope not.

I readjust my headphones and wipe my forehead with the hem of my T-shirt. It tugs at my nose as I let it drop, and my eyes flit to the TV screen in the corner. Some politics shit on the news, as usual. No fucking thank you. They couldn't put on sports high-lights or something? Hell, I'd settle for golf, and golf makes me want to poke out my eyeballs.

Gus walks over as I finish my set and rack the weight. I pull my headphones down to my neck and the din of the gym whooshes around my skull.

He jerks his chin at the TV. "What's this dickhead yappin' about now?"

"Fuck if I know." I lift my gaze to the screen again, where red-nosed Senator Pete Brennan drones on about urban density regu-lations and preserving the character of town centers. "Probably a bunch of whiny boomer shit."

"So fucking oblivious," Gus sighs, smoothing over his mustache. "Can't believe this guy is running for governor."

"Yeah, more like Gover-no-thank-you."

He smirks at the weak joke—admittedly, not my best work. "You almost done?"

"Uh, I was gonna do a bit more, actually. They need you at the station early?"

He rolls his shoulders. "Yeah. Nothing major. Just some lines down and shit after last night. More overnight calls than usual. Figure the crew could use a hand unloading."

Typical October in this small town. Rain, windstorms, power failures. Keeps Gus and the rest of the Lennox Valley Fire Department busy, though.

"Shay's gonna stop by too. Pick up the last of her things."

I pause, spray bottle and towel in hand. "She didn't change her mind about Lumpy, did she?"

I've gotten quite attached to Gus' long-suffering black cat. Officially named Coal—but unofficially Lump of Coal, Mr. Lumps, Lumpy, Sir Lumps-a-lot, or any variation on the theme—he's my favorite fuzzball, next to my brother's golden retriever, Murphy.

Gus cracks a smile. "Nah, you're good. I got Lumps in the divorce."

It's still weird to hear him say he's divorced. At least it was amicable—which is also weird, to me anyway. I've never managed to stay friends with an ex.

"Okay," I say, lifting my chin. "Catch you... what, Thursday, I guess?" Gus' shift work always fucks with my head. I don't know how he copes with working twenty-four hours straight.

"Yeah. Send me a selfie or something when you get here tomorrow."

I do a mock salute in response.

"And not a pic of your ass this time, dipshit." He chucks me on the shoulder and heads for the shower.

"You said you wanted proof I got my ass to the gym!" I call after him, but he doesn't look back.

Gus could work out at the station instead, but he knows the accountability is good for me, so he tags along whenever he can swing it. Plus, we both have physical jobs; working out together keeps us on our game—and helps keep me sober.

I unlock my phone and pull up the Lump-sized lobster costume I found online, tapping my way through the checkout.

Something to celebrate their bachelorhood? Honestly, any excuse to dress up that ridiculous fucking cat. I double-check I got the biggest size, make sure the shipping address is set to Gus' house, and place the order.

Lumpster. Nice.

Beside me, the moaner drops his weights with a loud crack and I flinch. My amusement instantly evaporates when I watch him walk off without wiping down his machine, because of course he fucking doesn't. I clench my fists, then let go.

The guy's probably in his twenties but has kind of a dad-bod going on. Curly blond hair sticks out from under a newsboy cap— of all fucking things to wear to the gym. He doesn't seem like your average gym rat. I hope with every fiber of my being that means I won't have to put up with his weird bullshit again tomorrow— sounding like he's gonna come in his pants on the damn treadmill.

Reminding myself to focus on my workout, I scroll through my playlists.

I'm pulling my headphones back up when I catch sight of a blonde near one of the stationary bikes across the room. I haven't seen her here before; I'd definitely remember her if I had.

You know that phrase *a sight for sore eyes*? I'm suddenly living it. Everything offensive around me dulls, my senses now tuned to supple curves and long, toned legs. I let out a slow exhale. *Fuck me*, she's got a nice pair of legs.

But she also looks like she probably spent more on that fancy-ass water bottle dangling from her manicured fingers than I did on whatever random T-shirt and shorts I grabbed on the way out the door. I glance down to double-check my shirt isn't on inside-out. Thankfully, I seem to have had two functional brain cells to rub together when I zombie-lurched out of bed this morning.

Catching myself staring, I thumb at my phone and crank my music, now needing to drown out two very different distractions.

But I've barely finished one set of lunges when the moaner rolls up beside me again and grabs a couple twenty-pound dumbbells, setting up at the bench to my right.

Lord, give me the strength.

I get through another set of ten reps before letting my attention wander again to the stationary bike. Well, technically, to the bike's current occupant.

Her curly hair is tied up in one of those on-purpose messy buns girls do, with little ringlets framing her face in all the perfect places. It's less *I woke up like this* and more *I spent an hour in the mirror getting this right*. One neon yellow sports bra strap peeks out from under a loose-fitting crop top that slips off her shoulder. When she leans forward onto the handlebars, I remind myself not to look down her top. This gym has reached its creeper quota in spades today; I don't need to be *that guy*.

Plus, I'm sure the last thing she wants is some scruffy dumbass like me ogling her. She looks fancy and put-together—my polar opposite.

When the moaner gets back on his bullshit beside me, louder than before, I cut him a wary glance. I have half a mind to say something, but I let it slide; I don't have the energy to take on a gym creep before six-thirty in the morning. This guy isn't gonna scare me off, though. I return to my lunges, determined to put my head down and wrap this up so I can get to work.

Finished with my last set, I rack the dumbbells and wipe my brow again, unable to resist flicking my gaze to the bikes as I let my T-shirt drop—and try not to react when I catch a certain someone looking back at me.

She quickly averts her eyes.

We both do, though I can't suppress a private smirk.

Caught ya.

Focusing on my reflection in the mirror, I stretch my quads, frowning as the moaner ramps up again beside me.

Fuck, buddy. Give it a rest.

I'm determined to block out his weird ass.

Ass.

That girl has a great ass.

Fuck. No. Focus up.

Movement in the mirror catches my attention, and I drop my leg as the blonde climbs off the bike and heads for the cleaning spray. Her cheeks are flushed pink from her warm-up and... Damn. She's beautiful.

I'm about to set up for calf raises when she settles into the chest press machine nearby, and my lats suddenly feel like they need some attention.

It's Tuesday. Tuesday is leg day. It's *always* leg day.

Or... it was until this girl walked in here.

On a whim, I abandon my calf raises plan and set up shop on the other side of her machine.

What am I doing?

Sure, I might be single, but single and fit for consumption are very different things. But, when our gazes lock and she gives me a sheepish smile, I hold my breath.

Oh, yeah. Calf raises can get fucked.

I've never seen eyes like hers before. They're like a damn tropical ocean, or maybe one of those glacial lakes up in Canada that are almost turquoise. Like pools of light and calm. They're fucking gorgeous.

Aggressive moaning cuts into the moment, and we both turn to the asshole nearby. When she looks back at me, eyes wide in a bewildered kind of amusement, I have to suppress a laugh. I screw up my face, hoping my expression reads half *that guy's a fuckwad* and half *sorry about men, generally.*

With another small twitch of her lips that nudges my attention toward places it can't go, she returns to her workout, tapping at something on her watch.

Her watch.

Shit. What time is it?

Checking my phone jars me back to reality; I've gotta be at work in half an hour or Dave will chew me out and I can't let that happen. That was the old Miles. Showing up late and hungover was the kind of crap that got my ass fired back in Seattle. Mouthing off to the foreman didn't help, either. While my impulsive and smartass tendencies are partly my ADHD and can't solely be blamed on drinking, still—that shit ain't cute when you're pushing thirty.

New Miles, though? New Miles is sober. Healthy. Going to therapy and AA. Sticking to the rules. Taking his meds. Learning about how his damn brain works. Grinding away at the gym every day and eating fucking vegetables and showing up on time for work.

I'm not gonna let myself fuck it all up again. Rock bottom isn't a place you wanna visit twice.

I'm about to go hit the showers when the moaner strolls up beside me with his hands on his hips, staring right at her. Sliding my headphones off one ear, I turn down my music, already on my guard. I've put up with this obnoxious prick long enough.

"Y'know," he says to her, "you should really watch how much weight you're lifting. You don't wanna get too bulky."

The fuck?

Her weights clack down and she cautiously pulls out an earbud. "Pardon me?" she asks, her tone far more polite than this dude deserves. "I couldn't hear—"

"I was saying," he says, and I push off my machine to stand, "women shouldn't lift too heavy if—"

"This guy bothering you?" My voice comes out louder than I meant it to.

"Uh…" Her eyes flit between us, lingering on mine for a beat.

The moaner immediately takes a step back and, when he

clocks all six feet, four inches of me, visibly swallows. "Naw, man, sorry, I was just—"

"You were *just* giving unsolicited advice to a woman trying to work out in peace." I barely stop myself from blurting out that he doesn't look like he knows the first thing about how—or how not —to get bulky.

"I wasn't—"

"Do better," I cut him off. "I promise you, my girl can make her own fucking decisions about how she exercises."

I glance her way, seeing surprise light her features at the words that fell out of my mouth. *My girl.* She's not mine. Hell, I don't even know her name. But this dickhead doesn't need to know that.

"Sorry," he says, holding up his hands. "Didn't realize you were with—"

"Doesn't matter who I am. You shouldn't be approaching women at the gym, period."

"Sorry, man," he repeats, then throws a contrite face her way. "Just... sorry."

When he fucks off, I open my mouth to check if she's okay, but she speaks first.

"Thank you," she says, her gaze slipping from mine, lingering for a beat on the honeybee inked on my left thigh before darting between the few onlookers nearby. She seems nervous.

Awareness slowly settles in—that I assumed she needed my help. Maybe she wanted to handle the moaning dingus herself.

Crap. Did I misread this?

"Sorry, I didn't mean to..." I gesture uselessly at the retreating asshole, second-guessing everything. "Wasn't sure if..." I glance at the clock again and pull off my ball cap to smooth back my sweaty hair. I gotta get out of here, but I don't wanna run off on her yet— especially when I can't finish a fucking sentence. Replacing my hat, I ask, "You okay?"

"Oh, yeah, I'm..." She makes a gesture like she's waving it all off. "He was..."

I arch a tentative brow as I pick up my water bottle. "Fucking weird?"

Her eyes snap to mine, and she lets out a little laugh. "Uh, yeah. That's one way to put it."

I catch sight of the guy heading for the exit. *Good riddance.*

"Uh, look," I say, turning back to her, "I hate to just take off here, but I need to get to work."

"You know what?" Her shoulders drop and she stands, coming around from the machine. "I'm actually leaving too. I can walk you out."

"You sure?"

"Yeah, I'm... I'm not really feeling it today. The wind kept me up last night." She quickly wipes down her machine, then hands me the spray bottle and towel. "I also haven't been here before, and I'm feeling kind of... I dunno,"—she scrunches her nose, looking around the place—"out of my element, I guess?"

"Yeah, well," I say, wiping down my machine, "I bet that asshole's sex noises didn't help."

She tilts her head.

Fuck. Why did I mention sex?

"So, you wanna get outta here, or...?" I quickly replace the cleaning spray in its wall bracket and lift my chin toward the elevator. When she nods, we do an awkward little start-stop routine as we head for the exit. She's taller than I thought. I could probably rest my chin on her head.

Whoa. What the fuck am I thinking?

Dismissing the mental image, I throw a glance toward the men's locker room as we collect our gym bags. Guess I'll have to change in my truck, and the guys on the job site will have to deal with me skipping the shower, because smelling good just took a back seat to spending another few minutes with...

I still don't know her name. Shit.

"I'm Miles, by the way." I hit the elevator button.

"Caroline." She slings her gym bag over her shoulder.

Caroline.

"Like the song, right? Sweet Caroline?" I narrowly avoid belting out the iconic *baah-baah-baah,* calling it a win that, for once, I didn't blurt the first thought in my head.

And that I didn't fucking *sing.*

"Ugh, no," she groans, dropping her shoulders as the doors slide open in front of us.

"No?" I follow her into the elevator, a bit thrown by her response.

Did I hear the wrong name?

"I mean, yes, Caroline, no to..." Juggling her water bottle and phone, she pulls a thick-looking hoodie out of her gym bag. "Sorry, I just really hate that song."

Shit. She probably gets called *Sweet Caroline* all the time. And I should know better; I've had more than my share of song references because of my name. Regret flits through my stomach and I drop my gaze to her feet.

"Oh, uh," I start. "Your shoelace is untied."

"Oh?" She looks down, moving like she's gonna fix it, but stops when she realizes her hands are full. "Okay, I'll get it in a minute, I—"

"Nah, I got it." On impulse, I swing my gym bag out of the way and kneel. It's only when I'm halfway through tying her shoe that I realize I've just met this woman and I've literally dropped to her feet. And, *God damn,* now her beautiful legs are inches from my face and all I wanna do is slide my palms up these perfect calves...

I swallow, my movements slowing as I snug the bow tight. I flick an uneasy glance upward, catching the surprise in her expression.

What's wrong with me?

"Um, thanks," she says, her voice a little breathy.

C'mon, Miles. Be less of a wang. Fix this.

Slowly, I push to stand, but can't seem to tear my eyes from hers as I straighten to my full height. When the elevator door opens, I force myself to put some space between us and follow her through the lobby. Momentarily distracted by the sight of her ass in those yoga pants, I have to rush to grab the door for her, willing myself to get my shit together.

Outside, the sun hasn't come up quite yet, but the sky is already glowing in warm tones that contrast with the crisp fall air.

"So, you hate *Sweet Caroline*, huh?" I ask as she turns to face me on the sidewalk, her blonde curls catching the golden, orangey light. "Is that 'cause you're not sweet, or what?" When she hesitates, I forge ahead, hoping I can smooth things over. "Or you don't like classic party songs? Or did Neil Diamond, like, murder your second cousin or something?"

"Can't believe you'd bring up the unsolved murder of my second cousin."

Her grin is infectious, and I'm flooded with relief that I seem to have swerved *awkward weirdo* and landed on *awkwardly charming weirdo*. She's doing nothing to dissuade me, even if every flirtatious word falling out of my face goes against my better judgment.

"Wow," I say, rocking back on my heels. "I've really done a number on you, huh? First I put my foot in my mouth about your name, and now this."

"Right? I'm gonna have to unpack this in therapy later."

"Rough!" I laugh, clutching at my chest like she's wounded me. I can't tell whether she's got a snarky, teasing side or she's actually in therapy—or both. Green flag, any way you slice it. "Starting to think you aren't sweet after all."

"Maybe I contain multitudes," she fires back.

Okay, I guess this flirting thing can go both ways.

"Well, if it's any consolation, my therapist will be hearing all about you too."

"Yeah?" Her brows quirk in confusion as she tucks her water bottle and phone into her gym bag.

"Y'know, about how I bravely rescued you from the moaning gym creep."

"Right, right." She readjusts her bag on her shoulder, then drapes her hoodie over it.

"Aaaaand then biffed it by being completely unoriginal and bringing up a song you can't stand." I take a swig of my water, still kicking myself. It's one of those small things that doesn't matter but, thanks to my anxiety, will haunt me nonetheless.

"You didn't biff it," she reassures me.

I tilt my head, not so sure. "Rookie move, really, because I actually get the song thing. My best friend likes to find any excuse to torture me musically. *500 Miles. Miles Away. I Can See for Miles...*" I should stop, but I don't. "*Miles to Go. A Thousand Miles...* Honestly, if I ever tell him I'm going downtown, it's over."

She squints in thought. "Because you're... making your way downtown?"

I nod. "Bingo."

There's an amused wonder in her blue-green eyes. "How often does that come up?"

"You'd be surprised how much Gus sings. He's uh... kinda aggressive about it."

"Well, I guess that explains why you're seeing a therapist." She tilts her head, one brow arching up.

Laughter puffs out of me when her joke lands. "I'm gonna tell him you said that."

"Oh, God, please don't!" She holds out her hands like she can wave her words away. "I was just joking!"

"No way. It's too good. He'll find it funny. Promise."

A chilly breeze kicks up, sweeping her blonde curls forward. She tucks a stray one behind her ear.

"So, what do you think that guy's deal was?" Caroline asks, juggling her bag so she can pull on her hoodie.

In her moment of distraction, I let my own attention wander. My gaze slips down her neck and across her collarbone to that neon yellow bra strap before traveling even lower. Her shirt looks so soft and—*shit*. I snap my eyes skyward when I notice her nipples have hardened from the chill outside.

"Sorry, what?" I swallow, willing my thoughts to stop spinning through a thousand ways I could warm her up.

"That creepy guy."

"Right." I remind myself not to get lumped into that same category, grateful when she zips up her hoodie—though I can't help but notice the way it hugs her curves.

Caroline shrugs against the cold as she shoulders her gym bag once more. "Like, do you think he travels around town, moaning inappropriately everywhere he goes, or…?"

I rub the back of my neck. "I dunno. Yeah, maybe tomorrow he'll be at a restaurant or some shit, alienating everyone with his foodgasms."

Her eyes dance with amusement. "Just leaving abject horror in his wake."

"Yeah, like some kind of… socially repellent motorboat." I almost wince as the words leave my mouth.

Great. Impress her with some unhinged brain connection. Women love that.

She does that cute nose scrunch again and her full lips quirk with uncertainty.

Forcing myself to stop looking at her mouth, I remind myself I'm not trying to impress her. I shouldn't still be flirting with her, even if my execution is a little rusty and she's getting more verbal diarrhea than anything else. And I better not mention *motorboats* again if I'm gonna have any hope in hell of keeping my mind off her boobs.

Look anywhere else, dumbass.

"Uh, listen…" I lean in, dropping my voice slightly. "Didn't mean to call you *my girl* back in the gym. I wasn't thinking. I just—"

"No, no, it's fine. Really. It was effective, right?"

"Yeah, I guess he backed down pretty fast," I admit.

She rubs her arms, snagging my focus. Her hoodie looks warm and, like everything else she's wearing, expensive.

Once again, I find myself hoping I'm not too scruffy in comparison. Probably should've shaved. My stubble is quickly approaching beard territory, and I'm starting to look like my fucking brother.

Another cold breeze sweeps past and, when Caroline shifts slightly, her gym bag slips off her shoulder.

Without thinking, I step toward her and gently set the strap back in place.

Those ocean eyes lift to mine as her lips part slightly, and her subtle, sweet scent—*vanilla, maybe?*—has me inhaling a bit longer, a bit deeper, like I might hold on to it.

For the second time in the last few minutes, I'm acutely aware of how close we're standing. As I let my hand drop, my fingers lightly graze her arm.

Accidentally. Probably accidentally.

"Sorry," I mumble, taking a step back, and rub my jaw.

"It's okay. Thanks." She brushes the spot where I touched her arm with her fingertips, then steps aside to let an old man pass between us on the narrow sidewalk. The interruption is insignificant, but it's enough to snap us both out of whatever trance we'd fallen into. "Wait. Didn't you say you had to get to work?"

"Oh, fuck." My heart kicks at the realization, and I look over my shoulder toward my parked truck. We're only down the block from the construction site, but I still need to change. I quickly check the time; I'm gonna have to jog there at this point. "Yeah, I should go." Walking backward a few steps, I keep my eyes trained on Caroline, reluctance to leave battling with the need to get to work.

Fucking New Miles and his adult responsibilities.

"Hey, thanks again for telling that guy off," she calls after me.

"Oh, yeah, uh, no problem." I smile, the moaner already a distant memory.

"See you around?" There's a hopeful note in her voice, and my blood starts thrumming.

Shit, that's a bad sign.

I can't risk this kind of distraction. Not yet.

"Yeah, hope so." As I turn to leave, I stumble slightly on a fallen twig but manage to recover with my dignity intact. Mostly intact.

Fucking windstorm did me dirty.

3

———

CAROLINE

It takes about ten seconds to recognize that Dad's in damage-control mode. The video call's intermittent, pixelated glitching does little to hide how red-faced and worked up he is.

"This is unacceptable timing, Caroline!" Dad booms. "This arrangement between you and Fletcher was supposed to last until the election! Now you're caught on camera canoodling with random men?"

My jaw drops. "Canoodling? Dad, that's unfair. And it wasn't *men*, plural. Besides, we weren't even..." I trail off, staring at the photo on the infamous local gossip blog, *The Wash*.

There I am, standing outside the gym with Miles yesterday morning, his hand hovering as it grazes my upper arm. We're standing close enough that, thanks in part to the angle, we could easily be mistaken for a couple. Plus, the way I'm peering up at him looks almost intimate. If I'm honest, those few seconds when he'd stepped closer had left my heart pounding and, even through my thick hoodie, the light touch of his fingers had sent a skittering sensation across my skin that lingered for long seconds after he pulled away.

"It doesn't matter what you were or weren't doing with this musclehead," Dad presses, interrupting my thoughts.

"*Musclehead?* Dad! I—"

"What matters," he continues over me, "is how it *looks*. I can't have my daughter sleeping around town when she's supposed to be happily engaged to my campaign manager!"

"Dad—" I try again, grasping for my usual mask of placating calm as hurt slices into my chest. For years, I've been supporting my father's career, pouring every ounce of energy into what my family wants. Showing up when and how they want me to. Dressing how they want me to. Acting how they want me to. Heck, *dating* who they want me to. And this is what I get back?

"Peter, I think that's taking it a little too far," Mom tries from beside him—unsuccessfully.

"What's too far, Valerie," Dad huffs, his bluster eclipsing her, as usual, "is my own daughter compromising my campaign. I don't care how upset she is about her situation. We had an agreement!"

An agreement I'm regretting more and more with each passing minute.

"You're making it sound like I did this on purpose!" I counter. "You know I would never knowingly jeopardize your career, Dad."

After everything I've done for him, that's the part that cuts deepest. Swallowing past the knot in my throat, I try to stomp the feelings down. I scroll down, skimming the article and willing myself to process just how bad this situation is.

Not-So-Sweet Caroline spotted with new mystery beau

The headline alone has me cringing in more ways than one, but I read on.

Caroline Brennan, daughter of Washington gubernatorial candidate Senator Pete Brennan, was caught in the early hours of Tuesday morning cozying up with her new mystery man in downtown Lennox Valley. Sporting the latest line of organic bamboo fitness finery by Seattle designer Joon Bishop, Ms. Brennan's looking sharp—but her ring finger is notably bare. Could this have anything to do with her having kept a low profile most of the last year? We smell drama! Sources speculate her engagement to Sen. Brennan's campaign manager, Fletcher Brady, has been called off. Reportedly living in the small town to take care of family, Ms. Brennan seems to be getting "taken care of" plenty herself—by the friendly locals… or one friendly local in particular.

"Caroline," Dad presses, pulling my attention back to the stern set of his jaw, "how do you intend to fix this?"

I have no idea how to fix this.

"Okay, I understand this doesn't look good," I say, stalling for time. "But I swear to you, it was an innocent moment." I scroll back up to the photo, arranging it on my screen beside the video stream of my father's ruddy, exasperated face. The contrast between the two images is striking, but I can't dwell on that right now. "Maybe we could put out a statement, or—?"

Dad's phone rings and he answers the way he's answered every phone call since I was a little girl. "Pete Brennan." I quickly gather it's Linda, his PR consultant. He excuses himself and, for a moment, I can breathe again.

Mom swivels the laptop to face her straight-on. "Your father will calm down. You know how he gets right before an election."

"I know," I say, shoving aside the memories of how he could *get* when I worked for him in Seattle. That side of him I never really saw growing up.

Maybe I'd just been sheltered from it, between my mother

acting as a buffer and all the time I spent with my grandparents. I was a teenager when I started helping out at Dad's office, trying my damnedest to forge a connection with him by making myself useful. But, by the time I was out of college, those rare crumbs of praise I craved from my father had only dwindled and his expectations of me had only grown. I was working my butt off for him and it was never enough.

Deep down, I know he wants the best for me and for us as a family. He's always said so. Mom's right; the election stress is amplifying everything right now.

Mom puts on her brave face. "We'll find a way to spin this, sweetheart."

"I'm not so sure," I say with a small grimace.

"Sweetie, we have the best PR team in the state; they'll come up with a way to dispel this nasty little rumor."

Nasty?

A sickly sensation twists through me. How is the idea of me being involved with Miles—even if untrue—somehow *worse* than the reality of my relationship with Fletcher?

Still, I can't shake the feeling I've done something wrong.

"I'm so sorry I messed this up. I shouldn't have..." I trail off, not really knowing what I'm apologizing for but feeling that familiar pang of guilt all the same. Trying to look at things rationally, I push aside the way it felt—the way it always feels—to know I've disappointed my dad. Because there was no way I could have anticipated this. Sure, I'd known there was a possibility of photographers lurking around Lennox, but what was I supposed to do? Maintain a solid four-foot radius of space around me at all times, never letting a single human enter my bubble?

"You simply need to be more careful," Mom says. "You never know who's watching. How things might look."

"Right," I say, masking the way my stomach sinks hearing her confirm I should have done something different. Something *more.*

I know she means well—know she's simply trying to keep the peace between me and Dad—but it also feels like putting this on me is giving him a pass. Enabling him to continue with his unreasonable expectations. I catch myself fiddling with my gold dragonfly pendant and consciously stop my fidgeting before Mom gives me grief about it.

Human-repelling force field it is.

And the only one allowed in is Fletcher. The last man I want anywhere near me. Sudden, aching dread washes over me at the thought.

Just a few more weeks, I remind myself, wishing I had a time machine to fast-forward my way out of this.

"Mom, I should go," I lie, avoiding looking directly at the screen. "I've got some work to catch up on. Let me know what Dad thinks we should do about the story." Straightening in my chair, I paste on my best mask of people-pleasing optimism—the one I've honed and perfected over a lifetime in the public eye. "I'm up for whatever he thinks is best."

After all, I've spent my whole life doing exactly that—whatever my father thinks is best. Always putting Team Brennan first. *Do it for the family,* Dad would always say. *Be a team player.* And I was. For years, I'd worked for Dad's various political campaigns, doing everything from fetching coffees to organizing fundraisers.

But that all ended last year. Grandpa's fall was minor and he's fully recovered, but it had been a wake-up call: living alone was no longer wise at his age. While he didn't need constant supervision or hands-on care, he did need someone around regularly. Grandpa's sudden need for a roommate had finally given me the perfect excuse to put some space between me and my father's controlling ways. It was long overdue—but I knew Dad would talk me out of it if I tried to quit on him for simply *wanting* a change. Helping Grandpa was not only something I genuinely wanted to do, but it made for a firmer leg to stand on in the face of my father's objections. It gave me the courage to finally break free.

With another forced smile, I end the call and close my laptop, sagging into the kitchen chair. I head to put the kettle on, determined not to fixate on my father's disappointment.

As I flick on the cold water, realization hits me.

That feeling of freedom I've always associated with Lennox Valley—summers with my grandparents, running around their backyard and roaming the riverside with my cousins—has been elusive since I moved in with Grandpa. I may be here, but I'm not *free*. Physical distance hasn't put a dent in my father's control; I'm still bending to his whims—still bound to what he wants, obediently shelving what *I* want.

What do *I want? Do I even know? And does anybody care?*

A wave of loneliness hits me. I try to let the feeling take root so I can feel it in my body—like my therapist taught me—but old habits being what they are, my mind quickly searches for a way to disprove it. In practical terms, the idea is ridiculous. I've got my job at the art gallery with Julian and Sunny. I dutifully attend every fundraiser and campaign event with my parents. I have Grandpa and his care aide, Sadie, who I see here at home. Adrian and I talk all the time. I'm not alone.

On paper, at least.

But below the cheerful surface? There's a profound emptiness, like the inky blackness of outer space—and it's been there for longer than I care to admit. I've been floating, untethered, unable to bump up against anything tangible to ground me.

My thoughts drift back to the image of me peering up at Miles, then to the light brush of his fingers on my arm. It had felt so different with him compared to Fletcher. Even in the beginning, Fletcher had never given me that warm, buzzy feeling. He'd fit into my world. Or my parents' world, at least. But Miles...

Water overflows from the kettle, splashing into the sink. I

gasp, snapping back to the present. Shaking my head, I pour out the excess and dry everything off with a dish towel.

No. I'm imagining things. There was nothing between me and Miles yesterday. I'm grasping at straws—flustered by his flirty attention and the thigh tattoo peeking out from under his gym shorts. Okay, so he's incredibly sexy. But he's not my usual type. I tend to go for buttoned-up prep-school guys—the ones who've always been in my orbit. Men who keep their dress shoes polished and know how to order expensive wine.

That's the kind of guy I always expected would be right for me, anyway. A man who would effortlessly impress my parents, hold his own rubbing shoulders with politicos, and—hopefully— be easy on the eyes. The kind of man I've always been steered toward.

Have I ever even let myself entertain the idea of a man who didn't fit that mold?

I turn the knob for the front burner and, in a few clicks, the flames jump to life.

"There she is!" Grandpa's rough voice cuts into my thoughts. "Don't suppose you've got enough in there for two cups of tea?"

"I do," I say over my shoulder as I pull open a cupboard. "I'll get another mug."

"How was work?" he asks as he slowly makes his way toward his usual spot at the kitchen table. "Those stuffed shirts give you any grief?" He stashes his walker nearby and slowly lowers into his chair.

"They're hardly stuffed shirts, Grandpa," I say, sitting down beside him. "It's an art gallery, not an insurance company."

He gives me a shrewd look. At ninety-two, he's as sharp and observant as ever, and I know he's shared my frustrations with the direction at the gallery.

"Actually, I've been mulling over some new ideas for events. I was gonna brainstorm tonight—maybe draft a sort of proposal." I pause, remembering my plan to stay in my lane and keep my curatorial suggestions to myself. Maybe if I wow Julian with a few successful events, he'll be open to more of my ideas. "Sunny's in my corner, but I'm not sure Julian will consider looking at it."

"Well, he'd be a fool not to!" Grandpa places a weathered hand on my arm. "It's about time someone breathed a bit of life into that place, kiddo. They need it, and you're the best person to do it."

I smirk, both amused and flattered by the unwavering faith he's always had in me.

When I was growing up, it was my grandparents who showed up to cheer me on at every school play, swim meet, and dance recital. My biggest fan and cheerleader, Grandpa never blinked at the hour-long drive into the city. And he'd always make sure he and Grandma stopped by a bakery on the way to buy me a cookie, saying I deserved a treat for trying my best.

"I am?" I ask. "How do you figure?"

Grandpa shrugs, his tone matter-of-fact when he says, "Well, you've done it here already, haven't you?"

I roll my eyes. "You're an old charmer, you know that?"

He winks, only proving my point.

Grandpa's been on the gallery's board of directors since the place opened over two decades ago—well before Julian and Sunny took the reins a few years back—and he'd urged me to apply for the event planning job when I first moved to Lennox. After all, I had the perfect credentials: I've loved art and design my whole life, minored in art history in college, and was the de facto event planner for my father for years—never mind the business experience I got through Found Family. It really was an ideal match. After Grandpa put in an enthusiastic word with the Gareth Mason board, the job basically fell into my lap.

The kettle starts to whistle, and I stand to make the tea, glancing at the clock. "Sadie should be here soon."

"Good! I've reached an impasse with my crossword puzzle."

Grandpa's health care aide comes to the house a few times a week to help him with physical therapy exercises and various other tasks he finds challenging on his own. She's a puzzle wizard; the two of them have a friendly rivalry about which of them is better at crosswords. "Maybe she knows an eight-letter word that starts with S for *dormant or immobile*."

I search my brain as I fill our mugs, steam winding around my wrist as the little pillowed tea bags bob upward. "Stagnant?"

Grandpa slaps the table so hard I almost drop the spoon in my hand.

I turn to him with wide eyes and find him inspecting the folded crossword puzzle he's pulled from his walker basket.

"Stagnant!" He grins up at me, fishing out a stubby pencil from his sweater pocket. "Brilliant girl. You're gonna give Sadie a run for her money."

I finish making the tea and take our mugs over to the table.

"Thank you, darling," he says.

Stagnant. I roll the word around in my head. Life in Seattle had been exactly that. After years of chasing my father's approval, I'd felt burnt out and trapped. And my relationship with Fletcher—even before I'd discovered his cheating—wasn't much better. We may have officially called it off last month, but we were just going through the motions long before that. We barely talked. Had forgettable sex.

That apathy was why I'd been so reluctant to set a wedding date. We were a practical match, but something always felt off. I'd never been sure what it was—or what I was hoping might change. It turned out, I couldn't reason my way out of what was wrong between us. Fletcher had never really loved or respected me. I'd been his ticket to my father's inner circle. Arm candy. Social currency.

My move to Lennox Valley had driven the wedge between us

deeper. Sure, we'd done the long-distance thing—he was always traveling for work, anyway, so it wasn't a stretch—but the time apart had only made it clear: distance wasn't a hardship. The cheating shouldn't have been that surprising to me, in hindsight.

"I'm gonna take this to my room and work on my proposal," I tell Grandpa, stooping to plant a kiss on his cheek.

"Don't let me keep you."

Balancing my laptop and my scalding mug, I pad across the sleek hardwood floor to my end of the house. Although we call it a cottage, Grandpa's house is modern and far from quaint or rustic. Built into the hillside overlooking the river, the house has a long set of stairs leading to the front door, with a driveway sweeping up and around back to provide the more level entrance Grandpa now exclusively uses. Dad had footed the bill to have the place built for my grandparents a few years before Grandma got sick, and he'd spared no expense—he'd even had the foresight to include an accessibility ramp at the back entrance. Grandpa and I have a pretty good setup with our rooms being at opposite ends of the house, giving us each the privacy we need.

I set my mug on my nightstand and flip open my laptop as I settle onto my bed.

I'm only jotting down the beginning of an outline when several notifications chime in quick succession, Adrian's name multiplying in a stack in the corner of my screen. Instead of reading it all, I call him, switching on my video.

"Caroline, have I got some bullshit for you!" It's Adrian's classic move: skipping the small talk and diving right in. From the jostling of his camera and the background blurring past, I'd guess he's walking somewhere in downtown Seattle.

"Hey," I say with a soft chuckle. "Well, spill."

Smirking, he pauses to check over his shoulder, scanning the traffic before continuing to walk. "You remember Portia Stanhope?"

I squeeze one eye shut, trying to remember. "The donor with the... the property in Vancouver? The ceramics retreat thing?"

"Yeah, her. So, there was this whole misunderstanding. We thought she was gonna donate the proceeds from the retreat, and she did, which is great, but get this: she also donated the ceramics themselves."

"Wait, what?"

Adrian comes to an abrupt stop, eyes widening dramatically. "*Exactly*! What the fuck am I gonna do with fifty-plus shitty clay pots?"

"Why would she give them to us?" I almost laugh.

Us. Old habits die hard. I still think of the charity as ours, even though I'm essentially a silent partner now.

He starts walking again. "No fucking clue. I don't think she's really tuned in to what a youth mentorship charity needs. Money is good. Donate money, please and fucking thank you. Does she think underprivileged youth want shitty clay pots? What's she smoking?" He drops his voice to a discreet mumble, lifting his brows. "Probably something she keeps in a shitty clay pot, is all I'm saying."

I suppress a laugh. "She sounds... unique."

He dead-eyes the camera. "Well, she's gonna be there Saturday."

"Oh." I give Adrian a cautious look. "Delightful."

"And she wants to discuss it with you, bestie." He drags a hand through his short brown hair, scanning the street.

"What? Why?"

"I dunno. Says you'll understand her vision or some shit. *Woman to woman.*"

"Hoo boy," I sigh.

"So, anyway, I need you to turn on that thousand-watt smile and work your magic, or this hippie granola lady is gonna send me to an early grave."

"I'll take care of it." I slouch back onto my pillow, propping the laptop on my raised knees. "But you're lucky I love you. And lucky I have to be there for my dad, too, or I'd ditch out on you and this hippie granola lady *so fast*."

"Nothing like crushing obligation, right?"

"Ugh, don't remind me." Despite the truth in his words, Adrian's gallows humor cheers me up a little. "You bringing a date?"

"Babe, I'd be *your* date if you didn't have to play happy couple with that lying asswipe."

"Wish you could."

As it stands, it appears I'll have to lean harder into this ridiculous scheme with Fletcher—dig deep so I can tolerate at least a few chaste public displays of affection Saturday night. Anything to make sure we're caught on camera looking like a couple.

"What happened to Casey, though?" I ask, reaching for my tea. "Thought things were heating up between you two." I take a cautious sip.

He scoffs. "Casey is an overgrown toddler. He's fun, like a big, sexy puppy, but... not the black-tie fundraiser type. Even if he would look cute as fuck in a tux."

"What about what's-her-name? The girl from grad school? Emma?"

"What? Sorry. Just picturing Casey in a tux." Adrian seems to shake it off. "Emma, uh, no. Funny story, though. I'll fill you in when I see you."

"Okay. Oh, hey, speaking of funny stories... You don't read *The Wash*, do you?" I grimace.

"Uh, no, I have a *life*, Caroline." He gives me a suspicious squint. "Why?"

"Hang on." Reluctantly, I send him the link. "It's not a big deal for the charity, but..." I let the dead air hang as Adrian pulls up the website, cringing when his eyes bug out. "Figured you should be aware?"

"What the fuck is this?" he asks, his voice rising in pitch. "You let me go on and on about clay fucking pots when there was *this* to talk about?"

I press my fingers against my temple, trying to fight off a laugh. "It's not a big deal."

"Who is this guy? He's hot as hell!"

My shoulders sag. "Just a guy I met at the gym. Literally like ten minutes before this. Nothing happened."

"I call bullshit. You're serving some serious bedroom eyes in this picture."

"Am not!"

"*Moony*, Care. You look *moony*."

Rolling my eyes, I try to bite back a grin.

"And like you wanna mount him like a mechanical bull in a dive bar. I mean, *I* would. Wait... *Do I spy a slutty little thigh tattoo*?"

I laugh, setting my tea back on my nightstand.

"Hang on, shit," Adrian says, the other shoe obviously dropping. "Is your family pissed?"

"Yeah, I talked to my parents, and it's a whole... *thing*." An email notification crops up. "Speak of the devil. Dad just emailed me about it."

I open it and quickly skim the message he forwarded from Linda's PR firm. As I process what I'm reading, the contents of my stomach slowly turn to a block of concrete.

"Oh, God," I groan. "They want me to *what*?"

4

———

MILES

"Jude, hang on. I can't hear for shit out here." I pull open the door to my truck. When I shut it behind me and the buzz of traffic muffles to comparative quiet, I yank off my hard hat. "Okay, what?"

"You got a girlfriend now?"

"Uh…"

"Thought you weren't dating."

"I'm not." Frowning, I switch my phone to the opposite ear, shoving my empty lunch bag and gear onto the passenger seat. "What the hell are you talking about?"

"Olena sent me this link Nat saw. Some political gossip blog thing. She came across it through her government job, I think."

"Wait. Gossip blog? The fuck?" My phone chimes against my ear and I switch to speakerphone, my mind already scrambling to make sense of what I'm hearing.

Dating? Girlfriend?

I can't even think of any women I've been around lately.

"Uh, it's called *The Wash*," Jude says as I open the link. "It says:

Airing the dirty laundry of Washington state elite." His sigh whooshes static through the phone. "Who reads this shit, man?"

Jude's one to talk; he reads landscaping blogs.

The site finally loads and my stomach drops when I see the photo of me outside the gym yesterday. With Caroline.

"Who the fuck took this?" I wonder out loud, zooming in. More importantly, why?

I quickly zoom out and scroll down, my eyes tripping a scattered path through the article.

Caroline Brennan, daughter of... Pete Brennan? Jesus. Engagement called off...

What the fuck is going on?

My mind races to make sense of this. The thought of a paparazzo type lurking around town is laughable. Nothing ever happens in Lennox. Definitely nothing that would qualify as celebrity gossip. That's part of the reason I moved home. It's slow here. I need slow.

"Alright, out with it," Jude says.

I roll my eyes.

My older brother has a bad case of BDE: Big Dad Energy. Though I guess he comes by it honestly, having basically stepped into the role after our parents died eleven years ago. "What's the deal?"

"Okay, look, I met her at the gym. There was this asshole talking to her and— Y'know what? It doesn't matter." I balance my phone on my thigh and start the truck, too hungry to go down this particular rabbit hole right now. "Anyway, I walked her outside and helped her with her bag. That's it. Haven't seen her since. Some creep obviously snapped a photo of us."

"Miles, how the hell do you, of all people, get tied up in a scandal with the daughter of some blowhard politician?"

"Scandal?" I echo through a skeptical chuckle. "Fuck off."

But also… *shit.* So much for trying to keep my head down here. I pull out into the street and head for home. "It was, like, a five-minute conversation. And I had no idea her dad was a senator."

Pete Brennan. Of all fucking people.

It does explain the rich-girl vibe I got at the gym, though. She probably *is* rich. Elite, like the blog title said. In other words, nothing at all like me. I exhale, already kicking myself for the way the thought deflates me. Disappointment is pointless; she might be way out of my league, but I'm not even playing ball.

"It says she was engaged or something?"

"I guess? Maybe?" I catch my shoulders creeping up to my ears and consciously lower them, shifting in my seat. "I don't know anything about her."

"She's pretty!" Olena calls out in the background, audibly enjoying the whole situation. "Did you get her number?"

"No," I say, but I can't help but admit it: she's not wrong. Caroline *is* gorgeous. Those long, toned legs… those perfect tits—on the small side, the way I like them. There's a reason I couldn't stop staring at her Tuesday morning—why I skipped showering before work so I could spend every last second with her. "Still not dating anyone. Not until I get my one-year chip, at least. Tell Olena to cool it."

"Alright," Jude says with an amused-sounding sigh. "I think I'll find some way to distract her."

Olena lets out a delighted shriek and I grimace. Ever since they got engaged, they're all over each other.

"Gross. Can you two please save your weird sex stuff for after you hang up?"

"Fucking relax, would you? I don't want you on the phone for that, either." There's a shuffling sound like he's sitting down on the couch. "Hey, I was gonna ask if you wanted to plan anything for your one year."

"Aw, c'mon, man. Don't jinx it. It's like two months away."

"Not trying to jinx it, Miles. You're getting there, though. It's an idea, anyway. Sober for a whole year is a huge milestone. So we should, y'know... celebrate."

"Celebrate?" I frown, turning onto my street. Jude suggesting a party is not exactly his style. "Did Olena put you up to this? Or Nat?"

That, or my brother really does think this is a pretty big deal. And... fair enough. He's probably the one who deserves a party— for keeping me alive for over a decade while I put us both through hell with my drinking.

"Uh, there might have been a nudge," Jude admits. "But they're right. We gotta do something."

"I mean, I guess? I dunno, man."

"Ooh, I can bake a cake!" Olena calls out.

"Look, I'll think about it, but later. I'm fucking starving." I park outside my building and kill the engine.

"Alright, alright. Go eat before you get pissy. Just wanted to put the bug in your ear. And don't worry, I won't let Olena bake anything."

I tilt my head. Food isn't exactly her forté.

After we say our goodbyes and hang up, I grab my bag and head for the front door of my apartment building. I lunge past one of my neighbors on her way out, catching the lobby door with my boot before it shuts. Trying to reassure the frowning older woman, I wave my keys in the universal sign of *don't worry, I live here* and make for the elevator. Since I leave so early for the gym each morning, I'm sure half my neighbors have barely laid eyes on me over the last ten months.

The clunking whir of the old elevator barely registers as I ride up to the fourth floor; I'm too engrossed in staring at that picture of me and Caroline to notice much else.

The timing of the photo—the placement of my hand, how I'd stepped in close to fix her bag—made it look like there was more between us. Though there *had* been something there. An intangible draw. Attraction, I guess. I shake my head, remembering how I'd fallen all over myself to help her out. I'd tied her shoe, for fuck's sake, like I was goddamn hypnotized.

I push inside my apartment and chuck my things onto the chair near the door, then duck into the tiny galley kitchen to throw a container of leftover pad thai in the microwave, like I can sense this new development in my life is gonna require brain fuel. But my willpower doesn't last long, because I'm only halfway through unlacing one steel-toed boot before I'm dropping into the nearest kitchen chair and flicking open my laptop with my free hand. I'm still typing her name in the search bar when my phone pings, pulling my eyes from one screen to the other.

GUS

Never thought you of all people would be anyone's "mystery beau"

Pretty fucking fancy, buddy

ME

Fucking hell. How'd you see this shit already?

GUS

My mom sent it to me.

This fucking town. I find the blog post right away and open the article.

GUS

Gotta say, calling your ass "elite" is fucking hilarious

Girl in the photo though… damn. *whistles*

ME

> Ok well laugh it up. It's all just a stupid misunderstanding.

GUS

> Tell that to the way she's looking at you

I zoom in on the photo again.

He's right. There's something in her eyes. I'd seen it—felt it—that morning. And I know I wasn't imagining things. Call it an ADHD sixth sense, but I've always been able to read people well.

I try to let it go. It doesn't matter if there'd been a fleeting attraction between us. Or if some gossip blogger thinks we're together after one misleading picture. I couldn't give two shits about what some local rag says, anyway. The rumor will probably be a distant memory by tomorrow.

By late morning, it's become clear I *can't* shake this rumor thing.

Despite my best efforts to brush it off, that photo of me and Caroline kept me up last night, and something about it was still humming away in the back of my head when I woke up. Working out hadn't shifted it, and my distraction level on the job site this morning was becoming a liability. I fumbled my hammer at least twice and praised the inventor of steel-toed boots when I nearly bit it tripping over a pile of rebar. Thankfully, Dave didn't witness any of this, but some of the guys gave me shit. I played it off like I missed my morning coffee, but, the truth is, my brain has been MIA all morning.

When I'd found her profile on the gallery's website last night and I realized she worked across the street from me, it felt like the universe was handing me a big, blinking invitation to go talk to her. I figured this weird rumor warranted a conversation, at the very least.

But I'd also paused. Sure, it'd be easy to pop by, but how would it look? Like I was just another asshole invading her space? With no other way to get in touch, though, I decided to risk it.

I have to take a huge step backward to avoid getting hit by the gallery door when a stylish older couple suddenly pushes outside. Pulling up short, they quickly swerve around me, throwing me a pair of cautious side-eyes.

They're not the only ones wondering what I'm doing here.

Stepping inside the bright, open space makes me strangely nervous. I probably shouldn't have come on my lunch break. I'm definitely not dressed to be in a place like this, in my dusty jeans and hi-vis. Nearly every surface in here is spotless and white, with one weathered brick wall at the back. A quick glance at the price tag next to the nearest painting confirms my suspicion: this little art gallery is bougie as fuck.

I rub my hands on my jeans, feeling like I'm sullying the place just by being here. It doesn't do much to shift the dirt from my sweaty palms and I make a mental note not to touch anything.

"Hello?" I call out into the empty space, hovering near the front door.

That older couple wouldn't have left the gallery unattended, would they? I'm pretty sure they're the owners. I recognized them from the website; their photos were alongside Caroline's.

"Be right with you!" a familiar voice calls back, and my heart rate ticks up a notch. It goes up another ten when Caroline rounds the corner from the back, stopping short when she sees me. Surprise lights her eyes. "Miles."

She's wearing this oversized, cozy turtleneck sweater-dress thing that seems to surround her in a glow of creamy fluff. It's short—like a miniskirt—and her smooth, bare skin peeks out over thigh-high brown leather boots.

Jesus, those boots.

Her hair is down, glossy blonde ringlets falling around her shoulders.

Stop staring like a dickhead and speak.

"Hey," is all I can think to say, still trying to process seeing her again, never mind those sexy fucking boots. "Uh, sorry, it's probably weird of me to just show up here outta nowhere, but I, uh—" I swallow, then breathe through a smile as I try to think of how to explain. Somehow, *I saw a rumor we were a couple and then low-key stalked you online* doesn't quite make the cut.

"You saw the article." It's not a question.

"I did, yeah. Well," I hedge, "pretty sure the whole town saw it."

Caroline lets out a heavy sigh. "I assume the internet filled you in on my family, then?"

"And where you work." I gesture at the wall of paintings next to where she stands, then rub at the back of my neck. "Didn't have your number or anything, but I'm working across the street, so I thought I'd, uh..."

Fuck, this is awkward.

She nods slowly as the silence hangs between us. At least she doesn't seem uncomfortable about me stopping by.

Thank God.

"You wanna come in? You look like you're about to run away any moment, standing in the doorway like that."

I laugh, glancing outside. "Not gonna run. Promise." Taking a few tentative steps forward, I peer around the gallery, stuffing my hands in my pockets as I inspect another painting without really taking it in. "So, you're some fancy famous girl, huh?"

She lifts her eyes to meet mine. "No, I'm not."

I tilt my head, giving her a look. "Says the girl getting followed by the paparazzi."

"Okay, I know, it's weird. But what am I supposed to do, tell everyone I run into, including some random man I met at the gym, that they might end up being political gossip fodder just for speaking to me in public?"

"I mean..." my lips curl up at the corner, "speaking as the random man in question... that actually might've been a helpful heads up."

"Are you kidding?"

I only shrug.

"Anyway, this whole thing is more about my dad than me. My family's been under a lot of scrutiny lately. Because of the campaign."

"So, we stirred up some shit." I try to look charmingly apologetic, not liking the idea that she might be in hot water because I tried to help her out. "On a scale of one to ten, how much did this fuck up your week?"

"Well..." she hedges, her face pinching.

"Oh, damn." My eyebrows shoot up. "How bad is it?"

"My dad... wasn't thrilled," she concedes, then, when she notices my surprise, rushes to add, "but it's not about you. I won't bore you with the details."

Her caginess is only making me want to know the dirt, though. I've always hated secrets. I lift my chin. "C'mon. Try me."

The front door pulls open, sucking a gust of air out with it. The older couple from earlier step inside, holding to-go cups from the cafe a few doors down.

"Can we help you?" the woman asks, sizing me up with obvious concern. "Is the water getting shut off again? Because, honestly, the disruption—"

"No," I say, holding up a hand. "That's, uh... not why I came by." I cast an uneasy glance at Caroline, who looks apologetic, before facing the older woman again.

"The power then?" She throws her free arm out at her side. "How are we supposed to run a business under these conditions?

This project has been an absolute nightmare! And don't get me started on the noise!"

"Uh…"

"Did no one consider the impact on local businesses?" the man asks.

"Well," I say, unable to stop the defensive clench in my stomach. "You could see it that way, sure, but what about the impact on the low-income families we're building this affordable housing project for?"

"Sunny, Julian," Caroline cuts in, elegantly diverting us from further confrontation. "Miles isn't here about the construction project. He's here to talk to me."

"Talk to you?" The man fails to suppress the surprise in his voice and gives me another assessing once-over, his gaze lingering on my dirty work boots. "What on earth about?"

I try not to be obvious about rolling my eyes. It's not the first time I've been judged by some snooty prick for having a blue-collar job.

"It's actually kind of a long story," Caroline explains. "I'll be happy to fill you in later but, for now, do you think you could give us a few minutes?" She gestures an elegant arm toward where she'd come from earlier.

Oh, she's good. Fancy girl's clearly got some managerial skills.

Visibly flustered and somewhat suspicious, the couple sweep past us with their coffees, probably headed to an office or whatever exists around the corner back there.

"Sorry," Caroline says when she turns back to me. "Where was I?"

"Uh, right." I have to tear my eyes away when she bites her lip. "You were gonna tell me about how I got you in trouble? So, what's the story there?"

Her brows quirk together. "How long do you have?"

I glance over my shoulder at the job site through the window. "Quick and dirty version?"

She opens her mouth, then pauses. "Okay, gosh, where do I even start? I guess the issue is—"

Something outside catches her attention, and she stops short, the color draining from her already-pale cheeks.

5

CAROLINE

I'm on guard even before he pulls the door open. "Fletcher. What're you doing here?"

"A better question is: what's *he* doing here?" He tilts his head at Miles like he's a thing rather than a person.

My confusion quickly morphs into understanding.

Right. Everyone and their dog has seen that photo by now.

Fletcher heads straight for me, holding a loaded, assessing kind of eye contact with Miles as he passes him. Neither man appears to like what he sees.

"Hey, Care-bear." Fletcher leans in to press a kiss to my cheek and I stiffen.

I flick a brief glance at Miles, whose expression hardens slightly, reminding me of the one he wore when that moaning weirdo approached me at the gym.

"Do you want me to..." Looking conflicted, Miles gestures over his shoulder and backs up a few steps toward the door. "Like, want me to take off? You seem busy. I can come back later or something."

"No," I blurt out, louder than I meant to. The last thing I want is to be left alone with Fletcher. Plus, my ex has gotten what he wants far more often than he deserves; I'm not letting him chase Miles off. "Don't go. Please."

He checks the time on his phone and I breathe easier when he gives me a small nod.

Fletcher shifts his frowning gaze between us and turns his back to Miles. "Look, babe, I happened to be in town and wanted to stop by and check in about the fundraiser on Saturday. You never answered my texts."

"There's nothing to check in about," I say, taking a small step backward, trying to hide my disgust at how Fletcher called me *babe* again. With all the political schmoozing he does, it's like he can't turn it off. But I refuse to be schmoozed.

"And why aren't you wearing your engagement ring?" he asks, jerking his chin toward my bare ring finger. "If we're gonna squash this story—"

"I forgot." It's a lie. And, I have to admit, the impulse to reveal the truth—that I've been wearing it as little as humanly possible because I'd rather swallow broken glass—is strong. "And I'll see you there. On Saturday."

He clenches his jaw. "No, I should pick you up. It'll look better if we arrive together."

I balk, but catch myself.

Don't make a scene, Caroline.

Squaring my shoulders, I say, "That won't be necessary."

He laughs, ugly condescension in his voice. "Don't be ridiculous. We always go together. The media will drag us over the rocks if they get wind of anything, and we need to nip this little"—he glances over his shoulder at Miles—"*rumor* in the bud. Pete was clear about our arrangement, Care."

"I know."

"Speaking of which, Linda's firm arranged the photographer for Friday."

My stomach churns at the reminder of the PR scheme proposed in Dad's email.

Fletcher continues, "They'll meet us at the restaurant and follow us to the hotel for some candid shots. You know, romantic evening away kind of deal."

A weight presses on my chest. Gritting my teeth through dinner is one thing, but being trapped in a hotel room with Fletcher overnight would be hell. Even thinking about it nauseates me.

I can't do this...

Scrambling for escape, my mind conjures up an image. A way out. What if, instead, I showed up Saturday with the same guy from the photo, so it would look real? Like an actual relationship —not just a fling. The prospect shimmers in my mind like an oasis in a desert, and I flick my eyes to the man who saved me from a jerk once before.

Could we pull it off? Could he?

"The photos will be leaked to the press," Fletcher drones on, and the oasis evaporates into thin air. "Discreetly, of course. That should take care of this unfortunate situation you've gotten us into."

Revulsion crawls up my spine.

"No." The word comes out before I realize what I've said.

"*No?*" Fletcher echoes, throwing his arms out at his sides like he's never heard the word before. "What do you mean, *no?*"

"I'm not going with you," I say, my voice flat. Crossing my arms over my chest, I tuck my shaking hands into the fluffy folds of my sweater. "I'm not doing the restaurant or the... the romantic hotel thing."

Panic and courage battle for control in my chest.

What am I doing?

"And I'm not going with you to the fundraiser Saturday, either."

"What?" Fletcher almost laughs. "Why not?"

"Because I'm..." Once again, my gaze lands on the pair of blue eyes trained on me from across the room—the safest harbor in this storm. "Because I'm going with Miles."

The silence hangs for an uncomfortable beat as we all process what I just said.

"What?" Fletcher turns, no longer ignoring Miles and instead pinning him with an incredulous glare.

Miles opens his mouth—probably to ask what the hell I'm talking about—then stops short when I paste on my best *please-roll-with-this* face.

"This guy?" Fletcher asks.

Miles shakes his head with a rueful smile, clearly picking up on Fletcher's derision.

"Fletcher, he—"

"Yeah, actually," Miles cuts in, stepping forward. He mocks Fletcher's tone when he adds, "*This guy*. I'm taking her. That gonna be a problem?"

Their gazes stay locked for a long moment.

What the hell did I just do?

And what's Miles doing?

I can't decide whether to feel relief or panic that he's going along with this. We don't actually know each other and he has no idea what this fundraiser is for. We could be raising money in support of some abhorrent cause, for all he knows. Clear-cutting the rainforest. Giving more white men podcasts. Wearing socks with sandals.

Instead of taking the bait, Fletcher spins back to me, eyes narrowed. "Is this your brilliant idea, Care? Your PR scheme?" He laughs joylessly. "You think the public is gonna buy that you're slumming it with some builder after being with *me* for three years?"

Disgust ripples through me, and I sneer right back. "At least *he's* building affordable housing for families who need it! Making an actual difference. Unlike you. And it's not like it's inconceivable, Fletcher. I'm a grown adult. The public will deal with the fact that I have a new boyfriend."

He huffs through his nose. "Oh, this is rich."

What did I ever see in this man?

Heck, maybe I never did see anything in Fletcher. Maybe it wasn't me choosing him so much as him being chosen *for* me.

"What's *rich* is you thinking I want to spend any more time with you than absolutely necessary after what you did. So I'll be there Saturday, and I'll be polite and professional in front of the cameras, but that's it. I'm done." My words are confident—convincing and committed. No spluttering or uneasy hedging. Even *I'm* impressed with my own acting skills right now, because they're all I've got masking the tornado inside my chest cavity.

"Care, I don't know who this guy is, but our arrangement—"

"Our arrangement is over, Fletcher." I swallow, well aware I'll be facing my father's wrath for going rogue. "I never should've agreed to it in the first place."

"Does Pete know about this little stunt of yours yet?" When I don't answer, he adds, "Or was that as impulsive as it looked?"

I set my jaw. Obviously, my dad hasn't been briefed yet on my harebrained scheme.

"Unbelievable," he mutters, then storms past Miles and out the door.

A shocked silence blankets the gallery as we both watch my ex climb into his Audi and peel out of his parking spot.

"I can explain," I say in a rush when I snap back to the present.

Miles' eyebrows are sky-high, but his lips twitch in amusement all the same. "I *was* kinda hoping you'd fill me in."

"Okay..." I press my fingers to my temples and try to steady my nerves.

Where do I even begin?

I open my mouth to explain, but he beats me to it.

"So, he's your ex, obviously." The wheels turn behind his eyes like he's making sense of what he just witnessed. "And, y'know, a self-important, dickhead, pretty-boy type. Gathered that much. But what was all the stuff about an arrangement and a hotel and shit?"

I can't seem to find the words, yet my shoulders almost sag with relief that Miles sized Fletcher up so quickly. "That photo of us," I finally manage. "Me and you, I mean. It was bad timing for my dad. Fletcher and I hadn't gone public about breaking up yet. We were trying not to rock the boat. For the campaign."

He nods. "And the photo rocked the boat."

"Exactly," I say, both grateful he gets it and momentarily distracted by the way the light catches on a small scar at the corner of his mouth. "Anyway, Dad's PR firm suggested we double down on being seen together as a couple. Overnight in a hotel... I guess it would make us look like a stable, happy family?" It's the image my father has always held dear—carefully curated for public consumption.

"And now?" he asks. "Is pretending I'm your boyfriend gonna help smooth everything over somehow?"

"Well," I say, begging myself to play it cool, "I guess it wouldn't seem like something so... casual?"

"Okay, yeah. Makes sense, I guess." He nods again, contemplating me as a long silence settles between us. "What'd he do? To you, I mean." He seems to catch himself and his eyes widen. "Sorry, that's a super personal question. Didn't mean to be that asshole. Forget I asked."

"No, it's fine. I roped you into this mess; it's only fair I explain why." I pause, trying to shrug off the stress of standing up to Fletcher. "We weren't..." I shake my head, then start again. "I mean, my family approved. Our relationship was good on paper." I puff out an exhale, hating how that sounded—and the way it made Miles grimace. "But then I found out last month he'd been cheating on me."

Miles clenches his jaw, his expression falling.

"Repeatedly," I add.

He looks out the gallery window, then lets out a long sigh. "Well, now I kinda wish I'd punched him before he left."

A surprised laugh bubbles up from my chest, pulling a smirk to Miles' lips when he faces me again. "Now *that* would be a PR nightmare."

"I was joking, to be clear. I don't go around punching assholes. Like, generally speaking."

"Okay," I say.

For a moment, we just stand there, holding eye contact, and a knot of tension takes root in my belly.

What was I thinking?

It's one thing to be caught on camera talking to a hot stranger, but it's entirely next level to lean into a flimsy rumor and invite him into my family drama—while under scrutiny from the media, no less. But the thought of spending a phony romantic evening at Fletcher's side seemed monumentally worse than taking a chance on said hot stranger.

"Sorry, again, for dragging you into this. It's not too late to back out."

"No way. Now I gotta see what all the fuss is about." He winks, and that smirk is back, pulling my attention to his lips, the square line of his jaw, and the cleft at the center of his chin under all the stubble. I school my features, trying to shake off the way Miles somehow flusters me without even trying.

This is business. Practical. A PR move to get the press off my back. Nothing more.

"Are you completely sure?" I ask.

"Yeah. You're stuck with me now, fancy girl."

THE NUMBER of times I have to pull my attention away from the construction site across the street after Miles leaves is borderline ludicrous. He needed to get back to work, so we'd quickly exchanged numbers and I'd promised to text him about Saturday. Then, I'd watched him jog across the street—definitely *not* admiring how he looked from behind in those worn jeans.

A few patrons wander in and I show them around, grateful for the distraction, although I find myself motioning at the paintings on autopilot, not really thinking too hard about the well-rehearsed spiel coming out of my mouth. Despite myself, my eyes drift, once again seeking out a glimpse of Miles through the front window. In a truly embarrassing turn of events, my breath catches when I think I spot him carrying a load of lumber over one shoulder.

What's next? Swooning? Fainting?

I need to get my head on straight before Saturday night. This fundraiser is going to be... rough. The idea of Miles mingling with my parents doesn't exactly give me warm fuzzies. And with Fletcher there, probably throwing me salty glances at every opportunity, I know I'm in for a world of awkwardness.

At least Adrian will be in my corner; God knows I need an ally in this whole mess.

But spending the evening with Miles? For some reason, that part doesn't feel as fraught. There's an easy openness to him—this up-for-anything energy that's both wholly unfamiliar and almost *magnetic*. He makes me believe I could be like that. Maybe I used to be.

And his deep voice... The soft sibilance each time he lands on an S. When he drops his voice low, it's like the ocean waves rolling gently over pebbles, somehow ragged and smooth at the same time. Rough with texture but time-worn, like any edges have been eroded away.

Okay, so, swooning and fainting might not be *entirely* off the table.

But who just spontaneously agrees to go on a fake date to a fundraiser they know nothing about? I can't tell if he's a fool or my savior. Heck, maybe he's both.

When I get home from work, Sadie's taken Grandpa for a walk and the house is quiet. I'm grateful for the silence so I can figure out what I've gotten myself into. What I've dragged *Miles* into.

I pull out my phone.

ME

You sure you're up for this fake date thing?

I try to bite back a smile when three dots immediately start to bounce on my screen.

Green flag.

MILES

We fooled that dickhead at the gym, didn't we?

Figure we can do it again.

Images of Miles in his gym gear rush into focus. Oh, God. He's gonna look *good* in a tux.

Then my stomach drops when I realize I forgot to tell him about the dress code.

ME

It's a black tie event. Will that be a problem?

MILES

Nah, don't worry, I clean up nice.

I bet he does. He's got this rugged, tousled-hair thing going where he looks like he's just tugged on a worn T-shirt between cups of coffee and a walk in the forest with his dog. Probably some derpy rescue mutt with a tongue bigger than its face.

Anxiety once again wraps around my chest. I don't even know his last name, for God's sake. Does he *have* a dog? Siblings? A meth lab?

I try to talk myself down from freaking out. Meth dealers probably don't hit the gym before seven in the morning—or need to work construction jobs.

My thumbs fly over the screen.

ME

What's your last name? And your address?

MILES

You gonna run a background check or something?

I can't tell if he's serious or not.

Should I tell him there's a real chance my father will do exactly that?

ME

I figured these are the basic facts I would know about my own boyfriend.

And I need to know where to pick you up on Saturday.

He sends his address, and I quickly save it to his contact info for later.

MILES

I was joking. It's Sharpe. Miles Sharpe.

(Just getting into character for Saturday.)

ME

I can practically hear the raised eyebrow from here.

MILES

Nice. I tried extra hard to pop that brow.

And don't worry, no criminal history.

Actually, full disclosure, I did shoplift a candy bar once in middle school.

ME

Really?

MILES

Yup. Coulda gotten away with it too, but I felt so guilty I couldn't even eat it.

Slept like shit that night and confessed everything to my mom in the morning.

ME

What did she do?

MILES

Made me take it back.

ME

Nice move. She sounds like a great mom.

The easy rhythm of our back-and-forth stutters to a halt when he doesn't respond right away. Ten, twenty, thirty seconds go by as I frown down at my phone.

Was it something I said?

Finally, he starts typing again. Then stops. Then starts again. The on-again-off-again nature of my relationship with those three little dots is getting worrisome. I exhale with relief when the text finally comes through.

MILES

You're driving Saturday? Assumed I'd pick
you up.

The change of subject surprises me, but I decide not to read
into it.

ME

Not necessary. My driver will take us into the
city.

MILES

Wait. Your driver?

Shit, you got a butler too?

ME

Very funny. No butler. And I only have a driver for
events like this.

MILES

Wow. I think you just out-fancied yourself.

Am I in over my head here?

ME

I told you it was black tie!

Don't make me use the facepalm emoji!

MILES

Whoa there, holster those big guns, partner. I
told you I clean up nice!

The mental image of Miles in a tux swims back into my mind,
and I bite my lip.

MILES

Don't stress. I can do fancy.

Can he, though? I've only ever seen him in gym clothes or dirty construction gear.

Oh, God. What if he thinks fancy *means clean jeans and a flannel?*

I need to relax. He's not clueless; the way he stood up for me at the gym proved that much. And the internet exists; he can find guidance on how to dress if he needs it. I don't need to micro-manage his clothing choices.

But my uncertainty gets the better of me, and I tap out another text.

ME

> If you have any trouble figuring out what to wear, I can help.

MILES

> Are you kidding? I've already got my monocle polished and my top hat…

What? My shoulders tense. I'm pretty sure he's joking. But, at the same time, I'm not entirely sure.

MILES

> …brushed. Did you know that's how you clean a top hat? Had to look it up.

His next text is a winky face emoji.

I drop my shoulders in relief.

Okay. Definitely joking.

Just to be sure, I fire back another text, aiming for a far more casual tone than I can muster right now.

ME

> If you're taking fashion cues from Mr. Peanut, we may have a problem.

MILES

> Shit, she's onto me!

Nah, relax fancy girl. I got this. Promise I won't embarrass you.

6

———————

MILES

This is at least the fifth load of soggy dead leaves and twigs I've hauled across this property and I'm sweating through my damn T-shirt. I wipe my forehead with the dirty wrist of my glove, then gather up the tarp and dump its contents into the bed of my brother's truck.

Jude's landscaping crew doesn't work weekends, but, since all the fallen leaves make autumn their busiest season, he tends to work an extra Saturday here and there to keep on top of it. He was hesitant to let me help at first, but it's a win-win situation: he gets free grunt labor, and I get to make amends—slowly pay him back for all the grief I caused him while I was drinking. The fresh air and exercise are solid perks.

So's Murphy. I pull off one work glove and crouch down to give Jude's sleepy old golden retriever a scratch on the head. He stirs, yawns, and gets right back to the important business: his mid-morning nap.

"Hey." Jude comes up behind me with another wheelbarrow full of crap. "Think there's probably one more load left over there."

"This place is pretty dope." I straighten and lift my chin

toward the open cliffside overlooking the river, adding, "Like a fuckin' postcard or something."

"Yeah." He follows my gaze, then scans around the yard. "This is where I met Olena, y'know." With a shove, he wheels the load of yard waste up the aluminum ramp and onto the open tailgate.

"Wait..." I throw him a skeptical look as I put my glove back on. The story of how they met—the version I heard, at least— didn't sound quite this picturesque. "Didn't she chew you out on the side of the road or some shit? In the pissing rain?"

Not that I'm one to judge; my first encounter with Olena wasn't exactly a meet-cute, either—showing up drunk and pounding on Jude's door like a shithead. We've patched things up since then, thankfully.

"Yeah. The road on the way *here*, though. This was our first project together." He empties the wheelbarrow, then brings it back down the ramp. "We got off to a weird start," he adds with a smirk. "But we figured it out."

I can't stop my thoughts from drifting to the way I met Caroline, but quickly shove aside any comparison. We aren't off to a weird start, because we aren't starting anything.

"What's with you?" Jude asks, lifting his chin with a brow cocked.

"What do you mean?"

"You're all..." He gestures at my face.

"I'm all *what*?" I grab a rake, ready to head off for the next haul of cleanup.

Jude passes me the tarp and picks up the wheelbarrow, following me along a gravel path toward a wooden arbor. "Something on your mind?"

"It's nothing." The white lie slips out easily—old habits and all. I give him a sidelong glance, my gaze falling to his tattoos; inked on each of his forearms is a tribute to the parents we lost too young—a hand planer for Dad, and a dandelion for Mom. Regret needles at me, knowing they'd want me to come clean.

Rigorous honesty. That's what they always say in AA.

"Okay, it's not nothing," I confess, gripping the rake tighter as we walk. "But don't get all judgy big brother on me about it."

Jude stops in his tracks and lowers the wheelbarrow as I turn to face him, giving me a long look. He's totally doing the judgy big brother thing. "Okay..."

"That includes your face, bro."

"I didn't say anything!" He throws his hands out at his sides, but I'm sure he's probably going through a laundry list of potential fuckups I could've committed.

"Dude, I'm not drinking again, if that's where your head went."

"Good," he says. "So, then, what's up? Do you need, like, more support or—?"

"What? No!" I say, realizing what he's thinking.

"It's okay if things are getting hard, Miles," he adds.

Fuck. Just my dick whenever I think about Caroline.

"It's not like that, man," I say, though I know full well I don't have a leg to stand on here. This thing with Caroline tonight has *hard* written all over it. And I'm partly to blame. She may have impulsively invited me, but I also impulsively leaned into it—too intrigued by the idea of spending an evening with her to take one of the multiple outs she offered later.

"This about that girl then?" Crossing his arms over his chest, he lifts his chin. "C'mon. Spit it out, scandal boy."

I set my jaw, hesitating another moment before I relent. "Alright. Fuck. So I might've... promised to go with her to this fancy, black-tie fundraiser tonight."

His eyebrows lift. "Thought you weren't dating."

"I'm not. It's like a fake... thing." I scrunch up my face, knowing I sound like a dumbass.

"A fake… thing," he repeats slowly.

"Like a fake boyfriend thing. She needs me to pretend for the…" I trail off, scrubbing my forehead with the back of my glove. "Shit, this is stupid, isn't it?"

"I mean, it's not sounding *smart*, I'll tell you that much."

"Fuck off! I said no judgy shit. It was a rhetorical question."

He holds up his hands in a silent *fine*.

"It's one night, okay?" I reason, my shoulders already tensing up. "Not a real date. It's fine. It'll be fine. It was either go with me or go with her dickhead ex, so…"

"Ah, right," Jude says with a nod. "So you're planning to, what, swoop in and play the hero? White-knight this thing?"

"I guess?" *More like white-knuckle this thing.* "I dunno. It was her idea. She was in a bind. Thought I could help."

Letting out a long sigh, Jude walks a few paces over to the cliffside, craning his neck to peer over the edge. He mumbles something I can't catch, like, "Forty-foot drop."

"What are you doing?" I ask as he wanders back.

"Oh, just trying to figure out whether I should throw you in the river." He tilts his head toward the cliffside with a smirk.

"Thanks," I deadpan.

"C'mon." He picks up the wheelbarrow again.

With a sigh, I follow him through the arbor and down a small set of stairs to a secluded garden, where we set up to do one last haul.

"So you must really like this girl, huh?" When I open my mouth to protest, he cuts me off. "Even though it's all *fake*, like you said, and blah blah blah, you're not dating yet, et cetera."

"I mean, she's… Like, she seems pretty cool and…" I trail off, unable to deny to *myself* that I'm ridiculously attracted to Caroline. That I haven't been obsessing about her, despite my best efforts not to. That I haven't come more than once thinking about pushing up that fluffy sweater dress and losing myself between those thigh-high leather boots.

"The dopey distraction isn't really reassuring, Miles."

Snapping back to the present—and my frowning brother—I remind myself *again* that it's not real. It's one night. And we have nothing in common, anyway. She's a privileged rich girl with a dad who's all up in her business, and I'm...

Well, it must be nice to have parents who *could* be all up in your business. The only one I've got all up in my business is Jude.

"Whatever, man," I say. "Doesn't matter. It's not a real date."

"Uh-huh." He doesn't seem convinced.

My phone rings from my back pocket.

"Don't be too long, 'kay?" Jude grabs the tarp. "I've got plans with Olena this afternoon."

I nod and tug off my gloves as I jog back up the steps to take the call. When I pull out my phone, the name on the screen makes me pause. Cautiously, I swipe to answer.

"Hey, Benji, what's up?" I haven't talked to the guy since I left Seattle. Haven't talked to *any* of my old friends, really. I'd needed a clean break from my old life.

"Miiiiiiiles, man!" he drawls. "Fucking settle a bet for me. Settle a bet. Okay. Okay. What was that chick's name?" There's shouting and laughter in the background. "Fucking get off me, man!" he says to someone. There are struggle sounds in the background, then a thud. More laughter. "Miles, fuck, who was that chick at Chap's work party? The one on the fuckin' boat or whatever. Houseboat. The houseboat. She had that... that fuckin' neck tattoo of the—"

"Uh, I dunno, Benj."

"—the snake—the cobra! Cobra. You remember her, man?" He sounds wasted. "Kayla? Makayla?"

I pull the phone from my ear to check the time. It's 10:20 in the morning and these guys are already pissed. I take a beat to scour my admittedly spotty memory. "Don't really remember that party, dude. Sorry."

"Aw, fuck," Benji says, sounding disappointed. "She was fuckin' hot, anyway."

"Okay?"

This is awkward.

"Thought we could hook her up with Chap. I think his virginity is growing back— Ow! Hey!" More laughter in the background. "Maybe try not being such an ugly piece of shit, Chap, ever thought of that?"

"Is that it? Like, is this why you—"

"Miles, what the fuck, bro? Haven't talked to you in like... in like... I don't even know. How the fuck are you?"

"Uh, I'm good..." I turn to Jude and hold up a finger like I need another minute—like this is an important matter of business and not some horrifying trip down drunk-memory lane.

Or no-memory lane, I guess.

"Yeah, I'm... I'm doing a lot better," I say.

"Yeah?" Benji coughs loudly on the other end of the line. "That's great, man."

"Thanks." I hesitate a beat, wondering whether to bother telling him. "I actually just met this girl and—"

"Fuck, Chap, will you stop with the goddamn ice?" Benji shouts, and I can't help the way his distraction deflates me a bit. "Bitch, if you come near me with that, I'll... Shit! Ah!"

"Hey, I should—"

"Chap just put ice down my shirt like a *fucking asshole*," Benji explains.

"Yikes," is all I say.

Yeah, fucking *yikes* is right.

Was this what I was like when I was sauced all the time?

"Hey, Benji," I say over more shouting and laughter on his end. "I gotta run. I'm uh... working here."

When I finally get a word in edgewise to say goodbye, I hang up and blow out a long breath, tapping my phone against my thigh a couple times before slipping it into my back pocket.

That was my life. Those were the assholes I called friends—too shitfaced to pay attention or listen. Or care.

My past life in Seattle suddenly feels like a parallel dimension to what I've built here. A fucking pathetic one. I make a mental note to thank Gus for showing up for me like an actual friend. We'd reconnected quickly when I moved home. Even when he was going through that rough patch, splitting up with Shay, he always made time for me. He's solid like that.

Do they make "thanks for not being a piece of shit" greeting cards? It's a pretty underwhelming sentiment, I guess, but it would probably still make him laugh.

When I collect myself, I jog down the steps to join Jude in gathering the piles of leaves he's raked up from around the fire pit in the center of the garden.

"Who was that?" he asks, probably picking up on my soured vibe.

"Just one of my old buddies from Seattle."

He lets a beat or two pass, watching me—probably remembering how stuff from my drinking days might be triggering. "You alright?"

"Yeah, fine."

Honesty, I remind myself.

"I mean, it was weird. Not in a good way." I throw a bunch of leaves onto the tarp. "Let's just say it made me appreciate being sober."

Jude smiles. "Good."

We work in silence, raking and collecting all the leaves until the tarp and wheelbarrow are both full. Slogging across the property, we haul everything back to his truck.

I cast my gaze sideways toward my brother, mulling over how

shitty it felt when Benji didn't give two shits about what I'd told him. I can do better—be present and ask questions and actually listen to the answers. "So, what plans do you have with Olena later?"

"Uh," he hesitates as he parks the wheelbarrow behind his truck. "I think they call it *afternoon delight*."

"Fuck, bro!" I groan.

He flings a twig at me, smirking at my reaction. "Hey, you asked."

"Then *forget* I asked,"—I chuck a handful of leaves back at him, but he only laughs—"unless you want a load of my puke mixed in with these leaves."

So much for my attempt at genuine curiosity and connection, because kumbaya just turned to kumba*yarf*.

"Wait, you *plan* that?" I ask. "No, nope, never mind." I grimace and shake my head. "Don't answer that."

"Hey, listen," Jude says when the disturbed look on my face has settled to something more like vague caution. He tugs off his gloves and reaches for his back pocket. "I know you wanted to help me out and, y'know, repair our relationship and shit, but, uh... We're good, man." He slips some cash from his wallet and holds it out to me. "Here."

"What's this?" I take a step back, wary expression firmly in place.

He balks. "What does it look like? A fuckin' Fabergé egg? Take it."

I scowl down at the cash. "Fuck off. I'm not taking your money."

He doesn't back down. "Miles, don't be proud. You busted your ass for hours here. I can pay you."

"That's not... Dude, that's not how this works." I push past him and heave the last tarpload into the truck, then turn back to face my brother. "Making amends in AA is about showing up for the people you've wronged. Behaving differently. Better. Y'know, actions speak louder than words, right?"

"I'm just trying to help you out."

"So stop," I say with a shrug. "You need to let me hold my own, alright? Stop trying to rescue me. I'm not needing that so much these days, if you haven't noticed."

"Yeah, Miles," he says, dropping his gaze with a nod. "Okay."

"And put your fucking money away. If anything, I should be paying *you* back. Not the other way around." I push the wheelbarrow up the ramp to dump its contents onto the pile of yard waste, then busy myself securing it to the truck.

My brother's covered a lot of my expenses over the years, including medical bills and paying for my move back to Lennox. Never mind all the times he's spotted me cash or bought me a meal because I've been broke or between construction jobs. The least I could do is offer up some free labor when he needs a hand.

"Alright. You're right." He slips the cash back into his wallet. "Sorry, man."

"Now let's get this shit cleaned up, 'cause I have a date with a hot-as-fuck shower when I get home."

"And what about your real date tonight? Your, uh... real fake date?"

"What about it?" I hop back down.

Murphy slowly pushes up and stretches, as if he can sense we're almost done here.

"You got a game plan?" Jude asks, folding up the ramp. "Where is this fundraiser thing?"

"Some hotel ballroom in Seattle, I think." I quirk a brow. "What do you mean, *game plan*?"

"There gonna be drinks there?" He slides the ramp into the truck bed. "You haven't really been around other people drinking yet, right?"

I hold his gaze and shove the tailgate hard until it latches.

Right. That part.

"Maybe chat with Barry before you go?" Jude adds.

Calling my sponsor is a solid suggestion. I should probably fill him in on this Caroline thing, anyway.

"Will do," I say with a nod, then smirk to myself as I peel off my gloves. "Bet he'll have a laugh at the idea of my ass in a tux."

Jude chuckles, pulling open the passenger door to his truck so Murphy can climb in. "Barry's what, like, sixty-something?"

"Yeah, think so."

He gives me a look. "Better make sure he's sitting down first."

THE TUX I borrowed from Gus fits surprisingly well and, to its credit, doesn't itch or pull on my skin in a way that'll make me seem twitchy all night. I've lost count of the number of work T-shirts I've got with a hole in the back of the neck from where I've torn out an irritating tag, but this tux is pretty fucking swanky. When Gus told me he had one I could borrow, I was so grateful not to have to hunt around for a crappy rental that I'd forgotten to ask what the fuck he's doing *owning a tux*. Dude must be living a second life as James Bond or some shit. Some kind of secret underground firefighter society, probably.

Do secret underground firefighter societies exist? Do they host black-tie parties?

Taking one last glance in the mirror, I shake myself out of that mental rabbit hole and straighten the bow tie I spent the last hour learning to tie. I try to stop fidgeting with everything I'm wearing, telling myself the clothes on my back are the least of my worries. Navigating this fundraiser will be enough stress on its own, no matter how much I'm looking forward to spending the evening with Caroline. I wipe my hands on my jacket, willing them to stop sweating.

Fuck, I could use a vodka. Or any drink, really.

The thought crops up, as it often does, straight outta left field —no doubt brought on by the anticipation I'm already feeling about this fundraiser.

I pull out my phone and text Barry. Sometimes just telling someone else that I'm having a craving is all it takes for the feeling to subside. It also helps me stay accountable since he'll make a point of checking in later. Knowing I may face temptation tonight is looming large in the back of my mind, though.

My door buzzer sounds, and I press the button on the intercom. "Hey. Be right down."

I'm too on edge to wait for the ancient elevator to chug its way to the fourth floor, so I push through the heavy fire door leading to the stairwell.

And, if the jog down three flights of stairs doesn't leave me a bit out of breath, the sight waiting outside the front door just about does it.

Caroline faces away from the glass front doors of the lobby, her eyes trained somewhere down the dark street. Her back is nearly bare, her glittering gold dress plunging in a deep V that ends right above her ass.

Holy hell.

It's realizing she must be freezing cold that has me pushing out the door.

"Hey." The word comes out slightly strangled, and I clear my throat, playing it off with a grin.

She turns, her soft lips slightly parted. "Miles." Relief rushes through me when she gives me—or Gus' tux, maybe—a small nod of approval, but my concern about the cold quickly swings back into frame when she rubs her arms and I notice the goose bumps dotting her skin.

"Jesus, you're gonna turn into an ice cube out here. C'mon." Without thinking, I slip my palm over her bare lower back, guiding her into the idling town car in front of us, but pull my hand away when the warmth of her skin spreads under my fingertips. I hadn't meant to touch her like that; I'm not thinking straight here.

This fucking dress.

I can already tell it'll be impossible to stop staring at her for the rest of the night—and I've only been with her for thirty seconds.

Shit.

I make a conscious effort to shove down the inkling that it's not just the dress flustering me.

The car is comfortably warm inside as we settle into the backseat and Caroline's driver pulls out into the sporadic traffic in front of my building.

"You look... uh..." I trail off and swallow, then shake my head, trying to stop from blurting out every description that comes to mind.

Stunning? Incredible? Sexy? Like that thigh-high slit could kill a man?

"Sorry," I say, tearing my gaze away only to have it land right back on her dress. On *her*. Willpower's never really been my thing. "I'm not sure how to..." I make a vague gesture between us.

"I'm not sure how to do this, either." She sounds almost sheepish. "It's weird, right?"

"Uh, weird isn't..." My eyes trace a path over her bare collarbone, her neck, her jawline.

Don't look at her tits.

Too late.

Fuck, they're perfect.

"Weird isn't what came to mind, honestly."

In the dim back seat, her light eyes are shadowed and unreadable, and I can only hope the darkness masked the path mine just took. Because it sure as shit isn't hiding the fact that I sound like I just crawled out of a swamp.

"I mean, you look..." I clear my throat, willing myself to string together a full sentence. "You look beautiful."

I hear more than see the smile on her face. "Thank you. And you did, in fact, clean up nice."

My ego practically purrs in response. "Told ya."

"And you shaved."

I instinctively rub my chin. "Yeah."

"Uh, sorry, I—" she cuts herself off, breaking eye contact like she's trying to shake off distraction.

I know the feeling.

"Alright," she says as she shifts in her seat, brushing my knee with hers, "we only have an hour to get you up to speed, so I should probably launch right in."

"I'm a fast learner. Hit me."

7

———————

CAROLINE

It all comes pouring out. I tell Miles about working for my father back in Seattle, starting Found Family with Adrian, and how Dad had thrown his weight behind our little charity from the very beginning. I don't go into details about his substantial annual donations, focusing instead on the basics Miles needs to know before stepping into a room with my father in it.

It all seems a bit over his head, but I think Miles gets the gist: this fundraiser is important to me, Adrian, my dad... and I owe it to my father to fall in line right now.

Which brings us to how I got wrapped up in a scheme to pretend Fletcher and I were still together—even after I'd found all those texts, confirming his flagrant cheating.

"So, that shitweasel didn't bother to cover his tracks?" Miles works his jaw for a second, like he's trying not to grind his teeth as he mulls over what I just told him.

"I guess?" I shrug, trying to brush it off, though I know I shouldn't. "Or he figured he didn't need to, maybe." It still stings. Fletcher isn't a man lacking in intelligence; it hadn't been a careless oversight but a choice. He'd been uncaring. Callous. I catch myself shrinking into my seat and consciously sit straighter. I don't want to dwell on it or let Fletcher get to me—let him ruin my night with Miles.

"And your parents know all this. About Fletcher cheating and shit."

"Yes."

He looks gobsmacked. "And they still wanted you to go along with this thing? Pretend to be with your lying fuckwit ex for show?" When I don't argue, he lets out a disappointed-sounding sigh. "Shit, that's brutal."

"Well, it was mainly my dad," I say quietly, as if that makes it any better.

Mom had objected to the arrangement at first, but Dad had gotten his way in the end—as he always does. His skill in debate, a politician's bread and butter, wins him just as many private arguments as public ones. Mom's developed a resigned kind of acceptance over the years; it's easier to let him have his way than make a fuss. If I'm honest, maybe I've done the same thing.

"The breakup came at a bad time for the campaign," I explain, trying to justify it. "Dad needs us in his corner right now. All hands on deck, right? Even if it means putting up with some"—I search for the right words—"uncomfortable circumstances."

Miles doesn't look convinced.

"Anyway, I think that's why I kind of... snapped. At the gallery. I know that sounds dramatic. But hearing Fletcher go on and on about all this time we needed to spend cozying up together to appease the press..." I trail off, gazing down at the gold brocade clutch in my lap. "It was too much. It had gone so far past uncomfortable for me. Honestly, it felt like torture." With tentative hope, I look up. "And then you were—"

"I was there," he says, watching me carefully. "Like, I was conveniently nearby."

"Yes." When I realize how that sounds, my eyes fly wide. "I mean, no! You were *there*, but that makes it seem like I would have roped in anyone within a twenty-foot radius."

He meets my gaze in the dark, smirking slightly. "Is that not what you're saying?"

"No! Of course not!"

He dips his head like he isn't sure whether to be amused or what. "You sure?"

"Look," I say, dropping my shoulders. "You were *nice* to me." Self-consciousness swelling in my chest, I throw a quick glance toward our driver, wondering how much he's overhearing. "At the gym. I know we only talked for a few minutes, but we seemed to get along, right? And you told that weird guy off, explaining exactly why he was being a human nightmare. It was enough that I figured you probably weren't gonna turn out to *be* a human nightmare."

"Probably not a human nightmare," he echoes, almost chuckling. "Should I put that on my resume, or—?"

"Miles! Dang it! You know what I mean."

He laughs. "Hold up. Did you just say *dang it*?"

"Yeah. So?"

He tilts his head, the orange glow from a streetlight passing over the crinkled corners of his eyes. "That's adorably wholesome."

I fail to suppress an eye roll. "But you get what I mean, right? You were— You felt... safe. Like a safe bet."

"Okay," he says carefully, like something clicks into place. "Good. Safe is... good."

"It wasn't only because you were there." Unable to maintain eye contact with that admission hanging between us, I sit back in my seat, training my gaze out the window. "That said, I'm sure anyone within a twenty-foot radius *would* have been a better option than Fletcher. It's apparently a pretty low bar." I huff out a breath. "Guess I really know how to pick 'em."

"Caroline," he says, waiting until I turn to meet his eyes. "I barely know that dick, but from what I saw and what you told me? It's time to raise the fucking bar."

I smile, still feeling a little uncertain.

"And, uh, I'm more of a high-jump guy, myself." He tilts his head. "Maybe pole vault, if I'm feeling fancy."

I laugh. "Well, this party is gonna be pretty fancy. Are you saying you're gonna... pole vault it?"

"Okay," he says with a lopsided grin, "that metaphor might have gotten away from me a bit."

"I liked it." Almost in wonder, I study Miles. There's something fascinating about the way he puts me at ease. After Fletcher, being with a man who doesn't keep me guessing is almost foreign. But it also feels a lot like relief. I've only sensed this kind of easy honesty from one man before, and he's ninety-two and loves crossword puzzles.

"Look, I know we basically just met," Miles says. "But I can definitely handle this fake boyfriend thing tonight. Hell, I look the part, right?" He throws his hands out at his sides. "I'm wearing my fancy pants and everything. Perfect for, uh, pole vaulting or whatever." Laughing through the last words, he shrugs, then drops his voice lower. "I'm just talkin' outta my ass here, but, point is, I'm up for this. So c'mon." He holds out his pinkie. "Trust me."

I stare at him in disbelief.

A pinkie promise? Seriously?

His brows shoot up. "What? You've never made a pinkie promise before?"

I scoff. "Of course I have. But I'm twenty-eight years old, Miles."

"And I'm almost thirty, *Caroline*," he teases, pinkie still hanging. "Your point? What, you too good for pinkie promises?"

"Fine." My shoulders sag as I hook my pinkie to his. "Deal. I'll trust you." Then my voice softens to something more tentative. "But there's one more thing we need to discuss."

"What?" He lets his hand fall back to his lap, and I can't help but wish he hadn't let go.

"We might need to act... affectionate. Tonight. At the event."

That gets his attention.

Warmth flushes my face and neck and I'm grateful for the darkness in the back seat.

"Like, touch each other, you mean?" He almost winces, like he regrets how those words came out.

"Yeah, I mean, we're posing as a couple. It'll be expected."

"Right. For the cameras?" He looks nervous.

"Exactly. Like, small stuff. Holding hands. That kind of thing. And... never mind. I'm not gonna ask you to—" I cut myself off, breaking eye contact. "The press can just be a bit pushy about getting a good photo and—"

"Hold up. You saying we might have to kiss?" He swallows, the movement caught in another swath of passing orange light from outside.

"Just for the cameras," I stress. "But we don't have to—"

"Right."

"If that makes you uncomfortable, I completely understand."

"No, it's—" He shakes his head, then clears his throat.

"Because we can figure something out if they—"

"Caroline."

The low tone in his voice cuts through my spiraling, and I press my lips together to stem the flow of words.

"Let's take it as it comes, okay?" Slowly, he takes my fingers between his own and gives them a squeeze. His hands are warm and a little rough, and he strokes his thumb over my skin. "Trust me, remember?"

The inexplicable thing is: I do. I do trust him.

"You're saying we should wing it?" My eyes flick from our joined hands to his face. "Are you sure we shouldn't..."

He shifts to interlace his fingers with mine. The movement is slow. Careful. As if he's testing the waters.

"... practice?" I finish the question in barely a whisper, then bite my lip.

Suddenly, all I want to do is bite his.

God, what am I thinking?

"Well, how's this?" He squeezes my fingers and his gaze settles on my mouth. Reaching out, he tugs my lower lip out from between my teeth with his thumb and I have to remind myself to breathe.

The car pulls to a stop, jarring us from the moment. Miles drops his hand and, like smoke suddenly clearing, whatever was materializing between us evaporates.

Trying to shake it off, I glance out the window before returning my attention to him and wetting my lips. "That was..." —I swallow—"good. A good start, I mean."

A slow grin unfurls across Miles' features as he opens the car door. "Alright, fancy girl. I think we're on."

8

MILES

My attention is split a hundred different ways the instant we enter the ballroom. The decorations. Shouting photographers. The warmth of Caroline's arm tucked under mine. Her soft vanilla scent. That clown Fletcher throwing me an unmistakable stink-eye. Pete Brennan's booming laughter as he schmoozes and back-slaps and shakes hands like a dickhead. He's shorter than he looks on TV.

A young woman in a server's uniform materializes at my side, holding out a circular tray full of fizzing glass flutes. "Champagne, sir?"

The question lingers between us for a long moment, my mouth watering as I watch the tiny bubbles scurry up to the surface.

"No, thank you," I somehow force out. But, the way I stare at that tray as the server retreats and winds through the crowd, it's amazing my eyeballs don't crawl out of my skull to follow it.

Fuck. Get your shit together.

I swallow the spit pooling in my mouth and focus my attention on Caroline—the whole reason I'm here. She's telling some story—something about unexpected donations, I think—to an older couple who are rapt with attention.

She looks like she was made for this place. Between her gold dress and blonde curls, she even matches the glittering decorations. Beaming bright, she greets all sorts of people, introducing me to each one. I shake their hands and immediately forget their names, too overwhelmed by everything my brain is tripping over.

There's being a fish out of water, and then there's me—a dumbass in a borrowed tux at a fucking gala, of all places.

In hindsight, it was beyond naïve to think I could pull off playing the role of boyfriend to a woman way out of my league several times over—never mind being at a fancy-ass fundraiser with her family and friends, her scowling ex, and the press who are snapping candid photos at every turn... Jude was right; I'd severely underestimated the booze factor. I'd planned to just steer clear of the bar area, but the ready-made drinks dangled within my reach have me obsessing about taking one. Just one. I could take one. Just one to take the edge off this stress.

No. Fuck.

I squeeze my eyes shut, clenching my fists at my sides, and try to steady myself.

"Miles, are you alright?" Caroline's voice is tinged with concern.

I should win an Oscar for the way I play it off like I got something in my eye, because all that rubbing and blinking is really the performance of a lifetime. Excusing myself to go to the bathroom, I squeeze Caroline's hand before turning away. I dodge an assortment of tuxes and ball gowns as I cut a path toward the men's room, gluing my gaze to the floor to avoid all the drinks in my eyeline. My breathing is labored by the time I push into the spacious restroom, and I prop myself over one of the half-dozen sinks, staring at my reflection.

Jesus. Get a grip.

I wash and dry my hands to stall for time—and to avoid seeming like a creep if anyone else comes in—then pull out my phone. I'm about to call my sponsor but, when a couple other guys come in to take a leak, I think better of it and text him instead.

ME

Probably shouldn't have come to this thing tonight.

Too many drinks being shoved my way.

BARRY

Sorry to hear. Can you leave?

ME

I don't know. I didn't drive here.

BARRY

I could pick you up if you can hang tight for a little bit. Maybe 20 minutes?

Thank fuck Barry lives in Seattle. I never did switch sponsors when I moved back to Lennox. But no, I can't ask him to rescue me. Hadn't I told Jude just this morning that I didn't need rescuing?

ME

Nah, I don't wanna interrupt your night. Thanks though.

I'll get my shit together.

BARRY

You sure?

ME

I'm sure. Promise.

For a moment, I consider calling Jude, but I can almost see the frown on my brother's face. The unspoken *told you so*. The silent *don't fuck it up*.

I can't fuck this up. *Won't* fuck this up. I've worked too hard to get this far only to throw it all away. And I couldn't stomach the disappointment from Jude if I did. We both know he has every right to doubt my promises. My track record hasn't been great. But, over the last ten months, I've been working to change that. To be a better fucking human.

Pocketing my phone, I head back into the crowd and spot Caroline with her dad and a woman about his age who must be her mother. Their expressions are solemn—serious.

When I finally get closer and she spots me, Caroline looks relieved. And the way she lights up? She's fucking gorgeous.

God, I wanna touch her. Maybe, if I can't have a drink, I can let myself have this one small indulgence at least.

I'm supposed to be the boyfriend, I remind myself. *Act like the boyfriend.*

"Hey, baby." The endearment falls from my mouth without a second thought, and I slip my hand over the bare skin of her lower back, dropping a quick kiss to her cheek. This time, I don't pull away.

Her startled "Oh!" is too quiet for anyone else to hear over the din of the room, and something inside me hums with satisfaction knowing that little sound was just for me.

I let my thumb linger, slipping it over the dip of her spine as I draw back to meet her eyes.

Caroline seems to catch herself and shifts her attention back to her father, whose focus, in turn, is fixed squarely on me.

I glance at her mother, returning the slightly strained yet polite smile she's got plastered on her face.

"Mom, Dad, this is..." she starts, pausing as she touches my arm before awkwardly trying again. "Miles, these are my parents, Valerie and—"

"Quick photo, Senator Brennan? Mrs. Brennan?" A photographer to my left croons, interrupting us. Her camera is already poised at the ready, and she must get some kind of nod of approval, because she gets right to it.

Flash. Flash.

"And let's get one with Caroline too."

I move to step out of the shot, but Caroline snags my hand and tugs me back to her side, whispering, "You too."

Right. This was the whole point.

I can't say no to this woman. Not with those blue-green eyes locked on mine, and certainly not when she slips her arms around my waist and presses against me in that fucking dress. When I catch sight of Fletcher watching us, I take the time to brush a stray curl back from her temple, my gaze locked on her mouth.

Flash.

I dip down to skim my lips over her cheek and whisper, "This okay?"

Flash.

"Yes." The word is nothing more than a breath. Her fingers tense against my back and she lifts her chin.

I shift just enough that my lips graze hers.

Flash. Flash. Flash.

"Caroline! Over here!" The photographer's call pulls us apart before we've really kissed—but tell that to the charge running through my veins when the heat of her mouth leaves mine. Remembering myself, I turn toward the camera, sliding an arm around her waist.

"You two look amazing; thanks so much."

Photos apparently complete, the photographer moves on while Pete and Valerie get drawn into another conversation—right as a man about our age approaches us. He's a couple inches shorter than Caroline, a clean-shaven, put-together type who clearly belongs here. And he's grinning.

"I think Fletch is about to have a coronary," he says, keeping his voice low enough to avoid being overheard, but unable to hide his delight all the same. "You've done a number on his ego tonight, Care. And I'm *so* here for it."

Caroline introduces him as her best friend, Adrian, and I immediately like the guy; anyone who's happy to see Fletcher pissed is good in my books.

"I keep telling Care she's entering her villain era," he adds, leaning toward me slightly.

"Adrian," she scolds quietly, although she can't suppress a smile. "I am not."

"Long overdue, if you ask me." Adrian's amusement is contagious. "Anyway, as much as I would love to enjoy this delicious *schadenfreude* with you two all night, we have a small problem." Adrian explains there's some issue with one of the donors in attendance—Portia something?—and pulls Caroline away to help smooth things over.

"Be right back," she promises, lifting on her toes to kiss me on the cheek. Our eyes lock for a loaded few seconds as she slips away into the crowd, and I realize I'm staring.

"Miles," a deep voice says behind me, and I whirl around. Pete Brennan's stepping toward me, slimy self-satisfaction oozing from every pore. He puts a hand on my shoulder and I immediately wish he'd remove it. "Miles Sharpe. Have I got that right?"

"That's me," I say, hackles already up.

"Good, good." He steps closer. Closer than I'm comfortable with, but I resist the impulse to step back. Touching me and getting in my space—it's is a blatant attempt at a power play. Bosses have pulled these stunts with me before, and I refuse to take the toxic masculinity bait. "Listen, I'm sure it's no surprise I've got contacts with the city."

"Uh," I say. "Okay."

"With law enforcement, specifically."

My hackles just grew hackles. Every cell in my body is at attention, my stomach already knotting over where this conversation is headed.

He lifts his glass, and I watch the amber liquid slip between his thin lips, wishing I had a drink of my own. "Found out some interesting information about you, son."

My jaw clenches at the term *son*. He can fuck right off with that condescending shit. Still, I have to bite back the impulse to scramble for an explanation. What would I even say? I was young, fucked up, and drunk? That much is probably obvious.

"I'll be plain with you, Miles," he goes on. "I'm willing to keep this under my hat. Caroline doesn't need to know, and the media doesn't need any help digging up dirt. So I've taken steps to keep the information buried."

I'm not sure what he wants me to say. *Thank you?* I settle on a cautious, "Alright."

"And I'll let this charade play out." He gestures toward his daughter with his drink. "You and Caroline."

Let?

I glance over my shoulder. Caroline and Adrian are speaking seriously with a middle-aged woman in a floral dress. Caroline's too engrossed in conversation to notice me talking to her dad.

"On one condition," Pete adds.

I turn back to her father, narrowing my eyes.

"You're on your best behavior from now until the election. No drama, no scandals, nothing. You treat my daughter right and play the doting boyfriend. Smile for the cameras and make it look like the real deal."

"We weren't planning to—"

"Caroline's forced my hand, Miles," he says, cutting me off, "by bringing you here tonight instead of coming with Fletcher like she was supposed to. And God knows I love my daughter, but I'm not a man who likes to be surprised. So you're gonna make this thing between you appear legitimate. Stable. Hell, I'd settle for *boring*. But this little game of yours ends when the votes are cast. You're gone. Out of her life when the election's over."

"Why?" I ask.

It's not like I had my sights set on being a permanent part of Caroline's life, but hearing her father tell me what I can and can't do has my rebellious side snarling like a cornered animal.

"Well," he says, looking me up and down, "you're just not her type, son."

Again with the *son*. Fuck this old prick and his bullshit. And fuck him for trying to make his daughter's decisions for her. At this point, I don't even care about our relationship being fake; she should be free to do what she wants. And so should I, for that matter.

"Caroline deserves a man who fits in with her... lifestyle. Her status."

There it is.

"And I don't, huh?" I stuff my hands into my pockets, desperate to appear casual and hide the way my fists keep clenching. I try to remember what Caroline told me on the ride here: this event is important to her and her charity. Publicly telling her dad to shove that scotch tumbler up his ass is probably not the best way to help her out.

Pete laughs as if we're old friends. I can smell the scotch on his breath and, for once, the scent is not the least bit tempting.

"I think we both know you're not that kind of man, Miles."

Fucking hell. I guess this asshole says the quiet part out loud.

"What she had with Fletcher made sense," he adds. "But you?" He shakes his head.

"Fletcher treated her like shit."

He makes a dismissive sound, then sips his scotch, his lips thinning as he swallows. "He made some mistakes."

I've had enough. Moving to push past him, I set my sights on Caroline.

Pete grips my arm, stopping me.

I force my gaze back to her piece-of-shit father and keep my voice low, not wanting to draw attention with so many cameras around. "Get your hand off me."

"You work construction over on Riverside. That new housing development, right?"

How the fuck does he know where I work?

"Yeah…"

"Nice little contract for Sitka Properties, that one. And for you." When my eyes only narrow, he goes on. "Must feel good to be making a difference."

I work my jaw. "Sure."

"Be a shame if something got in the way of you continuing to work there, wouldn't it?"

A roiling, seething anger takes root in my gut and I level my gaze with his. "You threatening my job?"

"Think of it more like an insurance policy." He gives the liquid in his glass a thoughtful swirl. "So I can trust you to follow instructions."

The nerve of this fucking guy.

I tug my arm from his grasp as discreetly as I can manage, then roll my shoulders to straighten my tux jacket, glancing once again toward Caroline.

"Now, you won't be causing a scene here tonight—or any other time for that matter. And you won't be upsetting my daughter."

"She should know what kind of man you are," I say quietly.

"But you won't tell her, will you, son?" He picks some invisible piece of lint from my shoulder. "Not if you want to keep that job of yours."

When I don't respond, he looks satisfied—like he knows he's got me cornered. "That's what I thought," he says, smug as hell. "This stays between us. You hear me?"

Fighting every instinct in my body and hating myself, I give the smallest nod.

And at that, he strolls off without a care in the world, as if he didn't just blackmail me like a fucking goon.

Jesus, I need a drink.

My eyes snag on the bartender pouring a glass of wine. It might be halfway across a noisy, crowded room but I can almost hear the liquid spilling into the glass, sloshing up to lick the sides before settling back down. I can practically taste it.

Tearing my gaze away, I search for Caroline again, the impulse to tell her everything fighting its way up my throat. When I find her across the room, I watch her for a few tortured seconds.

Shit. I can't tell her.

Can I? I'm trying to be honest here. Fuck.

A fresh wave of ugly resentment surfaces that her dad would put me in this position. I'd guessed from what I'd seen on TV that Pete Brennan would be an asshole, but this is next-level, top-shelf, above-and-beyond assholery.

"Red wine? White wine?" Another bright-eyed server appears at my side, presenting a tray.

Just one drink, a little voice in the back of my head whispers. That lying little voice I've spent all these months trying to shut up and stuff down. I grit my teeth, sweat prickling at the back of my neck. It takes everything I've got not to reach for a glass.

Taking one last look at Caroline, I force a step back, then turn and head straight for the exit. I hit the call button next to Barry's name before I've even pushed outside.

9

———————

CAROLINE

I've had an hour to spiral on the ride back to town.

Miles left. He just... left.

Nothing about it makes sense.

He swore I could trust him. He was confident—cocky, almost —about how he could handle being my fake boyfriend. And the night had been going well. We'd been having fun, he'd gotten along with Adrian, he'd played along for the photographer, and... he kissed me.

Well, almost *kissed me.*

Oh, God, and he'd pulled it off perfectly. I can still feel the way he'd whispered against my cheek, the way his words had fallen like silk on my skin. *"This okay?"*

It had been more than okay. For a relatively chaste and very public half-kiss, it had left me breathless. And there'd been regret in his eyes when we'd gotten interrupted, like he felt the same way. Wanted more.

But, when I came back from helping Adrian with Portia Stanhope, Miles was just... gone.

I should never have asked him to do this. It was too much.

Still, the need for answers tugs at me, and I scroll back through our texts.

ME

Where did you go?

MILES

Sorry. Something came up.

I can explain in person.

Can you swing by my place on your way home tonight?

ME

After midnight?

MILES

Anytime is fine. I owe you an explanation.

When the car rolls up to Miles' building, I tell my driver not to wait. He gives me a look in the rear-view mirror but says nothing. Let him think what he wants; it'll only help solidify the story that Miles and I are a real couple if he thinks I'm spending the night.

Dad had pulled me aside tonight and made it clear I'm in the doghouse for showing up with Miles instead of Fletcher. Despite his reservations—and his frustration over losing control of the narrative—he made clear what should have been obvious to me all along: this new boyfriend of mine can't just disappear without fueling the very rumor I was trying to dispel. Now that I've been photographed with Miles a second time—and destroyed any ambiguity about our so-called relationship—I've committed us both to making this look real until after the election.

The fact that Miles took off on me earlier isn't exactly boosting my confidence that he'll want to keep helping me out.

Neither is the uncertainty in his voice when he buzzes me in.

The elevator up to the fourth floor squeaks slightly, then the door opens with a grinding thump.

I'm still getting my bearings, inspecting the number on each door I pass, when I hear Miles' deep voice behind me. "Over here, fancy girl."

I turn and—

Ohhhhh boy.

He's standing in his doorway with his arms crossed over his chest—his bare, heavily inked chest. A cascade of tattoos snakes over his left bicep and shoulder, spanning from his collarbone down to wrap around his rib cage. It's not a single design but many smaller ones in different artistic styles, somehow merged and blended into a cohesive whole. I can barely process the details, though, because navy blue sweatpants are slung low on his hips, and *damn* if he isn't wearing the heck out of those sweats.

I swallow, ripping my eyes away from his skin. "Were you sleeping?"

"Not yet." He lets his arms fall, tucking his hands into his pockets. The movement tugs his pants slightly lower and all coherent thoughts seep out of my brain when I notice the treasure trail that disappears below his waistband.

Catching myself again, I snap my gaze upward.

"You gonna come in?" There's a hint of amusement in his expression. He definitely caught me looking.

"Yeah, okay." Hugging my arms, I rub them to dispel the chill still clinging to my skin and slip into his apartment. I take a moment to look around. His place is small and sparsely furnished, like he hasn't been here long. Or hasn't cared to decorate much, maybe. Small piles of clutter are scattered here and there, but it's not messy. There's a simple, lived-in warmth to it that suits him. What little I know of him, anyway.

"Can I get you a glass of water?" he asks, closing the door. "Or maybe… I dunno, a sweatshirt? You look frozen. I could make tea or—"

"No, I'm fine." I can't help but envy how comfortable he seems to be despite being shirtless. The contrast between my glittery dress and what he's wearing—or *not* wearing, rather—is stark. Was he in bed? Did he just throw on whatever he could find before I came up? That would mean…

Great. Now I'm picturing him shirtless and pantsless.

So… very… pantsless.

"You left," I say, pushing away the image of Miles naked.

"Yeah, I did." He doesn't elaborate, though my confusion and curiosity must be obvious. "Sorry 'bout that."

"Why?" I almost whisper.

"Uh, how long you got?" he asks, tilting his head toward the door. "Is your driver waiting out front, or—?"

"I sent him home."

"Oh." He nods. Then, the implication dawns on him. "*Oh.*"

I hold out a hand, eyes wide. "That's not what I— I didn't mean to imply any…"—a grin splits his face as he watches me scramble—"I wasn't planning to *stay*, I just—"

"It's okay, Caroline. I can give you a lift home."

"No, no, you don't need to. I—" I sputter. "I can get a cab or—"

God, I can't even finish a full sentence around this man.

"Like, after we…" He makes a generic gesture between us. My eyes must bug out, because the corner of his mouth starts to twitch. "After we *talk*."

"Yes! That's all I came here to do, I swear."

"Just messin' with you." Smirking, he guides me toward the couch. "C'mere."

We sink down onto the cushions, and I take a moment to un-fluster myself. "So? Why'd you take off earlier?"

He looks like he can't quite find the words.

"Was it something I said? Or did?" I ask quietly, the memory of our almost-kiss slipping back into focus yet again.

Did he not like it?

"God, no," he says quickly. He scrubs his hands down his tired face. "Shit. Is that what you thought?"

I shrug. "I didn't know what to think, Miles. You just disappeared."

A muscle works in his jaw. "It was shitty of me to take off on you. Especially after I said you could trust me."

I don't disagree with him. "How'd you even get home?"

"Took a cab about halfway. Then my brother picked me up." When I give him an expectant look, he goes on, his voice quiet. "Okay, so, the reason I left... *Fuck*." He closes his eyes for a moment. "I'm an alcoholic, Caroline."

"What?" I search his face.

"I'm sober. I'm in AA. And I'm doing good; I actually found a meeting online tonight when I got home, which helped... but yeah. I haven't been sober that long."

Why didn't he say something?

"How long has it been?" I ask quietly.

He runs a hand through his shaggy dark hair and sits forward, resting his elbows on his thighs. "'Bout ten months?"

Dropping my gaze to the scratched hardwood floor, I slouch back against the couch cushions as the puzzle pieces click into place. Drinks were all around tonight, offered up on literal silver platters from the moment we arrived. I can only imagine how intense the temptation must have been. "Miles, I'm so sorry. I never would've asked you to come if I'd known."

He turns sharply toward me. "Hey, no. Nothing about this is on you. You didn't know."

"Why'd you agree to come? You must've known there'd be drinks there."

Amusement plays on his lips. "Well, I was kinda... *voluntold*."

I grimace at the reminder. Still, he could have backed out. I gave him chances to back out.

Miles grows more serious. "Plus, it's not realistic to avoid it completely."

"Yes, but—"

"Look, when I saw you with Fletcher at the gallery... He obviously made you fucking uncomfortable. So I thought I could... I dunno. Help you out, I guess."

"You didn't have to do that for me."

"Yeah, but I wanted to." He meets my eyes. "I didn't like the idea of you stuck with him any more than you did."

"But it meant putting yourself in harm's way."

"Thought I could handle it." He pushes up from the couch, then paces a few steps toward the small galley kitchen, giving me a full view of his muscular back and another chaotic-yet-cohesive collection of tattoos: wavy, twisting kelp fronds; a feather, a cartoon character I can't place, and more I don't catch before he faces me again.

"Thought I could just steer clear of the bar. Didn't realize they'd be shoved in my face like that," he says, leaning his hips against the counter behind him. "And then when..." He rubs at the back of his neck, not quite able to look me in the eye. "It just got to be too much."

I study him, getting the feeling there's something he's not telling me.

"Couldn't risk it, y'know?" he continues. "By staying any longer. I'm sorry. Again. I hope you understand. This is... this is the only way this can work for me. I have to put sobriety first."

My eyes widen. "Oh my God, of course!"

"Even if it means running out on my fake girlfriend like an asshole, apparently." He looks apologetic as he returns to the couch and slumps down beside me. Rubbing his hand over the koi tattoo on the back of his arm, he turns to me. "Your dickbag ex give you any shit after I left?"

"No. He was probably busy hitting on some poor, unsuspecting woman." I roll my eyes. "Or women."

"Man, that guy's a real piece of shit."

I let out a resigned laugh. "Tell me about it."

His gaze licks over my collarbone, my neck, somehow heating my skin. "It's his loss, you know."

"What is?"

"You," he says simply—like it should be obvious.

My lips part, but I have no idea what to say. "Y-you don't know that," I finally stammer out. "You barely know me."

"Yeah, but I've got a good read on people. Always have."

I tilt my head in question.

"It's like an ADHD spidey-sense or some shit."

"You have ADHD?"

"Yup." He nods slowly. "And I know what you're thinking: ADHD, addiction... Man, this guy is the *whooole package.*"

My laughter takes us both by surprise and he gives my thigh a playful nudge with his, then catches it with his hand, squeezing gently. His palm lingers, warming my skin through my dress.

"Good thing I'm not your real boyfriend, huh?"

Our eyes lock then, smiles faltering. His gaze drops to my mouth before he looks away and removes his hand.

"About that..."

His attention swivels right back to me. "Yeah?"

"I know this was supposed to be a onetime thing," I start, suddenly hating the sound of my own voice. "And I know it didn't exactly go amazingly for you at the fundraiser..." My throat tightens and my palms feel sweaty.

God, why do I feel like I'm fourteen and asking Caleb Fraser to the Valentine's Dance all over again?

"But you need a fake boyfriend beyond tonight," he finishes for me.

My anxiety shape-shifts into confusion. "How did you—?"

"Just a hunch." He breaks eye contact, rubbing his thighs. "I have a good read on people, remember?"

"Right. Well, yeah, actually. But only for a few weeks—until the election. So the public thinks I'm in a stable, steady relationship. If you disappear now, it'll look like I'm... having casual flings. I'm sorry. I should have realized—"

"Casual flings?" Miles frowns, his jaw clenching in the dim living room light. "Is that what your dad said to you?"

"Not in those exact words."

The furrow in his brow deepens, the protective glimmer in his eyes from the gym back again. "What words did he use?"

Worse words.

"Doesn't matter." I wave him off.

He looks like he doesn't agree, but he doesn't push.

I study him for a long moment, my heart heavy with guilt for pulling him into all this. This man doesn't owe me a thing. How could I ask for anything more, especially after what he went through tonight?

"Actually, forget it." I push off the couch and head for the door. "I can't ask you to do this."

"Hey, whoa," he starts, standing to get a step ahead of me before I can get too far. His hands slip to my arms, holding me in place. "Where are you going?"

"Miles," I start, looking anywhere but into those magnetic eyes. "This is too much. It's late and you've done more than enough to help me out. I'll— I'll figure something out with my dad. I should go."

He doesn't let go or move aside. "Hey, look at me."

I can barely meet his gaze. When I finally do, there's an openness in his expression that I could get lost in.

"I didn't say no." He dips his head. "We could do this."

I start to protest, but the words catch in my throat.

"I mean, hey," he adds, letting go of my arms, "We did alright tonight. The photographer seemed pretty happy. Maybe the press will, uh... want more?"

More.

His eyes slip to my mouth, and the memory of his lips brushing against mine sends a tingling sensation straight to my core.

"Anyway, I'm up for it. If you are." I must not look convinced, because he adds, "And if you wanna leave"—he holds up his hands and steps back to give me a clear path—"I'm not gonna stop you. But I'll give you a ride, alright? We can talk more in the truck. Just... lemme take you home."

This man? At my house?

I swallow and nod, shoving away visions of being pinned to my bed under his tattooed chest.

When he disappears into his room to change, I drift toward the front door, kicking myself anew for pushing my way into his life like this. Miles is newly sober; the last thing he needs is to be dragged into political drama or forced to live under my controlling father's thumb. He should be taking care of *himself*, not my tarnished public image.

It's a good thing I've got a therapy session booked on Monday morning; I'll have more than enough material to talk about after this week.

My attention snags on movement in my peripheral vision. Miles' bedroom door is open a crack, and a soft yellow glow spills out, casting a strip of light on the floor of the dark front hall. I stare through the narrow opening as a sliver of muscle and tattooed skin disappears under a snug gray T-shirt. My gaze falls and, when I catch him tugging on a pair of jeans, I hold my breath.

No sooner have I registered the sound of his zipper than he's pulling open the door and stepping out, buckling his belt. A slow smirk plays at his lips when he realizes what I could see—what I was so obviously *watching*.

My cheeks flush hot, and that smirk splits into a full grin.

"Let's go..."

When he doesn't call me out, I exhale with relief.

He grabs a hoodie from a hook on the wall as he opens the front door, motioning for me to go first. I'm just stepping past him when—

"... ya big *perv*."

I groan out a mortified laugh as he locks up and we head to his truck.

MILES MANAGES to talk me down from my anxious state as he drives me home, and we hash out a few details of what fake dating could look like: being seen together out in public at least once a week until the election, doing whatever we can to present an image of committed stability, and avoiding anything that could compromise the Pete Brennan campaign. We brainstorm sober-friendly dates: restaurants without bars, activities that don't involve drinking, and family-friendly community events where we could be seen together, like Halloween Fest at Sonora Farm—a Lennox Valley tradition. Then we'd call the whole thing off after Election Day. Whether or not my father wins, there will be far less at stake for him after the votes are counted.

"There'd be no need to carry on with the ruse past then." I glance at Miles' shadowed figure in the driver's seat.

"Right." His grip twists on the steering wheel. "So we'd what, just... cut contact and go back to normal?"

"Yeah. I'd go back to my life, and you'd go back to yours," I add. "Unless... you wanted to stay friends?"

Miles flicks his eyes my way, his expression inscrutable as he returns his gaze to the road. "Is that what we are now? Friends?"

I open my mouth to answer, but I don't know what to say.

Are *we friends?*

The question hangs unanswered as we pull into my grandfather's driveway. Miles cuts the engine and quickly jumps out into the night, rounds the front of the truck, and opens my door.

I take his offered hand, careful to step out without the high slit of my dress revealing too much.

"You're quite the gentleman, huh?" I tease as I straighten.

"Oh, not even close," he says with a low chuckle. It's dark, but I don't miss the playful glimmer in his eyes. "But I can pretend."

"Are we really doing this?" I ask, my voice quiet.

"I think so, yeah." He quirks a smile that looks more laid-back than I can manage right now. "You in?"

Stuffing down a whole host of qualms, I let the side of me that genuinely likes Miles take the wheel. Hanging out with him for a few weeks could be fun. And it doesn't hurt that he's easy on the eyes. I nod. "Yeah. Okay. I'm in."

His broad grin has me in a choke hold for a moment. When I manage to shake it off, I climb the stairs to my front door ahead of him, feeling the burn of his gaze on my back with each step.

"Hey, uh, not sure how to say this," he starts as we reach the porch.

I turn, concern tugging at me.

He continues, "But, uh, just so we're clear from the start... I'm not in a position to date anyone. For real, I mean."

My stomach tilts. "Of course! I didn't— I wasn't—"

Did he think I was after more?

"Like, I know you only need a fake boyfriend for the cameras and stuff, but I wanna make sure you know that, right now, I can't offer anything more."

"Me neither," I rush to reassure him. "I'm not even remotely looking for a real boyfriend."

"No?"

"God, no. After what happened with Fletcher? No. Nope." I shake my head. "I don't want another relationship."

"Ever again?" he asks, his amusement turning to something more like concern.

"Pretty much." I lean into the lie, hoping it's camouflaging the aching void in my chest. "So bring on the cats and frumpy sweaters. It's the spinster life for me."

"C'mon," he laughs, puffing a cloud into the chilly night, "you're too pretty to be a spinster."

"Oh, so you think I'm pretty?" My tone is teasing, but I can't deny I'm grateful it's dark enough to mask my flushed cheeks.

He laughs again, rubbing his jaw like he regrets letting that piece of information slip out. "No."

Wait. What?

"No?" I scramble to school my features—cling to my dignity.

He meets my gaze. "I think you're fucking stunning, Caroline."

My chest feels like it's full of hummingbirds beating their wings against my rib cage. I've received my fair share of compliments about my looks—being in the public eye will invite that—but this simple praise from Miles feels different somehow. And so does the way he's looking at me. Appreciative, sure, but there's something more simmering behind his eyes.

"Anyway," he says with a definitive nod, leaning back on the porch railing. "It's good we're on the same page." It's like his words are trying to wrap this up, but his body is settling in to stay awhile.

I can't deny I'm feeling a similar push and pull. Setting my clutch on a nearby ledge, I lift my eyes to Miles. "So, why aren't you dating? For real, like you said." Realizing how that might have sounded, I rush to add, "Just curious."

"Uh, well, there's this rule in AA. Well, more of a guideline, I guess, but they tell us not to get into any new relationships for the first year."

"Why a year?"

He scrubs a hand over the back of his neck, looking thoughtful. "I think the idea is you need to get to know your sober self—kinda rebuild your identity without booze. Love yourself first, before you..." He trails off. "Point is, it takes time, y'know?"

"That makes sense."

I can certainly understand needing to find yourself—find your footing. Feeling cold, I rub my arms.

"I ignored the advice before, actually, which wasn't great. The first time I tried to quit drinking, I started dating someone right away and it blew up in my face. The breakup was pretty stressful. I kinda spiraled, and I relapsed pretty badly."

My brows pinch at the pained look on his face. "I'm sorry."

"Wasn't ready." He pauses for a moment, visibly shaking it off. "Still not ready. Still working on figuring myself out, taking care of myself better. So, I guess it's not a hard rule in AA but, for me, it has to be."

"I'm glad you're doing that. All of it. And congratulations, by the way. Ten months is huge."

He nods, a genuine smile touching his lips as he grips the railing on either side of him. "Thanks."

"I hope the kiss earlier didn't break any of your rules." I hug my arms, rubbing them again. "Sorry I kinda sprung the idea on you in the car, I—"

"What kiss?"

I balk. "What do you mean, *what kiss*? At the fundraiser."

He scrunches his nose. "Dunno. We got interrupted. Wouldn't say it was even a *kiss*, really."

"No?" I ask. "I thought it... I'm pretty sure it counted."

The corner of his mouth curls and he straightens, shoving his hands in his front pockets. "Caroline." He meets my eyes with an intensity that traps the air in my lungs. "When I kiss you, you'll know it." A muscle flickers in his jaw. "There won't be any doubt about whether it counted."

"Oh," is all I can manage. Those hummingbirds in my chest are back. And they're freaking out. And on fire.

"I mean," he shrugs, stepping closer, "we can do a hell of a lot better than that non-kiss."

I search his expression. "What are you saying?"

"Uh, well, you mentioned something earlier. About practice?"

I try to mask the way my stomach flips at the implication. "Yeah?"

He drifts closer still. "Well, we didn't really get to, y'know, do it right before. So maybe we need a do-over."

"You want to practice?" I huff a nervous breath into the small space between us. "Now? Here?"

"Just this one time," he adds with a one-sided shrug, like he's trying to convince himself as much as me. "Without an audience. No pressure, no interruptions. If we're gonna fake a relationship over the next few weeks, we're gonna have to get comfortable with this stuff, right?"

"Right." My voice isn't much more than a whisper. "So, how would you... um..." I swallow. "How would you do it differently? Do it right, like you said."

"Well," he says, slipping his hands from his pockets to rub gentle strokes over my bare arms, "first, I'd wanna warm you up." He gently fingers the strap of my dress and electricity skitters across my collarbone. "God, you must be fucking freezing in this."

"I am," I say, scrunching my nose. "Fashion over function, right?"

He unzips his hoodie, then shrugs it off and pulls it around my shoulders. Immediately, his clean, earthy scent engulfs me.

"Thank you," I whisper as I work my arms through the sleeves.

He reaches up to untuck a stray curl from under the fabric, and I shiver when his fingers graze my neck.

"Then…" He steps toward me and cups my jaw, brushing his thumb over my cheek and down to my lips. There's something hypnotic about the slow way he's closing the space between our bodies. "If this is a do-over—like, if this is a *first* kiss, I mean—I'd wanna make sure I have your… explicit… consent."

The way he's drawing this out is unfurling some long-dormant part of me that lives low in my belly. I lift my hands to his stomach, tentatively touching his waist. His T-shirt is buttery soft and he smells so good that I have to resist the urge to yank him against me. It would be too *take me now*—too forward.

"Consent is… very important," I say quietly, relishing the way touching his body heats more than my fingers; admittedly, it isn't just the evening chill pulling me into his chest.

"Mm-hmm." He nods, dragging his thumbs down my arms.

My body thrums with anticipation.

"So…" He tilts my chin up, exposing my neck. "Can I kiss you?"

I arch into him. "Like this?"

Cradling my jaw in his calloused hand, he slowly—so slowly—stoops to meet me. He grazes his open mouth over mine, heating my lips as he whispers, "Yeah. Like this."

"Yes." I close my fingers around handfuls of his T-shirt as a searing ache takes hold inside me, pulsing at my center and threatening to liquefy my knees. And when our lips finally meet, I think I could get lost in the warmth of his mouth. There's a deep rumble from his throat, and I let out a small whimper in response.

When he pulls back, something in his expression shifts. That heat was impossible to miss—or deny—and every line of his face tells me he felt it too. Long seconds pass, both of us barely breathing as an unspoken understanding hangs heavy in the inches separating us.

And then he dives for me, crushing me against him and

kissing me like he's been starving for it. Lips, teeth, and tongues all clash and coax and explore, drawing us somehow closer. I twine my fingers in his hair, gripping gently, then tightening as I lose all access to reason. His hands are on my throat, my waist, my back, hauling me closer, pressing that telltale hardness against my stomach.

This isn't the kind of kiss we'd ever do for the cameras. Not in public, and certainly not in front of my parents. This isn't a fundraiser kiss. A practice kiss.

This isn't a kiss at all.

No. This is my undoing.

10

———————

MILES

Walking back to my truck is torture. The ache between my legs is so intense it takes everything I've got to move them in a left-right-left-right pattern—like I've forgotten how to fucking walk.

"Fuuuuck!" I groan out the moment I slam the door shut, already ripping open my belt buckle with one hand as I start the truck with the other. There's no fighting it. Not anymore. Not after that kiss.

If you could even call it a kiss. It was so much more than a goddamn kiss.

What was I thinking?

She was so tempting in that dress, smelling so damn good with my favorite hoodie around her shoulders. And it was late. I wasn't thinking straight after a stressful night. I know suggesting that practice kiss was a weak-ass excuse... But, *fuck me*, I'd have done anything to touch her.

Gravel skidding under my tires, I try not to peel out of Caroline's driveway, swinging the truck into the road and scanning for the nearest place to pull over.

I can't remember how I managed to tear myself away.

Did I even say goodnight?

But Caroline in that fucking gold dress, kiss-stung and breathless? The image is seared into my brain.

In an asinine attempt to take the edge off, I rub myself through my jeans, but all it does is make it worse. My dick is fucking throbbing by the time I get to the turnoff for Cherry Park and pull onto the muddy shoulder.

I kill the engine, praying no one will be here at one in the morning. In some vain attempt at privacy, I grab a ball cap from the back and yank the brim down over my eyes, then slouch low in my seat. Stretching the waistband of my boxer briefs over the head of my aching cock with one hand, I firmly fist my shaft with the other. The first tentative, experimental stroke already has me letting out an involuntary moan.

Shit. I'm so sensitive it almost hurts. Precum immediately beads at the tip and I rub it in with a thumb before I stroke it again, nearly squirming in my seat out of desperation.

I can't believe I'm resorting to this. Jacking off on the side of the road is for teenagers and deviants, but I feel like some weird combination of both right now. Maybe I'm extra hard up for a release after tonight. That kiss... It pushed me past my limits. Just look at what it's reduced me to: a pervert in a truck, fogging up the damn windows.

Well, guess I'll have to face being *that guy* later, because I can't fucking stop. Can't stop thinking about Caroline. Her lips. Her body. How those long legs would straddle my lap if she were here right now, her perfect little tits pressed right in my face. I want to nuzzle into them like a fucking puppy while she scrapes her fingernails over my scalp.

This isn't gonna take long.

It's a wonder I have the presence of mind to grab an old work shirt from the back seat. *Thanks, Riverside General Paint Supply, I guess.* I might be jerking off in my truck like a pervert, but I don't need to be *gross* about it. Tightening my grip, I speed up, each stroke bringing me closer to oblivion.

God, if I could just touch her now...

I'd kiss and lick every inch I could reach. I'd bite her tight nipples—softly at first, then harder. If she told me it hurt, I'd lick them again. Kiss them. So gently. Make it better. And then I'd cover her mouth with mine when I pushed my fingers inside her, swallowing her moans. I'd whisper against her lips how good she was... or how bad—whichever she likes better.

That thought alone makes my dick stiffen even more.

What does *she like?*

Faster. Harder. *Fuck.*

I try to slow down—try to keep my shit together just a little— but my imagination is having none of it.

Would she like it if I called her a good girl? Would her breath rush out between those sweet, parted lips if I praised her? Would it make her thighs tremble and her pussy clench around my fingers?

As hot as that idea is, it also doesn't feel quite right. Something about the way Caroline had grabbed my hair tonight had shown a side of her that was almost wild. Animalistic. It hadn't felt like innocent, *good-girl* territory.

The devil on my other shoulder takes the mic and I swallow, barely holding onto control.

Fuck, I bet she'd like it if I told her all the dirty things I want to do to her. Teased her. Edged her. What if I wound her up and turned her into a needy little mess... then told her to let her inner whore out? Would she come apart for me? Would she soak my fingers if I called her a slut?

My ass practically lifts out of the driver's seat—like I could somehow get closer to her by thrusting upward. There's a rocketin-my-pocket joke here somewhere, but it escapes the disinte-grated pile of goo that was once my brain.

Oh, God. Tighter. Faster. *Fuck me.*

It's all I can do to contain the chaos as heat fans up my spine and sweat prickles my neck. With a shaky moan, I break, spurting in erratic, thrumming pulses as I slow my rhythm and wring every last drop of pleasure from my aching dick.

Chest heaving, I collapse against the cool, wet window beside me and try to come to terms with what I just did. As the waves of my release dissipate, the familiar weight of shame settles into me.

Jesus, that was fucking pathetic.

I haven't been this desperate to get off in... Actually, I can't remember ever feeling like this. About anyone. But it was either this or drink, and there ain't no way. *Shit.* A wry smirk plays on my lips. Guess if I'm gonna jack, it better be *off* and not *Daniels.*

I roll up the spare T-shirt, vowing to throw on a load of laundry the minute I get home, then hunt around the truck for something to clean up with—relieved when I find a pack of wet wipes in the glove box.

Ten wisdom points for past Miles.

As I drive home in the dark, the lingering stress from the fundraiser creeps back in. But it's way too late at night to be spiraling about how I was so tempted to drink—or how that shit-head Pete Brennan blackmailed me. Especially after what happened between me and his daughter. And after what I've just done.

My mind slips effortlessly back to Caroline and a singular pulse of pleasure travels through my body as my thoughts flash back to what she might like. Does she know? If not, *fuck,* would I love to help her find out. Would she like praise? Degradation? A bit of both? Something even kinkier? Or is she really the sweet, vanilla girl she seems on the outside?

There's no way. That kiss was...

Fucking hell.

I try to shake off the thought. It doesn't matter what she likes, because I'm in no position to give it to her. Besides, this is probably just my ADHD in search of the brain chemicals it craves. My therapist, Lydia, explained to me how novelty is a powerful source of dopamine for a brain like mine, making it easy to obsess over the new, shiny thing in my life.

I can't risk letting Caroline become that new, shiny obsession. My need for dopamine is running the show here, and I've gotta shut it down before I fuck everything up.

"You look like shit."

"Thanks, bro." I slap Gus on the shoulder, then hand him the paper bag and coffee before slumping into one of the seats around the huge table in the fire station's kitchen.

My alarm had been particularly grating this morning after only a few hours of fitful sleep, but I'd hauled my ass to the gym anyway. Because fuck if I'm gonna toss my entire routine out the window. After last night, I need normalcy now more than ever.

"What's this?" Gus asks, peering into the bag. "Aw, a cinnamon roll? Hell yes! Thanks, man."

I rub at my tired eyes, but I can still feel him watching me.

I was halfway through my workout when I realized I needed to talk this out. Exhausted and off my game, I was tempted to bail on the gym, but I pushed myself to finish up. Then, too antsy to wait until Gus was off shift, I'd hit up Bean Bag Coffee and driven to the station.

"Okay, what's with you?" He nudges my arm, dropping into the seat next to me. "You've got a face like a slapped ass."

I only groan in response, then straighten and blink hard, begging my brain to wake up.

"Last night not go great, or what?" He rips off a bite of cinnamon roll, then pops it in his mouth.

"Nah, it was... fine."

Fine doesn't even come close to describing it. Last night had swung wildly between catastrophic and incredible, but I'm not really sure how to explain or what I should share. Memories hit me in quick succession: Caroline glittering and perfect at the fundraiser, fizzing champagne bubbles, Pete's ruddy hand gripping my arm, Caroline wearing my hoodie. Those lips. Her body pressed against mine. *Those fucking lips.* Desperately jacking off into my shirt in the truck like I was—*Shit!* I forgot to put the laundry in the dryer. *Fuck my life.*

I clear my throat, willing the images away. "You, uh, gonna need that tux back anytime soon?"

Gus frowns. "What? Why? What'd you do to my fucking tux?"

"No, man." I wave him off. "Nothing like that. I just might need to borrow it for longer." Then my memory jogs. "Hey, wait, why do you own a tuxedo, anyway?"

"Calendars," he says simply around his bite.

I laugh. "What, like, you're a model now?"

"It's for charity, man! Fuck off." He shakes his head, then takes a sip of his coffee. "Anyway, what do you need it for? You seeing this girl again?" When I don't argue, he adds, "Thought it was a one-off thing."

I give him a long look. "Well, it was supposed to be."

"What? C'mon, what'd I miss here?"

"Alright, the nutshell version is she needs a fake boyfriend for the next few weeks, so I'm gonna keep helping her out."

He smooths down his mustache and straightens slowly, like he's not sure what to make of this.

Well, buddy, that makes two of us.

"Yeah, think I'm gonna need the non-nutshell version," he says as a couple of young firefighters file into the kitchen and head for the fridge. Martinez, I think her name is, and a new one I haven't met.

"Okay, but not here." I glance around, nervous about being overheard.

"Why are you being cagey?" He tilts his head toward the kitchen and leans in. "You think the rookie over there is gonna rat you out to the tabloids?"

"I dunno!"

"Well, you can't bring me gossip snackies and then refuse to give me the gossip." When I hesitate again, he sighs, pulling out the entire cinnamon roll. "Fine. Just gonna eat this while I reevaluate our friendship."

"Okay," I say with a grimace. "But I'm avoiding eye contact with you while you eat it."

He frowns. "What's that supposed to mean?"

"Let's just say I know where you got that nickname in college and *really* wish I didn't." I can't bring myself to say *CunnilinGus* out loud.

He barks a laugh, then looks thoughtful for a moment before he says, "Never had any complaints."

"Okay," I say, pushing up to leave. "Just remembered I gotta water my cactus."

"Aw, c'mon!" he grabs my arm and yanks me back into my seat. Craning his neck toward the others, he calls out, "Martinez, Abernathy, can you give us a minute?"

A MINUTE TURNS into about twenty when I'm finally done with the word vomit.

Gus shakes his head and stuffs the last piece of cinnamon roll in his mouth, then sucks the icing off his thumb. "I don't like this for you," he mumbles around his bite.

"No shit." I take my last sip of coffee and chuck the to-go cup into a nearby garbage can. "I step outside my comfort zone for *one* night and I get fucking blackmailed?"

"You don't need this stress."

"Hey, thanks for pointing that out. Not like it wasn't taking up ninety percent of my brain space already."

He holds up his hands. "I'm just saying, all that political fuckery right before an election—"

"Yeah, I know what you're saying. And you're not wrong." I rub my jaw. "But I'm telling ya, man, Caroline's not like that. She's not like her dad *at all*. I can feel it. She's..."—I try to find the words—"*good*."

Gus leans back in his seat, stuffing his hands into the pockets of his LVFD hoodie. "So, lemme get this straight. She's beautiful and *good* and you trust her and, aside from her asshole dad and having to flee the scene—good job, by the way—you had a great time together?"

"Pretty much. And I may have also... kissed her." I grimace as Gus' brows shoot up. "Like... a *lot*."

"For the cameras?"

A high-pitched sound sneaks out of my throat, like I'm a guilt-filled balloon with a slow leak.

His expression falls. "So, *not* just for the cameras."

"Shit." I scrub both palms down my face, knowing I'd taken it a bit too far with the whole *practice* thing. "I'd say it was an out-of-body experience, but my body was"—I bug out my eyes—"*definitely there*."

He points a thumb over his shoulder. "If you're gonna tell me about your dick, I'm out."

"Fuck off." I'm absolutely *not* telling my best friend about the masturbatory fever dream part of the night. The part where kissing Caroline had sent me into some kind of agonized sexual fugue state.

"But it was good?" Gus asks, cutting into my thoughts.

Damn, did I say any of that out loud?

When I don't answer right away, he adds, "The kiss, dumbass."

I puff air through my lips. "Let's just say I might go to my grave thinking about it."

He nods slowly, amusement tugging at the corner of his mouth. "Explain to me again how you're not really dating this girl?"

11

CAROLINE

It's almost a week before I see Miles again. He'd texted the morning after the fundraiser to apologize for taking things too far, joked that his moves were a bit rusty, sent a GIF of Homer Simpson disappearing into a hedge, then asked if it was cool if we waited a few days before getting together again.

I have to admit, the obvious panic spiral was kinda sweet.

And I'd agreed. Of course I'd agreed. He's not the only one who needed time to cool off. I'd been too worked up to sleep that night without a release, and desperate times had called for desperate measures. Perhaps a little *too* desperate.

Outside the narrow, brick-lined alley leading to El Taco Guapo, I scan the street for Miles and clutch his neatly folded hoodie against my chest. Not finding him anywhere, I shift the sweatshirt under one arm and pull out my phone. I scroll back past the few messages we've exchanged since that kiss—that brain-melting, time-bending, world-warping kiss—and confirm I've got the time and place correct for our fake date. I have. At a loss for what else to do while I wait, I reread his last messages from Sunday morning—for probably the twentieth time.

I know how I *should* react. I should accept his apology. I should agree the kiss was too much, too far, too intense. I should see Miles as a friend. A kind stranger who stumbled into a sticky situation and who—instead of bolting when I decided for us both that he could play the role of my new boyfriend—stepped up.

That's what I *should* see. And I can almost get there. Sensible Caroline is at the ready with her notebook full of reasons and facts and logic.

He's not available! she shouts. *He's just doing you a favor!* she scolds. *Stop thinking about kissing him!*

She waves her infernal logic in my face with increasing fervor every time I slip back into the memory of Miles' hands on my neck. Every time I picture that hungry look in his eyes before our bodies slammed together. Every time I foolishly give in to the urge to smell the hoodie he left behind. His scent is subtle yet intoxicating. Clean but earthy—like soap with a hint of sandalwood.

My fingers clench and I brush my thumbs over the worn fabric, transported right back to the warmth of his arms.

Cage the beast? God, no.

Because that kiss released something inside me that *had* been caged, cowed, and stuffed down for far too long. Was it messy, foolish, and wrong? Most definitely. But it was also incredibly freeing. I liked tasting freedom. And, more than anything, I want another taste.

But he's not dating right now. And neither am I. Although, I have to admit... dinner and a movie aren't really top of mind.

"Caroline!" a familiar deep voice calls out from the street.

Startled, I snap my head up to find Miles grinning at me through the open window of his silver pickup. "Hey!"

Heat flushes my cheeks, probably from the small jolt of adrenaline. Yes, definitely the adrenaline. Nothing to do with that backwards ball cap he's wearing or the boyish smirk on his face. Tearing his gaze from mine, he braces an arm behind the passenger-side headrest and throws the truck in reverse. The way he parallel parks in front of me in one smooth, effortless maneuver has me equal parts jealous and turned on.

Why was that sexy? Do I have a competence kink?

Before he rolls up the window, I step closer, offering him the bundled hoodie. "You forgot this."

"Oh, uh, yeah." He places it on the passenger seat. "Thanks. It's um... It's my favorite one. But you didn't have to— You could've held onto it. Like, for a while or whatever. No big deal."

I don't quite know how to respond, and a loaded pause hangs in the air before he finally seems to snap out of it and climbs out. As he rounds his truck, I take a steadying breath.

"You look nice," he says as he hops up on the curb. "I mean, you always look nice, but—"

"But?" I raise my brows, silently beckoning him to continue.

"But nothing," he says. "I like your dress."

"Oh, thanks." I glance down at my open wool peacoat and the plaid pinafore dress peeking out underneath, smoothing it under my palms. "This one's vintage, actually."

"You always wear such cool outfits. Makes me feel like I should've tried a bit harder." He runs a hand over his stomach, looking down at his clothes.

"Well," I say, "I think you're definitely passing the taco date vibe check."

"Yeah?" He cocks his hip and aims a model-like smolder somewhere into the street beside us. "Like what you see, huh?" He bites his lip.

I suppress a laugh and narrow my eyes in thought, scanning his black hoodie and dark jeans. "Mmm, yes. I'm getting comfort, I'm getting casual…"

He tosses his head and gives me a goofy, over-the-top pose, complete with peace sign and broody pout.

Playing along, I ask, "So, what inspired this ensemble, Mr. Sharpe?"

"Hunger," he deadpans, popping his hip to the other side. "For tacos."

"Very nice. Very nice." I nod sagely, struggling to keep a straight face. "And who are you wearing tonight?"

"I don't even know, actually." His eyes dance as he makes a grab over his shoulder, wrenching his hoodie around to check the label—only to drop it when he doesn't find one. "Shit, yanked the tag out. I mean…" He clears his throat, all casual nonchalance as he tugs his hoodie back into place. "It's an unknown designer. You wouldn't have heard of them. They're, like, so edgy they don't have a name yet."

"Ooh, underground. I like it." I laugh through the last words, both of us dropping the act.

His goofball routine mesmerizes me for a moment; there's something refreshing about being in the company of a man who doesn't need to wear a mask of pretentious seriousness at all times.

"If any photographers are around tonight, I'm sure we just confused the fuck outta them," he says, looking amused as he scans up and down the street.

But the reminder that someone could be watching us has our smiles waning.

For a second, I think Miles might step closer or kiss me—for the cameras, maybe—but the moment passes and he stuffs his hands in his pockets.

I swallow my disappointment, knowing it's ridiculous.

"You hungry?" he asks.

I nod quickly. "Ravenous."

FAMOUS FOR BEING the smallest restaurant in Lennox Valley, El Taco Guapo is impossibly small, wedged into the side of the alleyway and down a handful of stairs. It looks like an afterthought, as if it was carved out of the wall once the building was finished. There are exactly four tiny tables, each covered in bold, floral-printed vinyl, with smudged metal napkin dispensers and a bottle of hot sauce on each one. Savory aromas permeate the air and barely muffled hissing emanates from the kitchen, which is separated from the tiny dining area by a single swinging door.

Miles' eyes are all over the place, bouncing around the cramped room as we squeeze into our seats. He explains how the kitchen makes all the tortillas by hand and how, apparently, you have to know the inside scoop about the secret menu if you want to order the best tacos. He's got the enthusiasm of an overgrown kid as he sells me on the carnitas with the house-made hot sauce. "They slow-cook the pulled pork and then pan-fry it so it crisps up. Caroline, seriously, they're so fucking good. You have to get them."

I do. And he's right. They're incredible. And so messy. I quickly discover there's no way to appear ladylike while eating a greasy pulled-pork taco dripping with hot sauce and green salsa, and I awkwardly scramble for napkins to wipe the mess off my fingers.

"Hoooh my God." I fan at my open mouth, which increasingly feels like it's on fire. "So hot."

Miles laughs around his bite. "You gonna survive?"

"Nope. Dying." I reach for my water and take a long drink. "Might already be dead, actually. Can't say for sure."

"Here lies Caroline Brennan," he drawls, his voice solemn and deep, "who tragically met her end at the hands of some mildly spicy food."

"Mildly?" I echo, my eyes widening. "This is *mild* to you?"

"Maybe I'm just used to it." He shrugs, taking another bite.

I dab a clean napkin at the edges of my watering eyes, trying not to smudge my makeup. "You're not bothered by much, are you?"

Another shrug.

"How'd you get so comfortable in your skin?" When he tilts his head in confusion, I gesture to the alleyway outside. "Out there. The whole goofy fashion model routine."

Miles wipes his hands on a napkin and sits back in his chair, looking hesitant. "The palatable answer is I've always been a goofball. My grandpa used to call me a ham when I was a kid. I remember being confused about what he meant at first, thinking he was gonna eat me or something, because, like, who says that anymore, right? My dad had to explain it meant I was funny. Then I was like, well, shit, this is my entire personality now." He sits forward, leaning on his elbows, his gaze unfocused like he's revisiting a memory. "Grandpa was a cool old dude, though. He used to challenge us to make him laugh."

"Us? Do you have siblings?" I ask.

"Yeah. An older brother, Jude. You?"

"Nope. Only child."

He nods slowly, his expression assessing.

"What?" Self-consciousness has me sitting a little straighter; people always think it's weird not to have had siblings growing up.

"Nothing." He shakes his head.

I'm not sure I believe him, but I don't push it. "So, what's the unpalatable answer?"

"Uh, well," he starts, his tone turning more serious, "when I was still drinking, I did a lot of stupid shit. Dangerous shit. Don't even remember half of it. Some of the stories my friends would tell me the next day about what I'd done... They were pretty fucking embarrassing. I think I got used to kinda laughing it off, y'know? Maybe it was easier to make myself the butt of the joke so I could beat them to the punch. Like a self-preservation thing, I guess. So I didn't have to sit in the shame."

"So which one were you doing out there? The ham thing or the self-preservation thing?" Worry prickles at the thought that he might be hiding his discomfort with all this. With our arrangement. With me.

He chuckles. "That was just because I'm a big ol' dork who likes making you laugh."

I grin and my cheeks heat anew, though this time it has nothing to do with the spicy food. "So, the first one?"

"Yup." He watches me for a long moment, then seems to snap out of it like he's shaking off distraction.

I take another sip of water before carefully replacing my red plastic cup on the ring of condensation on the shiny tablecloth.

Miles insists on paying for dinner when we settle up, waving me off when I try to argue. "I got this one."

"But I'm the one who got you into this whole mess. Shouldn't I be paying?"

"Nah. Last time we hung out, I got a taste of your world. Saw how the fancy girls live." When I make a face, he winks.

I can't fight the way that wink sends a tendril of heat straight to my center.

"But, this time," he pushes up from the table and reaches for my hand, "you're in my world."

An accidental Aladdin moment.

I hesitate for a beat before I take it, then let him lead me out of the tiny restaurant.

"So this is your world, huh?" I ask as we emerge from the narrow alleyway and spill onto the sidewalk. A strong breeze sends my dress whipping at my thighs, and I tuck my scarf around my neck.

"Come on, Caroline. You'd never have gone to some hole-in-the-wall spot like that. Too sketchy. But if you know what to ask for..." He gives me a look—a silent *I told you so*. "So fucking delicious, right?"

"It really was... very delicious."

He narrows his eyes and repeats, "So *fucking* delicious. C'mon. Say it with me. So..."

"So..."

"Fucking..."

A laugh bursts out of me. "Miles, oh my goodness."

"First it was *dang it*, now *oh my goodness*?" His brows quirk together. "You don't swear, do you?"

I scrunch my nose in apology. "Not often, no. Not unless I'm pretty... worked up, I guess."

His eyes slip down to my lips before he seems to catch himself and snaps them back up. "'Kay, well, you're gonna have to elbow me in the ribs or something when I do, 'cause I don't even hear it come out of my mouth."

"It doesn't bother me. Honest."

He watches me for a moment. "It's cathartic, you know."

"What, swearing?"

"Damn fucking right." He grins and I can't help but mirror his delight. *God*, his eyes have no business crinkling at the corners like that.

"So, you think I need to *cathart*, or what?"

"Maybe." He looks like he's got more to say, but something's holding him back.

"Oh, right." I nod, folding my arms over my chest. "You think you have a pretty good read on me at this point, huh?"

He lifts a shoulder, noncommittal. "Yeah, I think so."

"Alright, and what has your spidey-sense figured out?" I tilt my head in amusement.

He stuffs his hands into his pockets, hesitating a moment before he speaks. "Well, if I had to guess, I'd say you've been working really hard for a long time to keep other people happy."

My smile falters.

"Maybe your parents," he adds. "Maybe that asshole, Fletcher."

I frown, the truth laid out so plainly that it takes me by surprise.

"And I'd guess," he continues, watching me carefully, "you're sick of no one asking what *you* want. Maybe you're not even sure, yourself, what that is."

My eyes fall away from his, losing focus.

"Caroline." In my blurred peripheral vision, Miles' feet move closer. "Caroline. Shit. Sorry. I didn't mean to— Ah, fuck."

A beat passes. Then another. And then, before I can react, I'm wrapped in his arms, surrounded by his earthy scent, his warmth, the press of his body. Reflexively, I snake my arms around his waist and cling tight as he rubs my back in rhythmic strokes.

"I'm really sorry." His voice vibrates low against my temple, his lips so close they heat my skin. I squeeze my eyes shut, trying to fight off the memory of the last time he held me this close, yet unable to pull away all the same. Because, God damnit, this feels good. To be held like this—to be *seen* like this. Even if his words did sting a bit.

How did he do that?

With just a few pithy sentences, he'd held up a mirror to all the uncomfortable truths I've been carrying around my entire life.

"You're right," I hear myself say against his chest.

"What?" His hands still. "No. I'm a dick who doesn't know when to shut up. Ignore me, please."

"But I *don't* know what I want." I finally work up the nerve to pull back, stepping out of his arms before I risk looking up. "Sometimes I feel like this puppet, just going through the motions, y'know? Other times I feel like I might explode. Or scream. And, even if I threw the fit, had the tantrum... what would it achieve?"

His expression pinches with concern, but his silence beckons me on.

"When I first moved here last year, I had this silly idea about starting over. I bought all these new clothes, trying to look less like a senator's daughter and kind of... lean into my own style a bit more."

"Did it help?"

"Kind of?" I shrug. "I mean, it's not like my parents picked out my clothes before; I'm an adult. But there was pressure to show up a certain way. Look a certain way. And I guess it never felt like me. Never felt right. Or good. I just wanted to feel *good*." Tears well in my eyes and I clench my hands into fists, fighting the way putting it into words brings back that suffocating feeling in full force. "It's like I've lived this neat little life that fits into this neat little box, and all of it has been what other people wanted me to do." My shoulders sag. "And I want out. I wanna live my own life, make my own choices, my own mistakes. I wanna have experiences. Be messy. Figure out what I like. What I don't like. Try stuff."

"Like sketchy, hole-in-the-wall tacos?" The scarred corner of his lips curls up slightly.

"Yeah! Like... like *fucking delicious* tacos!"

A broad grin splits his face.

I tilt my head. "Do you see what I'm saying? I'm just at this breaking point, and it all feels like such ridiculous, first-world nonsense to even be upset about it!"

"It's not." He shakes his head.

"Yes, it is! I've had this incredibly privileged life, and I'm still not happy? What's wrong with me?"

"Caroline, there's nothing wrong with you." He steps toward me, sliding his palms down my arms. "You deserve all of that. To be messy, to make your own decisions, to feel good. Wanting those things is like basic human shit, okay?"

I'm not sure I believe him.

"Listen," he says. "What's one thing you've never done?" When I hesitate, he squeezes my hands and adds, "One thing you always wanted to do but never felt like you could."

"What?"

"C'mon! Let's see if we can knock something off your list."

"Now? Tonight?" I look around us.

"Yes! A real boyfriend would help you do that stuff, right? Why not let your fake boyfriend take you on a few adventures while you've got him?"

"Uh, I... I don't..." A thousand thoughts careen and crash in my head, jostling to get front and center. I blow out a breath, pulling my hands away from his.

"Just hit me. Spitball style. Don't overthink it. Just blurt out the first thing that comes to mind. Something you wanna do."

"Skinny dipping!"

Miles' eyebrows nearly meet his hairline before shocked laughter stutters out. "Skinny dipping."

"Sorry! I panicked!" I press my palms to my cheeks, confirming they're on fire.

Did I seriously suggest being naked together?

"It's October!" He nearly laughs out the words. "The river is fucking glacial right now. Literally, it *is* glacial, pretty sure."

"I know! Forget I even said that. Oh my God." I search up and down the block, as if I might locate a hole I can crawl into.

His amused expression falls. "Wait, seriously, you've never been skinny dipping?"

"No!"

He drops his shoulders. "You poor, sheltered girl."

"Ugh, you don't know the half of it." I roll my eyes.

"What do you mean?"

No. I can't tell him.

Miles doesn't need to know Fletcher wasn't exactly adventurous in the bedroom. Not that any of my boyfriends before him were anything to write home about, either.

He studies me cautiously. "Are there other... *activities* you haven't tried?"

I stiffen.

Can he somehow hear my thoughts?

He dips his chin and drops his voice low. "Like.. *naked* activities?"

Oh, God. He can definitely hear my thoughts.

"Miles!" I look away, sure my cheeks are bright red. When he holds out his hands in an innocent shrug, I add, "What? You want me to list them for you? Oh my God, this is so embarrassing."

"There's a list?"

My shoulders drop. I can't do this—can't drag out all the details of my unremarkable sex life—especially in public. How can I confess to this sexy, tattooed, confident goofball of a man that I'm pretty sure I'm his polar opposite in bed? Inexperienced. Boring. Awkward. And so unbelievably desperate to be none of those things.

"Okay," he says slowly. "This feels like an indoor conversation."

I throw my arms out at my sides. "You think?"

"Then c'mon," he says, digging out his keys. "Let's get outta here. Find somewhere to talk in private." He opens the passenger door of his truck, chucks the folded hoodie out of the way, then gestures for me to get in.

I don't move. "Where?"

"I know a good place." He pumps his brows.

"Not exactly reassuring."

"Aw, where's your sense of adventure? Thought you wanted to *try stuff*." He makes a *come hither* gesture, a hypnotic kind of delight glittering in his eyes. "C'mon. Let's go make some mistakes!"

Biting my lip hard, I step past him and climb into the truck. Because... well, *fuck it*.

12

MILES

The old mountaintop fire lookout is more run-down than I remember, its wooden siding visibly weathered, even in the dark. The stairs to the top of the two-story tower creak a little under our weight, but any concern about safety is immediately replaced by the sight of Caroline climbing the stairs just ahead of me. I could bite those calves. Lick behind her knee, up to her...

Jesus. Get a grip, Miles.

She glances at me over her shoulder. "So, what is this, like a make-out spot for teenagers?"

"Kinda, actually," I say, impressed she caught on so quickly. Mount Makott was known as Mount Make Out when I was in high school. "But that's not why I brought you here, I swear." It's not a lie, exactly—more of a massaging of the truth.

She stops when we reach the top and peers inside. While these old living quarters used to have doors, they've been long since removed. The space is open to the public now, maintained by the parks department like a mini museum on stilts.

We cross the room to the expansive windows overlooking the

town, and Caroline's jaw drops as she takes in the view—the entirety of Lennox Valley spread out before us like a glowing tapestry. "This is…" She trails off, momentarily at a loss for words. "Gorgeous."

"I know." I take a moment to watch her in profile under the dim utility light—the gentle slope of her slightly upturned nose and the absentminded way she touches her neck. "So fucking gorgeous."

She tears her eyes away from the view to look at me. "This is where you wanted to talk?"

"Yeah." I shove my hands in my pockets, letting a small smirk pull at my lips. "About that list of yours."

She scrunches her nose and scans the room again, taking in the wooden pallet where a mattress used to rest, the tiny and practical kitchen, the bare cupboards without any doors, and the circular fire finder map mounted on a table in the center of the room. The place used to house whatever the forestry version of a lighthouse keeper is, I guess.

When she's quiet for long enough that I start to doubt myself, I break the silence. "You don't have to tell me if you don't wanna."

"It's not that." Caroline turns back to me. "It's just… I don't really know what to say."

"Well, you said you wanna try things." I cross my arms. "You got anything specific in mind?" I won't push her, but I get the sense she wants to open up. Maybe she doesn't know how.

She opens her mouth, then shuts it and lets out a long cringe-groan, like after I caught her peeking at me changing. She shakes out her hands like she can physically shake off the feeling. "This is so awkward, Miles!"

I laugh.

Embarrassed Caroline is fucking cute.

"Should I guess?" I ask.

"No!"

"Is it butt stuff?"

"Miles!" She drops her face into her palms.

"It's butt stuff, isn't it?"

"No-o-o-o-ooooo!" she whine-laughs, letting her arms fall. "It's not butt stuff!"

"Hey." Grinning, I step closer and tilt her chin up until she meets my eyes. "I'm just messing with you."

She gives me a look. "Okay, here's the thing: I don't actually know. I mean, sex has always been... fine for me."

"Fine?" I draw back a bit.

She throws her hands out at her sides. "Yes. Fine!"

I stare at her in horror.

"What?" She stares right back. "What's wrong with fine?"

I can't quite believe what I'm hearing. "Shit, Fletcher is a bigger dickhead than I thought." That asshole had this stunning woman in his life and never gave her anything better than *fine*? Never gave her the pleasure she deserves? And, to make matters worse, she doesn't even seem to know what she's been missing.

Now I *really* wish I'd punched him.

I groan and run a hand down my face, enraged by the injustice of it for her. "You can't just carry on like this. Not knowing."

"Not knowing what?"

"How good it can be!" I drop my shoulders. "Caroline, *fine* is for boring shit like traffic and the weather. But sex? Sex should be... fucking amazing. Incredible. So good you think you might die sometimes."

"Yeah, well..." She turns away and picks at the chipped paint on the windowsill. "Not for me, I guess."

"Not yet."

"Yeah, well, that's not likely to change anytime soon." When she finally looks at me again, her expression is cautious.

"I could help you."

"What?" Her eyes widen. Appropriately. Because...

What in the impulsive sex blurt did I just offer?

"No, Miles, you're already helping me plenty. I'm not gonna ask you to—"

"Well, we're already hanging out together."

Cool, yeah, I guess I'm doubling down on this.

"And I don't need pity sex."

"Oh my God. Whoa." I hold out my hands. "That's *not* what I was offering." When she doesn't look convinced, I step closer and reach for her cheek, brushing my thumb over her soft skin. "Hey. I don't pity you. I think you're fucking beautiful. And sexy. If that kiss was anything to go by... I think it could be amazing between us."

"Yeah?" Her eyes slip to my mouth.

"Yeah," I say, shoving aside the awareness that I offered this a bit impulsively. That I might have just cranked up the intensity on our already-complicated situation. I scramble for logic. "I mean, we might as well have some fun while we're pretending to date, right? And God, Caroline. You *need* to know what you've been missing. It's a fucking crime that you've never felt..." I trail off, distracted by thoughts of everything I want her to feel. To experience. How much I'd love to help her discover that side of herself. To be the one to experience it all with her, if she wants me to. "Look. You've been putting yourself aside for a long-ass time, right?"

"Yeah..."

"Isn't it time you did something that makes *you* feel good?"

She tilts her head. "And that something should be you?"

I huff out a laugh. "I, uh— well, that wasn't exactly where I was going, but, uh, yes?" When she rolls her eyes, it only encourages me. "I meant like, making sure *you* come first." I hear myself say it and wince. "Putting yourself first! But I'd make sure you came first, obviously—"

"Miles?"

"Yeah?"

"Stop talking."

"Yup." I'm trying not to grin like a fool here.

A few beats pass as she considers me. When she speaks, her voice is quiet. "Can I tell you something?"

"Of course."

"That kiss. Last weekend?" She bites her lip. "I kinda can't stop thinking about it."

Her confession releases something in my chest. The truth is, she isn't the only one who hasn't been able to forget it. "Me neither."

"I know we got sort of carried away." She looks up at me, almost shy. "But I've never been kissed like that before."

Another fucking crime.

"It was a *good* kiss," I say.

"So good." Her voice is barely a whisper.

"Can I tell *you* something?" I close the space between us.

"What?" Her shallow breaths mingle with mine, only drawing me closer.

"If you thought that kiss was good..." I dip down to brush my lips over hers and her eyelids flutter shut. "You should know..." I nip her full bottom lip, tugging gently until she whimpers and it pops from between my teeth. "I fuck like I kiss."

Right as she lifts to kiss me, I step back, failing to fight off a smile at the way she has to catch herself before she topples forward.

Wide eyes snap to mine. "That was so unfair!"

With a smirk, I tuck my hands into my pockets again, discreetly adjusting myself in the process. "You still haven't told me what you wanna try."

"What?" She still looks a little disoriented and it's fucking adorable. "Miles, this is bonkers."

Bonkers?

I'm completely failing to keep a straight face here. Mildly spicy tacos might have taken her out, but it's gonna be those cute fucking words that'll be the death of me.

"It's not bonkers!" I say.

It might actually be bonkers.

"I can't—" she blurts out. "We can't!"

I shrug. "Why not?"

Her shoulders drop. "We've known each other less than two weeks, I've roped you into this weird fake dating scheme with the press watching us, and now you wanna hop into bed together? This whole situation is wild, Miles!"

"So lean into it!" I throw my arms out wide. "Be wild! Hell, you said you wanted to find out what you like and try stuff, right? Break out of your shell?" I pump my eyebrows. "Maybe scream a bit?"

A crack forms in her composure. "Okay, yes, but—"

"How else are you gonna figure that shit out?" I reach out to squeeze her fingertips. "You won't know what you like until you try it. All I'm offering is a chance to try."

She contemplates me for a beat. "Alright. *If* we did this together," she starts, then holds up a finger when I grin, "how would it... Like, how would it work?"

"Well, it's not like I've done this before, either, but..." I think for a moment. "I guess, you gotta figure out what's on your sex list. *Our* sex list." I tilt my head, reconsidering my choice of words. "Or... our to-do list? Do-you list?" I make a dismissive face. "We'll workshop the name. But c'mon. You gonna tell me what I just signed up for?"

"Miles, I can't— I feel too on the spot, like if you want me to rattle off a list face-to-face like this—"

"You want me to turn around, or...?" I can't help myself; winding her up is too much fun.

"Stop!" she says through laughter. "I think I need some time to think about it. Maybe write it down?"

"Sure. Of course." I shrug, pretending I won't be obsessing about this thing until I see it. "Take as long as you need."

"Okay. And then, when you read it, I'll just quietly die of shame in the corner or something."

I reach out to give her fingers a quick squeeze. "Hey, you don't need to be embarrassed with me. I've got an open mind. Whatever makes you feel good, I'm game."

"But what if you aren't? What if you don't want to? Like, what if—" She balls her hands into fists, obviously a bit anxious about this idea.

"*And,*" I add, cutting into her spiraling with a pointed look, "if there's anything I'm not cool with, I'll tell you." I don't expect she'll put any non-starters on her list—not that I have many. "But what are we talkin' here, like ballpark style? Like, using toys and shit? Or are we gonna need to sacrifice an animal on a full moon?"

"Wha-a?" she splutters. "The first one. What kind of *weird*—"

"Hey," I deadpan, holding up my hands, "don't knock it 'til ya try it." When her eyes bug out, I bark out a laugh.

"Miles! Oh my God!" She stares at me, clearly both shocked and amused. "I can't believe you—"

I cut her off with a hard kiss, her indignation slowly surrendering with each stroke of my tongue. And, *holy shit*, she tastes like I could do this all night.

"Mmm," I hum against her lips, breaking away before going right back for more. "You sure you don't wanna start right now?"

Her laughter warms my cheek as she snakes her arms around my neck. "Are you serious? For real?"

"About fucking in an abandoned fire lookout?" My gaze falls to her mouth. "I dunno, sounds kinda hot to me."

"No!" she says, gently swatting my arm.

"Aw, c'mon. Thought you wanted to try stuff. Plus, you can't beat this view." My eyes are on her lips and I'm not even pretending to look outside.

"I meant this thing in general. This *sex* thing." I'd bet a million bucks her cheeks are flushed pink, but it's too dark to tell under this shitty utility light. "You seriously wanna help me explore what I like?"

"Why not?" There are easily a thousand reasons why not, but I couldn't name one right now if I tried. Not with Caroline in my arms, awkward and flustered.

"Wouldn't it be crossing a line for you?" she asks. "You said you couldn't date for real. And I'm not suggesting *that*, but"—her expression pinches with concern—"wouldn't it get blurry?"

I shake my head. "This wouldn't be a relationship. Think of it more like a... friends-with-benefits kinda deal. Just until the election, while we're already pretending to date. You need to have some amazing sex, and I'd get to have that amazing sex with you. It's a win-win, right? And I'd get to be, like, your sex sensei."

"My sex sensei?" She looks skeptical. "What, like a dirty Mr. Miyagi?"

"Hell yeah!" I chuckle, then put on an air of calm. "Now, young Grasshopper, where did we land on the ol' exhibitionism thing?"

"I'm ignoring that."

Worth a shot.

She cranes her neck to peer out the window once again. "So why did you bring me here, anyway?" When she turns back, she runs the pad of her thumb over my bottom lip, looking like she's still thinking about kissing me. "Other than to proposition me, obviously."

I smirk at the dig and nip at her thumb, though my amusement fades—along with any thoughts about getting under that dress of hers—as I think about how to answer. "Uh, my dad and I used to hike up here when we had something difficult to talk about. I think he found it easier to have awkward conversations when we didn't have to make direct eye contact, y'know? We could just stare out at the town instead of having to face each other straight on."

There's a sadness in the way she smiles. "Well, a hike and a heart-to-heart sounds a heck of a lot better than tense silences and lectures."

I frown. "Yeah, your dad seems…"

"Overbearing?"

I tilt my head, choosing not to finish my sentence. Calling her father a *twatwaffle* probably wouldn't go over well.

"I guess now we know why *I'm* in therapy, huh?" she dead-pans, then turns more serious. "My mom and I are closer. She gets a bit intimidated by Dad, though. I think she tries to keep the peace a lot…" Caroline trails off, then seems to snap out of it, forcing a change of subject. "Are you close with your parents?"

I hesitate a beat, then pull away. It still hurts, even though more than a decade has passed since the crash that took their lives. But I know I need to tell her. "I was."

"Not anymore?" she asks. "What happened?"

I hate this part, so I bite the bullet and blurt it out. "They died. I was seventeen."

My words hit her square in the chest, and her features crumple. "Miles…"

"It's okay." I look at my feet. "You don't have to—"

She crushes me in a hug, cutting me off.

Slowly, I wrap my arms around her shoulders and rest my chin on top of her head, grateful she isn't asking for details. I try to fight off the wince as the familiar script floats to the surface unbidden.

It was my fault. They'd still be here if it wasn't for me.

But I keep my mouth shut, swallowing past the lump in my throat. Caroline doesn't need to hear about my trauma—doesn't need to know how I tried to drown the pain in liquor, never managing to numb myself enough not to feel it.

What's within your control right now? That's what Lydia always says.

Inhaling the sweet vanilla scent of Caroline's hair, I stare out at the town lights, determined to focus on the present, not the past. There's good right here in front of me—right here in my arms.

"I'm so sorry." Her quiet voice drifts up from my chest.

"It's... yeah. Thanks." When I realize there's another awkward conversation we need to have, I step back, squeezing her chilled hands. "There's, uh, there's something else I need to tell you. If we're gonna do, uh, *naked activities*."

"What?" Caution etches her features.

I clench my jaw. It's a risk to tell her, but I can't keep this secret any longer. Not if we're gonna make this physical too. She needs to be able to trust me.

Honesty. Just tell her.

"Shit. Okay. Your dad told me not to say anything, but—"

"You talked to my dad?" Caroline stiffens. "When? At the fundraiser?"

"Yeah." My stomach is already halfway to bottoming out. I exhale slowly, trying to steady myself. "Look, I told you in the car that night you could trust me, and I meant it. I wanna be completely honest with you."

"Please spit it out." She searches my eyes. "Please. Just tell me what he said. Whatever it is, I—"

"He threatened me, Caroline."

"He what?"

"Well, he threatened my job, technically. Which is basically the same thing."

"Oh my God. Why?"

"To make sure I stuck around. Played the doting boyfriend. Behaved myself."

"Is that why you agreed to this?" Hurt flashes across her face. "I thought you were helping me. I thought you *wanted* to help me."

"I did and I do," I rush to clarify. "Even if he hadn't said anything before you'd asked me, I still would've said yes."

"I don't get it. He threatened you into doing something you would've done anyway?"

"Uh, there's more." When her brows lift, I add, "A condition, I guess. He wants me gone after Election Day. I think his exact words were *out of her life*." I grimace at the memory—and how it feels to watch those words land.

The resigned regret in her eyes says it all; she doesn't need to ask why. She digs through her purse for her phone. "This is *way* too far."

"Stop." I cover her shaking fingers with my own, stilling her hand, and her gaze snaps to mine. "Don't. You can't tell him. I can't risk my job."

"But he can't do this, Miles!" Her voice rises in pitch.

"I know." I rub her arms. "But he did."

Somehow, I convince her to breathe and let me explain. She looks numb listening to it all—numb and yet not surprised. My heart breaks a little for her; God knows how long this selfish prick has been meddling in her life. Someone who should have loved her unconditionally kept using her—manipulating her for his own benefit. Hell, she'd agreed to spend time with her repulsive ex just to avoid the possibility that her personal life could cost her dad votes. Based on, what, some bullshit idea about what women should or shouldn't do with their own bodies? It dawns on me why she wants to break free and try new things—and why she got so emotional outside the restaurant earlier about that whole making-other-people-happy thing; I'd hit the nail on the head.

And now she's quiet. Too quiet.

"Say something. Tell me what you're thinking."

She exhales hard. "I... Look, I know it probably doesn't make sense to you why I'd even *want* to help my dad—especially after he's done this."

"Hey, that's not for me to judge. Families are... messy sometimes."

"It's just complicated." She swallows. "He's my family. My blood."

"I know." Which is why it was such a dick move.

"There are also... business entanglements." At my obvious confusion, she adds, "He's a major annual donor to Found Family."

I nod slowly, remembering Caroline telling me about how her dad had supported the charity in its early days.

"He's dropped a casual threat more than once about pulling his donations if I"—she looks up at the ceiling—"step out of line."

I scowl and shake my head.

What a dirtbag.

"He nearly went through with it, too, when I told him I was quitting to move in with my grandpa here." She cuts her gaze out the window. "I had to beg him not to and promise to keep supporting him at public events."

"Fuck. I'm sorry he's been like that."

She turns back to me. "Maybe he won't win the election? Maybe—"

"He'll still be a senator," I say quietly. Whether or not Pete Brennan gets elected governor, he's got power, contacts, connections. Enough to fuck with my job no matter what happens.

"What are we gonna do?"

"Well, I think you're stuck with me for the next few weeks."

"What?" She looks dazed. "You can't be serious about still going along with this. Letting him get his way."

I shrug, knowing I've had more time to mull this over than she has. "Can't risk my job, though. If I don't have an income, everything else unravels. My rent, my meds, my therapist, my gym membership... Everything that keeps me sober."

"But—"

"*And* it sounds like you can't risk the charity donation stuff either."

Her shoulders drop. "Yeah. So, we what? Placate him and keep this up for weeks?"

"Okay, the placating him part obviously sucks, but would hanging out together be so bad?" There's no question we have chemistry.

"I guess not?" She bites her lip, thinking for a moment. "You'd keep your job, and I'd appease my meddling father." Her brows pinch together. "Is that a win for me? Why doesn't it feel like one?"

"You'd also be protecting Found Family. That *would* be a win. It's important to you, right?"

"It is." She nods. "And to Adrian. And to all the kids."

"See?" I tug on her dress and pull her into another hug, pressing my lips into her hair. "Plus, I can still help you out with your *sexploration* list. I mean, I heard girls with asshole dads deserve, like, extra orgasms and shit. So."

She laughs into my shoulder, though she sounds tired.

"C'mon, I'll drive you back to your car. You can work on your fuck-it list in the truck on the way into town."

She balks, pulling back to stare up at me. "My what?"

"Y'know, like a bucket list—but for sex."

"Okay." That awkward smile is back as I coax her toward the stairs. "But if you say butt stuff again—"

I hold up a hand in solemn promise. "I swear I won't say—"

Her eyes widen as she clamps a palm over my mouth. "Don't!"

When I stay quiet, she risks slowly peeling her fingers away.

Then, because my maturity level apparently never progressed past age thirteen, I whisper, "Butt stuff."

13

CAROLINE

Miles and I exchange a few flirty texts over the next week, mostly consisting of him begging for details about my sex list—and, nearly just as often, making ridiculous, unhinged guesses about what's on it.

MILES

Threesome?

ME

No.

MILES

Intruder role-play?

ME

No!

MILES

Me in a gorilla suit?

ME

No!!

MILES

It's butt stuff. I knew it.

ME

Miles!!

With each message, I shrivel into an increasingly tight, awkward ball of nerves, unable to bring myself to share much of anything.

And now I'm hovering inside his apartment door, list complete, thumbing the edge of the folded paper in my pocket. For a second, I think I might flee, burn the evidence, and enter the witness protection program.

I shouldn't be embarrassed. My brain knows sex is perfectly natural, but tell that to my body. Nothing screams *vanilla bore* quite like staring down an itemized list of all the sex acts you've been curious about but never tried.

With shaking hands, I slip off my heels. We'd agreed I'd come over tonight, and we both know exactly what I'm here for, but showing up at his apartment for the sole purpose of having sex fills me with a strange, simmering thrill. I'm nervous about actually going through with this, but under the nerves is excitement. Writing out that list was like drafting a blueprint for my own little sexual revolution.

Miles looks effortlessly delicious as usual, the jeans slung low on his hips and his worn T-shirt only fueling my thoughts of exploring what's underneath. But knowing I'm here to do exactly that is already giving me heart palpitations.

"You wanna take off your coat?" He gestures to the hooks near the front door.

"Um, not yet." Avoiding his gaze, I drop my small bag on the floor and snug the belt of my thigh-length trench coat. "I'm cold."

"Okay." Miles watches me for a moment. "Well? You finally finish it?"

My cheeks heat. "Uh, yes?"

"Cough it up, then." He holds out his palm with a smirk. "You've got me so fucking curious about this damn list."

With a grimace, I thrust the paper toward his handsome face and squeeze my eyes shut. "Just take it. Take it before I change my mind!"

Feeling him swipe it from my grasp, I crack an eyelid and watch as he slowly unfolds it and settles on the couch.

"Alright, let's see..."

He roughs his knuckles over his clean-shaven jaw.

Did he shave just for tonight? For me?

I shift on my feet, practically wringing my hands.

Studying the paper carefully, Miles flicks a few glances my way, a slow smile spreading over his lips. At one point, he raises his brows—but still doesn't speak.

When his silence becomes intolerable, I break. "Oh my God, say something!"

He looks up and does the faintest double-take, realization touching his expression as he pushes up from the couch. Letting my list drop to the coffee table, he strides toward me and, without breaking eye contact, starts to loosen the belt of my coat. His voice is rough when he speaks. "That last one..."

An involuntary sound leaves my throat. "Yeah?"

"Any chance you planned for that one tonight?"

As he undoes the buttons, he dips down to kiss me slowly, the clean, woodsy scent of him drawing me even closer. His lips are so warm, his tongue so deliciously distracting.

My heart jackhammers against my rib cage.

When my coat falls open, he hisses out the word *fuck*. Pressing his hands together over his mouth, he paces a few steps away from me—and my stomach sinks.

Does he hate it? Did I go way overboard?

I glance down. Intricate panels of red lace and satin crisscross over my breasts and delicate ribbing slopes down my waist, attaching to a high-cut, lacy thong. Crimson garter straps stretch from the lower edge of the bodice over my hips and bottom, clipped to the bands of lace at the top of thigh-high red stockings.

Self-consciousness flares hot in my chest as I smooth one garter strap over my hip. This getup suddenly seems ridiculous. Impractical and over-the-top, like a silly costume.

Who do I think I'm pretending to be?

"Do you like it?" I ask, my voice pathetically hopeful. "I wasn't sure if—"

He stops in his tracks, eyes snapping to mine. "Do I like it?" Brow furrowed as if he's in pain, his gaze slips down my body.

"Yeah, it's just—"

And then he rushes for me, cutting me off with a breath-stealing kiss. He wrestles the coat from my shoulders, letting it drop to the floor before pulling back enough to press his forehead to mine.

"Do I fucking like it?" He slides his palms up my arms, then cups my face in his hands and kisses me again. When he breaks away, his voice is a bit ragged. "Yeah, fancy girl. I like it."

"I didn't know if..." I trail off as his fingers find my hair and he grabs a fistful of curls, tugging my face up so I meet his molten eyes. He lets out a low growl, and delicious heat fans up from my core, engulfing my exposed throat. I might make a tiny whimpering sound in response.

He presses his lips to mine once more, and his grip on my hair has me arching into him.

I open my mouth so he can deepen the kiss, then gasp when he tears away and jerks my head back. A dark, almost thrilling tendril of pleasure slips from my scalp, spreading down from my nape to my shoulder blades as he kisses my neck. "I guess that answers whether I like having my hair pulled."

He lets go suddenly. "Shit, sorry, I didn't even— Was that okay?"

"Yes, I liked it."

"Oh, thank fuck." His cobalt eyes are nearly black in the dim light. "I uh... I think you melted my brain." He shakes his head like he can't quite believe what I'm wearing. "God, look at you."

"What?"

"Uh, I figured we were just gonna start by making out on the couch or something. But you've, um..."—he swallows—"really upped the ante, here." He explores my rib cage and waist with his fingers, his thumbs brushing reverent strokes over the lace covering my skin. "I mean, it's a helluva first move."

"Be honest. Is it too much?" I wish I still had my coat on so I could hug it around me. "Because I can change."

"Fuck no!" He peels off his shirt, flinging it across the room with a grin. "I just need to catch up." Taking my face in his hands, he kisses me again—intense, insistent, and hungry. "The only place this lacy little number is going"—he reaches down, tracing the satiny edge over my hip—"is on my bedroom floor."

I let out a small yelp when he scoops me over his shoulder, one palm squeezing and kneading at my thigh as he carries me into his room. The deep press of his fingers into my flesh is strangely intoxicating, and I want him to keep touching me like that—hard, like he can't help himself.

When Miles lays me out on his bed and climbs over me, all I can think is how badly I want to lick the cleft in the center of his chin. Or sink my teeth into his muscular, tattooed shoulder.

"You're so pretty in this." He dips down to nuzzle my breasts, inhaling like he's taking a long drag of a much-needed cigarette.

"I bought it for tonight." I thread my fingers through his hair, hoping he can read between the lines: no one but him has seen me wear this.

A rumbling sound escapes his throat, and my body hums in response.

Message received.

"Oh, God," I almost whine when he draws one of my nipples between his lips. Even through the fabric, the warmth of his tongue and the gentle scrape of his teeth send a pulse of longing through my entire body.

Apparently, I'm not the only one thinking about biting.

"Fuck, I love your tits," he mumbles around the peaked flesh and lace, palming and gently squeezing my other breast. When he switches sides, I whimper, but he just nips harder.

Urgency floods me; I need his mouth on my skin. *Now.*

Tugging down the straps of my lingerie, I free one arm, then the other, baring my chest and arching up. "More. Please."

Tendrils of pleasure spread through me when he groans, then licks and sucks my pebbled flesh, sending my heartbeat skittering. He hums against my skin, tugging gently before letting go with a soft pop before moving to my other side. "Mmm, fucking perfect." Slowly, reverently, he slides my lingerie down, kissing every inch he uncovers. His tongue and lips light fireworks under my skin as they sweep over my breasts, my ribs, then my stomach.

Settling between my legs, Miles tugs on the small bow at the top of one garter strap, frowning when it doesn't give. He tries again, running a finger under the elastic. "Fuck, Caroline," he almost chuckles, flicking his gaze up to mine. "How the hell do you get these things off?"

Skimming my lip with my teeth, I reach down to release the garter straps, then gasp when he shoves my knees apart.

"Y'know…" He feathers his fingers along my inner thighs and warmth blooms at my center when he nips me through my panties. "There's something else on your list that needs immediate attention."

"Which one?" I shiver when he repeats the movement, lifting the edge of the fabric ever so slightly. My skin hums in the wake of his touch.

"Coming your brains out." He pinches the thin lace between my legs, pulling it away before letting it go with a snap.

I flinch, letting out an involuntary whimper.

"Over and over again," he adds. He smooths his fingers over my center, soothing the sting and drinking in my reaction.

"Um, not sure those were my exact words." I try to tamp down on the grin he draws out of me.

"Fine. Multiple orgasms. Potato, potahto."

He increases the pressure, quickly turning me into a puddle. The mewling noises that slip out of me are so foreign; I don't think I've ever made sounds like this before.

I lift my hips as he frees me from the lingerie, sliding my stockings down with it.

He practically sighs the word *fuck* when he takes in the sight of me completely naked, dropping the red lace off the side of the bed before he crawls back over me.

I rake my fingers through his hair and down over his strong shoulders, pulling him into a kiss.

"How did it feel?" he asks when our lips part, then noses my cheek. "Walking around practically naked under that coat, knowing you were coming here to get fucked?"

I let out another small whimper as he drops a trail of kisses down my throat.

I've never been spoken to like this.

"Um, exciting?" I admit.

"Yeah?" He slides a finger between my legs, cursing when it slips easily through the slick wetness gathered there. "And you got yourself all wet thinking about it, didn't you? Thinking about me fucking you."

I press my lips together and nod, squirming at the light touch of his fingers.

"Everyone thinks you're such a good girl... but look at you." He rubs my clit and I tilt my hips against the bed, chasing the too-light pressure. "Making a little mess of yourself for me."

Enraptured, I stare as he sucks my taste from his fingertip, humming with pleasure.

"But you're not a good girl, are you, Caroline?"

"I'm actually"—I claw at the sheets when he dips his fingertip just inside my entrance—"really tired of being good."

He almost growls in approval. "Yeah? You wanna be bad, huh?"

I let out a faint moan, barely recognizing my own voice.

Oh, God. Who am I? What am I doing?

"Does it turn you on when I talk about how fucking naughty you are?" My lips twist, cheeks flushing hot as I nod, and he takes my nipple in his mouth again, sucking hard before he breaks away. "Showing up here, wearing almost nothing for me.'

Exhaling a rush of air, I try to fight the way his words send a wave of pleasure through my body.

"So bad. A good girl would never do that."

"I'm," I swallow, "trying new things."

He grins and kisses me, lowering his hips between my legs.

I writhe against him, urged on by the flick of his tongue and the hot press of his erection. I slide my hands down his back to squeeze his ass, encouraging him and wholly unable to stop grinding myself against his jeans. Even the cool sensation of his belt buckle against my skin has me gasping and squirming for more.

What am I, some kind of animal in heat?

His tongue slips and curls against mine in ever-deepening strokes until we're both lost in it, our moaned, animalistic sounds resonating in the space between our lips. When our movements become frenzied, he tears his mouth from mine, lifting his hips away.

"Hey, uh…" His laugh is shaky against my cheek. "I need to admit something here."

"What?" I smooth a dark lock of hair away from his forehead.

"I'm gonna be *real* easy tonight." He lifts a brow. "It's uh, it's been a while for me."

"Oh. Okay," I say. "Sorry, I—"

"Uh-uh," he warns, then kisses me again. "Don't you dare apologize. I just wanna last as long as I can. So let me take care of you first."

"Right. I'm supposed to… *come my brains out*, was it?" I bite my lip.

"Exactly." He grins. "Over and over again."

"Right."

He dips down to kiss my neck, then sucks my earlobe before running his tongue along the shell of my ear. "Fuck, Caroline," he says, his deep voice sending tingles straight to my core, "if I have anything to say about it, you're gonna be screaming into this mattress, begging for mercy when it's all too much."

My stomach hollows at his words.

Jesus.

"Helluva first move."

He laughs, the sound warm and rich. "Well, you set the bar pretty high with that lingerie." His amusement slowly fades as he gently strokes his thumb over my throat. "Fuck, the things I wanna do to you. You have no idea. The things I want you to feel…"

"Like what?" I almost whisper the words.

With a little moan, he scrapes his teeth over my neck and I arch against him. "I want you to come undone for me." His next words are slow and drawn out, dropped onto my skin between featherlight kisses. "I wanna turn you into a whimpering little mess."

I dig my fingernails into his back—certain my mind has already come undone.

Sweet baby Jesus.

"Obviously," he adds quickly, pulling back, "if you want me to stop, just, like, whack my shoulder or something." His warm exhale fans against my lips before he kisses me again. "You get to hit the brakes anytime, okay?"

I nod. "Okay."

"But"—he bends again to graze his teeth along my collarbone —"as far as I'm concerned"—he licks and nips his way up my throat, his words rumbling low over my skin—"my job isn't done until you're completely... fucking... spent." His lips wander back down my chest, and he sucks one nipple. "Shaking..." Then the other. "Trembling..." His deep, reverent voice reverberates against me as he continues moving lower, kissing a heated path down my stomach. "Now, how 'bout you spread these gorgeous legs for me."

I tense slightly but play it off like a squirm of pleasure.

Should I tell him?

"Can I taste you?" He waits for my consent as he settles between my legs.

I nod but, before he lowers his mouth, my uncertainty gets the better of me. "Miles, wait."

He freezes and quizzical blue eyes snap to mine.

"What if I..." I swallow. "What if I can't?"

He noses my inner thigh and mumbles against my skin, "Can't what?"

"It's just I've never been able to finish from... *that* before."

"Well..." He lifts a brow as he flicks his tongue over my clit, his eyes closing for a long moment as he exhales. "*Fuck*... Well, we're trying new things, right?"

The heat from his tongue was so brief but so perfect. It takes me a moment to get a hold of myself before I can speak again. "But what if it doesn't work for me?"

He lifts a shoulder, seemingly unbothered. "I mean, there's no rule saying you *have to* come." Pressing another kiss to my clit, he adds, "But I'm sure gonna fuckin' *try*."

"Okay," I manage through a smile.

"Just relax. I've got you." He pushes a finger inside me, curling it upward. "And I'm good with my hands."

I barely have time to register his cocky comment before he drives the point home, working me harder with his finger as his tongue meets my pussy in one greedy, delicious stroke. He sucks my clit into his mouth, flicking it side to side, and I cry out, the sudden burst of pleasure nearly overwhelming.

"Miles!" My back bows. "Oh my God!"

"Shhh," he cautions between strokes of his tongue. "The neighbors will hear you."

I press my lips together, struggling to stifle the sounds.

"Those pretty moans are only for me." He adds another finger in some kind of cruel challenge, doing everything in his power to test my restraint.

"I can't..." I whimper as he draws hard on my clit, pulling more strange, keening cries from somewhere deep inside me.

He breaks away and slaps my pussy softly, which only makes me buck up from the bed. "Such a bad girl. Making all that noise."

His words send me reeling, and another moan slips out. For him. Because of him.

"Acting like a desperate little slut for me."

My muscles tense and he stills.

"Shit, was that okay? You said you liked the whole naughty thing before, and..."

I'm reeling. It's like my brain is being rewired in real time. Being chastised like that isn't supposed to turn me on. Is it?

"I won't call you that again," he says, "if you don't want me to. Unless..." He flicks his tongue in tentative strokes, watching me closely. "Unless you liked it."

I let out some incomprehensible sound, unable to speak.

Oh, God. I did. Why did I like it?

"Use your words." He pumps his fingers inside me, nothing but heat burning in his eyes.

Just lean into it. We're trying new things.

Somehow, I find my voice. "Say it again."

He groans his approval, and his voice is deep when he drawls, "I fucking knew it." He grazes his teeth over my aching flesh. "Knew there was a needy little slut hiding in there all along."

That word has me inhaling sharply. It's so... dirty.

And hot. Yup. Emphasis on hot.

I can't take it anymore. Grabbing hold of his hair again, I grind against his mouth, my movements becoming more chaotic. Despite the undulation of my hips, he follows, working me with his tongue and fingers until I'm nearly shaking, the sensation somehow both too much and not enough. "Please!"

He pulls away and kisses my inner thigh. "What are you begging for, baby?"

God, I love when he calls me that. Fletcher calling me *babe* only filled me with rage, but Miles calling me *baby*? I can't explain it, but it just feels right.

"Please... Miles..."

"You wanna come on my tongue?"

Is he actually gonna make me say it?

"I—"

"'Cause I really fuckin' wanna know"—he licks a small circle around the center of my pleasure again—"what you taste like when you explode in my mouth."

When he sucks hard on my clit and adds another finger, I thrash so violently against the bed that he has to pin me in place with a thick forearm over my hips. "Fuck, Caroline," he says. "That's it. Let that whore out to play. Give her what she wants."

I think my eyes roll back in my head. I can no longer see or hear or think. There's only Miles. That tongue. Those fingers. Those filthy words. And that mind-bending, tantalizing sensation rocketing me toward a cliff, building and gathering, gripping and tightening, until...

I detonate. Shock waves rip through me, my throaty cries giving voice to the tension flooding from my core. Miles clamps tighter over my hips as he moans and sucks and coaxes each pulsing wave to the surface. He's playing me like an instrument, strumming every tightly drawn string just so—until I *sing*.

Blissful aftershocks slip through me as the chaos finally settles into a sweet warmth. I'm a puddle—boneless and trembling. I couldn't tell you my own name right now.

Miles breaks away, then licks one slow stripe up my center.

"That's one," he rasps, gently biting my inner thigh. When I can finally lift my head, I'm met with that crinkly-eyed smile and it nearly wrecks me all over again.

I drop back onto the bed, trying to catch my breath. "Pretty pleased with yourself, huh?"

He kisses my stomach. "Damn right I am."

"That's fair, I guess—" I gasp as I'm flipped over, yanked by the hips onto all fours.

Before I get my bearings, his chest is pressed against my back, his lips at my ear. "Can my needy girl take another one?"

I let out a delirious hum, already flexing my hips back into him.

How? How can my body want more? How can I take any more?

And yet, the way he's kissing the back of my neck has me aching to feel him inside me.

"Please…"

"There you go begging again," he rasps against my skin, reaching around to work my clit. "For what?"

"I want…" I try, unable to bring myself to say it out loud. "Fucking hell."

"Well, well, well," he rumbles, then runs his tongue along the side of my neck. His fingers speed up, threatening to take me on another trip to oblivion. "She says she only swears when she's worked up."

My eyes shutter as I battle for my sanity. "I'm—"

"You must be pretty *worked up*." He squeezes my hip, letting out a low growl. "Look at you, grinding against me like you can't even help it."

"I can't. I can't help it."

"You want me to fuck you, honey?"

"Yes!" I whine. "I need it."

"C'mon, then. Ask for it." His voice drops to a low rasp. "Ask for exactly what you want."

It takes everything I have to align my mind with my mouth. "I want you to fuck me."

"Fuck you until…?" His throaty drawl nearly obliterates any sense I have left.

Oh my God.

"Until you what, Caroline?" he asks again. He pulls his hand away and I sag, tensing up again with a gasp when he delivers a sudden slap to my ass. "Until you what?"

My voice is thin and desperate. "Until I come."

"Yeah? My dirty girl wants to come all over my cock?"

"Mm-hmm." I nod as the sound of him working his belt buckle and zipper floats through the fog of my arousal and my last two brain cells finally connect. "Condom."

"Right. Shit." There's a rummaging noise beside me, the tearing of foil, and the slick sound of him rolling it on.

"Put it in me," I hear myself say. *Put it in me?* "Please. Right now. I need it."

"So impatient." With a dark chuckle behind me, Miles delivers another slap—this time to my swollen center—sending a sharp pulse of pleasure through me. He nearly growls, "You'll take what I fucking give you."

"Yes, sir."

I don't know why I say it but, for a moment, everything goes still.

"Oh," he almost growls. "You did not just... Holy shit, Caroline." He nudges the crown of his cock at my opening and I almost buckle. "I'm gonna fuck you so hard for that."

"Yes! Do it!" I twist back to watch him and his free hand grips my jaw.

"Quiet, remember?"

I nod, willing to promise whatever he wants—anything if it means he won't make me wait another second. "Please. I'll be so good for you."

"My good little whore, huh?" When I only whimper in response, he asks, "You ready to get fucked?"

"Yes, oh, God, yes!" I shudder with pleasure, my arms nearly giving out as he slowly pushes inside.

"Oh, *fffuuuuck*," he groans.

He's thick and big—*God*, he's big—and I feel every aching inch. The stretch is delicious; I've never felt so full, so complete. I don't want him to pull away.

As if reading my mind, he stills for a moment. "Fucking... shit. Don't move for a sec. Fuck." He sounds like he's struggling to keep it together.

But it feels too incredible for me to stay still and, when I can't help but give in to temptation and rock my hips, another moan wrestles its way from my throat.

"Shhh, baby. Someone is definitely gonna hear you if you keep that up." As he starts to thrust, he reaches around me again to work my clit with his fingers. "C'mon. You can take it. Nice and quiet for me."

"I..." I try to summon enough lucidity to speak. "I don't know if I can."

"Take it? Or keep quiet?" He's enjoying this.

"Both?" I'm a sex-addled wreck. "I'm falling apart here."

"Not yet, you're not," he throws back. "But you will be by the time I'm done with this pretty cunt."

God, his words are so obscene. So dirty. And yet, hearing him talk about my body like this—like no one ever has—ignites me like nothing else.

Pleasure gathers quickly to a desperate peak and, when he increases the pressure on my clit, that little shift is all it takes. Already on the cusp, I feel it building, and my muscles tense around him once more.

"Miles!" I grip and twist at the sheets below me. "I can't— I'm gonna—"

"Yes," he growls, speeding up. "Come for me. Let it out. Fucking do it."

One strangled moan slips out before he clamps his palm over my mouth and pulls me up against his chest, still working my clit with his other hand as he thrusts into me. And, like I've been given permission to let go, something unlocks in my throat. I reach behind me to grasp at his hips and cry out against his palm as I erupt—explosion after explosion combusting, bursting, fanning out from my center to the tips of my fingers and toes.

"More. That's it," he whispers against the shell of my ear as I break apart. "I got you."

His words seem to pull pulse after pulse of ecstasy from inside me. When I'm unable to stay upright, he lets me go and I drop forward once more onto my palms—but the angle only sends me spinning all over again.

"*Oh, God,*" I manage between gasps.

"Shhh, baby," Miles pants out, gripping my sweat-slicked hips. He pounds into me from behind, faster, harder, both wringing me out and urging me on. "Just breathe."

"I can't..." Just when one pulse is fading, another takes its place, and I'm engulfed in bright colors, in heat, in spectacular, all-consuming fire.

"Oh, fuck. You're taking it so... damn... good."

My orgasm is barely slowing when he withdraws, flips me onto my back, and plunges inside again. There's nothing but panting desperation in the sliver of space between us, and his lips claim mine, swallowing the next wave of my moans. Clawing at his back, I cry out against his mouth as he grasps fistfuls of my hair and fucks me with everything he's got. The luscious bite of pain melds with the ecstasy into some hot, dark, drugging sensation I only want more of.

And, when Miles breaks apart over me, there's a raw beauty in the way he shudders, spilling into the condom with an almost pained, glassy look in his eyes. As the racking pulses of his orgasm gradually ebb, he slows, then collapses onto me. He kisses me with surprising gentleness, and the slow slip of his tongue against mine feels like reassurance—like the calm after a raging storm.

Our lips part, and he runs his nose along my cheek. There's a playfulness in his shaking voice when he asks, "Was that two? Or three?"

"I'm actually..." I swallow, then can't help but grin. "I'm not sure either. It was— it was chaos for a while there."

The satisfied look on his face makes me want to bite his lip, so that's exactly what I do.

"Well," he says, before nipping me back. "Let's be fucking sure." He slides out and quickly moves down the bed.

"What? What are you...?" But my words die in my throat when

his warm, incredible tongue finds my clit once more. "Oh my Gooooodddd..."

"Gimme one more." He slips two fingers inside me and, incredibly, it only takes a few strokes to get me right back on the edge, squirming at each flick of his tongue over my sensitive flesh. I guess he can tell I'm close, because he pulls back and blows a gentle stream of air over my clit.

And, just like that, I shatter.

14

———————

MILES

The multipurpose room at West Valley Community Center is pretty dead, but I'm early. Only one other group member is here—a guy I haven't seen in months whose name I can't quite remember... Nick or Chris or Mike, maybe? I'm shit with names—and he's out in the hall on his phone. Needing to do something useful, I set up about ten chairs in a circle, taking a seat in the one closest to the window. My knee bounces as I check my phone, waiting for everyone else to show up.

I try to ignore the way my heart rate picks up when I see her name.

Walk of shame? Fuck.

A slight sting spreads through my chest. But maybe it's just a saying, right? Last night there was no glimmer of anything like shame. Nerves, sure, but I'd put money on the fact that she had zero regrets about what we did. It was too good. Incredible, actually.

I'd found her list still on my coffee table this morning. When I picked it up for another perusal, I noticed she'd crossed off three items. The three exclamation points she'd added beside *multiple orgasms* had me grinning like a fool all through breakfast.

The little dots start jumping on my screen and I chew on my lip as I wait for her text.

CAROLINE

No actual shame though, for the record.

I had an amazing time with you. Thank you.

Relief has my shoulders sagging. *Thank fuck.* It wasn't my imagination; it *had* been amazing.

Okay, I just need to keep this casual, because that's what this is supposed to be. Casual.

ME

So... more like walk of fame?

And you're welcome. 10/10 would do you again.

CAROLINE

That was very frat boy of you...

I smirk at the teasing dig. There's nothing remotely frat boy about me, but I guess my attempt at casual worked out. Or... wait. Did I overshoot *casual* and hit *dumbass*? Now I can't tell if she's flirting with me or thinks I'm a turd.

Shit.

Attempting damage control, I type out another text, cursing myself for getting in my head about how I'm coming across.

So much for casual. Why do I have no chill?

ME

Hope you're okay today. Not too sore or whatever?

CAROLINE

Is that a humblebrag?

ME

Damn, you caught me!

But seriously, we really… went for it.

Until we passed out, basically.

I used to think I needed to drink to loosen up and get in the mood, but sober sex is surprisingly wild. Last night, I was so much more *aware*. So *present*. I felt every touch, every gasp, every little clench of Caroline's muscles. The way her body responded. And I noticed the subtle stuff. Checked in. Adjusted. Communicated. There was nothing sloppy or blurry about how we fucked. It was intentional. And I felt more connected and in control than I'd ever been while drinking. I was so in tune with my own body—and hers—that it lit me the hell up. And the pleasure was fucking unreal.

I think that's why we couldn't stop.

Neither of us had planned for Caroline to spend the night; it had kinda just happened. She'd been so shaky and exhausted after all those orgasms that I'd joked about having to carry her to the shower, and then we hadn't been able to keep our hands off each other once we got there. It had been well after midnight by the time we finally collapsed onto my bed and, by then, I *was* blurry—in the best way. I don't remember much after that, other than pulling her against me. She was so fucking cute all sleepy and disheveled. And I fucking love being the big spoon. I was defenseless.

Cuddle puddle: 1, Miles: 0.

The door creaks open and that Nick-Chris-Mike guy gives me a small nod as he takes a seat across from me.

CAROLINE

> I actually am a little… tender. I think that shower took a lot out of me.

Flashbacks to Caroline dripping wet thunder through me—how she'd clung to my neck, holding on with a death grip as she came on my hand. I have to cross my legs and discreetly adjust my half-hard dick as another few people file in for the meeting.

Not the time or the place.

ME

> Look at me resisting that "I can put a lot into you" joke setup like an adult

CAROLINE

> If you listen closely, you can hear my slow clapping.

ME

> So that's what that was!

> Listen, I gotta run here, but uh… maybe I can help with any "tender" spots after our date tonight? I feel responsible.

CAROLINE

> Looking forward to it, Mr. "I'm Good With My Hands."

A broad grin splits my face as I pocket my phone. Glancing around, I realize how the room has filled up without me even realizing it, and my amusement falters.

Fuck.

This is exactly why I'm here.

Ever since Caroline showed up at my gym, I've been off my game. Distracted. And last night, incredible as it was, also left me feeling a bit thrown.

When I realized she'd snuck out on me before I woke up this morning, disappointment had percolated in the back of my mind. But, instead of going down that rabbit hole, I reminded myself of the facts: this is fake dating and bonus sex. Temporary. Nothing deeper and nothing long term. I'm not ready for a relationship and neither is she. Plus, we come from different worlds and we're on completely different paths; she's trying to let loose and I'm trying to rein it in. Incredible sex or not, it would never work between us in the long run.

Forcing myself to stuff it and focus on things within my immediate control, I'd doubled down on all the shit I know supports my mental health; with all this change in my life, I need to use my fucking strategies now more than ever. I'd hit the gym with Gus, put protein and vegetables in my face, drank a ton of water, scheduled an extra therapy session, and got my ass to this AA meeting. I'll prioritize sobriety like my life depends on it— because it fucking does.

Russell opens the meeting with the usual preamble explaining AA, followed by a moment of silence. Then he asks that Nick-Chris-Mike guy—who I learn is actually Trevor, *cool*, not even close—to read a passage from the Big Book, which is basically the AA Bible.

Trevor reads aloud about how those who succeed in AA are the ones who are capable of "grasping and developing a manner of living which demands rigorous honesty." The wording in the Big Book is sorta old-fashioned, but the gist is clear: honesty is key. It is, after all, essentially the first of the Twelve Steps; admitting you have a problem means being honest with yourself.

Facing that truth hadn't been easy for me. I'd fought it for a long time. Lied and denied it more times than I can count. On some level, I'd fought it even after I first joined AA years ago. Sure, I'd admitted I had a problem, stuck to the program, and managed to quit drinking for a stretch or two that I was proud of. But some part of me had held back from fully committing—fully accepting I was an addict like the others. I'd held onto this irrational belief that I was different—that I could drink in moderation if I only learned to manage it better.

And, well, I was a fucking fool.

Alcoholics are incapable of *moderation* when it comes to booze, and I'm more likely to sprout a tail than develop the ability to control my drinking. It took breaking my arm after stumbling down the fucking interstate to make me realize I could never touch another drop of liquor for the rest of my life. That next morning in the hospital, my addiction had slugged me in the face. I couldn't deny it any longer: I was powerless over alcohol and, unless I found a way to take that power back, it was gonna kill me.

As I listen to Trevor read, I realize honesty has been the game-changer for me this time. Being honest with myself and with my friends and family has kept me accountable. Kept me on track, in check. Sober. I guess I've managed—or, more accurately, *am* managing—to adopt that whole "manner of living" thing, even if it did take me a while to get here.

Fuck. There's something else I need to be honest about—another uncomfortable truth I need to face.

I like Caroline. I *really* like Caroline.

That's... not great. I can't be in a relationship right now, full stop, and she doesn't want one either. Ours is fake and it ends after the election, whether Senator Shithead wins or not.

Maybe it's for the best. Caroline and her family are obviously complicated. I'm not looking to stress-test my sobriety by tying myself to someone with a family under constant public scrutiny—*and* a manipulative prickstain of a father on top of that. The guy's blackmailing me, for Christ's sake! Between the addiction and the ADHD, I don't need any help living life on *hard mode.*

Doesn't matter if I like her. That I haven't felt a connection like this in... ever. I can't have her.

But *fuck*, curling up with her pressed against me last night had felt as natural as if we'd done it a hundred times before. She'd fit in my arms like she'd always been there.

Reminding myself not to get carried away, I straighten in my seat.

Trevor finishes reading, and Russell invites a woman named Tiffany to share about herself.

I blink a few times, rubbing my thighs.

Focus. Be present.

"Hey, everyone," she says. "I'm Tiffany, and I'm an alcoholic."

"Hi, Tiffany," we all chorus together, the familiar call-and-response of it almost automatic to me now.

She starts to talk about her life, sharing a little about her recovery journey—and something about her new boyfriend, I think.

No matter how hard I try to stay present, Tiffany's soft voice takes a backseat to the way my memories of Caroline are screaming to get front and center.

I make a mental note to call Barry on my way home from the meeting. Maybe he can help me get my head in the game so I can stick to my priorities.

But Caroline in that lacy red lingerie... The image flickers into focus. Her long legs in those fucking thigh-high stockings, her mess of blonde curls, and those nervous, whimpered sounds she made when I had her under me on my bed... Then the louder ones she made when she...

Shit, I can't shake this off.

Maybe I'm just touch-starved? Keeping to my little routine, I don't have a lot of physical touch in my life. Jude shoving me in the shoulder for being a dumbass probably doesn't count. The most physical affection I get these days is probably cuddling up with Lumpy on Gus' couch. He's like a weighted blanket. A heavy one.

Which reminds me, I need to figure out what kind of unhinged Halloween costume to get for Lumpy. That lobster getup was hilarious, but I gotta get him something for spooky season...

Fuck, focus on Tiffany, you ass.

I straighten in my seat, willing myself to pay attention—as if that's ever worked.

"Anyway," she's saying, "I think maybe it's, like, infatuation? I dunno. I'm not sure, but... I'm working so hard to control one addiction, so I don't wanna just replace that with a new one, like being addicted to *him*, right?"

It takes a moment for Tiffany's words to land.

Is that what's happening here?

No, it can't be. At first, I'd thought my interest in Caroline was just my ADHD seeking a dopamine hit, but there's something real between us. I can feel in my bones it's more than the *high* of attraction or novelty or even mind-blowing sex.

Then again, that's all this *can* be. So I'll have to keep a lid on it and power through. Yeah, maybe it'll suck when this fake relationship ends, but at least I can go back to keeping my head down.

Gym, work, home, repeat.

My small, shrunken fucking life.

Shit.

Movement snaps me back into the room when everyone around me stands and begins stacking their chairs. I rarely hang around for the social chat part of AA meetings, but, after barely hearing more than a couple sentences of what Tiffany said, I feel like I should make the effort. I'm filling a paper cup at the water cooler in the corner when Russell appears at my side.

"Miles, how ya holdin' up?"

I nod. "Good, fine, yeah. I'm good."

Russell gives me a long look. "You sure?"

"Yeah!" I say through a chuckle. "Why?"

"You just seemed... somewhere else during the meeting today."

"Shit, sorry." Guilt swirls in my stomach for being a crappy listener. "Guess I'm kinda distracted."

"Anything you wanna talk about?"

I hesitate. Any explanation about Caroline and our situation would probably sound ridiculous but, before I make up some white lie about being busy with work, Trevor's passage about honesty snags in my memory. Guess I wasn't totally out to lunch after all. "Uh, actually... I met someone."

God, that line is such a cliché.

"Oh?"

It's such a simple response. No judgment, no pressure, but it reminds me of my therapist's way of letting the silence hang so I'll be compelled to fill it. It always fucking works.

"She's..." I trail off, blowing a breath through my lips.

How do I describe Caroline? How do I describe this feeling? I barely understand it myself.

"That good, huh?" Russell smirks.

Dropping my gaze to my feet, I work my jaw. "Doesn't matter, I guess." I stuff my free hand in my hoodie pocket and fidget with the seam inside. "I'm not ready to date yet."

Russell frowns in thought. "Remind me, you're, what, nine months sober?"

"Ten now."

He contemplates me for a moment and crosses his arms over his chest. "Y'know, the advice from AA about dating that first year... It's more of a guideline than a hard rule."

"It's a hard rule for me." I take a sip of water and swallow, letting a cool sensation spread through my chest. "Has to be."

"Oh?" He lifts his eyebrows.

Again with the oh? *Damn Russell and his trickery. Is he secretly a therapist?*

"Didn't work out for me last time when I rushed it."

He nods slowly. "Well, if it's something real, it'll be worth waiting for. Or worth going for when the time is right, anyway. When it's healthy. You don't wanna risk all the progress you've made on something—or some*one*—who isn't worth it."

"Exactly."

He's quiet for a moment. "So, I guess, the question is: is this girl a distraction? Or is she your future?"

"Oof," I say with a half smile, trying to hide the way his words hit me in the solar plexus. "Heavy shit for a Saturday afternoon, Russ."

He laughs and claps me on the back, like he didn't just take all my swirling thoughts about Caroline and sum them up in one pithy question. "What can I say? I'm dropping truth bombs here. You take it easy, alright?"

"Yeah, you too." I hold up my cup in a little paper *cheers* as Russell walks off, then drain the last of the water and toss it in the trash.

Take it easy.

As if anything about this is *easy*.

15

CAROLINE

"You've played before, right?" Miles sets down the cup of tokens on the edge of the air hockey table.

The arcade is a cacophony of bleeps, cheers, and chatter. A huge neon sign on the wall reads *Pinball Wizard* and casts the entire space in a pinkish glow.

"Um," I hedge, tucking my hands into the front pockets of my jeans. "No, actually."

"You serious?" His eyes widen. "You've been missing out. Here." He passes me one of the two plastic disc things and sets up across the table from me, slotting a few tokens into place until a whirring fan noise kicks into gear.

"What are the rules? Is there a technique, or...?" I try a few experimental strokes with the felt-bottomed disc, hovering my free palm over the table. Cool air blows up through the tiny holes dotting the surface.

"Not a lot to it. You try to score on me; I try to score on you. Pretty straightforward." Miles flips the thin plastic puck in midair and catches it, pinning me with a cocky grin before tossing it down on the table. It drifts slowly to one side, carried on the air like a tiny hovercraft. He leans forward. "But you gotta be fast."

"Okay?" I try for a brave smile.

"Just remember to protect your goal." He braces his arms wide on his end of the table, his corded muscles flickering with tension. "You'll get the hang of it. Trust me."

Trust me.

Images of locking pinkies with Miles in the car on the way to the fundraiser drift back into my mind and I bite my lip. It's hard to believe the man in the backward ball cap standing across from me is the same one who donned that tuxedo two weeks ago— though he pulls off casual every bit as well as the tux.

Who am I kidding? He'd make a paper sack look good.

"Caroline!" Olena calls from nearby, drawing my attention away from Miles' body. "Kick his ass for me!"

"I'll try my best!" I call back with a shrug. "Any pointers?"

Olena cups a hand beside her mouth, pumping her eyebrows. "Distract him!"

"Hey!" Miles shouts over to her. "Interference much? Whose side are you on here, anyway?"

"Hers, obviously!" Olena calls back, screwing up her face. "Hos before bros! Plus, if she doesn't beat you, I will!"

Miles had told me about his friendly rivalry with Olena on the drive over here.

I liked her the moment we met up with her and Jude out front of the arcade. Maybe it was the two pairs of sunglasses in her hair, or maybe it was the way she hugged me without thinking twice, but there's something warm and real about her that put me at ease right away.

Jude has been harder to get a read on. While Miles has the enthusiasm of a golden retriever, Jude's vibe is more guarded. Is German shepherd energy a thing? I guess I can't blame him for being protective of his little brother, knowing what they've been through together. And this arrangement between me and Miles is unusual, by anyone's standards.

Despite Jude's objections about driving so much for work, Olena convinces him to play a racing game with her. He casts an uneasy glance our way before letting her drag him off.

"You ready?" Miles asks. At my nod, he taps the puck into play, his first strike clearly somewhat restrained on my account.

"You don't need to take it easy on me, y'know." As we knock the puck back and forth, I start to get a feel for it and give it a bit more gas. "I'm not some delicate flower."

"Oh, okay," he says. "She's wearing her sassy pants today." To his credit, though, he picks up the pace and I catch a competitive set to his jaw when I risk a quick look up.

Not backing down, I take a hard swipe at the puck, and he rushes to block the shot, narrowly deflecting it at the last second.

"Shit, and she's a quick learner."

The awkward save sends the puck skittering sideways, bouncing back and forth across the center line. I lean forward, straining to make contact, but it's just out of reach of my clumsy swipes. "Dang it. I can't get it."

I'm practically climbing the table when Miles leans forward, his longer limbs giving him the advantage. He easily reaches the puck and sends it whooshing right under my stomach and straight into my goal. I raise my head, mouth agape. "What? Rude!"

"Hey!" He holds up his hands, tongue pressed into his cheek. "I told you to protect your goal."

I crawl back off the table, straightening my loose-fitting button-up shirt. "But I was in a compromising position!"

"Just how I like you." He smirks. "Oh, and uh... Nice boobs."

On reflex, I clutch my shirt to my chest. I shake my head, though I can't help the way my cheeks heat at his words. Remembering last night, I raise an eyebrow, holding his gaze in challenge. "You better watch it, *sir*."

His jaw clenches so hard, I wouldn't be surprised if he cracked a tooth.

If he's gonna say blatantly suggestive things to me, he's gonna get a taste of his own medicine.

I can barely hear him over the din of the arcade, but I'm pretty sure I catch him muttering something that sounds an awful lot like "bratty fucking girl".

Feeling satisfied, I toss the puck across the table. He traps it in place with his disc, giving me a long, heated look.

The rest of our game whips by in a haze of flirtation—punctuated by the occasional booty-shaking victory dance from Miles and eye roll from me. The score is tied at nine when Jude and Olena appear at the side of the table.

"Ooh, tie game!" she croons, wandering over to my end. "Come on, Caroline," she lowers her voice to a comical growl, "*finish him*."

I laugh, my amusement fading to something like a dazed appreciation when Miles pulls off his hat to smooth his hair before replacing it—the right way around this time. The few wisps stick out at his nape, reminding me of how it felt to run my fingers through it last night as he coaxed me over the edge time and time again—until I was shaking and spent, sure I couldn't take more. *God*, he was right about that whole *so-good-you-think-you-might-die* thing. It was everything I never knew sex could be. He was incredible. *We* were incredible. And, as much as it was hands-down the best sex of my life—as foreign as it was for me to come that often and that hard—what truly shocked me was how comfortable it had been. How easily I'd welcomed the idea of falling asleep in his arms. Sure, I couldn't exactly walk by that point, but there was something more than shaky legs keeping me in his bed.

I snap back to the present when I realize Olena's talking to me. "Sorry, what? Zoned out there for a sec."

"Oh, trust me, I get it." She waves me off, then drops her voice to a volume only I can hear. "But if you're gonna win this, you've gotta distract *him* and not the other way around."

"Yeah, but I don't really know how."

"I'd suggest unbuttoning your top, but that's too obvious." She twists her lips in thought. "Take down your hair?" Then, frowning to herself: "God, why am I such a horndog right now? I must be ovulating."

"I guess I could *frighten* him to distraction," I muse, knowing my curly hair would probably look more like a lion's mane than anything sexy if I took it down.

"What are you two yappin' about over there?" Jude calls over, crossing his arms over his chest with a smirk. "You gonna finish this game or what?"

I cast a glance at Olena. "Guess I'll have to win this the old-fashioned way: brute force."

"Hell yes! For feminism!" Beaming, she holds out a hand and we bump fists. Then she winds back around the table to whisper something in Jude's ear that makes him straighten and clear his throat.

I flick my gaze back to Miles, who's watching me intently.

"Good to go?" He raises a brow.

"Yes, sir." My tone is innocent enough that no one would catch the flirtation in my voice, but the way he breaks eye contact and blows out a long exhale tells me I hit my mark once again. I grin. Poking holes in his composure might be my new favorite thing.

Seconds later, when I sink the puck in his goal, he gives me a rueful look as Olena rushes over for a congratulatory high five.

"You hungry?" Jude wraps his arms around Olena's waist from behind, kissing her temple.

"Ugh, yes," she admits. "But I left my purse in the truck."

"Here," Jude says, digging out his wallet to hand her some cash. "Go grab something before you get hangry on me."

"I'll come with you." Miles lifts his chin at Olena. "I didn't eat enough dinner."

"The two of you, man," Jude says.

Miles passes me the cup of tokens. "You want anything?"

"No, I'm good."

Olena and Miles head off to buy snacks, leaving me alone with Jude.

He crosses his arms over his chest as we watch the two of them cut a winding path through the arcade. When they stop to mess with the claw machine, he calls out, "Hey!" They turn, and Jude mimes eating something, setting them back on task. He shakes his head, muttering to himself, "Like herding cats."

There's no doubt Miles and his older brother are related. Jude looks like a green-eyed version of Miles, but with the beard factor cranked up a couple notches. The brawn factor, too; his grip almost crushed my hand when he shook it earlier.

"Hey, listen," he starts, keeping his voice down. "I know this thing with you and Miles is all for show…"

"Yeah?" I can't help but glance over my shoulder, nervous that someone might be listening.

"But I'll be honest. I'm glad he's been hanging out with you lately. Getting out more." At my curious expression, he goes on. "He's been lying pretty low for a while now. He needs some decent friends in his life so he can branch out a little."

"Decent, huh? Should I be flattered, or—?" I smirk, trying to keep it light despite my unease.

He huffs a laugh. "Poor choice of words. I mean people who'll keep him on the right track. Not drag him into trouble, y'know?"

"Yeah, I wouldn't…" I trail off, not quite sure what to say. *Trouble* feels like a loaded term.

Am I dragging him into trouble?

Heck, maybe I already have. My stomach tilts remembering why Miles took off from the fundraiser—how he'd been too tempted by the drinks to stay a moment longer.

"His construction buddies are fine and all, but he needs stability." Jude tucks his hands into his front pockets, watching Olena and Miles across the arcade.

"That makes sense."

He turns to give me a thoughtful look. "I'll admit, when he first told me about agreeing to this whole pretending-to-be-your-boyfriend thing, I kinda had an *oh-shit* moment. Thought he'd gotten sucked into some soap opera drama that would be bad for him."

"I totally understand," I say honestly. "This situation is... odd."

"Yeah, but I can tell you're not gonna be the type to encourage him to, I dunno, steal a boat or something."

I arch a brow. "Can't say I'd even know how, to be honest."

"Perfect." His amusement fades to something more serious as he watches me. "Just... don't fuck with him, okay? He's been through a lot."

I open my mouth without knowing how to respond, but I don't get the chance, because Miles materializes at my side, shaking what's left of a small bag of french fries.

"Want some? I saved you a couple."

"No, thanks." I cast a glance over at Jude, who's busy snagging a fry from Olena's little paper bag. "I'm not hungry."

"Okay." He gives me a funny look, then polishes off the last of the fries before tossing the bag into a nearby trash can. "You ready to fuck shit up, Skee-Ball style?" He pumps his eyebrows in invitation, then grabs my hand, nearly bouncing with excitement as he drags me away from Jude and Olena.

"Uh, I don't have the best aim, but... sure?" I can't help but mirror his broad grin, although the shadow of my conversation with Jude hangs over me.

Don't fuck with him.

His warning is like a pinball bouncing around my head, and I cling tighter to Miles as we wind our way through the arcade.

Jude's right. I can't put Miles at risk—can't pursue anything with him beyond what we've agreed to. I won't compromise his job or his sobriety. If I hurt him, I'd never forgive myself. And he'd never forgive me, either.

I'm so lost in thought that I almost crash into Miles when he stops and turns to me in front of the Skee-Ball machines. "Shoot, sorry."

He steadies me by the arms. "You good, fancy girl?"

"Yeah, I'm…" I trail off when he lifts a hand to cradle my jaw, tilting my head up, and a little involuntary sound escapes my throat at the look in his eyes.

With a crooked smile, he spins his hat backward and stoops down to kiss me, everything inside me turning to warm honey when our lips meet.

Dear God. That spin-the-hat move should be illegal.

I kiss him back, not even thinking to question it, because the truth is, I've been craving this all night and it's soothing the twisting sensation in my chest to finally be in his arms like this. It's only when he breaks the kiss that my mind catches up. "What was that for?"

"I uh…"—he swallows, then shakes his head like he's coming back to his senses—"just uh… thought I saw a guy watching us."

"Oh. Right. Yeah." I school my features to hide how disappointment grips my stomach.

He was just acting.

But, as we set up to play, I can't shake the feeling that nothing about that kiss was fake. I try to let go of the idea. Maybe Miles is simply a great actor; he said he was a ham, after all. Maybe he missed his calling in the theater.

All it takes is a few rolls to see that Miles did, in fact, miss his calling—as a Skee-Ball shark. Being lost in my head probably isn't helping my hand-eye coordination but, my distraction aside, his aim is incredible and he trounces me easily. Several times over. Pride glitters in his expression, though he looks like he's trying to suppress grinning too hard.

"You know you can openly gloat about this, right?" I ask, lifting a brow. "You're wildly good at it, and I'm"—I roll my next ball and it doesn't even think about cooperating—"lousy." Deflating, I watch as it slips out of view at the bottom of the rings.

He moves to kiss my cheek, but I pull away without thinking —Jude's warning and the fake kiss still too close to the surface. Regret lands like a brick to my sternum when I catch the sting of rejection in his eyes.

Damn it.

The uncomfortable reality is I want him to kiss me more than anything right now. I just don't want it to be a lie for the cameras. What I told him before about not wanting to date anyone after Fletcher was true enough, but that was when my idea of a relationship was being treated like an afterthought by a man who never truly cared about me—and who I'd never really loved in return.

Before Miles, I'd never experienced wild chemistry like this. Never felt this kind of connection. Never been treated like I should be someone's priority—in bed or otherwise. It's all so new that it has me reeling. And it's making me question what I want.

I must look as conflicted as I feel, because he hands me my next ball with a frown. "What's up with you?"

"Nothing." I can't tell him the truth—that I'm starting to wish this thing between us wasn't an act. Wasn't only temporary.

"Bullshit. What'd I miss?" When I hesitate, he tries again.

"C'mon, you know I can sense when something's up. And you've been all quiet ever since I left to get—" Realization smooths his features and he steps closer. "Wait, did my brother say something to you?"

"Uh, sort of?" His eyes widen, and I rush to add, "He just reminded me you've been through a lot, and he said I shouldn't..." I take a breath, not sure how this will land.

"Shouldn't what?"

"Mess with you?" I may have softened Jude's sentiment in both tone and choice of words, but Miles' features harden all the same.

"Fucking Jude."

I touch his arm. "He's just looking out for you."

"Yeah, yeah, he does a lot of that." Miles furrows his brow. "Needs to learn how to turn it off, though. And keep his nose out of my business. Jesus."

"But be real, though," I press. "Am I already messing with you? Maybe we're playing with fire with this whole thing. I really don't want you to get off track because of me, Miles."

"Caroline, you aren't messing with me. We made this plan together, right?"

"Yeah, but—"

"And I'm having fun. I wanna do this with you."

"Are you sure?" I ask. "It's not too complicated? With my list? That's not, like, blurring the line a bit?"

I keep the rest locked in my chest—the admission that I'm feeling plenty blurry myself here. Between acting like a couple in public and the mind-altering orgasms in private last night, the roles of boyfriend and girlfriend aren't feeling too far-fetched.

Acting, I remind myself, though I can't help the doubt niggling at me.

He must feel this too.

No. I'm getting ridiculous ideas in my head. He's not ready.

Miles shakes his head. "You're overthinking this. And trust me, I overthink shit all the time, so if *I'm* telling you to relax... Listen, I'm here 'cause I wanna be, okay?"

"Okay, but you're sure it's not confusing? Because I can't stand the thought of you risking your sobriety. Or your job. Everything you've worked so hard for. I could never forgive myself if—" My throat closes up as tears well in my eyes.

"Hey." His stern tone is at odds with the gentle way he pulls me into his arms. "I'm not confused."

I bury my face in his warm hoodie, inhaling the earthy, clean scent of his soap and hoping this looks more like a loving embrace than me trying to fight off tears at an arcade like a teenager.

Mom might be right about me being dramatic.

"It's sweet that you're worried about me," Miles says. "But let *me* worry about me, alright?"

I nod, nuzzling closer.

"Here's how I see it." His voice rumbles low against my temple. "It's like we're two friends—two *sexy* friends..."

I grin against his T-shirt, hugging him tighter.

"... who landed this really cool gig where we have to hang out and have fun together a whole bunch and—*super cool bonus*—we get to boink while we're at it."

I lift my head, peering up at him. "Did you just say *boink*?"

"Yeah," he chuckles. "It's like being forced to go to Disneyland and ride all the rides. Like, *oh no*." He fakes a weak protest, adding, "Don't make me go."

A tendril of heat winds low in my belly. "Yeah? And which ride did you wanna try tonight?"

His lips tick up at the corner. "Aren't you the one with the list of things to try?"

"Yeah, so choose something from my list, then," I say, playing coy. "If you can remember what was on it."

"Is that a challenge?" When I shrug, he makes a *pfft* sound.

"What, you think I'm all *forgetty spaghetti* over here? I got that shit *memorized*."

"Oh, you do, huh?"

"Locked in."

"Then pick something."

He thinks for a moment, then holds my gaze when he says, "Splash Mountain."

I raise my brows, catching his meaning right away. "You're saying you wanna get... wet?"

He leans close and his lips graze my cheek. "Soaked."

With a slow nod, I hum, pretending to ponder this—pretending the way he said that word didn't just get *me* soaked.

"I'm not sure if that ride is... operational."

"I think we can get it working." He lifts a brow, all cocky confidence, and his gaze slips to my mouth. "Plus," he adds, "I said I'd help you with those, uh, tender spots of yours?"

I slide my hands over his chest. "I think I'm feeling all better, actually."

"Oh?" The scarred corner of his lips twitches. "Well, I'm sure we can find somewhere that still needs a little attention."

"I do have one spot that's been... not hurting, exactly. More like... *aching*?" The innuendo is shameless, but I can't resist liquefying his brain while we're in public.

Maybe he's right; Maybe I am *a brat.*

He almost groans, but doesn't kiss me. "Can we get outta here? I suddenly couldn't give two shits about Skee-Ball."

16

____

MILES

"Are you snooping?" Caroline stands in the doorway of her ensuite bathroom, arms loosely crossed.

"Damn right I'm snooping!" I lean in to inspect a framed photo of her and Adrian on the wall next to her bed; they're pulling faces outside what looks like one of the monorail stations in Seattle. I scan around her room, my gaze landing on the huge picture window above her bed. "You've got a nice place, fancy girl."

The nickname is particularly apt now that I'm seeing where she lives. Her grandpa's house is spacious and clean, decorated like something out of one of those magazines at the dentist's office. All luxurious and shit—well, compared to my crappy apartment, anyway.

"Thanks," she says, sheepishly shifting on her feet. She's beautiful; she's almost glowing in the orangey-yellow light of her bedside lamp. Reminding myself not to stare, I keep poking around.

It hadn't been hard to ditch Jude and Olena at the arcade; they'd been weirdly fine with cutting our double date short. I try not to think about why—not that it's been difficult, what with Caroline dropping flirty innuendos and smuggling me into her bedroom like contraband. She said it was to avoid waking her grandpa, but I'm pretty sure she just wants to jump my bones. I'm not complaining.

"Well?" Caroline asks. "Have you uncovered all my secrets?"

"I dunno." Skirting the foot of the bed, I meander over to her dresser and peer into a few little trinket boxes arranged in a neat row. "Nothing too juicy just yet. I mean, a girl like you having fancy lotions and 300-billion-thread-count sheets isn't exactly a surpri—"

I stop short when a box tucked into a corner catches my eye, the partially obscured writing on the side revealing only the words "an ocean of pleasure". I walk over and pull it out, my jaw dropping when I see what's inside.

"Oh my God!" Caroline's voice has a shrill edge as she rushes toward me. "No, that's—"

"Whoa-ho-ho!" I laugh, spinning the box to face her. "What's this now?"

She drops her face into her hands a moment before risking another look at me, her cheeks a deeper red than I've seen them yet. "It was an impulse buy. How did you even—?" She stares at me in wonder, probably trying to work out how I could've zeroed in on *this*, of all things.

I spin the package back around for a closer inspection. It's like a gift set but, instead of hot chocolate or bath bombs, it's silicone sex toys, all ocean themed: a seahorse vibrator, a tentacle-shaped dildo, a vibrating seashell butt plug, and a pair of little starfish things that might be nipple suckers.

This is an interesting development.

"These are..." I blow out an exhale.

"I had just broken up with Fletcher," she scrambles to explain.

"Maybe I was on the single-girl side of the internet or something?"

I lift my gaze, unable to hide my amusement. "It's fine. You don't have to—"

"This woman was raving about this set, and I guess I got, I dunno, *influenced*?" She does air quotes around the last word, rolling her eyes. "It's ridiculous, I know. But I haven't used them."

"It's not ridiculous," I say, the corner of my mouth twitching despite myself. "It's cute."

With a scoff, she snatches it out of my grasp and moves to tuck the box back in the corner.

"Don't put them away," I say, catching her arm. "Toys were on your list, right?"

"Yeah, but *these* toys? They look like they belong in one of those Japanese vending machines."

"Well," I say slowly as I take the box back to toss it on the bed, then slip my hands to her waist, thumbing the silky material of her shirt. "I've always wanted to go to Japan."

"Really?"

"Mm-hmm." I lean close, pressing a gentle kiss to her cheek. "And I mean, who am I to judge if you wanna get fucked by a glittery tentacle dildo?"

She gives me a playful shove.

"Wha—? Hey!" I feign innocence, clutching my chest. "I'm just trying to give the people what they want here!"

"Oh, yeah?" She steps toward me and drags her palms over my T-shirt, a challenge gleaming in her eye. "Well, this *people* wants something else, actually."

"Tell me." A smirk plays at my lips.

She shoves me harder this time, and my ass hits the bed.

"Shit, or... show me, I guess." I like her like this—bold and a little sassy. Taking what she wants. When she kneels at my feet, I let out a low hum.

"I've been thinking about this"—she slides her hands up my thighs, then flicks open my belt buckle—"all night."

My brows twitch together as my dick swells behind my fly. I cut a glance toward her bedroom door. "What about your grandpa?"

She shakes her head quickly. "He takes out his hearing aids overnight."

"Okay." I lean back to let her pop the button on my jeans, then sit back up, cupping her cheeks. "Then fuck... take it out." I've been half-hard since the damn arcade; by the time she tugs my belt, jeans, and underwear out of the way, I'm all the way there.

My eyes close at the first stroke of her hand, and I stutter out a shaky exhale.

Shit, that feels good.

She smiles up at me. "I like making you do that."

"Do what?" I ask.

"Breathe like that." Pumping my cock slowly, she drinks in my reaction. "I like making you... malfunction, I guess?"

"Like you even have to try." I let out a low moan at the pleasure already coursing through me. Her hand feels too good. *Hands.* Plural. Because she's working my balls now, too, and... *fuuuuuck.*

"I have a confession," she says.

"Yeah?"

"What I really wanted to do was *this.*"

She dips down and engulfs me with those perfect lips. The slip of her tongue sends a bolt of electricity up my spine that tingles the base of my skull, and I groan at the luscious heat wrapped around me.

"Jesus, fuck, baby," I say, unable to formulate a coherent sentence.

She squeezes on the upstroke and takes me deeper each time she sinks down.

Shit. It's building too fast.

"Stop, stop, stop."

Those beautiful eyes snap up to mine, and she pops off. "You don't want me to?" Her uncertainty is almost innocent. "Or... was I doing it wrong?"

"No," I say, then swallow as I snag her wrists, pulling her hands away from my aching dick before I lose it. "God, no. It was so right. *Too* right. Do you understand?"

She nods, biting that fucking lip.

"I wanna make you feel good first," I say, my voice rough. "Before you make me, uh, *malfunction.*"

Tilting her head as she considers this, she slides her palms over my thighs. "Okay..."

"I have an idea. Can we try something new?"

"From my list? What happened to Splash Mountain?" She brushes my shaft with her fingertips.

"Oh, we're still going on that ride." I twist around, snagging the box of toys. Ripping it open with all the care of a raccoon in the garbage, I feel wild. Feral. I pull the small, bright blue butt plug from the package and a tiny bottle of lube rolls out with it.

Well, that's convenient.

Caroline tenses up. "Miles, I'm not sure. I—"

"Okay, hear me out. I know I made, like, a thousand jokes about butt stuff, and I know it wasn't on your list, but have you ever tried it?" I experiment with its little remote, and the plug starts to hum against my fingertips.

"No," she says. "I mean, I guess it always felt sort of wrong? Or bad, maybe? Is that silly? It sounds ridiculous when I say it out loud."

"There's nothing wrong with making yourself feel good."

She softens at that, her hands drifting back to my hard cock, stroking gently.

"And, fuck..." I'm already struggling to concentrate. "I seem to remember you enjoying being a little bad."

A delicate pink flush creeps up her cheeks. "Okay, yes, but that's not why I bought those toys."

"I know, I know," I say. "It was the huge tentacle dick."

She freezes again and rolls her eyes, though she can't fight the grin working its way across her face.

"Do you trust me?"

She hesitates. "Yes, but—"

"We don't have to do anything you don't want to." When her gaze dips to the plug, I sense her curiosity and hold out my other pinkie. "Promise."

With resigned amusement, she hooks her pinkie to mine.

"Here. I'll go wash it," I say, moving to stand.

She grabs my thigh. "You don't need to. I... washed everything recently."

"Recently?" I raise a brow, a heated kind of suspicion thrumming through me when she won't meet my eyes. "Why recently?"

Her shoulders drop. "I thought I might... The night of the fundraiser?" She looks up, wide-eyed, like she's pleading for me to fill in the blanks.

Understanding sends heat straight to my dick and it pulses in her hands. Guess I wasn't the only one desperate for relief after that fucking kiss.

"But I chickened out, then put them all away."

"But did you get what you needed?"

"I told you, I didn't use—"

"Not what I asked. That night... did you get what you needed?"

"Mm-hmm." She bites her lip and nods, squeezing harder on the next stroke.

"*Fuck*," I whisper, images of Caroline touching herself flooding my brain. I curl down to kiss her, unable to help myself. "So did I."

A small whimper squeaks out of her at my admission.

Oh my God, this girl needs to get naked, stat.

"Take off your shirt."

"My shirt?" She eyes the plug still humming in my hand. "But that's for..."

"Yeah, I know what it's for," I laugh. "But we're starting slow."

Slowly, Caroline unbuttons her loose top and lets it drop to the floor, revealing her lacy, pale pink bra. I wanna take it off with my teeth.

"Bra too. I need to see those perfect little tits."

When she reaches back to unclasp it and it finally slips off, I have to keep from lunging forward to suck on those hard, pink nipples until she can't take it anymore.

I run my thumb over her lower lip, willing myself to focus on one thing at a time. "So, the trick is to relax. And to do that, you need to know what to expect." I lift the toy in silent question.

Can I?

She looks skeptical but nods.

"Here, touch it. It's on the lowest setting. Nice and gentle."

She brushes it with tentative fingers. "Okay."

Gently, experimentally, I graze the toy down the slope of her breast. "But, on somewhere more sensitive,"—it crests her peaked nipple and she startles slightly at the sensation—"it might feel kind of... exciting."

Lifting a brow, I drag the buzzing plug across to her other nipple.

"That's..." She hums a little sound of pleasure and slides her hands up my thighs once more. "That feels nice."

"We don't have to put it in unless you want it." I exhale hard as she starts to stroke me again. "You call the shots here. But... you wanna see how it feels, just on the outside?"

Another small nod as she stands, and my eyes drag up along with her. She unbuttons her jeans.

"Need to hear you say it," I say, tugging her closer before I kiss her stomach, letting my free hand slip down her thigh. No way in hell am I gonna pressure her into something she doesn't want. "This is your choice, okay?"

"I know," she says, cradling my face. "I wanna try it." Then she lifts a brow. "But don't act like you haven't been manifesting butt stuff all along."

I cough out a laugh. "Wha—? Oh, you think I was playing the long game?"

"Mm-hmm." Her teasing smile is everything.

"Butt-stuff manifestation, huh?" My jaw clenches as she strips naked in front of me. "Okay, but really. I don't want you trying this for me. This is for you. You'd said no butt stuff and—"

"Miles…" She straddles my lap, tangling her fingers in my hair. "Didn't you tell me not to overthink things?"

"Oof!" I chuckle, dropping my forehead between her tits, then press kisses against her smooth skin. "Called the fuck out." I drop the plug onto the bed, needing both hands to explore her. "C'mere." I suck one nipple into my mouth, smoothing my palms over her hips, her waist, her back—like I might memorize her skin by touch alone.

Fuck, she's perfect.

She reaches between us and guides my cock, moving closer so my shaft glides between her pussy lips and up against her clit.

I can't tear my eyes away, so I feel around on the bed until I land on the plug. Sliding it slowly down her lower back, I follow the trail of her spine. The moment it slips over her tailbone, she tenses up a little.

"Try to relax," I whisper. "Just tell me how it feels."

"Mmm," she hums, though her voice is pitched higher than usual.

"It's okay to be nervous. And hey,"—I pause, lifting the toy away—"if anything is too much, just say *pomegranate*, okay?"

"That's the safe word?" Her brows quirk together. "Pome-granate?"

"First thing that came to mind." I shrug, grinning before pulling her into a teasing kiss. "Now—and I appreciate the irony of me saying this but—*focus*."

Watching her closely, I gently drag the plug down again, her reaction telling me when I've found the spot.

"Oh!" She pitches forward a bit, resting her forehead against mine.

"You're doing so good," I whisper, experimenting with only the smallest movements, the lightest pressure, as she lifts and lowers, sliding her wet pussy up and down the length of my dick. "You're making me feel so good too. Look how fucking hard I am for you."

Mewling moans escape her throat, and I pulse against her with need. When she starts to push back against the toy, I move it away, drinking in the frustrated pinch between her brows.

"You need more?" I rasp against her cheek. When she nods, I reach for the lube and coat the plug generously. "Okay. We're gonna make you feel so good, baby." I slip it back between her cheeks. "There?"

"Yes," she whimpers. "Right there."

"Just a little bit," I murmur against her neck as I angle the plug, pressing in gently. "So slow."

"So slow," she echoes in agreement, though she tilts her hips, subtly increasing the pressure.

I follow her lead, pushing in slightly more each time she flexes back against my hand, letting her adjust. "So proud of you," I whisper into her hair as she gasps through the last push and it slides inside. "How does it feel?"

"Good. Buzzy, obviously, and... heavy. Full."

"You did so good." My pulse beats like a drum through my cock and I fist it for her in long, slow strokes.

Arousal flushes Caroline's cheeks as she watches me, rolling and pinching her hard nipples. "This is the dirtiest thing I've ever done."

Her words are tentative—whispered and unsure—but they slip up and down my spinal cord. There's something about knowing she's testing her limits with me that sets my brain and dick on fire simultaneously.

"Yeah?" I kiss her long and deep, swallowing every delicious whimper she makes. "Do you like how it feels?"

"Yes." The word is like a sigh of relief.

"Then maybe dirty's what you like." I take her nipple into my mouth and suck hard as she arches into me, running her fingers through my hair. I let go, grazing her taut flesh with my teeth. "Maybe you shouldn't fight it."

She reaches between us to work her fingers over her clit, looking almost pained.

"You like breaking the rules, don't you? Playing with those gorgeous tits for me... touching yourself and taking a plug in your perfect ass when you're supposed to be such a good girl."

She tries to stifle a whine. "We're being so bad."

"I know." I love watching her like this but, *fuck*, I need more. Grasping her jaw, I pull her in for a kiss and flick my tongue against hers. "Mmm, baby, can you do something for me?"

"What?"

"Get up here so I can taste you." I lean back to peel off my T-shirt.

She slowly crawls off my lap and I turn, unable to tear my eyes away when I catch a glimpse of the bright blue plug between her gorgeous ass cheeks.

I nearly stumble trying to tear off my pants and socks. By some miracle, I remember to grab the tiny remote before I dive between her legs, lapping at her cunt like I'm dying of thirst. "God, you taste so fucking good."

"I wanna taste you too," she says between little moans.

My resolve falters. "Fuck, okay, fine. Turn around." I scoot up the bed and she spins, dropping her knees on either side of my head. Greedy for more, I yank her hips down, sucking her clit hard and fast.

"Miles!" she cries out, gripping my thighs. It's got to be a lot—the vibration in her ass and my tongue working her clit.

I break away. "Sorry, that okay?"

"Yes," she says quickly.

"You said you were a bit tender from—"

"Please," she cuts me off. "Don't stop."

"Oh, thank fuck."

With another sweet mewling sound, wet heat envelops my cock and my eyes roll. She sucks me in long, deep strokes, playing with my balls with her free hand, and it feels so good I almost lose track of what I'm doing.

Almost.

I click the vibration up a notch and her back bows as she lets out a muffled cry. Reluctantly, I tear my lips away from the soft, wet warmth of her pussy, practically panting. "Still okay?"

She pulls off so she can answer. "Yes! Oh my God!"

I slip my fingers inside her and dive for that swollen, perfect clit again. "Fuck, Caroline. I can feel the plug vibrating inside you." I add another finger, stretching her.

Oh, God. This fucking pussy.

"Does it feel good when I fill you up like this?"

She gives me a muffled whimper in response.

"Such a good little slut for me." I tap gently on the end of the plug and she jolts, letting out another strangled cry of pure pleasure.

I lick and suck and tug on her clit, working my fingers faster until she's keening over me, her own rhythm falling apart in her distraction.

It's funny; sixty-nine is a position that always riles up my competitive side. It's like a mind-melting tug-of-war where each of us tries to do such a good job that the other can't keep up their end of the deal.

Picking up the pace, I push her closer to the edge. I don't even care that my jaw is cramping or that my cock has slipped out of her mouth and she's only absentmindedly kissing and licking the tip between shaking gasps. I'm out to fucking *win this*.

She tenses up, digging her nails into my thighs. On another beautiful moan, her release floods from her cunt, soaking my face.

With a groan, I lap up every drop. Or at least, I try to, before she wiggles away.

"Sorry!" she squeaks. "I'm so sorry! I didn't mean to— Oh God!"

"Uh-uh." I haul her back by the hips, sinking my tongue back into her wet slit. "Don't you fucking dare." I swipe my tongue, pressing my face into her, slipping against her, coating myself in her release. "This is all mine."

Her nervous little sounds quickly melt into throatier cries, and another pulse drenches me, the tension in her finally yielding. Her lips close over my aching dick again and glide down—*deep* down —until I bump up against resistance. She's silent but keeps pushing. Then I feel something give.

Holy. Fucking. Shit.

Gripping my hips, she hauls me even closer, opening her tight throat for more, and I nearly blow right then and there.

It's only when her stomach hollows in sudden tension that I tear myself away and pull her off.

"Fuck, are you okay?"

She sucks in a huge gulp of air before exhaling a laugh. "Yes."

"Please... Don't hurt yourself for me." Untangling our limbs, I sit up and tug her closer, needing to check in face-to-face. "Hey..." I cradle her cheek, searching her eyes. "I don't want you to do that just for my sake."

"I'm okay," she reassures me. "Did it feel good though?"

"So fucking good. C'mere." I pull her into a kiss, mumbling against her swollen lips. "You did so fucking good. But I don't like the idea of hurting you."

"You didn't," she reassures me, taking my face in both hands. "I'm fine. Promise. I wanted to try that too, remember?"

Right. Another one to cross off her list.

She slips her fingers over my wet stubble. "Sorry about— Are *you* okay? I didn't think I'd lose control like that while you were... *down there.*"

"Baby, *okay* doesn't even touch how good I am." I lean in to kiss her again. "'Cause you squirting on my face was the sexiest fucking thing."

Her face pinches up. "You sure?"

"You don't need to be embarrassed," I reassure her. "You leveled the fuck up."

She laughs.

"In fact," I say as I guide her onto her back. "I think I might need you to do that again."

"Well," she says, peering up at me, her light eyes dark with desire. She reaches for my hips. "Maybe I want more too."

"Yeah?" When she nods, I let her guide me into position so I'm straddling her rib cage. "Where do you want it, baby?" I let my gaze drop to her peaked nipples, imagining streaks of my cum over her chest.

Slowly, almost reverently, she strokes me with both hands, biting her lip. "I don't know."

"Well, y'know," I muse, "good girls... get cum on their tits." I pinch both nipples hard.

With a whimper, she arches up. "But... I'm not a good girl, remember?"

"Oh," I say, pretending like I'd forgotten. "That's right." I slip my hand up to gently collar her throat. "Well, *naughty* girls... they get cum on their necks."

She tilts her head back, her voice breaking. "Yeah?"

"Yeah. But... *bad* girls," I continue, tugging her chin down as I brush my thumb over her parted lips, not missing how her grip tightens on my cock, "bad girls get cum on their faces."

Her breath stutters at my words.

I take over, stroking myself above her, my jaw clenching as I try to draw this out. "So tell me where you want it. Tell me what kind of girl you wanna be tonight, Caroline."

"Bad." The word rushes out without hesitation. "I wanna be bad. Please."

I almost growl in response.

She tucks her arms between my legs as I shift my knees higher, getting into position. "Tell me. Tell me you want it on your pretty face." I speed up, squeezing myself tighter with each stroke. "Fucking say it."

"I want it on my face." She nods quickly. Only one of her arms circles around my thigh, and I can tell from the desperate way she's writhing under me that she's touching herself with her other hand.

"Say you want it"—my voice gets rougher as my release builds —"on these perfect lips."

"All over my lips." She practically whines the words—those dirty, feral words I know she's been aching to let out. "My lips. My tongue. I want it dripping off my fucking chin, Miles, *please*!"

"Fuuuuuck," I practically groan out, my neurons momentarily liquefied by the filthy image my girl just served up. "You wanna be my messy... little slut?" I barely get the words out. I'm about to burst. About to combust.

"Yes! Please. I need it." She curls up toward the aching, throbbing head of my dick. "Make me messy."

Everything whites out as pleasure lights me from head to toe. I tilt forward, spurting over those beautiful lips with a deep moan, painting her cheeks, her chin, her delicate nose… and then I sink into her mouth, muffling her cries.

She sucks the last of it eagerly, drawing out the incredible, dizzying sensation until I'm shaking. It isn't long before her own stifled gasps pitch up to tell me she's coming again too.

The moment I can see straight again, I reach back and sink my fingers into her pulsing cunt, curling them and quickly coaxing her into another ecstatic wave that soaks my palm.

"Fuck, you love being so full, huh? You can't stop coming."

She can only whimper around my cock.

"You're making such a mess with all your pretty holes filled." I shift my hips back and she lets go of me with a slick pop, then lets her head fall back on the bed in a tangle of blonde curls.

Her flushed cheeks and swollen lips are painted in my release, and I've never seen a more beautiful sight.

Still slowly working my fingers inside her as her orgasm wanes, I use my free hand to wipe the cum from her cheek, slipping my finger into her mouth. "Clean it up."

She licks and sucks it with a low hum, her eyes rolling as her pussy clenches around my fingers.

"You like how I taste?" My voice is ragged.

"Mm-hmm." She wiggles an arm up between us and catches my hand, holding it as she licks my fingers clean.

"More," I command quietly, scooping up another bit from her chin and pushing it between her lips.

She slips her fingers over mine, sucking my cum off us both. Wiping up from her chin and over her plump lower lip, she holds my gaze as she sucks her own fingers clean, getting every last drop she can find into that gorgeous, perfect mouth.

"God, that's so fucking hot."

Her slow grin makes me want to kiss her. *Need* to kiss her.

Fuck it.

I shift down and she lets out only the barest squeak of uncertainty before she melts into the long, slow kiss, wrapping her arms around my neck. We're sticky and sweaty; I can taste myself on her tongue, my veins still pulsing with the memory of spilling onto her lips.

Her words echo in my head. *"Bad. I wanna be bad. Please."*
Well, fuck. Same here.

This girl makes me want to do nasty, raunchy, utterly depraved things to her—then hold her close and nuzzle into her hair, talk with her, take care of her, wake up with her, make cringey jokes with her, and have slow, sleepy morning sex with her.

When our lips part, I find the remote and turn off the plug.

Caroline lets out a contented little sigh and I smile down at her. She returns it when my stomach rumbles a protest, a sudden pang of hunger cutting into my thoughts. Those arcade fries are a distant memory.

"Uh, what are your thoughts about post-coital snacks?" I ask.

"Coitus? Is that what we just did?"

"Uh, I guess not, technically," I say on a laugh. "Post-sixty-nine snacks? Post-facial snacks?" I gaze down at her, brushing the hair out of her eyes.

"Facial? Sounds like I've been to the spa or something," she says with a shy smirk.

"Shit, yeah, sorry. You probably wanna..." I look around the room. "Can I get you a wet washcloth or something?"

"It's okay. I got it." She glances toward the bathroom door. "But, after we clean up, yes, post-orgasmic snacks." She gives a playful poke to my chest. "Gotta feed the beast."

"Is that me? Am I the beast?" I let out a low, rumbled growl and, when she nods, I gnash my teeth, diving for her neck as giggles squeak from her throat. Snuffling and snarling against her skin, I relish in the way she squirms under me, carrying on until my playful nips turn into kisses and our laughter yields to soft hums against each other's lips. The moment settles in my chest, simmering and warm. I draw back and look into her eyes.

Shit. I'm falling for this girl.

I tear my gaze away and let her out from under me—though I can't help but catch the little peek of bright blue still nestled between her ass cheeks as she heads to the bathroom. When she closes the door, I fall back on the pillow and blow out a huge breath.

17

———————

CAROLINE

I'm hovering outside my father's home office, trying to steel myself for whatever he wants to talk to me about, when his housekeeper quietly emerges carrying an empty whiskey bottle and a small bag of trash.

We exchange polite smiles as she gathers her cleaning supplies, and I absentmindedly reach for my necklace—Grandma's dragonfly pendant. As I work my fingers over the fine gold chain, my eyes fix for a moment on the last drops of amber liquid in the bottom of the bottle, remembering countless nights Fletcher came home after working late to paw at me, his breath hot and reeking of scotch. Not wanting to reject his advances, I'd lean into it, going through the motions even if I wasn't really in the mood. I'd never orgasm those nights, but Fletcher didn't seem to mind and it was over soon enough, anyway. I'd told myself it was fine, but Miles was right. It was anything but fine. And, until recently, I had no idea what I'd been missing.

Miles.

My heart squeezes a little, remembering how he'd insisted on going home last night. How he'd taken the spoon from my grasp in the dark kitchen, set it gently in the sink, and held my face as he kissed me like he didn't want to leave. I'd clung tightly to his waist, knowing I had no right to feel disappointed that he wouldn't stay the night. Maybe it was the vulnerability of having tried something so new and so intimate with him. But I couldn't ask him to stay, no matter how much I was dreading being alone.

When I realize the cleaner left Dad's door open a crack, I peer in. He's at his desk, poring over some papers with a glass of whiskey in one hand.

Reminding myself to stop fiddling with my necklace, I rap tentatively on the office door.

Dad pulls the reading glasses off the end of his nose as he sits back in his chair. "Caroline. Come in."

"Mom said you wanted to see me?" I take the seat across from him and smooth the fabric of my pleated linen skirt. The setup feels strangely formal, like a job interview.

"I spoke with Michael this week," he says, returning his gaze to the papers on his desk.

"Okay..." I say slowly, trying to work out what my father's financial advisor has to do with me.

"He's done an analysis of my charitable contributions and he recommended I make some adjustments to my portfolio."

An icy sensation spreads over the back of my neck. "What kind of adjustments?"

He spins one of the papers around to face me and slides it across the desk. "This will be the last year I'll make my annual contribution to Found Family."

"Wait. What?" My eyes jump between my father and the paper in front of me, which I'm not really digesting. He's threatened this before but never gone through with it. Panic needles my stomach, knowing Dad's substantial yearly donations are crucial to Found Family's operational budget.

How did I screw this up?

Pretending to date Miles was supposed to avoid this— supposed to appease my dad and keep Found Family afloat. I thought I'd done enough: I'd followed his directives, been on my best behavior.

"Why?" I ask, bewildered.

"Return on investment, mainly." He collects the remaining documents into a neat pile, then reaches for a paper clip from the caddy of office supplies near his computer.

I frown.

That's not how charity donations work. You aren't supposed to expect anything in return.

"Michael suggested some other philanthropic strategies that may... *align* better."

"Align better with what?" My expression falls when I realize what he means. "The campaign? But this is a personal donation. These aren't campaign funds."

"Of course not," Dad agrees. "Look, I've supported your little project since day one, sweetheart."

My little project?

I sit back in my seat. "And so, what, you're just done now?"

"It's a business decision, Caroline," he says. "Nothing more. With you no longer at the helm, it's a natural time for this to happen."

"And what's Adrian supposed to do?"

"Adrian will find another donor." He says it as if it'll be easy. An afterthought. "He's a charming young man. I hear he has no trouble getting what he wants. From women *and* men, apparently."

My brows draw together. I've never known Dad to be biphobic. "Are you making a dig at Adrian's sexuality?"

"Don't be dramatic." He drops his gaze to his paperwork, avoiding the topic.

Attempting to shelve my frustration is getting challenging; at this point, the shelves are full-to-bursting.

"So, let me get this straight: you're pulling a substantial donation from a small charity that relies on it, all because it's no longer *my little project*, and supporting underprivileged youth isn't winning you any points with voters? Have I got that right?"

He shakes his head. "Caroline—"

"Wow." I search his face, trying to make sense of this. Dad's been trailing slightly in recent polls. This has got to be a strategic attempt to sway voters. Free up funds to make promises to the right people.

Gross.

"Don't make this out to be something bigger than it is," he says. "It's simply a restructuring of my finances."

"But you wanted to tell me in person." He had to know this would be a big deal for me—and a major blow to Found Family. To Adrian.

"I didn't want you to find out secondhand." He pulls the sheet of paper back from in front of me and clips it to the front of the rest. "I'll be letting Adrian know once Michael has things finalized."

My heart breaks at the thought of Adrian having this bomb dropped on him.

"Don't bother," I say, pushing up from the chair. "I'll tell him myself."

I owe my best friend that much. Starting the charity had been personal for Adrian, having grown up without the kind of opportunities we've been able to offer thousands of kids through Found Family. For my part, not only had I believed supporting at-risk youth was a worthy cause in and of itself, but it seemed like a perfect way to bolster my best friend's dreams while also complementing my father's political aspirations.

My father, who just turned his back on what I built.

I guess this is *my* return on investment.

"Suit yourself," he huffs. "Though I assumed you'd be too busy."

"Too busy with what?"

"Gallivanting around town with that boy toy of yours."

"Boy toy? You can't be serious."

He swirls his glass of whiskey before taking a slow sip. "Where to next? An amusement park?"

I set my jaw, though I can't say I'm surprised Dad's been keeping tabs on me and Miles.

That's when it occurs to me: with Dad's donations withdrawn, there's no longer anything in it for me when it comes to continuing this fake relationship with Miles. Well, except propping up my father's election chances.

And the best sex of your life, a little inner voice reminds me before I can squash it.

But, with Miles' job still at risk, I can't bail on our arrangement. I wouldn't do that to him. Plus, it's only another nine days until the election, and it's not exactly a hardship spending time with him. Especially the part where he's helping me come out of my shell—and lose my mind with pleasure. I try to shelve the thought.

Dad types something on his computer, and my vision hazes over when he turns the screen to face me. I don't have to read the article; seeing the photo is enough. It's a shot of me and Miles, hand in hand, laughing as we left the arcade last night.

"He's not at your level, sweetheart." He swivels the monitor back to face him.

My lips part, but I find I don't have the words to respond. Unable to maintain eye contact with my father, my gaze flits around the room, landing on framed photos of Dad playing golf with various high-profile politicians, the enormous mahogany desk with hand-carved detailing, the expensive watch on his wrist. It suddenly feels like I'm choking on the stuffy opulence in this office.

Not at my level? Is this *my level?*

"You're wrong," I say, my voice quiet with restraint. "You don't know anything about him." It crosses my mind that maybe it's *me* Dad doesn't know anything about. Has he ever bothered to ask?

"I know enough."

"What's that supposed to mean?"

He doesn't get a chance to answer, because Mom pops in, interrupting us. "You ready to go, darling?"

"Uh, yeah," I say, slinging one last disillusioned look at Dad. I don't want to spend a minute longer in his presence. "I think we're done here."

The short drive to Mom's tailor is quiet, the usual bustle of traffic in downtown Seattle barely registering as I try to process what Dad told me. Is this really who my father is? Donating to charities only out of performative obligation or to sway voters into thinking he values them? I've never related to him less.

"Magda has all your measurements, so there shouldn't be any alterations necessary." Mom's voice reaches me as though I'm underwater.

"What?"

She throws me a sidelong glance. "Your *costume*, darling."

"Oh, yeah." I try to shake off my distraction, gathering my cashmere cardigan tighter around my chest.

Halloween is in five days.

I don't normally put a huge effort into my costume unless I'm attending a high-profile event, but when Mom had gotten wind of my idea for the local Halloween Fest, she'd pushed for having it custom-made. She always insists on me showing up looking as polished as possible—even for smaller-scale public appearances. I'd argued it was overkill for a family event held at a small-town farm, but she wouldn't back down.

I'd only gone to Sonora Farm once or twice as a kid, when my parents would make the trip to Lennox for Halloween Fest, but I still have vivid memories of running around the pumpkin patch with my grandparents and cousins. It's grown since then; nearly the whole town shows up every year to partake in the train ride, corn maze, live music, and haunted houses. The seeds of my fascination with fashion may have been sown at Sonora when I was little, marveling at all the creative, intricate costumes people would wear. In Lennox Valley, it isn't only the kids who dress up for Halloween.

"You're quiet today," Mom finally says, breaking another awkward silence.

"Just tired," I lie.

The truth is, Dad's condescension about Miles had felt personal. Miles has single-handedly brought me out of stagnation, waking me up to a life I'd always wanted but had been chasing in all the wrong ways. He's funny and real and, *God*, when I'm with him, I feel like I can breathe. He encourages me to do what I want, like what I want, try what I want. It's like I'm the best version of myself when he's around—finally spreading the wings I've been keeping closely tucked at my sides for most of my life.

"Are you not sleeping well, darling?" Mom asks, pulling me back to the car once again. "Or is this about that fellow you've been seeing?"

"What? No, I... I told you I'm just tired. I'm fine, really. And I'm sleeping... fine. I'm fine."

I'm sleeping better than I ever have, but I don't tell her that. I don't want to invite any more questions about why.

Concern cuts lines in her expression as she turns into a parking spot outside Sew Bespoke, letting a long silence stretch between us. "He's not"—she lowers her voice—"taking advantage, is he?"

"Mom! No!" I sputter. "Of course not!"

"Well," she says, glancing my way as she unclips her seat belt and reaches for her clutch, "this arrangement between you two is rather unusual. I hope he's being respectful."

Respectful?

My cheeks heat as I remember last night, and my gaze cuts to somewhere—*anywhere*—outside the car. I can almost hear Miles' voice. "*Such a good little slut for me.*" A shiver ripples through my entire body and I close my eyes, willing myself not to react. I turn back to my mother.

"Mom, don't worry, he's being very... He's been great. Please don't worry about that."

"Well, I'm glad to hear it." She reaches for my hand and gives it a quick squeeze. "I worry about you, my love."

"I know, Mom." I slap on a brave face, then tilt my head toward the shop window with the minimalist needle and thread motif. "Shall we?"

I move through the costume fitting in a sort of trance, following Magda's instructions and responding politely to my mother's fussing with a people-pleasing automaticity.

The costume itself is, unsurprisingly, perfect. I still think it's a bit much for this kind of event, but Mom won't be dissuaded. And the dress *is* beautiful. As I stare at my reflection in the three angled mirrors in front of me, I can only think one thing: I can't wait for Miles to see me in it.

THE WHOLE HOUSE smells like cookies when I get home. I peel off my scarf and coat and venture into the kitchen to find Grandpa and Sadie standing at the island, cleaning up a few mixing bowls smeared with the remnants of cookie dough.

"Well, hey there!" Grandpa says when he sees me. "How was

your big-city adventure?"

"Fine," I say, lifting the large, somewhat rain-spattered paper bag from the tailor. "Picked up my Halloween costume."

"Your mother convince you to spend a fortune on it?"

"Of course." I do a little eye roll as I set down the bag. "But you know clothes are my weakness."

"Caroline," Sadie says, catching my attention as she finishes loading the dishwasher. "Since you're back, I wonder if I could slip out about ten minutes early today? I have an appointment and the traffic in this rain is just—" She makes a face.

"Oh, absolutely! Go for it!"

"Thank you." She looks relieved. "The timer for the cookies should go off in about five."

"Gotcha."

"Now, George?" She turns to Grandpa, leveling her index finger his way in a friendly threat. "You be on your best behavior with those cookies, you hear me?"

He holds up his hands with a shrug, the picture of innocence.

Sadie pauses as she moves past me to whisper, "I told him he can have two max, but watch out because he sneaks 'em when you're not paying attention."

I laugh softly. "Okay, noted."

Sadie heads off and Grandpa settles in his usual spot at the kitchen table, pulling out his crossword puzzle. I fill a glass with water from the fridge and savor the way the cool sensation trickles down my throat.

"You'll be going to Halloween Fest, is that right?" Grandpa asks, eyeing the bag from the tailor in the doorway.

"That's the plan, yeah. Do you think you'll go this year?"

"Ah," he answers, his head tilting. "Tough going with the walker on uneven terrain, especially in the dark. Think I'll leave the Halloween hijinks to the younger crowd."

"That makes sense." I nod, albeit a bit sadly. "Tell you what, then. I'll bring back a pumpkin for you and Sadie to carve. Sound good?"

"Perfect." He smiles before dropping his gaze back to his puzzle. "That new boyfriend of yours going with you?"

"He's not my boyfriend, Grandpa. You know that." The oven timer beeps, and I use the cookies as a convenient excuse to avoid more scrutiny about Miles. Slipping on an oven mitt, I try to suppress a grin as I add, "But, yeah, he's coming with me."

"Well, you're certainly spending a lot of time with him lately. When do I get to meet this lucky fellow, anyway?"

"Soon, I'm sure." I open the oven, letting out a waft of caramelized heat. I pull out the tray of golden brown chocolate chip cookies, setting them gingerly on the stovetop. "He was actually here last night, but you were already in bed." When Grandpa's bushy white eyebrows lift, I rush to add, "He dropped me off after we went out."

That's not all he did.

I will myself not to think about everything else that happened between us before he left. The flashbacks today have been intense enough to stop me in my tracks.

"Tell me what kind of girl you wanna be tonight, Caroline."

I busy myself with a flipper, hoping I can blame the oven's heat if my cheeks are bright pink. One by one, I gently lift the cookies from the pan and shift them onto a wire cooling rack.

"Well, I'm sorry to have missed him," Grandpa says.

I've missed him, too, as ridiculous as that is. It had felt so lonely crawling between my fresh sheets after he left last night.

Trying to shake off the memory, I slide two cookies onto a plate for each of us and settle in beside Grandpa at the table. "Here, eat your cookie quota."

"Thank you, dear."

"Careful," I warn. "They're hot."

"Ah, you know that expression *strike when the iron's hot?*"

"Yeah…" I narrow my eyes, not sure what he's getting at.

"Sometimes you need to *eat* when the *cookie's* hot."

I laugh. "But won't you get burned?"

"My dear," he says, leaning toward me as he lifts the edge of his cookie from his plate, "that's how you know you're alive."

I tilt my head in acknowledgment. But, as I bite carefully into my own nearly molten cookie, huffing air through my teeth to cool it down, I ponder his words.

Something tells me he isn't just talking about the cookies.

18

MILES

Sonora Farm is where I formed one of my earliest memories: my mom lifting me up to sit on a pumpkin bigger than I was. The place is nearly unrecognizable now—nothing like the quaint local pumpkin patch I remember going to as a kid. Over the years, it's ballooned into something more like a fairground. Attendants wave glowing orange batons to direct traffic in and out of a field that's been converted into a parking lot. The ground is a mix of mud and hay, and it takes me a good five minutes to trudge through the mess to get from my truck to the festival itself. I'm glad my costume involved work boots.

Not knowing where to look for Caroline, I pull out my phone. My background photo—Lumpy, aka *Lumpkin*, thanks to his new pumpkin costume—has me smirking as I send her a text.

ME

I'm here. This place is wild. Where are you?

She doesn't text back right away, so I pocket my phone and wander between the big marquee tents, one of which covers a roped-off, snaking lineup for the small train ride. A live band plays a cover of Monster Mash for a burbling crowd of kids, their parents seated on bales of hay around a dance floor of sorts.

People stream around me in all directions, most wearing costumes, some carrying pumpkins. Twin girls walk past hand in hand, dressed up like the ones from *The Shining* and playing the part a little too well. They're creepy as fuck. Just to be safe, I give them a wide berth.

Caroline wouldn't reveal what her Halloween costume was, saying she wanted it to be a surprise, so I have no idea what I should be searching for as I scan the crowd. I'd decided to dress up as a lumberjack, though I basically look like my brother on your average Tuesday. He'd reluctantly let me raid his closet, which was probably ninety percent plaid flannel. He'd even dug out a pair of suspenders for me. Olena's delight had been borderline unhinged, especially when she'd had a light-bulb moment and practically sprinted to get a squeaky toy of Murphy's—one in the shape of an axe—to hang from my belt loop. I absentmindedly give it a squeeze and smile to myself when it squeaks.

My phone pings in my pocket as I make my way past the entrance to the corn maze.

CAROLINE

Turn around, handsome…

I stop in my tracks and straighten, craning my neck before I spin around fully, my heartbeat pounding in my chest just knowing she can see me. I almost miss my back pocket with my phone when I spot her, and my hard exhale forms a cloud in front of me in the cold night air.

Little Red Riding Hood.

Caroline's blonde curls peek out from under a bright red, warm-looking cloak that flows almost to her ankles, the hooded cape covering an old-fashioned, lacy white dress under a maroon corset top and... *fuck*, I don't know what else because she's walking toward me and melting my brain more and more with every step. She shifts a small wicker basket from one hand to the other, grinning as she slips her phone into some hidden pocket in the billowy fabric.

I don't even consciously reach for her, but I find my hands on her waist somehow, sliding under the warmth of her cloak as she lifts to press a gentle kiss to my cheek.

Damn, she smells so good. Like cookies, but classy somehow?

All I know is I'm already hungry for more.

"Hi," she whispers, wiping my cheek with her thumb.

"Fuck," is all I can say in response, not giving two shits if I have red lipstick on my face. "I mean, hi."

She laughs, dropping back onto the heels of her brown ankle boots. "You look great." She steps back slightly to give me a lingering once-over, tugging at my plaid flannel jacket. "People are gonna think we planned this."

"Huh?"

She gestures between us. "Little Red Riding Hood and the Woodcutter?"

"Oh! Yeah. Gotcha..." I blow out a long breath, and she grins. "You're enjoying making me malfunction again, aren't you?"

"Oh, I haven't even *started* to make you malfunction yet." She lifts a coy brow.

"What do you mean?"

I'm in. Whatever she wants to do, the answer is yes.

She leans in close. "You should see what's underneath this."

Oh, fuck me sideways.

My dick presses against the fly of my jeans, already convinced it's go time.

Taking my hand, she pulls away, leading me through the crowd.

Reminding myself this is a family place, I will myself to get it together. I'm definitely *not* scanning the area for spots I could take Caroline to be alone. Definitely *not* considering how the loud music and the crowd noise would drown out any sounds.

Nope, not this guy. Family. Place.

"Caroline!" A woman with turquoise hair in a bright orange dinosaur onesie and Converse high-tops jogs over to us from one of the game booths. "Hey!"

"Ada!" Caroline sweeps her into a hug. When they draw back, Caroline touches my arm. "Ada, this is my boyfriend, Miles."

Her words crackle in my stomach like I've just swallowed a handful of popping candy. I don't know why I'm surprised—this fake dating thing is the whole reason we're here tonight—but still, as I go through the motions of shaking Ada's hand, I'm distracted by how right it felt to hear Caroline call me that.

"So, how do you two know each other?" I ask, forcing myself to stay present.

"Ada's an artist," Caroline explains. "I'd been following her online for ages and then we bumped into each other last year at the gallery."

"Found Family also funds my volunteer gig," Ada adds. "Speaking of which... Hang on." Ada turns back to the game booth to shout, "Roly! You got everything under control?" When a dark-haired teenage boy dressed as a mummy gives her a thumbs-up, she spins back to us. "Sorry. Vaguely supervising the teens tonight."

"Weirdly enough," Caroline says to me, "Ada and Adrian also go way back, so, I was like, well, you're my friend now."

Typical Lennox Valley—it's always six degrees of Kevin Bacon around here.

"So, do you make a habit of adopting people into your life without asking, or what? Hey! Ow!" I wince when she elbows me in the ribs, but I can't wipe the smirk off my face. "Ada," I say, lifting my chin her way, "blink twice if you're here under your own free will." Ada barks a laugh as I dodge the next elbow from Caroline, snagging her arm instead, a teasing seriousness in my voice when I chastise, "Violence is never the answer."

"I like this guy," Ada says.

Rolling her eyes, Caroline lets me tug her into my side, then yanks my beanie down over my face in retaliation. "It's a good thing he's cute."

I grin as I fix my hair and settle my hat back into place.

"Quick photo for the Lennox Valley Chronicle?" A photographer interrupts us, lifting his camera in question.

"Uh, sure," I say.

"You all look great," the guy says as we pose for the photo. "Don't remember the dinosaur from Little Red Riding Hood, though."

"Oh, that's 'cause I ate the wolf," Ada deadpans. "And the grandma."

Flash.

Ada and I take turns spelling our names for the guy and swiping out wobbly signatures on a simple release form he's got on his phone.

Caroline starts to spell hers out when the photographer cuts her off, shaking his head. "Oh, you need no introduction, Ms. Brennan."

And she says she's not famous.

He passes her his phone with the waiver ready to go. "Just sign here and I'll be out of your hair."

"Hey, any headway with that curator of yours?" Ada asks when the photographer leaves.

"I wish," Caroline replies, her shoulders drooping slightly. "I'll keep trying, though. The gallery needs a shake-up so bad."

"Well, if he doesn't listen, it's probably 'cause his head is stuck too far up his ass to hear you."

I tilt my head. Having crossed paths with Julian at the gallery, I'd say she's not wrong.

Ada gets called back to her game booth duties and promises to meet up with us later.

When I notice the train line has died down, we duck under the ropes to wait under the marquee tent for the next ride.

"So, you got some kind of mutiny planned at work, or what?" I ask as the train chugs slowly to a halt.

She laughs. "Kinda? I'm hoping to get Ada's pieces in for a local artist exhibition, along with some others... if I can swing it."

"What's stopping you?"

"Well, it's not *strictly* my role." She does a cute little nose scrunch. "I drew up this proposal for some new events a couple weeks back, which went over well, but I'd love to take on more—plan something bigger."

People stream out of the small carriage and Caroline smiles softly at a tiny princess who darts off in the wrong direction before her dad snags her hand.

"Sunny loves having my help and wants Julian to include me in some of the curation decisions, but he isn't very... receptive to input, shall we say?"

"You mean he's a dick?"

Her jaw drops, though amusement glitters in her eyes. "I did *not* say that!"

"Didn't have to." I shrug.

I love this. Bantering with her. Flirting with her. Joking around and flustering her with my bluntness. It'll only be a few more days, I remind myself. The election is in less than a week, and I've been trying not to think about how it'll feel to have to drop out of Caroline's life.

"Anyway, Sunny's working on him for me. For now, I'm trying to stay in my lane and be patient."

I lift a brow. "Ah, 'patience, young Grasshopper.'"

"Hey, put that sex sensei voice away," she teases quietly. "There are children here."

As we squeeze into our bench seat on the train, I accidentally sit on the dog toy I'd forgotten was attached to my belt. I can't tell which is worse: the sudden, shrill squeak when all my weight deflates it, or the slow, drawn-out honk as it reinflates. Caroline and I share an embarrassed laugh.

The little kid in the seat ahead of us turns around at the weird sound. He must be about four, and he's cute as hell, dressed in a bright yellow firefighter costume. As he climbs up to kneel on the seat, his mom throws a polite, somewhat apologetic glance over her shoulder. I wish Gus was here so I could introduce the kid to a real firefighter—blow his tiny mind.

I catch the kid's eye, wiggling the axe from my belt to show him. "It's a dog toy," I explain, giving it a gentle squeeze. "It looks like an axe, but it doesn't actually work. See, I'll show ya." I bang it on the back of his seat a couple times, then spin it around. "You try. C'mon, hit it as hard as you can." When I notice his mom's hesitation, I quickly add, "Don't worry, I washed it."

She looks relieved.

His grabby hands quickly claim it and he gives it a little squeeze, then proceeds to whack the thing with comical vigor against the wooden bench, yielding only a few strange, honking squeaks that make us all laugh.

"See? Not even a *dent*," I say when he stops, smoothing my fingers over where he'd attacked the seatback. "I think it's broken, dude!"

A tinny safety announcement crackles over a small speaker above us and the boy's mom tells him it's time to turn around and sit down. She passes the axe back to me and, when her son starts to protest, she's saved by the train slowly chugging into motion, distracting him.

"You're good with kids," Caroline says, keeping her voice low

—even though a private conversation on this cramped little train car is impossible. "Do you want kids someday?"

"Nah," I say honestly, scrunching my nose. "Don't think I've got it in me. I mean, taking care of *me* seems to be a full-time gig here." I flick my eyes to Caroline, the corner of my mouth curling up. "Still trying to be my own grown-up, y'know? Wouldn't be fair to throw a baby into that."

I'd say more, but this isn't really the place for a deep dive about my mental health and all the reasons parenthood would be a bad idea for me.

"Well, pretty sure throwing babies is frowned upon, anyway," she teases, nudging my knee.

"See? What the f…" By some miracle, I stop myself from dropping an f-bomb in earshot of our tiny firefighter buddy. "What the heck do I know?"

Caroline's red lips twist in amusement and I resist the urge to kiss her.

"I think Jude and Olena'll probably have kids someday, though. He's already basically a dad, personality-wise."

"I can see that." She tilts her head, I'm sure remembering the protective shit he pulled at the arcade.

"So, I figure I'll be fun Uncle Miles, y'know? Spoil 'em, get 'em all wound up on candy and then just…"—I make a pushing away motion—"give 'em back."

"I'm sure your brother will *love* that," she teases. "Be sure to buy them lots of super noisy toys too."

"That's the plan." I laugh. "What about you? You want kids?"

"No."

I have no business feeling relieved to hear her say that. But tell that to my fucking *relief*. I can't deny how my heart twisted in the milliseconds after asking the question, and how her simple *no* had let me breathe again. I clench my jaw.

This is hypothetical. Not about us.

"No?" I repeat, searching her beautiful eyes as the train rounds the haunted houses.

Fuck, if I wasn't already falling for her...

Creepy music and witchy cackles drift out from the smaller shack and strings of orange lights swing in the wind above the entrance where a line of families waits to go in.

"Never had the interest, to be honest." She casts a guilty glance toward the mother in front of us. "I didn't exactly get the best example growing up, either."

"Then how'd you turn out like this?"

"Like what?"

The train chugs along past the second haunted house—the bigger and scarier of the two, a two-story converted barn geared toward teens and adults. A group of teenage boys clusters in the line to get in, bullshitting and joking around, one of them fucking with a lighter.

"Sorry, what?" I ask when I realize Caroline's waiting for a response.

"How'd I turn out like what?" Her expression is open—genuinely curious. She really doesn't know how incredible she is. How taken I am with her.

"Uh," I hedge, dangerously close to spilling my guts. "Well, probably not a human nightmare."

She lets out an adorable snort-laugh. "I deserved that."

"I mean, jury's still out!" I shrug and she whacks me gently in the ribs, reminding me of how she elbowed me earlier. Bumping my knee against hers, I drop my voice low. "Hey, why didn't you tell Ada the truth back there?"

She looks sheepish but doesn't answer.

"You called me your boyfriend."

"I know." Her gaze drops to the basket balanced on her lap.

"Thought we were, y'know, being straight up about this whole thing with—"

"I know," she says again, cutting me off. "It's just... Ada's kind of a newer friend, and I guess it felt complicated to explain in the moment." She fidgets with the edge of the little checkered cloth in her basket, unable to meet my eyes.

"That's not it, is it?"

She sets her jaw. "Maybe someone was eavesdropping. I dunno."

That's not it, either.

"Okay," I say, pushing down the thousand questions fighting their way up my throat. Maybe if I offer up a slice of truth, she'll cop to the real reason. "Can I admit something?"

She looks up, seeming nervous about what kind of bomb I might drop between us. "Of course."

"It felt nice. To hear you say it. To pretend. It's *been* nice to pretend. With you." It's as close as I can get to admitting it. That *pretend* slipped away from me somewhere along the way. That I carry an aching regret about the clock running out. That I wish I could be a better man for her—the type who can give her everything she deserves. "And maybe... I dunno, maybe it felt nice that way for you too."

She swallows and threads her fingers between mine, like I did in the car on the way to the fundraiser that first night—careful, slow, exploratory. "Yeah. I think it did."

Just holding hands like this—for the sake of it—feels strangely intimate considering we've done it a dozen other times before. Because, this time, there aren't any cameras. No one's watching.

"Only a few more days, huh?" The thought claws at my heart.

"Right." Her features cloud over slightly and she nods.

I remind myself she doesn't want a relationship, either. Or, at least, that's what she told me the night of the fundraiser. But something about the way she's looking at me has me wondering if it's still true.

"I was actually thinking," she adds quietly, throwing a hesitant glance my way, "maybe we could stay friends after? I know that wasn't what we talked about, but…"

Hating myself for it, I shake my head. I can't risk my job and everything riding on it. "Your dad was really clear—"

"He doesn't need to know."

I lower my gaze, not trusting myself to stay steady with those crystal eyes pleading with me. I'm fucking tempted, my desperation to keep some scrap of Caroline in my life locking horns with everything logical about our circumstances. But what are we gonna do? Have some secret, half-assed friendship? Risk her dad finding out I didn't follow orders?

"I mean, we could at least talk on the phone or—"

"I can't," I force out. Frowning, I shake my head again. "As much as I want to, I can't risk it."

"I'm sorry. Of course." She blinks, as if trying to snap herself out of getting carried away. "I shouldn't have suggested it. I told you I wouldn't—"

"No, I get it. I do. It's just…" I clench my jaw as I search for the words. "It has to be a clean break, okay?"

"Yeah." Brow pinched, she nods. "Okay." But the slight catch in her voice and the pain in her eyes have me regretting my words.

Her full red lips tremble slightly, and it tugs at something inside me; I've never wanted to kiss her more. And not because I wanna get under that dress.

It's because I'm scared shitless I've found the perfect woman at the wrong fucking time. And, even though I know I have no choice but to let her go, all I wanna do is pull her closer.

The train's brakes screech, jostling us to a stop.

Ride's over.

As we climb off the little train, I keep my fingers entwined with hers, needing her touch to ground me, to anchor me, to keep me from spiraling over this ending too soon. I refuse to spend my last few days with her lost in my head, spinning out and grieving what's still right in front of me. It's like the opposite of that old Joni Mitchell song. I *do* know what I've got, and it's *not* gone. Not yet.

We walk in silence, an unspoken weight between us, until we spot Ada up ahead.

She's talking to a tall, beardy guy dressed like the Dread Pirate Roberts from The Princess Bride, who she introduces as her boyfriend, Jesse. He seems almost confused as he shakes my hand.

Ada cuts a glance over at the teens running the game booth. "Hey, so, I think I can leave the kids to do their thing for a bit. You folks wanna check out the haunted house?"

"Sure," Caroline says, peering up at me with a question in her eyes.

"Oh, hard pass."

"What?" She almost chuckles at my blunt answer.

"Uh, yeah. If you people find scaring yourselves entertaining, fill your boots, but I've got enough trauma for one lifetime." I wink to soften the brutal honesty behind my words. But it's true: I've never liked haunted houses, gore, or thrillers—even before my parents died. My idea of a good time has always been having a laugh, not giving myself nightmares. After all the shit I've been through, I don't need to add any fuel to my anxiety by traumatizing myself on purpose. My nervous system doesn't need that shit.

"Okay," Caroline says. She looks hesitant about leaving me— no doubt still mulling over our conversation on the train.

I'm not thrilled about letting her go either, but I'm not gonna hold her back from having fun tonight.

"Jess?" Ada tugs on the loose sleeve of his black shirt. "You in?"

"Nah, once was enough for me. I went earlier with Marcus and Renee. Think I'm gonna get something to eat."

Caroline kisses me goodbye and, for the brief moment when her lips press against mine, I want to stop time, sink my hands under her warm cloak and haul her against me—make the kiss endless. But, just as quickly as she rose up on her toes, she pulls away, her eyes lingering on mine before she turns to follow Ada across the grounds.

When the girls have left, I turn back to Jesse.

"You wanna grab a bite?" he asks.

"Uh, sure. I could eat."

"Ever had a Japanese hot dog? There's this stand over by the pumpkin patch. It's surprisingly good."

"A Japanese hot dog?" I give Jesse—and this concept—a hefty dose of skepticism.

"Trust me. I used to eat them all the time in Australia. You haven't lived until you've had seaweed on a hot dog."

"Alright, I'm game."

As we head to the hot dog stand, Jesse gives me a sidelong glance. He hesitates another few moments before he breaks the silence. "Hey, uh, this is super weird, but... you look so much like someone I know. It's tripping me out."

"Oh, yeah?" I shrug. "People say I look like my brother, Jude."

Jesse stops in his tracks, yanking up his mask to rest on his black bandana. "You're Jude's brother? No fucking way!"

"You know him?"

Jesse's eyes go wide. "Uh, I work for him!"

"Fuck all the way off. You serious?"

"This town, man." Jesse shakes his head, then inspects me again as we resume our quest for the hot dog stand. "I was gonna say, I'm pretty sure I've seen him wear that exact shirt."

"This *is* his fucking shirt!" I pinch the plaid flannel. "I borrowed it for my costume."

Jesse laughs. "What the shit?"

"I know!"

We pay for our food and find a bench near the stand to sit down and eat. I marvel at the unexpectedly delicious combination of flavors on my tongue. "Shit, this *is* good."

"I know, right?" Jesse asks before taking another bite. He chews for a few moments before talking around his mouthful. "So, what do you do for work?"

"Construction."

"So safe to assume that's not how you met Caroline?"

"No, we, uh..." I pause, settling on the simplest explanation. "We met at the gym. A few weeks ago."

Jesus. Has it only been that long?

My mind sifts through everything the last few weeks have brought—how Caroline has opened up my world just as much as I've opened up hers. I must look like I'm on another planet as we eat, because the sound of Jesse crumpling up his hot dog wrapper and chucking it into a nearby trash can eventually interrupts my thoughts.

I take the last bite of my hot dog and push off the bench to toss out my garbage.

"Is that smoke?" Jesse asks, tilting his chin. He sniffs the air.

"Where?" I swallow and scan the crowd. I can't smell anything other than the hot dog I just ate, but the energy around us starts to shift. Worried murmurs intersperse with a few indistinct shouts. With a quick glance at Jesse, I reorient my gaze to follow his.

Someone runs past us.

"Shit, is that—" he mumbles, then more urgently, "is that the fucking haunted house?"

In the distance, the old barn flickers in a distinct orange glow and a dark gray plume steadily rises into the night sky, lit from below.

No.

Jesse's already taking off running, dodging the throngs of people now streaming in the opposite direction. "Ada! *Ada!*"

It's his terrified shouts that finally cut through my frozen state and get my feet moving—a jog at first, then a sprint.

Caroline.

19

CAROLINE

Fight, flight, or freeze.

The last one seems to be running the show, because I'm stock-still, feet cemented to the wooden floorboards and my heart jackhammering against my rib cage like there's some faulty circuit between it and my brain. Adrenaline floods my system and blood redirects to my limbs. *Biologically,* I'm primed to fight or flee.

But I'm not fighting. Or fleeing.

I'm frozen.

And the building is on fire.

There's shouting and shoving. Someone slams into the wall of the stairwell, letting out a cry of pain in the crush of bodies all trying to get out at the same time.

"Caroline!" Ada grabs my arm, the urgency in her voice bordering on confusion. "Caroline! Come on!"

The curtains had gone up first. It had taken only seconds.

"Caroline!" Ada pulls harder, her panicked face flickering in the fire's orange glow.

Move. You have to move.

My feet finally shift, the rest of my body following suit. Blocked by the mayhem in the stairwell, I search frantically for another way out. The dim red glow of an exit sign catches my eye through the accumulating smoke to my left.

I claw for Ada's arm and haul her back. "This way!"

It's dark, but we keep low and feel our way through a narrow hallway, dodging a ghoulish zombie and shrieking skeletons lit in disorienting flashes of purple strobe light. Creepy music still plays over unseen speakers—an ominous soundtrack to our actual terror. I cover my mouth and nose with my cloak, gasping through the fabric as I cling to Ada's hand.

Finally, *finally,* the back door pushes open and we drag in desperate lungfuls of fresh air as we barrel down the stairs and away from the tinderbox of a building quickly succumbing to the flames.

The screaming and shouting intensify as we round the side of the haunted house and, as we near the front entrance, I claw the hair out of my face and chance a look back. The entire upper floor of the barn is ablaze, sparks and acrid smoke rising into the night above the roofline.

Oh my God.

I can only hope everyone's getting out before it's too late.

Ada coughs and grabs my arm again. "We're still too close! Come on!"

As if to illustrate her point, something cracks from inside the upper level and a bulge of flame billows up, the blast of heat reaching our faces. I shuffle backward before turning to run with her among the crowd of people fleeing the scene.

Along the sides of the path, strings of lights flicker and die out, no doubt having lost their power source to the inferno behind us. It reminds me of that scene from *Titanic,* when the lights extinguished on the ship as it sank—a strange reminder of the way nature can reclaim us, swallow us into the night.

Someone running beside me jostles my shoulder, trips, and grabs at my long cloak, yanking me downward. I stumble and crash into the dirty grass at my feet. The impact triggers a coughing spell and I can't get up again right away.

"Caroline!"

I lift my head, my lungs straining for oxygen.

Miles.

I push to my feet, my eyes darting in every direction.

Where is he?

"Miles!" I call back, voice ragged from the smoke. I drift forward once more but have to stop again to cough.

Wait. Ada. Where's Ada? I know she got out, but I've lost her. I scan the chaotic, panicked crowd—and that's when I see him.

He's backlit against the festival lights, but the silhouette struggling through the crowd of people running in the opposite direction is unmistakable. When he sees me, he muscles past the last few bodies and we collide.

"Oh, fuck, thank God!" His deep voice against my temple is full of pain and relief.

I can't breathe, and I'm not sure if it's from smoke inhalation or the way he's crushing me so tightly in his arms. Maybe both.

He pulls back to look me up and down. "Are you hurt?"

"No, I'm okay," I say; my scuffed knees and palms are inconsequential. "But I lost Ada. She got out... she's..." I scan around us, relief flooding me when I spot her with Jesse about fifty yards away. "She's okay. It's okay."

Sirens wail in the distance and I twist in Miles' arms to face the inferno behind me. Flames lick up from the roof and into the smoke-filled sky, and every window on the lower floor reveals roiling orange flames inside.

Minutes. It only took minutes.

My stomach twists with worry at the thought that someone

might have gotten trapped inside. I want to help but I have no idea how.

My arm is pulled yet again, and I turn to find that, this time, it's Miles.

His stricken face hollows my stomach. "Come on. Please. I need to get you out of here."

"But I think we're—"

"*Please*," he says again, a terrified urgency in his voice. "Just come with me. Caroline, *fuck! Please!*"

"Okay," I say quickly. "Okay."

He drags me through the crowd, weaving us between shocked onlookers and groups of people rushing past with buckets and hoses. Miles ducks us through a gap in the fencing and into the parking area, away from the festival-goers, the noise, the mayhem.

"Miles!" I say, but he keeps tugging me along. "Miles!"

It's only when I dig my heels in that he finally gives in and stops in his tracks, gasping for air. He bends at the waist with his forearms propped on his knees, still clutching my hand. "I just..." He can barely speak. "I just need you to—"

"It's okay," I reassure him, finally wrenching free from his grasp so I can hold his face in my palms. "I'm okay. We're okay."

He straightens, crushing me against him once again, cupping the back of my neck in his trembling hand. "I'm sorry. I'm so sorry."

Why is he apologizing?

"It's alright," I say carefully, getting the distinct feeling that this is about something bigger than the fire. Bigger than my safety. "You're okay."

Still, his shoulders heave and his heart hammers under the palm I have pressed to his chest.

"Hey, hey, look at me. Miles. Look at me."

His face twists in anguish when he draws back to meet my

gaze and then he's suddenly pushing me away, lurching from my arms and toward the space between two parked cars—where he vomits onto the ground.

The faint flicker of fire truck lights reaches us across the dark night and, when Miles finally emerges, wiping his mouth, his face is strangely ashen in the red glow.

"We should sit down," I say. Now I'm the one dragging him along. I find a bale of hay next to the fence and figure it'll be better than the muddy ground. "Sit down with me, okay?"

He slumps down hard and I sink onto the hay bale beside him, tugging him against me.

I squeeze his shoulder, his hand—anywhere I can reach to ground him.

"I'm sorry," he grits out. "You shouldn't be—"

"It's gonna be alright," I whisper, kissing his temple. "I've got you. We're both safe now."

"C'mere." He draws me into him. "Please. Closer. I need you."

Climbing onto his lap, I straddle him, and he pulls me flush with his chest. I kiss his cheeks and his forehead, then bury my face in his neck. "I'm here."

When I turn to cough into my cloak, he stiffens, drawing back to search my face. "We need to get you checked. The smoke..."

"I'll be fine."

"No, it could still make you sick. How long were you in there?" The worry in his expression is intense. "Exposed to it. How long?"

"I dunno. A couple minutes? It's just a cough. I swear I'm fine."

"Are you sure?" He holds my face in his hands, his eyes darting back and forth between mine.

"Miles, I'm sure." I pause, wishing I could reassure him—infuse him with calm. I've never seen him this upset before. This distraught. My next words are tentative. "Are *you* okay?"

He frowns down at some indistinct spot on the muddy ground

beside us. "Yeah, I just... I had this weird hot dog and—" He cuts himself off with a grimace.

I don't buy for a second that he threw up from what he ate, but I don't argue.

"Caroline, I'm so fucking sorry." He looks up at me, his eyes burning and glassy. "I wasn't there. I should've been there."

"Why?" I ask. "You keep apologizing, but none of this is your fault."

"No, I should've come with you. I could've... *fuck*."

"But I wouldn't have wanted you to do anything that made you uncomfortable."

"It doesn't matter! I should've kept you safe! If something had happened to you..." His voice falters as he trails off, the emotion in his words cutting into my chest. "It was my worthless brain that stopped me from going with you. My goddamn fucking anxiety! I should've been there!"

"Miles!" I raise my voice so he can hear me over his own spiraling and fist his t-shirt underneath his flannel, tugging it to get his attention. "Your brain is *not* worthless and this is *not* your fault!"

He pushes against me to get up, and I climb off his lap so he can pace in front of me. He yanks off his beanie and drives his fingers through his sweaty hair. "It *is* my fault."

"How can you say that?" I plead. "You didn't even—"

"No," he says, cutting me off. "My messed-up fucking life is *all* because of me, Caroline! This piece-of-shit brain..." He stabs a finger at the air between us. "It's why I'm a fuckup and an addict, it's why my parents are dead, and it's why I almost lost you!"

My jaw drops. "Hold on. Your parents?"

"Do you know why they died?" He steps closer, welling up with anger and anguish.

I shake my head. He knows I don't.

"Because my ADHD ass forgot my meds at home and my lazy,

selfish fucking solution was to call my mom and beg her to bring them to me. It was dark and raining, and I was too fucking pathetic to walk home to get them myself."

I hate the vitriol in his voice. I've never heard him like this. "Miles—"

"My fucking *uselessness* is the reason they were even driving on that road."

My heart twists for him—hearing the ugly way he talks about himself, the shame and disgust laced in every word. "But you didn't know—"

"It doesn't matter! *I'm* the one who killed them, Caroline!"

"No!" I reach for his face, but he steps out of my grasp like he doesn't deserve to be touched or comforted. "It's *not* your fault!"

"Yes, it is. And I know I don't fucking deserve you. Not for a *minute*." He presses his lips together, his expression anguished. A tear slips down his cheek, lit by the faint festival lights behind me. "But if I'd lost you, too, all because I couldn't suck it up and do the most *basic* fucking thing—"

"Stop!" I plead, rushing to him. I take his face in my hands and force him to look at me. "Stop. Please. Just... God, stop." Tears stream down my face, dripping off my jaw and onto my dress.

Dropping his forehead against mine, he closes his eyes.

"Breathe," I whisper.

He doesn't fight it, and the rigid lines of his body slowly soften against my tentative embrace.

I'm not sure how long we stand there in silence, just crying and holding each other.

"You're wheezing," Miles eventually says.

Instinctively, I clear my throat. "A bit, I guess."

"We're getting you checked out. Come on." He grips tight to my hand as he leads me back to the subdued festival grounds and toward a pair of ambulances parked a safe distance from the fire.

I don't fight him on it; God knows what kind of dodgy chemicals were in those plastic Halloween decorations, after all.

From here, the fire looks like it's under control, but a small crew of firefighters are still working to put out any hot spots.

"Miles!" a voice booms from nearby. "Hey!"

Sitting in the back of the ambulance is a firefighter with his gear off and a blood pressure cuff around one arm. He's big, built like Miles, and his shirt is soaked with sweat.

"Shit, Gus, you hurt or something?" Miles asks.

"Nah, just standard procedure. Gotta cool off and get cleared to go back in." He pauses, scrutinizing his friend. "You good, buddy? Look like you've seen a ghost."

"Not now, man."

"Okay." Gus watches Miles with concern for a moment, then turns to me. "You must be Caroline?"

"Mm-hmm."

The EMT hands Gus a bottle of water before returning to check his vitals.

"And you're Gus?" This isn't exactly how I imagined meeting Miles' best friend. "The one who famously sings to annoy Miles?" I flick my gaze to Miles, but he barely cracks a smile.

Gus chuckles. "My reputation precedes me."

"Is... Is everyone...?" I half ask the question, throwing a pointed glance at the smoldering haunted house.

"Everyone got out safely."

"Oh, thank God." I exhale and fold my arms over my chest, hugging myself in the chilly night air. "Do you know how it started? I didn't see anything when I was in there, and it..." I make a vague gesture, unable to find the words.

"You were *inside*?"

I nod.

Realization transforms Gus' features and his eyes jump to Miles, something unspoken passing between them.

The EMT pipes up. "I heard it was some kid messing with fireworks. Thought it'd be funny to scare his friend and—"

"Wait. What kid?" Concern tinges Miles' raspy voice. "I saw a kid waiting to go in and fucking around with a lighter. He was blond, I think? Kinda stocky. Skeleton T-shirt?"

"Uh, I didn't see him but, apparently, the fool lit the thing, then tried to chuck it out the window. But he missed and it got caught in the curtains."

"Shit," Miles says quietly, almost to himself.

"The curtains..." I say, remembering how they'd gone up in flames almost instantly. "It happened so fast."

"Yeah. You good?" Gus asks. "Any trouble breathing? They'll check you out over there." He tilts his head toward the second ambulance.

"I dunno, I—"

Miles cuts me off. "You're getting checked out."

"Better safe than sorry," the EMT says as he takes Gus' temperature and pulls off the blood pressure cuff. "Go for it. Doesn't take long."

"Okay."

"And hey, nice to meet you," Gus adds. "I mean, minus the shitty circumstances." When I give him a small smile, he returns it and lifts his chin. "Take care of my guy, alright?"

"Yes. Will do." I squeeze Miles' hand, still more worried about him than myself.

"Catch you tomorrow, buddy." Gus stands and heads off, presumably to gear up and get back to work.

It doesn't take long for the EMT at the next ambulance to check me over and declare me fit to avoid a hospital visit. She passes me a bottle of water and sends me on my way.

Miles paces nearby.

I take a drink as I walk over to him, then pass him the water bottle. "Here."

"Thanks." He takes a swig and swishes it in his mouth before spitting into the dirt, then has a proper drink. "I should've said something." Miles frowns at his feet. "About the kid."

"No," I say, grabbing his face to make him look at me. "Not everyone in possession of a lighter is a safety risk. This isn't on you, either."

Why is he so hard on himself?

His voice is hoarse when he finally speaks. "Can we just go? I wanna take you home." He sounds so tired.

"Okay," I whisper.

"And I wanna stay with you tonight." It's not a question.

I nod, pulling him closer, and lean in to kiss his cheek. As I draw back, I slide my palms down his chest, wishing I could erase everything that hurts his heart—knowing that wishing isn't enough. I peer up at him. "Come to my place? I'll draw us a bath."

He gives me an intrigued look, a glimmer of the Miles I know cutting through his still-pained expression. "Bubble bath?"

"Yeah, if you want." I circle my arms around his waist. "Anything you want."

"Anything?" He tucks a stray curl behind my ear.

I nod. "Anything you want from me. Anytime."

He closes his eyes and slips his hands to the sides of my neck, pressing his forehead to mine. "Baby, you can't say shit like that to an addict."

I gently kiss his cheek again, letting my lips linger on his skin. It's an apology. A promise. A plea.

20

MILES

I'm pulling on a T-shirt when Caroline rolls over, her sleepy little frown making me round her bed to crawl back in, big spoon style. Slipping my arm around her bare waist, I skate my fingers up over her ribs and palm her breast, squeezing gently.

"Morning, fancy girl." I nose her neck, breathing her in.

"Mmm?" Caroline stirs, barely awake.

Fuck. She still smells faintly of her fancy lavender bubble bath, and the soft, clean scent brings everything back. Soaking in the tub last night, we'd barely spoken as we slowly scrubbed away every trace of the fire—all the fear, the relief, the vulnerability. She rested against my chest as I washed the smoke from her hair and kissed her warm, wet skin.

Later, she straddled my lap on her bed, never breaking eye contact as she sank down onto me and drew the air straight from my lungs. We kissed the whole time, hair dripping onto our still-damp skin as our tongues tangled in slow, deep strokes that were as unhurried as they were intense.

I held her tighter than I needed to.

She came so hard she sobbed, taking everything from me until we were both wrecked and shaking. Hell, maybe we were both crying. All I know is, for the first time, sex hadn't been about some list. Hadn't been about anything other than *us*.

"Come with me?" I whisper against her bare shoulder, then raise an amused brow when I remember uttering those exact words about eight hours ago—under much sexier circumstances.

"What? Where? What time is it?" Caroline's disoriented questions have me nipping at her neck, kissing her skin with smiling lips.

"The gym. It's about five-thirty, I think."

The idea of leaving her here makes my chest ache. Our connection last night—not only physical, but emotional—rocked something deep inside me. Inside her too; I'd put money on it. And there's no way it was just the fear factor or some kind of trauma bond.

Would that be trauma bonding or bonding over trauma? Is trauma superglue a thing?

Whatever you'd call it, there was already something real growing between us even before last night. The fire didn't create it out of thin air. Only cemented it.

She rolls over to face me. "Aren't you meeting Gus there?"

"Yeah, but you should come with me." I kiss the confused furrow on her forehead, certain I'm clinging too hard, but unable to stop myself all the same. I'm not sure at what point this inability to let her go becomes unhealthy, but that'll have to be a later-me problem. For now, I'm just grateful my gym bag was in my truck so I could stay here a little longer instead of having to drive home. "Please? Promise to punch any jackasses who try to talk to you."

"What about Gus?"

"Alright, Gus gets a pass. Unless he sings."

"Tell you what: *I'll* punch Gus if he sings." Wiggling closer, she kisses my cheek. "To protect your honor."

"Okay, deal." I chuckle. "Buuuut"—feeling my dick start to get the wrong idea, I shift my hips back—"you're gonna have to get less naked in a hurry, unless you want us to be late."

Raising a coy brow, she drags her fingers down my chest to the waistband of my underwear. "Can't you be my cardio?"

"Oh, don't you fucking tempt me," I murmur against her temple, then tear myself away, climbing out of the bed to grab my shorts. "Come on. We can grab breakfast after. Maybe the deli?"

She sits up quickly, her hair a fluffy, messy halo.

"Oh, *that* got your attention?" I smirk.

She squints as if she's weighing the pros and cons. "And I get to watch you work out in your..."—she gestures at my lower half—"little shorts?"

I'm just pulling on said shorts, but I slow to inspect them. "What do you mean, my *little shorts*? They're normal shorts."

"I dunno. That's, what, a five-inch inseam at most?" She lets out a long exhale, openly ogling me, then crawls over the bed to slide her palms up my thighs.

"You like my slutty little shorts, huh?" I lift her chin.

"Mm-hmm." She nods, then presses a kiss to my stomach, her lips warming my skin through my T-shirt.

"See? Knew you were a big perv."

She grins up at me, then slips her fingers under the hem of my shorts, sliding them up a bit. Tracing her thumb over the tattoo on my left thigh, she sinks down on the bed to inspect it closer. The entire design is about the size of her palm—a detailed honeybee, surrounded by wildflowers. "Why do you have a bee tattoo?"

"'Cause my head's full o' bees?" I draw back, dodging the subject. "Now c'mon. We gotta go." I curl back down to kiss her, then force myself to tear away and wink. "Go get those slutty little yoga pants on."

Amusement dances in her eyes, but there's something more

lacing her expression: a kind of *cut-the-crap* look I'm all too familiar with. She doesn't move from her perch.

Honesty.

"Okay, fine." I step toward her again and brush a frizzy curl back from her forehead. I attempt to tuck it behind her ear, then frown when it springs back. "It's for my mom. She was big into gardening. Loved the bees."

"It's beautiful," she says quietly. "I assume you've got one for your dad as well?"

I contort my left arm so she can see the simple semicolon on the back of my triceps—one of many in my hodgepodge of a collection. "He was a high school English teacher. But it also means... y'know, I could've stopped, but I didn't. Didn't give up." When she's silent for a beat too long, I add, "Anyway, congratulations, now you know my secret; I'm a huge dork with a punctuation tattoo for my dead dad. Can we get going now?"

Without speaking, Caroline climbs off the bed and tugs me into her arms. She kisses my neck, then my cheek, before nuzzling into my chest. Her voice is muffled against my T-shirt, but I can still hear the emotion in it when she says, "I'm so glad you didn't give up."

I've barely been home in three days, Caroline and I having come to some kind of unspoken agreement to spend these last few days before the election together. Ever since the fire at Sonora, it's like we've dropped every pretense of our relationship being fake. I can only assume it'll hurt more to pull the plug this way, but I can't seem to get enough of her and I refuse to sleep at home unless she's with me. I think we're both milking this little bubble of denial for all it's worth, but staying at her place has also made practical sense, what with her needing to be around for her grandfather. At least I finally got to meet the guy. Now I understand how Caroline got to be so kindhearted, despite the judgy, bullshit example her parents set.

"Smells great in here!" George shuffles into the kitchen with his walker.

"Hey," I say, throwing him a grin over my shoulder. "Almost ready here." I turn back to my task, scooping steaming portions of spaghetti and meatballs onto three plates. I'm not usually a fan of cooking for myself but, for some reason, it's easier when Caroline's keeping me company. And I make a kickass spaghetti—when I'm motivated, anyway. It's one of the dishes Mom made sure Jude and I learned to cook for ourselves. We survived off a lot of spaghetti in those early days after our parents died. It's like a weird mix of grief and comfort to eat it now, which is probably why it felt right to make it tonight, on the cusp of this thing ending.

Right now, Caroline is the source of all my comfort and, in a matter of days, she'll be the reason for all my grief.

"Grandpa," Caroline starts, turning from the sink where she's washing a few dishes, "did Sadie ever let you know if she could pick up that extra shift next week?" She places a pan on the dish rack and stoops to dry her hands on a nearby tea towel.

"No, I don't think she can. Sounds like that boy of hers is keeping her busy. Teenagers, y'know." He raises his bushy eyebrows, settling into his seat at the table.

"How old is this kid?" I ask. I'd met Sadie in passing the other night; there was definitely an exhausted mom vibe behind her kind eyes, although it was obvious she has a great relationship with George.

"Thirteen, I think?" Caroline answers. "Fourteen, maybe."

"A baby!" I say with a smirk. "I remember being thirteen. When Gus and I weren't falling off our skateboards, we were just trying to figure out a way to see some boobs."

Caroline pauses gathering cutlery from a drawer to nudge me, glancing toward George with wide eyes.

"Shit, sorry. I mean..."—I clear my throat—"or... dang, sorry."

"Believe it or not, darling," George says to Caroline as I place the plates of spaghetti on the table, "I was once a young man, myself."

She takes a seat across from him. "I don't believe you were anything but a fine, upstanding young man." Twirling her fork through her pasta, she throws a pointed look my way.

"What was that for?" I ask, faking shock. "Are you implying you don't think I was *fine and upstanding* in my youth?"

"Oh, please," she teases. "You've got *former teenage menace* written all over you."

"Wha—?" I scoff. "Me?"

She only lifts a brow.

"Yeah, alright." I cave immediately, reaching for my water as I throw her a wink.

George swallows and wipes his mouth on a cloth napkin. "Appearances can be deceiving, Caroline."

"Yes, I know, which is why Miles here isn't fooling me for a second."

"No, sweetheart," he says, leaning closer to her. "I meant *me*."

"*You?*" Caroline sets down her glass.

"You think I was born with white hair and a crossword puzzle in my hand?" At the amused tilt of her head, he adds, "I got up to mischief back in my day, like any young man."

"What kind of mischief?" I ask, too curious not to press for a story.

"Well, I met my late wife when we were juniors in high school."

A soft sadness takes shape in Caroline's features at the mention of her grandma.

I reach under the table, gently stroking her thigh through the silky, billowy fabric of her skirt.

George places his fork beside his plate, sitting back in his chair. "I used to sneak out every Sunday night, run the five blocks to her house, and hop the back fence just to see her. I'd throw pine cones at her bedroom window."

Caroline's face lights up as she listens. "Why every Sunday?"

"Couldn't wait to see her at school Monday morning," he says simply.

The corner of my lips lifts, and I can't help but cast my gaze to Caroline, catching a flicker of something like understanding in her eyes when they meet mine.

"Nancy would always tear a strip off me for taking the risk," George continues. "Risking waking up her parents, that is. But I could tell she was just as happy to see me as I was her."

"See, but that's romantic," Caroline says, propping her chin on her fist. "Sounds more sweet than mischievous."

"Oh, don't give me too much credit," he cautions, picking up his fork again. "I also enjoyed getting a glimpse of my girl in her nightgown, if I'm honest."

Caroline's jaw drops. "Grandpa!"

I point at George and throw a knowing look her way. "See? Boobs."

She knees me under the table and I flinch. "Hey!"

We return to our food, exchanging a few casual comments between comfortable silences. It's nice having a family meal like this. Jude and Olena have me over for dinner often enough, but sometimes I feel like a third wheel—or like they're trying to check up on me by inviting me around.

"How did you know Grandma was *the one*?" Caroline asks George out of nowhere.

Don't say boobs. Don't say boobs. Don't say boobs.

"Oh! Well..." he starts, taking a moment to think before he

finally says, "I suppose I just knew, darling. No question in my mind. It was easy with her. I was always happiest when we were together and, when we were apart, well, I was always thinking about her."

"So, you two were together a long time, then," I say, doing some rough mental math. "If you got together in high school, that's what—?"

"Seventy years." He nods. "Sixty-five married."

"Wow," I say, raising my brows in genuine awe.

"My first love and my only love." George straightens in his seat. "When you find a good thing, you don't let it go. Even during hard times, you make it work. You know, when I was stationed in Korea, we'd write to each other every chance we got. I carried a picture of her in my breast pocket. Told her in my letters she had me on cloud nine... when, really, I took her up to cloud nine with me." He pats his chest, giving me a wink.

Catching his meaning, I ask, "Air Force?"

He nods. "Flew an F-86 Sabre in '52."

Under normal circumstances, I'd have a thousand questions about what it's like to be a fighter pilot, but all I can do is give him a small smile—hoping like hell my face doesn't give me away. That it's not obvious I'm thinking about his granddaughter.

When you find a good thing, you don't let it go.

"I know you miss her." Caroline reaches out to squeeze George's hand. "I do too."

The emotion in her eyes is raw. I can't know for sure what's going through her head right now—whether her grandfather's words have also hit *her* on a deeper level—but the only thought running a loop in mine is: I don't want to let her go. I don't want to fucking *miss* her.

Stuffing another bite of spaghetti into my mouth for something else to focus on, I try to let them have a moment. Try not to stare.

Gus had called me out just this morning for staring at Caroline across the gym, reminding me not to let him drop the barbell on his throat when I was spotting him on the bench. I told him to fuck off, of course—but he wasn't wrong. He could tell from the dopey look on my face what I've been trying not to admit to myself: I'm gone for this girl. *So fucking gone.*

Caroline excuses herself to use the bathroom and I stand to clear our plates, almost grateful for the interruption so I can get a handle on my thoughts.

I'm busy rinsing a few dishes at the sink when George sneaks up on me.

"Oh, hey, I got this," I say. "You didn't need to get up."

"Nonsense. I may be slow, but if I sit around all day like a lump, I'll go batty." He parks his walker and shifts his grip to the counter beside me. "Now, you pass me whatever you've got there, and I'll load the dishwasher."

"Okay," I start, then pause when I realize I'm not sure how to word what I want to say next. "Uh, this might sound weird, but you seem so... different... than Caroline's mom." I pass him a dripping plate. "I mean, from what I know of her, anyway."

I'd only briefly crossed paths with Valerie at the fundraiser, but the impression I got has been tough to square with this sweet old man offering his help with the dishes. It's easy to forget she's George's daughter—especially knowing she chose to marry a judgmental ass like Pete Brennan.

"Yes, well..." He slots the plate between the prongs on the lower rack. "My daughter was born for the finer things in life. Finer things than we could give her, to be frank."

"Yeah?"

"Oh, yes. Always had stars in her eyes, that girl. Wanted the latest fashions, the most expensive shoes. When Pete came along... well, he was able to provide something we couldn't. She went headfirst into that life and never really looked back."

"You two close at all?" I ask, remembering Caroline saying things are often strained between her and her mother. But there seems to be a kernel of love between them despite it all; Valerie had been shocked and upset—and rightly fucking so—when she found out about the fire on Halloween.

"Wish I could say we were," George says. "But I'm glad she's found something that makes her happy. At least, I hope she's happy. I'm not sure sometimes, to be frank." His expression is a bit sad. "But I'll give credit where credit's due: she looks after me. She's a good daughter, even if we don't relate much, you know?"

"Of course."

"And she gave me one very special treasure," he adds, leaning in slightly. "I know I'm not supposed to have a favorite grand-child, but,"—he pats a weathered hand on my arm—"between you and me, Caroline's had that title since she was knee-high to a grasshopper."

I grin, dropping my gaze to the dish I'm holding before passing it to George.

"She's always been easy to love," he adds—like it's an afterthought.

My amusement falters.

Shit, a little warning before you drop that mic next time, George.

I can only nod as I shut off the faucet. Wiping my hands on a tea towel, I try to figure out how to respond.

"What are you two talking about?" Caroline's voice rescues me from over my shoulder and we both turn.

Between that flowy navy skirt, her striped T-shirt, and the little scarf thing she's got tied around her neck, she reminds me of a flight attendant—in all the right ways. She's perfect.

"And Grandpa," she adds, "you don't need to help clean up. Miles and I can—"

"Bah," he says, waving her off. "It's good for me to get off my duff. Plus, now it's all done and you two can go enjoy the rest of your night. I'll get out of your hair."

She flicks a glance my way before returning her attention to George. "You gonna go read?"

"You bet." He turns to me. "Thanks very much for dinner, Miles." As he shuffles past Caroline to grab his walker, he nudges her arm. "This one's a keeper."

I drop my gaze to my feet and let my hips fall back against the edge of the counter.

If only I was.

My shame-filled confession on Halloween sharpens into focus, knotting my throat.

In my peripheral vision, Caroline moves away, clearly no more eager than I am to address the topic of whether we get to *keep* each other. Because we don't.

When I look up, she's wiping down the counter with a far-off expression on her face.

Gus warned me earlier to keep my priorities in check.

Sobriety first.

I know he's right. And maybe I'm replacing one addiction with another, like Tiffany had said at the AA meeting. Still, something in my chest reaches for her—something that runs deeper than any craving.

I come up behind her slowly, closing my eyes as I graze my nose over her temple. "Leave it for tomorrow," I whisper.

"It'll only take a minute," she replies, her voice slightly breathy. "I shouldn't"—she inhales as I gather her hair in my hands, lifting it from her neck—"shouldn't procrastinate."

"Oh," I rasp against her neck. "Don't be so sure."

She laughs and drapes the cloth over the faucet, then turns to face me.

I let go of her hair, brushing it back from her cheeks.

"Is that right?" she asks, arching a brow.

I cradle her face in my palms. "Trust me, I'm an expert procrastinator."

"That another one of your ADHD things?"

"Yup. And I know we can find something better to do than fucking *cleaning.*"

"Well, then," she starts, playing with the small buttons on my Henley, "you'll have to tempt me away with something better than a clean kitchen."

"Pffft," I huff immediately, sweeping my thumb over her cheek. "Easy."

But my teasing tone is a bluff, because what I truly want to offer her is anything but easy. The easy version of me isn't the one standing in front of her. Not yet. Instead, I focus on what I *can* give her. Leaning in close, I slip my fingers into the hair at her nape and grip tight, a slow smile spreading over my face when she gasps.

"How 'bout I make you come so hard you can't *remember* the kitchen." I let go and back away, sliding my hands down her arms until I finally let go of her fingers, one cocky eyebrow raised.

Yeah. Proud of that one.

Borderline cheesy but still pretty hot—and the look on her face is priceless.

I hold her gaze as I continue to walk backward, motioning for her to follow me. But the universe humbles me almost immediately, because I clip the sharp corner of the countertop. "Ah!" I buckle slightly and grab my hip as the impact zings up to my brain.

That's gonna leave a mark.

"Shoot. You okay?"

Rubbing my hip to dissipate the pain, I play it off like the Black Knight in *Monty Python and the Holy Grail.* "It's just a flesh wound."

"Alright, smooth operator," she deadpans, walking toward me with her lips twisting in obvious amusement.

I throw her a flirty smirk, still not turning around as I continue to back up because I *never fucking learn*. "Would you believe me if I said I wasn't watching where I was going because I was so"—I whip out the finger guns—"*distracted by your beauty?*"

"Riiiiight." She lifts her chin, clearly not convinced, and guides me to turn around and walk forward to her room. "It's too bad I wasn't filming that, actually, or your little yelp could've been the next viral mashup."

"*Little yelp?*" I pull an over-the-top, incredulous face as we push through her bedroom door. "What am I, a chihuahua?" I drop my voice deep. "You mean *great big manly guffaw!*" With a growl, I spin to pick her up, booming cartoonish and increasingly ridiculous sounds of surprise between the kisses I pepper over her face and neck.

"Miles!" she pants between peals of laughter, wriggling in my arms and slapping at my shoulders. "Put me down!"

I toss her onto the bed and crawl over her.

Her eyes catch on the inside of my left arm, and she does a double take. "Wait, wait—"

"What?"

"Your tattoo..." She scrambles to sit up, pushing me back so she can grab my arm and shove my T-shirt sleeve out of the way to get a better look. "Is this a *ham*? How have I not noticed it before?"

"Uh, I dunno." It's small and blends in pretty well with the rest of the ink covering my shoulder and upper arm; I'm not surprised she missed it. I raise a brow. "Maybe, when I've had my clothes off, you've been a little distracted?"

"Yeah, but- but—" she sputters, searching my face. "You have a *ham* tattoo."

"I do." I grin at the wonder in her eyes. "For my Grandpa. Remember? He used to call me a—"

"Oh my God!" she laugh-groans, pulling me by the neck until we both topple back down to the bed. "You're killing me here."

"What?" I ask through a chuckle, though it's muffled by the way she's smushing my cheeks together.

"You have no business being this adorkable *and* sexy at the same time."

I laugh again. "You're one to talk, with all your *oh dangs* and, y'know, getting me hard just by existing and shit."

Biting her lip, she runs her fingers through my hair, and I drop my forehead to her sternum, kissing her between her breasts through her T-shirt. She rests her arms lazily over my shoulders, and I lift my head.

As I smile up at her, two truths hit me at the same time: I'm deeply, painfully, irreparably in love with this woman... and losing her is gonna hurt like hell.

21

———————

CAROLINE

I'm unpacking a shipment of art supplies for the paint-and-sip night I've got planned at the gallery when Miles pulls open the front door, and I can't help the way my entire body lights up when I see him. And I need light. Election Day has felt nothing but heavy so far.

"Hey," he says, holding up a plastic bag. "I know it's not your break time yet, but I grabbed you lunch from the deli."

"Aw, thank you," I say, closing the distance between us before I push up on my toes to kiss his cheek.

I'd woken up to my period this morning, unsure whether the dull ache in my belly was cramps or dread. Likely both. Miles had been so sweet when I told him and rubbed my lower back as I curled up in the fetal position, waiting for the painkiller to kick in.

We'd voted before the sun came up, swinging by the ballot drop box before Miles started work. With only the faintest orange glow over the mountains across Black Bear River, it had felt almost clandestine and yet somehow so anticlimactic. We could have waited to mark Election Day by casting our votes in person, of course, but I'd shied away from any chance of facing the media at a voting center. I'd wanted to be alone with Miles one last time —and wanted privacy when I, for the first time in my adult life, saw my dad's name on the ballot and left the little circle beside it blank. As acts of rebellion go, it's minuscule, but it felt symbolic. I'm trying new things—like supporting politicians who've earned my trust rather than broken it.

Miles hands me the bag, squeezing my fingers in a way I know means he'd show me more affection if I wasn't at work. "Figured you could put it in the fridge for a couple hours?"

I peer inside, catching a glimpse of something that looks like dark chocolate beside the wrapped sandwich.

"Got you a cookie too. Chocolate's good for period time, right?" He cups my jaw, brushing his thumb over my cheek.

"It's perfect."

His sweet gesture would be swoon-worthy if it wasn't a painful reminder that today's our last day together.

My heart heavy and raw, I search his eyes for reassurance and finger the edge of his hi-vis vest. "You still okay to come with me tonight?"

He draws back a bit, like the answer should be obvious. "Of course."

Election results at Pete Brennan headquarters. Our final photo op together. My throat tightens at the thought.

"Caroline, darling?" Sunny's voice wrenches me back to the present, and I turn just as she rounds the corner into the main gallery space, trying to hide the way my stomach sinks when I feel Miles put some space between us. Sunny pulls her reading glasses down from her hair to peer at the open binder in her hands. "We need to finalize the table arrangement for tomorrow night. We've got an odd number of registrations, so we'll have to stagger the —" She stops short when she finally looks up and sees Miles. "Oh! It's you again."

Sunny's observation is neutral enough, but my expression is

somewhat pinched as I send her a silent plea not to go on about the noise or the service interruptions this time—as if Miles is personally responsible for any of that.

"Yeah, hi," he says. "I was actually just taking off."

I spin to face him, sure the disappointment is written all over my face. "Already?"

"Yeah." He shoots me an easy smile that I know is covering up something neither of us want to face in front of Sunny.

He's already pulling away from me.

"Gotta get back to work." He squeezes my hand again. "See you later, okay?"

I nod, my gaze lingering on his back as he pushes out the door and jogs across the street.

When Miles disappears from sight, a surge of anguish lurches up and there's a burning feeling behind my eyes. I take a deep breath, reminding myself that my hormones are amplifying everything.

Needing a moment to collect myself, I make my excuses to Sunny and go to put the sandwich in the office fridge.

Last night, while Miles was out at an AA meeting, I'd talked with Adrian for over an hour on the phone. We'd been well overdue for an epic heart-to-heart and, given everything that's gone down in the past week or so, there was plenty of material to cover. By some miracle, my name had—for once—stayed out of the news coverage that followed the Sonora Farm fire. I suppose it was thanks to the darkness and general mayhem that I'd escaped notice, but it meant having to drop a bomb on Adrian. Unfortunately, it was only one of two.

He took the news about Dad withdrawing the donation about as well as learning I'd been caught in a burning building. And, as if that wasn't enough heavy reality for one conversation, I told him about what happened afterward: Miles' panicked vulnerability. The shift between us. The way we've barely left each other's sides since.

Explaining it all—and admitting how hard I've fallen for Miles—had me in tears. I know I have no business feeling disappointed that this thing is ending, but my heart is breaking all the same.

"Care, you have to tell him," Adrian said. "This doesn't sound one-sided."

I know he's right. But hesitation twists at my stomach all the same.

Miles had been clear from the start that he couldn't get into a real relationship; he even said on Halloween he needed a clean break. So what's the point of laying my heart at his feet when I know he's gonna walk away? He *has to* walk away.

Still, I feel like I'm losing something incredible in slow-motion and I'm powerless to stop it.

When I finally drift back into the gallery space, there's a shrewd look in Sunny's eyes that reminds me of Grandpa. She closes the binder. "Have I ever told you about how Julian and I got together?"

"What?" I say, almost on reflex, then remember myself. "Uh, I mean, no?"

"Believe it or not, he wasn't always a stuffy old grump."

I stifle a laugh at her unexpected bluntness and tuck my hands into my trouser pockets.

She leans closer, dropping her voice a little and peering up at me over her glasses. "He was a stuffy *young* grump once upon a time."

This time, I do laugh. "Okay?"

"Our families didn't approve. And not just because of his mumbly grumbling." She winks. "My parents wanted me married off to a good Korean boy, and his parents, well, I don't think they knew what to make of me, swanning about the place with my *emotions*." She clutches her chest, her features drawn and dramatic. "It wasn't easy being an interracial couple in the eighties, let alone being such polar opposites. But you know what they say…"

"Opposites attract," I finish for her, unable to resist a quick glance across the street.

She nods. "Julian wouldn't even propose for years. He loved me, don't get me wrong, but he didn't think we'd ever be accepted. We came from different worlds, you know. And the more I badgered him, the more he dug in." She rolls her eyes. "You know how he is. God love him, but the man moves slow as molasses."

I smirk, almost to myself.

Ain't that the truth.

"But, little by little, he saw things were changing. He eventually came around. And darling,"—she pats my arm—"it hasn't always been easy, but he was *worth waiting for.*"

A tight sensation squeezes my throat and I can only nod.

"Now!" Sunny claps a hand on the binder in her arms, and I almost jolt. "Let's sort out this infernal table chart, shall we?"

In a trance, I drift to her side and peer over her shoulder as she flips to the registration list for tomorrow night, blinking to clear my vision when the names blur. I try to steady myself as Sunny's words sink in.

She's all sweeping arms and jangling bracelets as she gestures about the gallery, talking through her thoughts on where everything will go. Once we've agreed on a physical setup, she snaps the binder shut and passes it to me.

"Thanks," I say, hugging it against my chest. "For your help, obviously, but also for sharing with me about you and Julian. I had no idea you'd had a whole star-crossed lovers backstory."

"Yes, well, thankfully ours didn't end in tragedy." Her face suddenly lights up. "Speaking of good news, though, Julian said he'd be open to looking at suggestions for a few new artists. The ones you've been following?" She waves vaguely in my direction. "The young local artists."

My eyes widen. "What, really? Are you serious?"

"Yes! But remember, darling," she says, a note of caution in her voice at my obvious excitement, "*molasses*. I promise nothing immediate. You'll have to give him time."

"Of course," I rush to say. "But it's a first step."

Sunny pats my arm again. "It's a first step."

I DON'T HEAR Miles come into the bathroom; everything is drowned out by the hiss of water, the overhead fan, and the ache in my lower belly. I'm turning under the shower spray, trying to angle the heat to take the edge off, when I hear a distinct clink of metal on tile. A few moments later, he drags the curtain open and I look up.

Oh, hello, beautiful naked man.

I may be in pain, my brain exhausted and my emotions raw, but I'm never too tired to drink in the sight of this man without his clothes on.

He climbs in silently, then hisses at the temperature I've adjusted to, scrambling to lower the heat to something more human-friendly.

"You're gonna cook yourself in this, Jesus Christ!"

"Sorry," I say and, when the temperature settles, I fall forehead-first into his inked chest, tucking my arms up between us.

Don't leave me. Or this shower. Not ever.

He wraps me in his embrace and kisses my wet hair. "You okay?"

"Not really."

"What can I do?"

"I dunno. *Remove my mutinous uterus* seems like too big of an ask."

"*Mutinous Uterus.* Sounds like a punk band."

I laugh, albeit a bit sadly, and try to get closer, wishing I could climb into his skin. "I guess it does."

"Sorry to say, I'm definitely unqualified for that level of surgery." I can hear the amusement in his voice without even looking up. "I could probably manage splinter removal at best. Any less invasive options?"

I groan into his skin.

"Hey," he says quietly. "I know this sucks." I'm not sure if he means my cramps or the unspoken dread looming over us both.

"Yeah."

He reaches down between us to adjust his erection, pressing it against my stomach.

There's something strangely comforting about knowing that simply being with me makes him hard.

"There is one thing we could try."

I lift my head, a skeptical pinch between my brows.

"They say orgasms help." He dips down to kiss me before I draw back.

"What? But I have my period."

He shrugs. "I mean, we're already in the shower. And a little blood doesn't bother me. Between my job and my clumsy-ass ADHD brain, I'm always bruised or bleeding and I don't even know *why* half the time."

"Is that supposed to be encouraging?"

He grins and kisses me again, slipping his palms down over my ass. "I'm just saying. I could help you out. It's not a big deal for me."

I think for a moment. "Maybe it would be okay. I don't think there'd be any... I mean, I use a cup, so..."

"And I can, y'know, stay on the outside." He squeezes my ass hard, then chuckles softly against my cheek. "Why do I feel like we're talking in code here?"

I smile, then let out a little moan when he squeezes again. "That feels really good."

"Yeah?" He does it again, kneading into the muscle as I slide my arms around his neck. Slowly, he works his way to my hips, his firm grip distracting me from the dull ache I've been living with most of the day.

"Thank you," I murmur against his lips.

He turns us so my back faces into the shower spray and starts to massage my thighs.

I groan at how good it feels, but my breath catches when he slowly drops to his knees. "Are you...?"

"Not gonna do anything you don't ask for, don't worry." He blinks up at me as tiny, rogue droplets jump past my shoulders to speckle his cheeks. He gently kisses my tummy, lingering there like he can erase the pain. "You're in charge."

Still massaging my hips and thighs, he lowers to rest on his haunches, then works his strong hands up to my glutes again. Anticipation moves through me in dull pulses, everything about today making me feel sluggish and slow. I want him to draw this out. Suspend time so we can stay in this moment, never having to face the cooler air, getting dressed, traffic, my parents, cameras, questions.

Goodbyes.

He's hard and ready but he doesn't push me. Doesn't seem to have his sights set on any outcome other than making me feel good—whatever that looks like.

"Tell me what you want." He kneads my calves, and I comb the wet hair back from his forehead with my fingers.

I want you.

I love you.

Holding the words back makes my heart feel like it's dying. I can't have him. So I settle for what I can have—what he can give me.

"I want you to make me feel better." Shifting on my feet to widen my stance, I run my thumb down his rough cheek, over his small scar, then his bottom lip. "You're so good at making me come."

His cock pulses. "You want my fingers?"

"No." I shake my head. "Just your mouth."

I've barely got the words out when he groans and dives for my clit, the warmth of his tongue making me suck in air and scramble for purchase on the cold tile. "Miles, oh my God."

He breaks away for a second to say, "Hold on to my hair. I've got you," then again to add, "Don't be shy about pulling it, either." Eyes burning with heat, he buries his face between my legs again.

"Yeah?" I thread my fingers into his wet locks, gasping with every flick of his tongue as pulses of blissful sensation course through my body. "I guess we can both like having our hair pulled." I drag my fingernails over his scalp before grasping tight —tugging him closer—and relish the low, satisfied moan that rumbles from his throat.

He keeps kneading my muscles as he coaxes me to the edge, and I can't get enough of the hard press of his fingers or the way he's working my legs so thoroughly I think my knees might give out.

Both literally and metaphorically, there's freedom in trusting that, if I collapsed completely, he'd scoop me up. Put every piece back together.

It's not long before I'm completely lost to the pleasure, coming undone in mindless, convulsing, shaking waves on his tongue. Letting myself go in this moment feels like succumbing to beauty and despair all at once.

La petite mort, the French call it. *The little death.*

I'M quiet when Miles zips me into my simple navy dress. I duck back into the bathroom to start on my hair while he gets ready, and I'm midway through slathering mousse between my palms when my phone rings.

Miles brings it over to me, turning it so I can see the call display.

I hold up my mousse-covered hands, gesturing to the phone. "Can you answer it? Just put him on speaker."

He swipes and taps at the screen as I drag the product through my hair.

"Hey, what's up?" I ask.

"*Finally!*" Adrian says. "I've been trying to call you forever."

"Sorry, I was in the shower."

Miles smirks and rubs the back of his neck, the movement dragging my eyes down the strip of bare, inked skin peeking out from his unbuttoned dress shirt.

"Have you talked to Lover Boy yet?"

I freeze, feeling all the blood from my face drain into my toes. My gaze jumps to Miles, whose brows twitch together in obvious confusion.

"Adrian—"

"Like, polls closed, Care. If you haven't told him yet—"

"Adrian!" *Oh, God, please shut up.* "I need to call you back."

"What? What's going on?"

Mousse be damned, I smear a sticky thumb over the red button on the screen.

"Care—" Adrian's voice cuts to silence as the call drops.

"Told me what?" Miles asks carefully.

I swallow. "Nothing."

He studies me. "Bullshit."

"It's nothing. I... It's..." I'm looking everywhere but into those blue eyes. "Damnit, Adrian." I hurry back to the bathroom to wash my hands, scrubbing them a bit aggressively as I panic-spiral about how to explain.

My feelings are *my* problem, not his. I wasn't supposed to fall for him, and telling him will only hurt us both.

"You can talk to me." Miles' voice comes from the doorway behind me. "You know that, right?"

"Not about this, I can't." *Do I sound bitter?*

"Caroline." His voice takes on a harder edge than I'm used to. "Come on."

Frowning, I crack open my hair gel and rub it over my palms. I tilt over to one side and scrunch it into my curls, avoiding the figure looming in the mirror—leaning against the door frame, arms crossed over his tattooed chest. Those arms I've kissed. Those arms that have carried me and pinned me down and held me as I fell apart.

Those arms that won't be wrapped around me tonight. I already ache at the thought.

"We're gonna be late." My voice is quiet. I keep my gaze trained on my reflection in the mirror, though I can feel him staring at me. "You should finish getting dressed."

Eventually, the silence drags my eyes over to his.

"I'll get over it," I add, barely trusting my voice to stay steady.

"Caroline..." His brow pinches, emotion touching every line of his face. He looks like he wants to say more but knows, like I do, that going there will wreck us both.

"I'll be okay." I slap on a brave smile, willing myself to breathe—fighting the way my throat knots around the lie.

Another little death.

22

MILES

The Brennan property is the kind that makes me wonder if it should be called an estate. Surrounded by huge maples shedding leaves in vivid shades of orange and red, the house itself is probably three times the size of the one I grew up in. There are at least a dozen vehicles parked out front, including a local news van, all spattered with rain. A few dead leaves are plastered to their windshields, as if clinging on for one last wild ride before the November temperatures claim them.

Look at me getting all poetic and shit.

I guess falling in love really fucks you up.

I cling tight to Caroline's hand as we head inside, less sure than ever about where we stand but not quite ready to share her with anyone else all the same. Showing up for the Pete Brennan campaign tonight will be our last public appearance together—one last photo op for this fake relationship that's become anything but fake to me.

To *us*.

George decided not to make the trip with us tonight. He

claimed it would be too late for him to stay up, but I suspect he has no more interest in showing public support for Pete than I do.

"You sure you're up for this, fancy girl?" The endearment rolls off my tongue as naturally as my next breath, a bittersweet reminder of how easy everything is with her.

George's words about his late wife drift back to me: *"No question in my mind. It was easy with her."*

My chest feels like it's about to cave in. I may have found *the one*, but that doesn't magically make me ready to be the one she deserves. Doesn't make me *easy* for her.

"Uh, yeah. I think so." Her features are tinged with a sadness that makes me want to pull her into my arms and make promises I can't keep.

Caroline drove us to Seattle in heavy silence after our almost-conversation back at her place. Hearing her tell me she'd *get over it* had been like swallowing hot solder—a burning sensation seared my throat at the implication that there's something here to get over. And, *fuck me*, there is. I'm in so deep I might as well be lying at the bottom of the Mariana Trench. With a shovel.

She'd all but confirmed she's fallen just as hard. The pain in her eyes had said it all.

But, no matter what happens after tonight, and no matter how much it'll hurt to say goodbye, Caroline's given me a gift. She's helped me realize I don't need to keep hiding from what life has to offer. My routines have kept me sober, of course—no doubt about it. But she's helped me see I can loosen my strict death grip on structure without sacrificing sobriety. And I'll never be able to properly explain to her the freedom she's given me.

Not that I'll even get the chance to try.

Fuck.

It hits me all over again that this is it. I don't know how I'm gonna sleep tonight. Alone. I've gotten so used to having Caroline in my arms, her fingers absentmindedly playing with my hair when I lay my head on her chest. The way her heartbeat hammers, then slowly settles after we—

Okay, God, I need to stop thinking about it or I'll fucking cry.

I hang back, letting her lead us into her father's office, suddenly aware that this is her family home—her turf. Naturally, the first person my eyes snag on is Fletcher, probably thanks to some hypervigilant part of my brain scanning for threats. Threats or, y'know, nearby assholes.

The room is busy, full of chattering people huddled in small groups, most of them on phones or laptops. Pete's staff, I assume. Maybe some friends, if the bastard has any.

I squeeze Caroline's fingers tighter when Fletcher heads in our direction.

"Caroline," he says, flicking a level glance my way. "You look nice."

"Fletcher."

The dead-eyed way she greets him—no *hello*, no pleasantries, just his name—makes my chest swell with so much pride that it's hard to keep a straight face.

Fuck him up, fancy girl.

Letting go of her hand, I slip my palm to her lower back. Even through her dress, the warmth of her skin is a familiar anchor in this room teeming with strangers.

Her eyes slide to mine and linger there for a moment.

I hold her gaze, hoping she can read my silent words: *You got this.*

When it becomes clear Fletcher isn't fucking off, Caroline breaks the silence. "So, did you need something, or—?"

"I was actually hoping we could talk. Alone, if possible." Another glance my way, like he's wondering why I'm still here.

"I don't see the point." Caroline's gaze only lands on her ex for the briefest pause before she scans the room, as if showing him she'd rather be talking to anyone else. That, or she's searching for the emergency exits like a nervous passenger on an airplane.

"Please, Care-bea—" He seems to catch himself. "Caroline. Please."

She turns to me, clearly uneasy and probably remembering what went down the last time she left my side at a busy event.

"I'll be right here," I reassure her, despite the way my entire body bristles at her spending even a second with this douchebag. Remembering the cameras—and, let's face it, as a final fuck-you to Fletcher—I dip down to kiss the corner of her lips.

The temptation to keep Caroline away from Fletcher is strong, but she's gonna be navigating this shit on her own soon enough. And, I remind myself, I have no claim on her, despite the way every cell of my body screams she's mine. As of tomorrow, she won't be in my life anymore. Won't be in my arms when I wake up in the morning. My heart twists at the thought.

Fuck, I'm gonna miss the shit outta that.

She cautiously crosses the room with Fletcher and I finally let my eyes jump to the election coverage on the huge TV. The graph of early vote counts shows two nearly intersecting lines, although, I note with satisfaction, Pete's is the lower of the two. But, with heavily overlapping error margins, it's too early to say how the race will pan out.

"Miles." Pete appears over my left shoulder and sidles up beside me, swirling the remnants of a glass of whiskey.

Shit. This is the worst kind of déjà vu.

"Surprised you came tonight," he adds, then drains the dregs.

I frown, darting a quick glance Caroline's way before focusing back on the TV. "You said until the election."

"I did, didn't I?" I can hear the asshole smiling like he just remembered that tiny detail. But I know, like a damn elephant, this fuckwad never forgets. "I have to give you credit, though," he drawls. "You did what I asked you to. You and Caroline seem to have gotten pretty cozy together."

"That's what you wanted, wasn't it?" I can't help the sharp edge in my voice.

"Yes, well." It's one of those responses that says it all without saying much of fucking anything. He gives me a look of low-grade disgust and sucks his teeth. "Maybe a little too cozy."

"It's none of your business how *cozy* we are."

"Ah, Miles, that's where you're wrong."

My teeth grind together involuntarily, and I work to keep my tone even when I speak. "Ever thought about letting Caroline decide what she does with her life?"

God, I need a fucking drink.

The familiar thought floats easily—too easily—into my mind as my eyes fall to the empty whiskey glass in Pete's hand.

He shakes his head as if the idea isn't worth contemplating. "Don't mistake a few weeks of playing house with my daughter for knowing what's in her best interest."

I shouldn't let his comment sting, but it burrows under my skin anyway. *A few weeks of playing house.* I know it's been more than that. To me *and* to her.

"I've indulged this little rebellious phase of hers for too long," Pete says, almost to himself, training his gaze on the TV screen across the room.

"Rebellious phase?" I ask, almost laughing. "She's twenty-eight."

Christ, everything out of this man's mouth is laced with privileged dickhead judgment.

"All the more reason for her to quit acting like a teenager so she can get her life back on track."

"What are you talking about? She has a life in Lennox."

He tilts his head, regarding me with amusement. "Now, Miles, if I didn't know any better, I'd think you were hoping to be a part of my daughter's life. But you wouldn't have forgotten yourself, would you?" He inches closer, lowering his voice. "Wouldn't have forgotten the terms of our deal?"

"*Our deal?*" I echo, trying to keep my voice down. "Don't make it sound like I willingly signed up for this."

He ignores my comment. "It'd be foolish, wouldn't it? To fall for a woman you can't have?"

I huff out a breath, trying to hide the way his words kick me squarely in the chest. Is there anything worse than someone you despise being *right*?

"My daughter deserves fine wines and penthouse suites, Miles." He stares me down, scrutinizing me. "And we both know you're more of a... *tacos and arcades* kind of guy. Isn't that right?"

I knew he'd been keeping tabs on us—through the press and by God only knows what other means.

"You don't even know her." The words feel thin on my tongue. Pathetic. Maybe I'm the one acting like a teenager.

He tilts his head like that's debatable. "Well, starting tomorrow, you certainly won't."

My neck heats, every shred of decency I've worked to build suddenly draining from my body, replaced by a white-hot rage and the overwhelming impulse to punch that smug look right off Pete Brennan's face. "What's your problem with me?"

"Pete!" Valerie appears at her husband's side, smoothing her short gray hair. "The reporter from Cascade News wants a quick interview in about five."

"Excellent." Pete quickly lacquers on a phony mask as his gaze drops to his empty glass, then he looks up at me again, placing a hand to his chest. "Goodness, where are my manners? I haven't offered you a drink, Miles."

Shit. No.

"Uh, I don't—"

The room erupts in cheers and back-patting as the news

update reveals a small surge of Brennan votes, and a camera operator pans around the room, capturing the delighted reactions of Pete's lackeys.

"Well, that's cause for celebration right there." Pete motions to a bright-eyed staffer who looks barely old enough to vote.

The kid hurries over. "Sir?"

"Ethan, top me up, will you?" He glances my way before turning back to the young man. "And bring another one for my friend, here."

"No," I say, but it comes out quieter than intended and the kid is already hustling off, following orders. Across the room, Ethan opens a cabinet and pulls out a decanter, filling two glasses with a generous measure of scotch.

I take a conscious step away, clenching my fists at my sides, and try to command my breathing to steady.

Caroline is still deep in conversation with Fletcher, a frustrated frown marring her features.

What the fuck is he saying to her?

My heart thumps wildly against my rib cage like it's jumping between the two sides of the room, just like my eyes. It's like watching my past and my future.

No, it's not, I remind myself. *Because Caroline isn't my future.*

But she sure as shit isn't just a distraction, either. If things were different... If I was different...

The distinct clink of crystal glassware pulls my attention back to Ethan and the two tumblers he's carrying back to Pete. Saliva pools under my tongue even as my stomach roils.

No. Say no. Leave. Push it away. Anything.

But I can almost feel those familiar neural pathways wake up, yawn, and stretch before blasting electricity through my brain, lighting up every reason to accept the drink.

I'm losing the woman I love. Nothing else matters.

What's one more fuckup, really?

It's what everyone expects from me, anyway.

Relapses are common.

It's only one drink.

Time seems to slow as Ethan passes Pete the glasses, the older man's leathery fingers curling around the second tumbler and lifting it in my direction. As he extends his arm toward me, the amber liquid undulates like an invitation.

It's just one drink. Just one.

"Dad!" Caroline suddenly pushes between us, forcing me to take a step back. "What are you doing?"

"Offering your guest a drink, sweetheart." Pete's smile is as slimy as his fucking personality, but he's holding my kryptonite in his hand and my attention keeps jumping back to that glass of scotch.

"He doesn't drink." Without turning, Caroline reaches back and grasps at me, clumsily interlacing our fingers. An anchor point. I try to let it ground me, but I'm drawn in by something with a much stronger pull.

Fuck me. I just want one drink. Just one sip.

"Oh, what's the matter?" Pete catches my gaze over her shoulder. "Can't hold your liquor, son?"

I swallow the twin flames of anger and shame burning a path up my throat.

"Dad, stop," Caroline begs, her voice breaking. "Put it away."

"See, this is what I mean, Miles." Ignoring his daughter, he steps closer, the whiskey sloshing gently as it encroaches on my space like it's trying to reach for me. Pete drops his voice to avoid being overheard. "You're just not the kind of man who fits in here."

He's right. I hate that he's right.

"Dad!" Caroline turns, her hands finding my waist and her glacial eyes blazing up at me. "We're leaving. Right now."

I don't move, my attention jumping between Caroline, her

father's hateful smirk, and the crystal tumbler still held in his grip.

He swirls the whiskey again and I hate myself for wanting it so much. But I fucking do.

"Miles," Caroline says again, digging her fingertips into my ribs to get my attention.

I finally snap out of it, but shame instantly cuts trenches into my guts. For being tempted. For being an addict in the first place. For letting this asshole bait me, manipulate me, and treat me like trash. Still, however fucked up her family is, the thought of taking her away from them to deal with my bullshit is a bridge too far. "Uh, no, I don't wanna be the reason you—"

"No," she says, cutting me off, her tone leaving no room for argument. "I'm *not* making you go through this again." When she clasps my hand tight, I let her lead me out of the room, down a long hallway, and into the massive foyer. My coat is shoved into my arms and the front door opens to a blast of icy wind. Darkness cloaks us as we cross the driveway to Caroline's car and I welcome the jarring bite of cold, the spatter of rain on my cheeks. Anything to put some distance, some new sensation, between me and what just happened. What *almost* happened.

As I slump into the passenger seat, I try not to cry. Or rage. Or scream. It wouldn't change a damn thing if I did, anyway.

I can't fight this. Can't tell Pete off, can't keep the woman I love. None of it. Not with my livelihood at stake.

Losing my job would be exactly the kind of stressor that tiny voice in my head would love to exploit. He only wants one drink, and I'm terrified that, unemployed and unable to pay the bills, he'd get what he wants.

Because, of course, it'd never be just one.

Caroline takes angry swipes at her wet cheeks, then guns it out of the driveway, throwing me back into my seat.

Jesus, this little electric car can go.

"Whoa, whoa, whoa… Slow down." Eyes wide, I brace my forearm against the door and my throat tightens as the memories flash through my mind.

Dark. Rain. The pair of police officers on our front porch.

"Slow the fuck down, Caroline!"

As if snapping out of it, she eases off the accelerator and the car slows to a less-frenetic speed. "Oh my God, I shouldn't have—"

"You fucking scared me." Heart pounding, I try to reason my way back to calm, clenching my fists to stop my hands from shaking.

Speed hadn't been a factor, the investigators had told us.

But still.

"Sorry! I'm— I just wanted to get as far away as I can from—" With a pinched frown and tears in her eyes, she wrenches her attention back to the road. "I'm so sorry."

"It's okay. We're okay," I say, though we both know it's not and we're not.

Long seconds pass before she speaks again. "Dad was way out of line."

I don't argue.

"He's been difficult plenty of times before," she adds. "Coercive. Controlling even. But I've never seen him be outright *cruel* like that. Maybe he didn't know about you being in recovery. I didn't tell him."

"No," I say, my voice low. "He knew what he was doing."

I'd seen it in his eyes; it was no accident. Plus, he admitted he'd looked into my past the night of the fundraiser. Offering me a drink had been a blatant power play.

She sags against the headrest. "I should never have brought you here."

"I would've come anyway."

Confusion shadows her face. "You can't tell me you wanted to be around these people. My Dad. Fletcher. All the—"

"No." I shake my head, cutting her off. "Fuck those assholes. I wanted to be around *you*."

"Miles..." My name on her lips sounds tired, and she grips tighter to the steering wheel.

"Well, it's fucking true, Caroline!" My chest threatens to crack open.

"Don't." She shakes her head. "I can't have this conversation in the car. Not now. I can't drive while I—"

"When, then?" I ask, cutting her off.

Her shoulders shoot into her neck. "I don't know!"

"There's no good place. No good time. This whole thing has been the wrong fucking *timing*..." My voice breaks on the last word —right as her phone rings.

The goddamn irony.

Sniffing back my emotion, I gesture at Adrian's face on the car's touchscreen and drop my hand in defeat. "Answer it."

She gives me a long look, then draws in a steadying breath before accepting the call.

"Hey," she says, her voice soft.

"Hey. Can you talk?" His voice is cautious this time, like he might have sussed out why Caroline hung up on him so fast earlier.

"Yeah, it's fine." She flicks a glance my way.

"How's your dad taking the news?"

"What?" She frowns. "What news?"

Adrian scoffs. "*What news*? Aren't you watching the election results?"

"No, I... We were, but we had to leave. What's going on?"

"They're calling it," Adrian says. "He lost, Care."

23

CAROLINE

There's nothing but a strange numbness in my chest, which should surprise me given how much I've supported my father my entire life. But there's also relief in knowing this campaign is finally over—and that he won't be holding a higher position of power, especially after what he did to Miles tonight. The truth is, my dad doesn't deserve the role. Doesn't deserve the public's support. Or mine.

Miles shuts down for the rest of the drive home, like Adrian's call interrupting us gave him the chance to think better of what he seemed on the verge of saying. He texts back and forth with his sponsor while I drive, and I'm grateful he has someone who understands the temptation he just faced.

But, the longer neither of us speaks, the more my anxiety prickles and an all-too-familiar coil of dread squeezes my heart. Growing up, tense silences always meant I'd done something wrong.

I'd felt the beginnings of it in the gallery earlier today. Rationally, I know I'm losing him, but my heart can't take the emotional withdrawal. Not from Miles. He's never once made me feel alone, ignored, or abandoned, and I can't stomach the grief I already feel creeping in. There's a cruel loneliness in finally being seen only to have it ripped away. It's like being stabbed with a barbed spear—it does more damage on the way out than on the way in.

I pull into my driveway and park a few feet from Miles' truck. I try to catch his eye but the blue glow from the dashboard lights his cheek as he turns away from me to step out into the night.

Heart sinking, I climb out of the car, tugging my jacket tight around me. The night is cold but clear, the nearly full moon casting a cool glow all around us. We meet behind my car, stopping short of falling into each other like we're trying to get used to something about as natural as trying not to breathe.

I let my unfocused gaze settle on the center of his chest.

"Well," he says, rocking on his heels as he swings his arms in front of him, "it's been a slice."

My head snaps up as he turns toward his truck. "Miles!"

He spins back to me, his smile teasing but laced with pain. "C'mon. Did you think I would really just walk away?" As he shakes his head and closes the distance between us, the moonlight catches the way his eyes have welled up. "Fuckin' c'mere."

I can't pull him against me fast enough—squeeze him tight enough—and I bury my face in his coat to silence my inadvertent sob.

"I dunno how to do this goodbye thing." His voice is a familiar deep rumble against my cheek, even through his thick jacket. He sniffs back his emotion. "Can I be a selfish prick for a sec?"

I lift my pinched face, and he thumbs a tear from my cheek.

"I wish..." He swallows and tries again. "Look, I have no right to say this to you. But I wish this wasn't it. Wasn't goodbye."

I close my eyes. "Me too."

The words are barely a whisper, and I nearly crumple against him when he takes my face in his hands. And then his lips are on mine.

I can't tell what's breaking my heart more—the kiss or the gentle way he's holding me.

Don't leave me. Please.

I never want it to end. Never want to let go. But I know, despite every fiber of my being trying to find some way to ask him to stay, I can't do that to him. I can't risk his job, his sobriety—his *life*—by asking for more of him than he can give.

When our lips part, his regret is potent. "Can't believe I don't get to see you again."

"Maybe we'll cross paths?" The prospect sounds pathetic the moment the words leave my mouth, and I wipe at my wet cheeks. "God, is that the best we can hope for, if we can't even stay friends?"

"I don't think I could ever just be friends with you." The creases in his brow deepen, and he cradles my jaw, brushing a thumb over my cheek. "Wouldn't know how."

I drop my head, feeling like the pain is pulling me into the ground.

"And I fucking hate this, too, okay?" he adds.

My ribs squeeze at his words, but I force a nod.

"Caroline." He lifts my face, but I can't look him in the eye. "You need to know... Fuck, if I could do this—for real, I mean—"

"Stop. Don't say any more, okay?" I shake my head, trying to fight off a fresh wave of tears. I reach for his face, willing time to stop yet resigned to having no such power.

"I'm sorry," he whispers, dropping his forehead to mine. "I'm so fucking sorry."

"For what?"

"Sorry I'm not better. Not ready. Not good enough for you."

"Miles, no... You're everything I—"

"No." He pulls back, his brow pinched in pain. "Your dad... As much as I fucking hate it, he's right. You deserve so much more than this broken mess."

"You're *not broken*," I plead, gripping handfuls of his coat. "*God*, I wish you could see yourself through my eyes."

"No, baby... I'm too fucked up."

Breath rushes out of me. "Aren't we all?"

"Not like this." He inhales like he's trying to steady himself. "Fuck, I wish I was better enough to do this right. But just look what happened earlier. I'm not... I don't deserve you, Caroline, I'm—"

"Stop! I love you!" The words tear from my chest, hollowing me out. "I love you." I say it again, quieter this time, searching his face.

A puff of warm air clouds the small space between us before his mouth meets mine, the taste of salt slipping between our lips. Whether the tears are his or mine, I don't know, and I couldn't care less. Because this kiss cracks me in half. And it's anything but a clean break.

I finally pull away, kissing his cheeks, his jaw, the cleft in his chin. I can't seem to wean myself from his skin as I command my heart to accept what it never will—that I love him and I can't have him.

"Caroline..." The way he whispers my name as he pushes his fingers into my hair threatens to destroy me. I touch his lips, shaking my head.

I don't need him to say it back. And, if he did, I might not be able to do what I need to do.

"I know I told you I didn't want a relationship. And, yeah, what I want changed, but I'm not asking you for one, okay? Because I meant what I said. Back at the arcade." I swipe at my wet cheeks. "I could never forgive myself if I hurt you. If I compromised your recovery. And I've come close enough as it is. Twice now."

"No," he says, the word not much more than a whisper. "It wasn't you. It was never you."

I'm not sure I believe him. It was being in my orbit, after all, that brought him so close to breaking.

And if I'd broken him…

I can't keep doing this to him. Can't keep dragging him into temptation.

"I wish loving you was enough." My voice wavers, and I fight to keep it steady. "I wish *I* was enough."

"God, don't say that. You're fucking amazing."

"I'm not fishing for compliments." I touch his face again. "I just mean, this isn't the movies. Love doesn't fix everything. Cure everything."

"It's really fucking annoying that it doesn't."

A watery laugh burbles out of me and I kiss him again. "Super fucking annoying."

He grins that crinkly-eyed grin I love so much and I try to memorize it. Memorize *him*. The earthy, intoxicating way he smells. That scar at the corner of his mouth. The way he can make me laugh, cry, and melt all in the same moment. He's perfect.

"You were clear from that first night you couldn't do this."

He nods, looking thoughtful. "Almost like I had a feeling this gorgeous fancy girl was gonna trick me into falling for her or something."

"Is that what I did? Trick you?"

"Definitely. I was minding my own business until you showed up. And then you were all like, *be my fake boyfriend!*" He does air quotes, pulling a face. "*It'll just be for one night!*"

I can't help but laugh—as blurry, tearful, and heartbroken as I am.

"See? Trickery." He cocks an eyebrow, sliding a hand down his chest. "And don't get me started on how you took advantage of my body— Hey!" He steps back when I poke his stomach.

"You *offered* me your body, may I remind you."

"Oh, right." His smile is lopsided as he tugs me back against him. "I did that. God," he sighs, looking thoughtful, "I'm a little bit slutty."

I sniff. "In the best way."

"Obviously."

"Thank you," I say, my voice quieter than before, although I can't help the way my lips twitch when I add, "for being my *sex sensei*."

"You're welcome," he murmurs against my forehead. "Sorry we didn't finish everything on your list, though... but, y'know, not a bad gig, in the end."

The end.

The reminder that we're delaying the inevitable makes me feel colder than seconds ago and my amusement fades. I tug up the collar of my coat against the chilly night air.

"I should go." Miles hooks a finger under my chin and lifts my face. His kiss is lingering. Apologetic.

Like they never stopped, hot tears stream down my cheeks once more, cooling quickly in the night air. I scramble to pull him closer, not wanting to let go. When we finally break apart, I step back, forcing some distance between us that feels like fighting gravity. "You're never gonna get out of here if we keep—"

"Okay, okay," he says, squeezing my hands and pressing his lips to my forehead one last time before heading to his truck. He's just opening the door when I call out to him.

"Miles."

He turns.

"I love you."

My words hang between us for a long moment. Maybe I do need to hear him say it back.

Moonlight catches on a tear slipping down his cheek. "Love you, too, fancy girl."

24

———————

MILES

There's this thing with ADHD where you can forget people. *People.* Not some old can of beans at the back of a cupboard—actual human beings. People you care about. People you love. And, if you don't see or talk to them often enough for them to occupy your thoughts, they can just... fall out of the sieve that is your brain. It's basically the most guilt-inducing version of *out of sight, out of mind* imaginable.

Of course, it's not that you *literally* forget they exist. There'd be freedom in that. This is worse. I'll remember I haven't talked to my cousin in a few years and should probably email him but, inevitably, the thought is so fleeting that it's gone before I can do anything about it. I'll be hauling rebar or taking out the trash, and then... distraction. Or, more likely, seventeen different distractions and... *poof.*

It's awful. It's humiliating.

And I've never wished harder for it to happen.

Everything reminds me of her. Fucking *everything.*

It's not like she'd spent that much time at my place but, still, traces of her live in every room, squeezing the life out of me at each turn. The couch she'd sat on in her stunning gold dress, the bed she'd slept in, curled against me… Hell, even opening a drawer to find the hoodie I wrapped around her the night of the fundraiser takes me out. It's been like living with a ghost for the past two weeks.

My phone chirps beside me.

GUS
Gym time.

ME
No

GUS
Be there in 10.

Gus had let me off the hook all of twice before he started showing up at my apartment and muscling me out the door to go work out. Increasingly concerned about my state of mind, he'd dragged me to the beach last week for a change of scenery. The *beach*. In *mid-November*. It was fucking miserable and was *not* made any better by being surrounded by seashells that reminded me of… Well, I hadn't really told him that part. When he'd caught me turning one over and sniffling to myself, I'd started to make up some excuse about Caroline loving the beach, then tearfully confessed the truth. I didn't get too far before he stopped me, looking horrified. Pretty sure he was considering throwing me in the ocean. He probably should've.

Not that it would've helped.

Getting up to answer the buzzer feels like walking neck-deep in tar, every movement taking so much mental and physical energy that I collapse onto the nearest chair, sure I could fall into a coma.

"Get dressed," Gus says when he comes in.

"I told you no," I mumble into my hands.

"It's for your own good. Come on."

I groan and slump lower in my chair. "Fuck off."

"I'll fuck off when you don't look like the guy in the ad *before* he takes the flu meds. Get the fuck up."

I've tried everything in my toolbox. Water, diet, therapy, exercise. Hell, I was even desperate enough to try meditation once. Nearly threw my phone three minutes in. *Imagine filling my body with shimmering, golden light?* Been there, lost her, miserable. Thanks for the fucking reminder.

Somehow, Gus bullies me into gym clothes, his SUV, and, finally, into the gym itself. I wince under the fluorescent lights like a vampire thrust into sunlight, the prospect of lifting anything heavier than my head filling me with catatonic dread.

I'm an orphan and an addict. I've been through grief and withdrawal. This feels like both—compressed, folded, and compounded together in inextricable layers like butter in a croissant. Only instead of light and delicious, it's dark and bitter.

It's possible I haven't eaten much today.

"Do I have to?"

"Yep." Gus shoves me over to the bikes.

The bikes. Fuck.

I stiffen, the memory of Caroline on the bike stabbing me in the sternum. "Not bikes."

He gives me a funny look. "Then get your ass on the treadmill."

"You're a dick." I schlep onto the belt and Gus takes the one to my left. Some sloppy, half-baked part of my brain ponders the possibility that I could run away from this feeling.

"A dick who cares about his best friend. Now move."

My chest threatens to cave in, but before I can start crying about what a good friend he is, he cranks up the speed on my machine and forces me into motion. With legs that I'm sure are ninety percent sand, I clomp along, holding the side rails at first until I find my rhythm and can trust myself not to bite it.

"I hate this," I puff out between breaths that stab my ribs.

"I know, buddy. I know."

It's dark in the grocery store parking lot. Using every available mental resource, I'd mustered up the fucks to buy a few easy meal things, but the prospect of driving home with the food is soul-crushing. I've fallen into the sit pit and can't make myself start the truck just yet.

It's been two weeks since election night. Two weeks since I told Caroline I loved her—*love* her, present tense—and forced myself to walk away. I've lost track of the number of texts I've almost sent, every one deleted when I remembered *I'm* the one who said I couldn't do this. It would be cruel to string her along by staying in touch, but the temptation to call her is goddamn relentless.

I've sat like a zombie through every AA meeting, only catching disconnected snippets of the readings and stories people share. Jude forced me to set up a daily check-in with Barry for extra accountability. Good idea, probably, but I hate needing that much hand-holding from my sponsor.

And I do.

I could really use a session with my therapist, too, but that ain't happening. Lydia picked the worst time to go out of town.

Parked beside me, an exasperated mom loads her kids into a minivan, shouting at them to stop fighting. Her voice is muffled through the window, but I catch something about the noise.

My tired eyes slip from her weary face to the neon sign flickering above the liquor store next to Lennox Foods.

Stop fighting.

The noise.

Temptation is an opportunistic motherfucker and I've taken so much emotional damage that, at this point, I'm an easy target.

I don't remember getting out of my truck, but my pulse pounds in my ears as I pull open the door to Riverside Liquor & Wine, the surge of anxiety an almost welcome change from the depression boulder that's been crushing me into the ground.

It's both a wildly terrifying and completely ordinary thing to do, buying a bottle of vodka like a regular person.

You're not a regular person! the voice in my head screams.

If the checkout guy notices I'm shitting myself, he doesn't let on.

By the time I'm home with the groceries and the booze, the impulsive rush has eased to something more intentional, and a numb detachment settles over me. I set the bottle on the counter next to my phone and keys, then get out a glass, hands clenching as I stare at the curve of the bottle, watching the tilt of the liquid inside settle before I twist off the lid. Closing my eyes, I inhale the familiar smell, blurred and disconnected memories of my drinking days rushing past. The parties, the women, the hang-overs. The drunk tanks. The hospitals. The shame.

My memories of Caroline, in contrast, are crystal fucking clear. Painfully clear. I wish I could blur them. Numb them out. Find relief.

I try for a deep breath, anguish squeezing my lungs.

I've suffered for so long. Worked so fucking hard. And for what?

Sure, my job is safe, but I've lost the best thing that ever happened to me—all because I'm an addict. Just look what I'm about to do, for fuck's sake. I'm weak. Pete was right; I'm not on her level.

My fingers clench around the bottle.

Don't do it.

Images of her flash in my head.

Caroline stepping in front of me, shielding me from the drink in Pete's hand. Caroline's fierce, worried eyes when she insisted we leave. Caroline dragging me the fuck out of there.

Yeah, well, she's not here to save me now.

The bottle shakes slightly in my grasp as I pour a measure into the glass, not bothering to cap the bottle when I set it down.

This is poison. For me, it's poison.

I gently swirl the clear liquid, my vision losing focus.

Pour it out. Call Barry. Gus. Jude. Anyone. It's not too late.

"Miles."

Caroline's tearful voice behind me.

Her sad eyes when I'd turned around.

"I love you."

Then, through tears, I watch myself cave.

25

———————

CAROLINE

When I answer the phone, there's only jagged breathing on the other end of the line. Anxiety tingles in a cascade from my scalp to my toes.

Something's wrong.

"Miles?" I ask softly, slowly pushing up from my bed. "Miles? Are you there?"

"Hey," he finally bites out, his voice thick and rough. "Yeah, I'm here."

"Are you alright? Where are you?"

"At home." He sniffs, letting my first question hang, though I already know the answer. "I know I wasn't supposed to call you."

"It's okay," I say, my throat already knotted with worry.

It's not okay. He's *not okay.*

"I'm sorry." There's a rustling sound, then a whoosh of air. "Just needed to hear your voice."

I pad over to my bedroom door and close it gently, knowing Grandpa might still be up. "Need me to come over?"

"No," he says quickly, then swallows. "Just... just stay on the phone with me, okay?"

My brow pinches. "Of course."

"I just need you. To hear you." A long silence follows before he speaks again. "Tell me something true."

I love you. I miss you. I've been in pieces for weeks. I can't sleep without your arms wrapped around me.

"Like what?"

"Anything. Something small. Something boring. Just talk to me, so I don't... just talk."

So he doesn't what?

The vulnerability in his voice stops me from asking what he was about to say. He sounds too fragile. Too fraught. And, even though I'm sure I know the answer, I can't accept it. Icy fear slips up my spine as I scramble for denial.

"Alright, let's see..." I search my brain, wanting to tell him everything and nothing all at once. I decide against sharing about how my parents booked a last-minute cruise and ditched me and Grandpa, leaving us to navigate Thanksgiving on our own for the first time ever. Whatever our differences, we've always put them aside to spend the holidays together—although I must admit, I'm relieved to have a bit of space from Dad after what happened on election night.

I also decide against telling Miles about Fletcher trying to worm his way back into my life. When he'd pulled me aside in Dad's office, he'd proposed the ludicrous idea of us as some kind of political power couple—getting back together for the optics alone. He even had the gall to suggest we could be non-monogamous if I still wanted to keep Miles on the side. I'm still reeling from the way my soul recoiled.

No. Anything to do with my parents, my dumpster fire of an ex, or the election feels too loaded to share with Miles right now.

Stick to neutral territory.

"I'm working on planning an art show fundraiser just before Christmas."

"Oh, that's great," he says quietly. "From your proposal thing?"

"Yeah. And Julian agreed to let me organize an exhibition in the spring. Young local artists." I wander back to my bed and sink down, tucking my feet under me. "Sunny finally wore him down, I guess."

"I'm happy for you." I know he means it but, somehow, it doesn't sound like he can muster up *happy*.

Not that I've managed to lately, either. I've tried to bury myself in work over the last two weeks, but I end up numbly staring at my laptop most nights, trying to wish away the ache in my bones, the silence in my bedroom, the urge to call or text Miles every time it hurts too much not to. I've sobbed through multiple therapy sessions, never feeling any relief or release. Working across the street from Miles' work site all day has been a torturous exercise in trying to keep my gaze from wandering outside the gallery walls. A thousand times a day, I find myself wondering if he's over there, hating himself for trying to catch a glimpse of me too.

"Ada's working on a few paintings for it." I switch my phone to my other ear, sweeping my hair out of the way. "She's pretty stoked."

"Awesome."

More silence.

"Miles?" My voice feels small, and I bunch the loose fabric of my sweater sleeve in my fist.

"Yeah?"

"Tell *me* something true?"

Static whooshes through the phone.

My heart sticks in my throat, but I manage to squeeze out, "Please?"

Tell me you're okay. Please be okay.

"I'm so tired, Caroline." His voice catches when he says my name. "I've been working so hard. Fighting so hard."

Guilt grips my stomach. I put him in this position—being with me, loving me, being apart from me, is what led him to this wretched, exhausted moment. I've stayed away, knowing it was the right thing to do, knowing he needed to protect his job and focus on himself again. But that doesn't mean it's been easy for him to cope.

"I'm so proud of you." I barely get the words out. "You know that?"

"You shouldn't be. I'm so fucked up."

"No." There's an edge to my voice I can't hide. "You're brilliant and kind and fun and funny, and you work harder on yourself than anyone I know. And you're my favorite fucking person in the world."

There's a long pause before he speaks. "You swore."

I swipe the tears from my cheeks. "Someone once told me it was cathartic."

"Smart someone." He sniffs.

"He's handsome too."

He huffs out a breath—almost a chuckle. "The whole package."

"Exactly."

"I miss you." His strained words catch me off guard, and the air rushes from my lungs. "So fucking much."

I try to steady my voice, sensing he *needs* steady right now. "I miss you too."

"I know I'm an asshole for saying that—"

"No, you're not an asshole." I shake my head, looking up at my ceiling as I roll the hem of my sweater between my fingers. "You're honest."

"I'm scared, Caroline."

"Yeah?" The pain in his voice is almost more than I can bear.

"Scared I'll never be right in the head. Scared my heart will never feel whole. Scared I'll always be too broken for…"

My eyes close.

"Fuck, just listen to the shit coming out of my mouth." His voice is tight. "This is why. This is *exactly* fucking why."

"It's okay to be scared. Or feel like everything's awful. But it doesn't mean you're irreparably broken."

"How do you know?"

"Because I fell in love with everything good in you." My voice breaks as I wind the fabric of my sweater into my fist. "And there's *so much good* in you, Miles."

"I dunno if I can do this." He pauses. "Without you. Fuck, it hurts."

I want to run to him. Wrap him inside my heart and keep him there.

But I know I can't.

"You have to. Promise me you'll keep going. Keep trying. Keep getting better. Because I need you—" I cut myself off before I sob, then try to collect myself. I could stop there: *I need you.* That's it. That's the truth. But I push more words past my lips. "I need you to exist in this world. I need you to be okay."

"Baby, I'm not okay."

The way he calls me *baby* has me squeezing my eyes shut, letting loose a cascade of fresh tears. He sounds so tired—so *done*—that my anxiety spikes again. "Then… I need to know you *will be* okay. Someday. Even if I can't be there to see it. Even if I have to stay away from you to let you get there."

"What if I never am?"

"It'll get easier," I say quietly, unable to entertain his question. I tuck myself under my blanket and pull it up under my chin, wishing I could hold him instead. The solidity of him. The muscle and bone and weight and warmth of him. "With time, I mean."

"Will it?"

I close my eyes again; the last two weeks apart haven't eased the grief crushing my chest. But I have to believe it'll get better—have to convince him it will, at least.

"It has to. So promise me," I say once more. "Actually, no. Scratch that. You owe it to yourself to keep going. Promise *yourself.*"

A memory drifts back to me and I quickly switch the call to speaker so I can take a selfie. The lighting's bad, my hair's a mess, and my eyes are bloodshot, but I don't care. I hit send.

"Did you just send me..." A pause. "Oh, fuck." He lets out a sad sound and inhales hard. "Hey, gorgeous."

"Pinkie promise." My voice breaks. "Send me one back. Please."

"I look like shit."

"Hey," I almost laugh through my tears. "I went first."

"Shut up. You're beautiful."

A few moments later, the text comes in. In the photo, like in mine, Miles is holding out his pinkie.

My chest threatens to crack open at the sight of his tear-stained cheeks and his tired, crooked grin. His hair is shaggy and he's let his beard grow in. I touch the screen, wishing I could touch his face. Wishing I could kiss him and take this pain away.

"Did you get it?" he asks.

"Yeah." I sniff, trying to find my voice. "Sorry, just... distracted by your beauty."

"So fucking cheeky."

I smile to myself. "You look like Jude, though."

Jude.

My eyes land on my laptop as Miles makes a wounded sound. "Well, if that isn't motivation to shave, I don't know what is."

"But seriously." I flip open my computer and quickly search for Jude's contact info online. "Pinkie promise?" I'm not letting him dodge this. "That you'll do it for you?"

"What, shave my sad-boy beard?"

"Miles!" I laugh, wiping at my tears.

"Okay, I promise, I promise."

"Say it properly."

"Oh my God. I already sent you my ugly mug."

"What, you too good for pinkie promises?" I ask, echoing his own words from the night of the fundraiser. "Just say it!"

A long exhale. There's rustling, then a clink of glass on his end of the line—and something that sounds like running water. When he speaks, his voice breaks a little. "Pinkie promise."

26

———————

MILES

Nothing says *I'm in a fucking state* like booking the earliest possible therapy session on the first day your therapist returns from vacation, but I guess I'm that guy. Lydia had given me contact info for a couple backup options while she was away, but I didn't have it in me to start fresh with anyone. So I waited.

Too long, in hindsight.

I'd come dangerously close to throwing it all away the night I called Caroline. The closest I've come in almost a year. But, *thank fuck*, the only place I'd poured that poison was down the sink.

I'm not a religious man but, as cheesy as it sounds, I can't help but think of Caroline like some sort of guardian angel. Not that she'd done anything magical last week; there was no miracle. No divine intervention. All she did was see me and love me and remind me there's good underneath all the hard, ugly stuff. That there's a life to fight for. And, when my brother inexplicably showed up at my place to check on me that night, I'd known she'd also found a way to make sure I wasn't alone.

I've looked at the picture she sent every night since—those

teary, gorgeous eyes, and that outstretched pinkie. She was right. Dorky pinkie promise photo aside—I couldn't keep fighting just because she asked me to. Couldn't rely on her as my motivation. I need to find the fucks within, so to speak. Need to do this for myself.

Step one of *Operation: Find the Fucks* was to get in with my doctor, who tweaked my prescriptions. It'll probably take another few weeks to feel the full effects, but there are glimmers that the worst of this shitstorm might be lifting.

Step two? Therapy.

Lydia listens to my tale of woe, scribbling notes.

I wonder what kind of lingo therapists use to describe this kind of situation. How do you say *heartbroken hot mess* in thera-pist-ese? I stuff down the impulse to ask, not wanting to waste my precious—and expensive—time with her.

Unable to help myself, I'm compelled to fill the silence as Lydia writes. "There was this woman at AA a while back." I shift in my seat, my jeans squeaking slightly against the faux leather couch. "Talked about how she'd been dating this guy but thought maybe she was too attached. Figured she could be replacing one addiction with another. Is that a thing? Like, can you get addicted to a person?"

Lydia sits back in her seat, looking thoughtful. "Is that what you think happened with Caroline?"

"I dunno. Maybe." Then, I hedge. "No?"

She pulls her horn-rimmed glasses off, perching them on her head. "Well, before I answer your question—before I launch into the neurochemistry of addiction—perhaps you could tell me more about what got you thinking about that."

Ah, *tell me more*. She's good. Or that's, like, Therapy 101.

Regardless, I take the babble bait.

"I guess I'm just... worried what we had wasn't healthy?" Fuck. *Had.* The past tense makes me wince. "Like, maybe I got way too attached. I think the fire fucked me up. Brought up some shit about losing my parents."

Lydia nods and pulls her glasses back down to scribble some more.

"How do I know if it was healthy? How do I know if I'm ready for something like that?"

"A sober relationship, you mean?"

"Yeah. Like, AA says wait at least a year, right?"

Lydia tilts her head in thought. "I think, Miles, instead of arbitrary timelines, you'll find out more about your readiness by examining evidence from your own life."

I frown. "Like what?"

"How you've handled various stressors recently. How you've coped."

"Okay…" Spiraling into depression after losing Caroline doesn't feel like an A+ in coping, somehow.

"Why don't we look back at some of the things you've shared today?" Lydia scans her notes. "You said at the fundraiser, there'd been a strong temptation to drink, made worse by Caroline's father."

"Right."

She raises her head. "What did you do when that came up for you?"

I puff air between my lips, slumping back in my seat. "I left. Called my sponsor, then called a cab, then called Jude. Did an AA meeting online when I got home."

"So you distanced yourself from the trigger and reached out to your support network."

I take a moment to think about it. "Yeah. Guess so."

She nods and writes a note on her paper. "And the fire?"

I drag both hands over my face, then scruff them through the back of my hair. "Uh… well, I got scared. Wanted to get Caroline the fuck out of there. Y'know, to keep her safe, I guess. So we went back to her place."

"You said the fire brought up memories of losing your parents."

"Yeah." I scrub at my scruffy beard. "It was... fucking rough. I told her about how they died that night. How I blamed myself..." I flick Lydia a guilty glance, like I'm doing therapy wrong. "I know it wasn't my fault, but I was in a shitty headspace."

She nods. "And that night, or in the days that followed, were you tempted to drink?"

I think back, dazed by how the memories have blurred in the weeks since. "I mean, the thought must've crossed my mind. Like, it's always there in the back of my head. But I was really focused on her. On being with her. I dragged her to the gym the next morning." My lips twist as I remember how she'd bolted upright when I mentioned breakfast.

"And you'd say Caroline is someone who's supportive of your sobriety?"

I raise my eyebrows. "Absolutely. Yes."

"Okay. So, again, after the fire, you surrounded yourself with supportive relationships, sticking to your healthy routines and coping mechanisms. These have all been key tools for you, Miles. Exercise, especially."

"Right." I frown, pondering all this.

"What about the night of the election? You said you were offered a drink outright."

"Yeah." I shake my head at the memory.

"Did you take it?"

"No, but Caroline came over pretty much right away." My knee starts to bounce.

"But there was a chance to accept the drink before she intervened?" Lydia asks.

"Yeah."

"So you could have taken it, but you didn't."

"I was tempted."

"But you didn't act on that temptation."

I frown again. "No, I guess I didn't. And we got outta there."

"Good. And more recently... The night you almost drank. What was that like?"

I feel myself sink into the couch. "Fucking awful."

Lydia nods slowly. "Say more about that."

"Caroline convinced me not to give up."

"Was she there with you?"

"No, I called her."

"Why?"

I take a moment to think about it.

"You didn't have to call her. You could've just taken the drink. Or called someone else. But you called her instead."

Tension chokes my throat and I try to swallow past it. "I guess I knew she wouldn't judge me for fucking up. Or she'd understand why I was hurting so bad. And," I swipe the tears from my eyes, "I dunno, maybe she'd give me a reason not to go through with it."

Lydia, like the pro she is, silently extends a box of tissues. I take a couple, and she gives me a few moments to breathe. To process all this.

"Miles, what's the pattern you notice here?"

I give her a look—borderline annoyed, mostly good-natured. "That I've been through stressful shit and stayed sober? Like, used healthy coping strategies instead of drinking?"

She nods, contemplating me before she speaks. "The reason relationships are discouraged during the early stages of recovery is they often involve emotional highs and lows. It's important to be in a place where you can navigate those stressors without falling back into unhealthy habits. In your case, drinking."

"So you're saying I've done that?" Something like hope creeps into my psyche. "Shown I can handle my shit?"

"I'm saying you've been tested. Especially recently. Put through some very stressful experiences—some significant temptation—and still chosen the sober path."

I chuckle wryly at the wording. "Sounds like some kind of choose-your-own-adventure shit."

Lydia smiles. "Something like that."

"I guess that's life, right?" I muse. "A bunch of fucking choices."

PEOPLE TALK about a breakthrough in therapy like it's some transformative *a-ha* moment. A spark, a sudden light bulb, or the clouds suddenly part and you can see everything with perfect clarity. But they don't talk about the fatigue—the soul-level emotional drain of processing your shit. The sheer effort of bushwhacking new neural pathways to get out the other side of the mess. The way your past still claws at you, your old patterns none too keen to let go or let you embrace new ones.

Brains are dicks like that.

"So, wait." Gus sounds confused. "You think you could go for it?"

"Not what I said." I jab the button for the crosswalk and sling my bag over my shoulder, switching my phone to my other ear. "It's not like all my problems magically disappeared here."

Cowed though he may be by losing the race for governor, Pete Brennan is still a powerful, influential man; he could still use his position as a senator to fuck up my livelihood. This isn't only a question of my mental readiness.

"Okay, but what I'm saying is, it's more of a job thing than a sobriety thing at this point, right?"

"I guess?" My anxiety spikes just thinking about that. But there's something else there. Something warmer, lighter. Something that feels like relief. "I dunno. I literally just got out of therapy. I need some time to think."

"You gonna talk to her?"

"Dude, what did I just say?" Shaking my head, I jog across the street toward the construction site, reminding myself not to look at the gallery. I usually arrive at work earlier than Caroline would, but, after therapy this morning, I'm starting later than usual.

"Just sayin', man..." I can practically hear Gus smiling on the other end. "You've been a miserable fucking mess lately."

"Thanks," I say dryly.

"Listen, I saw how happy Caroline made you, back before... y'know. I just mean it'd be cool to get your girl back."

Fucking understatement of the century.

He goes on, "Is the job thing really make-or-break? There have to be other construction gigs. Like, if he were to screw you over with that one."

"I dunno. In this town, it's pretty much all Sitka builds. Trust me, I've looked into it." I pin the phone against my shoulder and fish my hard hat out from my backpack. "If he can fuck with me here, he could fuck with me on any job site in Lennox."

Gus hums a little sound of understanding and pauses. "Well, if it's a paycheck you need, the station needs new recruits. A couple older guys are retiring this year."

"What, seriously?" I squint against the low morning sun. A career change is too much to integrate into my exhausted goo-brain.

"Yeah. And like, I dunno if you'd be open to switching things up at that level—and I don't wanna downplay the stress of that—but you'd pass the physical no problem. And if that old prick ever tried to fuck with anything LVFD-related, I'd back you up."

Whoa. Becoming a firefighter?

Having heard a bit about the kind of calls Gus gets, I don't know if I could hack it—especially considering how I lost my shit on Halloween. Of course, that was more about who was involved than the fire itself, but... *God*, the prospect of finding a way back to being with Caroline?

Could I change jobs?

"And hey," Gus adds, "you know I love a happy ending."

"Um, gross?"

He puffs a laugh. "Not like that. Shit. Happy ever after? You know what I mean. Plus, it's almost Christmas."

I have half a mind to brush him off, but a fuzzy kind of realization simmers in my head. Maybe I'm not as trapped in this situation as I thought. Aside from income, nothing's tying me to this work. I was already an addict back when I started out in construction, too far gone by then to give a shit about making an intentional career choice. Construction work was a paycheck—a thing I could do. Keeping at it was the path of least resistance. I'm good at my job, but it's not like a *calling*.

"Look, I gotta get to work. I can't process any of this right now."

"Could be a Christmas miracle..."

Jesus. Gus' sap factor really goes off the charts when it comes to the holidays.

"Bruh, you sound like a six-year-old girl."

"Hey," he chuckles, "normalize grown men believing in the magic of Christmas, and—"

"Gotta go!"

"And true love, dude!"

"*Bye!*" I hang up on his sappy ass with a smirk and head into the site office.

27

———————

MILES

Freezing rain spatters Caroline's porch, the erratic staccato basically a match for where my heart's at. I shrug my coat up around my neck and stuff my shaking hands into my pockets, so nervous that I feel like I might throw up. The only glimpse I've had of her since election night was that photo she texted me, and I don't know how I'll react when I see her in person. I don't know how *she'll* react when she sees me here, either—on Thanksgiving of all fucking days.

I spent all day at work yesterday mulling over my therapy session. All day with a roiling feeling building in my gut until I felt like the nervous energy was gonna do me in.

Lydia hadn't come out and said *you're ready*. Being that direct would probably break the rules of therapy or something. But she's right; I'd been clinging to the one-year mark, this arbitrary date, to prove that I made it. That I followed the rules. That I did the right thing, for once in my life. But nothing magical happens on your 365th day of sobriety and I don't need my bronze chip to prove I'm ready for a relationship. I've already proven it to myself. Sure, it's been dicey, but that's fucking *life*.

It had taken all my effort to force myself home for dinner after work yesterday, but I'd barely touched my food, too preoccupied to eat. The restlessness got so bad, I'm surprised I managed to stay there all night. To sleep.

Jude had been brining a turkey for the last two days and the rest of the Thanksgiving dinner prep was gonna take all afternoon before Olena's parents joined us. She'd put me to work peeling potatoes, which helped a bit, but you can only zone out and get caught staring into the middle distance so many times before people notice you're acting weird. Hell, even Murphy could tell something was off and parked himself at my feet, staring at me like he was begging me to act normal. Eventually, Jude and Olena had to sit me down and prod me until I spilled about what was up.

In the end, I didn't even stay to eat. Probably muttered something about coming back or picking up leftovers—fuck if I know. I just needed to see Caroline and couldn't wait any longer.

I drove to her house with zero plan, my heart feeling like it was gonna short-circuit. All I could do was hope she'd be home and we could figure this shit out together. Because *together* is all I want.

I'm not gonna lie to myself about a relationship with Caroline being all sunshine and rainbows. Shit, especially with her dad in the picture. But I know in my bones any stressors between us would pale compared to this gut-wrenching separation. I think some part of me has known all along that she could never be dangerous for me—which is why it's been so hard to accept being apart.

When no one answers the door on my first knock, I frown, peering back at the driveway, where I'm parked next to Caroline's car.

She should be here.

I knock on the door again. Again, no answer.

The rain turns to hail and I tuck myself under the eaves to avoid the icy sting. That's when I hear it. A faint groan from inside.

Instantly on alert, I shout through the door, "Hello?"

Another groan. Louder. This time it might be the word *help*.

Shit.

"George!" I try the door, but it's locked, so I hunt around the usual hiding spots for a spare key. Under the mat. In the plant pots. Above the door frame. *There.*

I let myself in and barge through the house in my wet boots. "George?"

A pained sound. Then, with effort, "Over here."

"George!" I spot him in the kitchen, lying on the floor on his back. "Shit. Okay, I'm here. It's Miles."

"Miles... I've had a fall."

"I can see that." I rush over, but I don't touch him right away, remembering the first-aid training I did for work.

Fuck. Come on, brain.

"Did you hit your head?" Taking a quick glance around the place, I can tell Thanksgiving dinner was in progress. There are carrots and parsnips on the cutting board, a bowl of cut potatoes soaking in water, and a few errant onion skins have fallen on the floor near where George fell. Everything smells savory, like rosemary and garlic.

"No. I'm okay. Well, not *okay*..." He tries to adjust his position and cries out in pain.

I hold out my hands, feeling useless, then pull out my phone. "Shit. Don't try to move. Hang on."

"I was just trying to clean up a few things. Caroline's been cooking up a storm for us and I wanted to help."

He seems lucid. Probably not a stroke or a head injury. Can't rule out spinal injury, though.

"I'm calling for an ambulance, alright, George?" I punch 9-1-1 into my phone, racking my brain for a way to make him more comfortable without moving him. "We're gonna get you some help."

He nods, wincing in pain.

As I connect to the dispatch operator, I spot a throw blanket in the living room and jog over to grab it before returning quickly to George's side. I relay the basic info to the operator and get asked to wait on the line.

"Where is she?" I ask George, tucking the phone into my shoulder as I carefully lay the blanket over him. "Caroline. Her car's outside."

"Out for a run."

I frown and tilt my head, glancing at all the half-prepped food. *In the middle of making dinner?*

George must notice my confusion, because he adds, "She's been... running a lot lately. Working through some things, she says."

My heart squeezes at his words, but I try to shake it off.

He goes on. "Dinner was under control and she thought—"

"Don't—" I cut him off, "Don't worry about explaining, okay? I'll call her when I'm off the phone."

"Thank you," he says, visibly relieved.

I grab his hand, squeezing tight, and nod. "Of course."

It doesn't take long for the ambulance to arrive and I can end the call with dispatch. Paramedics take over with practiced ease, splinting George into a supported position before transferring him onto this two-part plastic stretcher, which they carry outside.

"It's good you didn't move him," one EMT says as she passes me. "You don't wanna mess with a hip fracture."

"Shit, yeah," is all I can manage, then force a reassuring smile for George. "You're in capable hands, alright? I'll follow you to the hospital."

"Thank you," he says again, shaking a little as he reaches for my arm. He gives me a light squeeze. "You're a good man, son."

Son. Somehow, when George calls me that, it carries none of the condescending vitriol I'd felt from Pete. If anything, the older man's stoic approval fills me with a sad kind of warmth that makes me miss my dad—and my own grandpa.

I make sure the oven's turned off, then follow them outside to lock up, replacing the spare key above the door frame as the paramedics carefully navigate George into the ambulance.

Jogging through the rain, I try to brace myself to hear Caroline's voice. I slide into the driver's seat and pull out my phone, my stomach clenching as I hit the call button next to her name.

"Miles..." She sounds out of breath and a little uneasy, surely remembering the last time I called. "Are you okay?"

"Yes, I'm fine," I say quickly, trying not to fixate on how her voice—her concern—is like a salve for the wound that's stubbornly refused to heal these last few weeks. "But George isn't."

CAROLINE RUSHES through the emergency room doors, wild-eyed, with her puffy winter coat billowing unzipped around her running clothes.

She doesn't see me right away. Quickly zeroing in on the reception desk, she jogs over.

I can only watch from across the waiting room as she exchanges frantic-sounding words with the nonplussed nurse behind the desk. The magnetic pull in my chest begs me to go to her, but I know it isn't my place.

Caroline rummages in her purse before thrusting her ID through the hole at the bottom of the plexiglass divider. The nurse eventually returns it, gesturing toward the waiting area.

And when Caroline spins around, our eyes lock.

I slowly stand, clutching my bunched-up coat in my hands. "Hey."

She crosses the waiting room with tentative steps, like she doesn't know what she'll do when she reaches me. Her approach stutters to an awkward stop about a foot away.

"Hey," she says, her voice breaking a little.

We share a pained look before she launches forward, wrapping her arms around my waist.

I tuck her in close, my thumbs gently stroking her back through her damp jacket, and she squeezes tighter, burying her face in my hoodie.

"They wouldn't let me go in with him," I murmur with my lips pressed into her hair. Closing my eyes, I inhale her familiar vanilla scent and it's like the wound tears open all over again.

Keep your shit together. Only one of us can fall apart at a time here.

"I tried," I add, "but they'll only let family back there."

"Thank you," she manages to say, sniffling. "For helping him. For being there." Drawing back, she searches my expression. "Why *were* you there, anyway? It's Thanksgiving."

"Wanted to talk to you." I shake my head sadly. "But now's not— It can wait."

"Do I have family here for George Nickerson?" a voice calls out from my right and we turn. A door reading "*authorized personnel only*" swings shut behind a black woman in scrubs holding a clipboard.

Caroline steps out of my arms and toward her, swiping at her eyes. "Me. I'm his family."

My arms already feel empty and useless, and she's just a couple feet away.

"Is he okay?" she asks.

"If you come with me, ma'am," the woman says, "I'll go over his X-rays with you. Right this way."

Caroline nods, moving to follow, then turns back to me. The look she gives me breaks my heart.

"Go." I tilt my head toward the woman, then cover up the burning in my throat with a soft smile. "Get outta here."

Taking a few steps back, she whispers, "Thank you" once more, then turns to go.

28

CAROLINE

I awkwardly pivot around Grandpa's hospital room with a small potted plant in one hand and a book of Sunday Times crossword puzzles in the other.

"There's no room to put it anywhere," I mumble to myself.

"Maybe we can tape some of the cards to the wall?" Grandpa ventures.

After only three days in the hospital, every available surface in his room is covered in bouquets of flowers, gift bags, and get-well-soon cards—a testament to how well-loved Grandpa is despite keeping more to himself since his first fall last year. Word must've gotten around that he was in the hospital.

I shuffle a few things around to make enough space to set down the fern, then place the puzzle book on his bedside tray table. With a sigh, I take off my coat and drape it over a nearby chair, then lower down to perch next to Grandpa's outstretched legs, careful not to bump him.

"You just missed your parents, darling," Grandpa says, his voice a little rougher than usual.

"Oh?" I pass him his water cup. "Too bad."

It's not; I've kept our interactions to a minimum since election night. When I'd called my mother to tell her they'd have to cut their cruise short and fly home, the conversation had been clipped and awkward. I haven't seen either of my parents since they got back.

Grandpa watches me closely, probably picking up on my unease, and sets his water on the tray table. "Miles stopped by this morning too."

"He did?" I can't help the way I perk up at the mention of his name, like a hopeful puppy who just heard the word *walk*.

He nods. "It was awfully kind of him to check in on me. He's a good one."

"I know." I busy myself smoothing out the rumpled edge of the blanket. "How did he look?"

"Like a broken heart on legs."

A surprised, sad sort of laughter escapes my throat, though my stomach twists at the reminder that he's been struggling.

"Same as you," he adds, patting my knee.

"Yeah?" I smile sadly, knowing I've been about as put together as I feel lately. If not for my job, I wouldn't bother doing my hair or makeup. I've been wearing cozy pajamas and oversized scarves like a uniform at home, like I've been trying to bundle myself in softness, cocooning myself to find some scrap of comfort. But it's futile. Nothing compares to being in Miles' arms.

Grandpa gives me a slow nod. "He was telling me a bit about getting sober. Mentioned his one-year mark is coming up this weekend."

"This weekend?" A pang of guilt hits me for not putting two and two together about the milestone. "He never mentioned a specific date to me."

Grandpa shrugs. "Something worth celebrating, certainly. You know, a few of the boys I flew with in Korea had trouble with drinking after the war. After seeing what we saw..." Grandpa trails off, then shakes his head as if choosing not to go there. "Not an easy thing to kick, in any case, though a few of them tried."

My heart squeezes. For those men who suffered through trauma and addiction. For my grandfather, who saw his friends struggle that way. And for Miles, whose call almost two weeks ago still weighs heavily on my heart.

"Have you called him yet?"

"No, I've been focusing on you." I've been busy researching all the assisted living facilities in Lennox Valley. His doctors say recovery will be long at his age and, given how much assistance he needs with transferring from bed to chair, he'll need more support than he can receive from me and Sadie. On top of that, living as remotely as we do, it may not be feasible to get all the therapies and services he'll need to come out to the house.

We all knew this could happen someday, but I wasn't ready for someday to be now.

"I think I've found a place that seems promising, actually."

"Oh, your parents dropped off some brochures. I guess they've had someone look into it too." He gestures vaguely at the crowded table beside him.

"Really?"

"They said it was no rush—that I could read them over when I was up to it."

I stand and peer into the labyrinth of petals and cards, shifting things around until I spot the brochures tucked between two small vases. I somehow extract them without knocking anything over, then drop into the chair next to Grandpa's bed.

"Let's see... Mason Seniors Lodge." Not recognizing the name, I flip it over to read the address on the back. "Oh, this one's in Seattle." I frown and set it aside, picking up the next one. "Hearthstone Gardens... Seattle?" Grandpa appears as confused as I am. I shuffle through the rest with a cold, tingling sensation rising on the back of my neck. "Seattle, Seattle, and..." My shoulders drop. "Grandpa, these are all in the city.."

"They are?"

"Is that what you want? I didn't think—"

"No, darling, the thought had never occurred to me." His expression is baffled. "I thought I'd stay in Lennox. I've lived here my whole life."

"Mom and Dad didn't ask you what you wanted? Just assumed and—" I grit my teeth, cutting myself off before I say any more.

"No, they didn't," he admits.

I blow a breath up at the ceiling, trying to contain my anger.

"They probably think it'll be easier if I'm closer to where they live."

"I don't care!" I throw up my hands. "This is *your* life. They should ask you what *you* want. Respect *your* wishes."

I hear myself say the words before the obvious slams into me: this is exactly what they do with me. Treat me as if my opinions don't matter or I don't know what I want for myself. They've pulled this nonsense for so long, they've trained me to second-guess whether I truly know what's best for me. My therapist was right. I've learned to defer to their guidance. I've been living for them. Bending to them. Like an obedient child.

Well, I'm not a damn child anymore.

I push to stand and snatch up my coat. "This is unbelievable. I have to go."

"Caroline, wait."

I spin back to face Grandpa. "I need to talk to them! They can't keep doing this."

"Darling, I know better than to get in front of a woman on a warpath and I'm in no shape to stop you, regardless. But before you go ripping into your parents..."

"What?" Immediately concerned, I sink back into the chair. "What is it?"

"Wherever I end up—" he starts. "Seattle or Lennox Valley or *Timbuktu*—"

I can't help but smile.

"I want you to know the house is yours."

My amusement vanishes. "What?"

"The deed's already signed over. The place is paid for. So you'll only have maintenance and repairs to deal with."

"Grandpa," I say, shaking my head. "This is… No, I can't accept—"

"Nonsense," he says, squeezing my fingers. "I know how much you love it here, Caroline. You've come alive since you've been living with me. You're finally chasing after what you want and building your own life, on your own terms. It would make me happy to see you stay."

"What about my cousins? Is it fair to—"

He lifts a hand, cutting me off. "I've evened things out with their inheritance. And, if any of them give you grief about it after I die, I will personally haunt them."

I blow out a laugh. "Quite the threat."

He winks and pats my arm. "Anyway, just keep that in your back pocket."

"What do you mean?" I tilt my head in question.

"Well," he starts, his demeanor turning more serious, "something tells me your parents might think moving me to the city will sway you to do the same."

My face falls. Of course. They're trying to make my decisions for me, as usual. Dad's always seen my move to Lennox as some kind of rebellious phase that would eventually end. And, without Grandpa here, he'd assume I'd have no reason to stay.

Setting my jaw, I get up once more and move to leave.

"Oh, and, for the love of God," he calls after me, "find a way to work something out with Miles."

I open my mouth to protest, knowing there are multiple reasons we can't be together, but he holds up a finger to stop me.

"Don't argue with a broken old man. I've seen how that boy looks at you."

"Wha—? How does he look at me?"

"Like you hung the damn moon." He picks up the book of crosswords and waves me away. "Now go give 'em hell."

29

———————

CAROLINE

The drive into the city does nothing to calm me down; it only gives me a chance to stew and get more worked up. Maybe it's the heartbreak of the last few weeks, or maybe the lifetime of bending to my parents' will, but I'm exhausted. And, while my personal demons aren't contained in a liquor bottle, what I said to Miles still applies to me too: I owe it to myself to keep—or rather, *start*—fighting.

When I get to the house, I head straight for Dad's office and barge inside.

"You think you can just decide where Grandpa lives?" I stride across the room, closing in on his obnoxiously huge desk. "Without even asking him? Or me?"

"I'll have to call you back." He hangs up the phone. "Caroline..."

"Where do you get off, thinking you know what's best?"

Dad puts his hands up as if trying to slow me down. "Sweetheart, what's gotten into you?"

"Caroline." My mother's voice comes from behind me. "I heard shouting. What are you doing here?"

My eyes jump between my parents as Mom drifts into the room. "You don't care about Grandpa or what he wants, do you?"

Dad stands. "Alright, now stop being dramatic and calm down."

"I'm not being *dramatic*!" I grit out—okay, maybe a touch dramatically. "Grandpa doesn't want to move to Seattle. Why would you think he would?"

"Of course we care about your grandfather," Mom says. "That's why we want to find him the best care possible. And, as for location, Seattle has more options and it's more convenient. We're here, and living in a care home won't be that different for him, whether it's in Lennox Valley or the city."

"Lennox Valley is his *home*." I stare at my mother. *Has she really forgotten growing up there?* "Just like it's *my* home now."

"Jesus," is all my father says.

I round on him. "Don't."

"Caroline," he says, having the nerve to sound exasperated. "The whole point of you moving there was to help George. That's over now, so you can get back to reality. Back to your life here."

"You think Grandpa was my only reason for moving away from here? Away from you?" I shake my head in disbelief. "I worked my butt off for you, Dad. For as long as I can remember. And it was never enough. I was suffocating here."

"Don't be ridiculous," he says. "We gave you everything you could ever ask for."

"Yeah, everything except your basic fucking respect."

"Caroline," Mom cautions. "Language."

"Stop!" I nearly groan the word. "Stop trying to fit me into some neat little presentable box! In case you haven't noticed, I'm an adult. I can manage my own life. So, unless you're gonna support that, stay the hell out of it. I'm done with being your photo op or your..."—I search for the right term—"trophy child."

"Trophy child?" Dad drags a hand through his gray hair. "And you think you're not being dramatic. Unbelievable."

"No, Dad. What's *unbelievable* is how you can't stop downplaying and undermining the life I've made in Lennox because you think this is some kind of childish rebellion. Or that you can get me back to doing your bidding. I've got friends, a home, a job, a *life* there, Dad. People who actually care about me. *Love* me."

He holds up a hand. "If this is about that ridiculous fling of yours—"

I scoff, his dismissive words only stoking my rage.

He raises his voice. "You think you've found yourself some fairy tale? He's a drunk, Caroline!"

He *did* know.

"He's *sober*, Dad! No thanks to your cruel bullshit on election night! What is *wrong* with you?"

"Caroline," Mom cautions again, but I ignore her.

"I don't know why you're defending someone like him," Dad says.

"Someone like him?" I echo. "What's that supposed to mean?"

"As I've said, he's not on your level. Our level."

"If *this*"—I gesture between my parents—"is *our level*? You can keep it. Hard pass."

"Now, listen—"

I cut him off, recoiling. "On *our level*. Gross. What, like Fletcher? Look how that turned out."

"It could have turned out differently if you hadn't pulled this temper tantrum—"

"He cheated on me! Repeatedly! And he barely made an effort to hide it. All I had to do was pick up his work phone and it was all there, plain as day. Real A-plus character, that Fletcher."

"That damn phone," Dad grumbles, sitting back down. "I always told him to be more careful with—" He cuts himself off and I stiffen.

"More careful with what, Dad?"

Guilt flickers across his features before he breaks eye contact, clenching his jaw.

The blood drains from my face. "*You knew.*"

When he doesn't deny it, it's as good a confirmation as any.

Betrayal slices into me. "I can't believe this. You knew all along."

"Peter, is this true?" Mom asks, blinking in obvious shock. "You knew about Fletcher's"—she pauses, choosing her words delicately—"*indiscretions?*"

Dad doesn't respond, keeping his gaze trained on me. "Look, Caroline, he made some mistakes."

"Oh, yeah," I say through a joyless smile. "Boys will be boys, right?"

"That's not what I said."

"Didn't have to." Disgust knots my throat. "You would've let me marry him."

"Sweetheart—" Mom starts, like she's torn between comforting me and arguing with Dad.

"Save it." I cross the room and yank open the door, then think better of it and whirl back to face my father. "And I know about you threatening Miles."

The glance he casts at Mom is telling. Yet another piece of information she was in the dark about, I guess.

"You did what?" Mom asks, but I can't deal with her milquetoast level of surprise right now.

I step past her to get in Dad's face. "I'm gonna be very clear," I say. "If you so much as *breathe* near Miles or his job, we're done. Mess with him in any way and you've lost me for good."

"Sweetie, you're getting carried away," Mom says. "You're saying things you don't mean."

I turn to my mother, narrowing my eyes. "Oh, I'm dead serious."

"Enough!" Dad shouts, only bristling when my angry gaze snaps his way. "You think you can just go it alone?"

"Gladly!" I throw my hands out at my sides. "Don't you see that's what I've been trying to do this entire time? Live my own life? For me?"

"What I see is a tantrum." Dad jabs a finger against his desk. "I see my daughter laughing in the face of everything she was given so she can skip off into the sunset with a deadbeat. This nonsense ends now, Caroline. You're moving home."

"I have a home!" I fire back, disappointment sinking deep in my gut as I realize Grandpa knew this would happen. "And it sure as hell isn't here."

"George no longer requires assistance, Caroline," Dad says. "His house will be put up for sale."

"No, it won't." I shake my head. "I'd never sell that house."

Dad's brows draw together. "What the hell are you talking about? It's not your decision to make."

"It is now."

The confusion marring Dad's expression would be delicious if I wasn't so nauseated by this entire conversation.

"Grandpa's given me the house."

"You can't be serious."

"Well, unlike you, Dad, he cares about what actually makes me happy."

"Christ." Dad closes his eyes for a moment and pinches the bridge of his nose.

"And, unlike you, I care about what makes *him* happy too. So I'll be handling his care going forward. I'll find him a place to live —a place *he* wants to be."

"Caroline, you can't—"

"Fucking *try me*, Dad." I clench my jaw as a tear slips down my cheek, begging my voice not to break. "I'm done putting up with your meddling, toxic bullshit."

"Toxic?" Dad balks. "I've worked my whole career to support this family. Always done what's best for you."

"Oh, was it best for me when you let my fiancé disrespect me? Humiliate me?"

Dad lets out a defeated exhale.

Mom cuts in, "Sweetie, I'm sure your father never meant—"

"Was it best for me when you pulled funding from my charity?" I cut her off, too angry at Dad to back down or entertain her attempt at placating. "Was it best for me when you called the man I love a deadbeat and a drunk?" I step toward him. "If you're keeping track, that last one was only a couple minutes ago."

"Caroline, listen—" he starts.

"No. No more listening to you." I take in the picture before me one last time: my father sitting behind his big, obnoxious desk, surrounded by the artifacts of a life lived for his own gain. And I don't see power or prestige: just a pathetic, weak old man. "Earn a place back in my life or don't. That's your choice. But I can't even look at you right now. I need space."

I'm midway through storming out to my car when I come face to face with the last person I want to see.

"What are you doing here?" My voice is terse, a barely controlled rage searing the back of my throat.

"Nice to see you, too, Caroline." Fletcher finishes climbing the front steps, regarding me coolly as he adjusts the leather strap of his shoulder bag. "And to answer your question, I'm moving next week."

At least one positive of my dad losing the election is his disgraced campaign manager getting the boot.

Good riddance, Fletch.

"Got a new position at Delta Consulting." He smooths down his tie as if he can sense how I'm fantasizing about choking him with it. "In Olympia."

"Good for you." I give him a withering smile. It's joyless and phony—concepts he should be well-acquainted with.

"So," he continues, "I'm dropping off my work phone, laptop... a few other things."

That infernal phone.

The mere mention of it fans the flames of my anger all over again. "Well, I hope the women of Olympia are ready for you, Fletch." It's possible I could incinerate him with a look. "And I hope they get off on mediocre sex and snoring."

He rolls his eyes and I turn to go. "Care, come on," he calls after me. "Don't be like that."

Stopping halfway down the stairs, I face him, my jaw working. "And how should I be?"

"Here." He digs out his wallet and slips a glossy business card from inside as he comes back down a few steps, holding it out to me. "In case you lost my number." When I only gape, he does a disgusting little smirk and adds, "For when you get over your Bob the Builder phase and need a man who sits at the grown-ups' table."

It takes everything in me not to punch him in the throat.

This guy just won't let the dream die.

I give him an icy once-over. "If anyone's a child here, Fletcher, it's you." I take one step up—as close as I'm willing to get—and drop my voice low. "You selfish, entitled..."—I pause before landing on the perfect term for my ex, courtesy of my favorite wordsmith—"... *shitweasel*."

Plucking the business card from his grasp, I tear it in half, then turn away to jog down the last steps. As I cross the driveway to my car, I flick the pieces from my fingertips like they're not worth the dirt they land on when they flutter to the ground.

Twisting the gift bag's handle between my fingers, I peer past the fire engines, unsure whether I'm allowed to just walk in. I've never been to a fire station before, and I'm on edge.

Of course, being on edge is a near-constant state of affairs for me lately.

My nerves feel like they've been raked over a bed of nails. It's been five days since I stormed out of my father's office. A lifetime of repressed emotions and people-pleasing finally broke me, detonating some part of my brain. I haven't found a way back to normal yet.

Not that anything about the last month has felt normal. Between losing Miles and the stress from Grandpa's accident, I was already a mess. Blowing up the status quo with my parents has only tightened the twisting grief gripping my chest for the last few weeks.

My indecisive loitering outside eventually summons a young woman in a thick LVFD coat and navy cargo pants, who emerges from a wall of equipment in the back corner of the fire station. "Hey! Something I can help you with?"

"Yeah, hi," I say, stepping toward her. "Sorry for just dropping in. I wasn't sure where to go, but I need to talk to Gus. Is he here?"

"Oh, yeah. Come on in. Shep's upstairs. Follow me."

"Shep?" I follow her inside, toward a narrow staircase.

"Yeah, Gus Shepherd, right?" Climbing the stairs ahead of me, she glances at me over her shoulder. "That's who you're looking for?"

"Yeah, uh..." I thumb the handle of the gift bag as we reach a kitchen area. "I actually didn't know his last na—"

"Caroline! Hey!" Gus calls over from the stove. Stirring a huge, steaming pot of what smells like chili, he lifts his chin at the woman who let me in. "Thanks, Martinez."

She nods and disappears the way we came.

Gus lowers the heat on the stove and turns to face me. "What're you doing here?"

Great question.

I open my mouth to answer but get interrupted when a young, muscular firefighter comes up the stairs carrying a tray. I step out of his way so he can set it on the counter beside Gus. "Hey, Shep! Brought some fresh bread from my Nonna."

"Oh, hell yes!" Gus peeks under the cloth covering the tray and takes a huge whiff. "Damn," he sighs, "that smells good."

"Figured we could have it with the chili," the young guy explains.

Gus cocks a brow my way. "Nicolosi's Nonna is a damn saint."

The guy, who I gather is called Nicolosi, finally cuts his gaze to me and his expression shifts. "Well, who do we have here?"

"Nicolosi?" Gus gives him a long, warning glare. "Wrong tree."

"Roger that, Shep." With a polite nod, Nicolosi excuses himself and ducks back into the stairwell.

"So, what's up?" Gus asks again once we're alone. He gives the chili another stir.

"Um, well, I didn't have your number, so I thought I'd take a chance that you'd be working." I look around, feeling about as comfortable as a wet sock. "I won't keep you, but I was hoping you could give this to Miles for me."

Even saying his name seems to knock the wind out of me, but I force myself to hold up the little gift bag in explanation.

I had to do something for him. He made it to a year sober and I'm so damn proud of him. It had taken me a few days and some begging, but Ada came through for me—gem that she is.

"Uh, okay?" Gus throws a skeptical glance at the bag.

"For his sobriety anniversary?"

Realization smooths the confusion from his face. "Ah, gotcha."

"Yeah, uh, he saw my grandpa at the hospital the other day

and mentioned it was this weekend." Awkwardly, I hold out the bag. "So if you could..."

He moves to reach for it, then pulls his hand back. "Actually, I'll do you one better. You can give it to him yourself."

"What? No, I—"

"We're doing a bonfire in my backyard Saturday night."

I drop my arm. "Oh, no, I don't wanna intrude. We haven't been..." I try to mask the way my throat tenses up just remembering the last time we spoke—those few heartbreaking moments in the ER. "I'm not sure he'd want me there."

The look Gus gives me drops into *duh* territory. "Promise you he would."

"You sure?"

"Listen, between you and me," he says, "he's had a hell of a month. Doing a bit better lately but, let's just say, it'd do him some good to see you again." Gus leans back against the counter and folds his arms over his chest, watching me with something glittering in his eyes. Then his expression turns more serious. "Unless... Would that whole situation with your dad be a problem? Or do you think we could steal you for one night?"

"No," I blurt out. "That's not— I mean... that won't be an issue." I don't go into details, not trusting my composure yet on the subject. Processing my father's toxicity in therapy has been an emotional ride—and one I'd rather not get on at this moment.

"Alright, then you have to come." Gus pauses, probably watching the cracks form in my resolve in real time. "I can double-check with Miles if it'd make you feel more comfortable."

I bite my lip, anxiety already swirling inside me about seeing Miles again. "Um, yeah, okay? As long as he's alright with it."

"Nice! I'll text you the details." He turns to snag his phone from the counter behind him. "Supposed to be cold this weekend, so dress warm." He stops whatever tapping and swiping he's doing on the screen and looks up with a smirk as he hands me his phone to get my number. "You ever been up on Westview Crescent in December?"

I frown as I take it from him. "Don't think so? Why?"

He sticks his tongue in his cheek, clearly trying to fight off a grin.

"Specifically in December?" I ask, confused. When I finish typing in my number, I pass the phone back to him.

He winks. "We'll keep it as a fun surprise."

30

MILES

"Where should I stand, like, up here? Or—?" I take another step up onto Gus' small gazebo—the *Guszebo*, I call it, 'cause I'm an absolute cheeseball. "Nah, that's too high. Feels weird, like I'm Lord Farquaad or something." I move back down a step.

Gus shoves a mini doughnut in his mouth as he kills the music from the small speaker on the back porch, then gestures for me to go ahead. "Alright," he mumbles around his bite, "let's hear your little speech, Lord Fuckwad."

"Okay, whoa." I clutch my chest. "Didn't realize there'd be hecklers at my own party, but alright, alright."

Gus gives me a shit-eating grin as he jogs down the porch steps, then spins one of the camping chairs around to face me. He sinks down with his back to the fire, uncapping his thermos of hot chocolate.

Strings of golden lights are draped all around Gus' yard and the gazebo, making it look pretty damn magical back here—and helping me see my audience, who are otherwise backlit by the bonfire.

"Gotta hand it to you guys," I say, nodding to Jude and Olena, who've snuggled up close in a double-wide camping chair, a thick blanket spread across their laps. "This is pretty dope." I can't help but check over my brother's shoulder one last time, toward the back gate.

She's still not here.

It's been nine excruciating days since I held her in the ER. Despite being desperate to see Caroline again, I've held off on reaching out, figuring she was stressed and busy with George. When Gus told me she'd come by the station a couple days ago, my palms started sweating instantly. And, when he asked if it was cool for her to come tonight, I thought I might throw up. In the best way.

Digging out my speech from my coat pocket, I decide to just go for it. No sense in waiting any longer. Maybe something came up. Or maybe she decided not to come. That second possibility stabs me in the gut.

"I did have a few things I wanted to say." I take a steadying breath as I unfold the paper, orienting myself, and angle it so I can read in the dim golden light.

"You got this!" Olena calls out.

The reassurance is sweet, but I'm actually pretty good at talking in front of people. The nerves I'm feeling have less to do with the three sets of eyes on me and more to do with the absence of Caroline's. I glance at the empty camping chair beside Olena and clear my throat.

"In AA," I start, "the first step is admitting you have a problem. Doing this took me a while. Well, way longer than it should've, anyway. Y'know, no one loves having to admit they've lost control and need help. But I've been working hard this past year on being honest. With myself, and with the people I love." I flick my gaze to Jude, knowing I owe him a lifetime of honesty and then some for what I've put him through.

He ducks his head slightly and Olena slips her arm around his. It's then that the gate finally clicks open.

For a moment, my stomach feels suspended in midair, like when you're going up in an elevator and it overshoots slightly before settling to a stop—like simply seeing Caroline again has fucked with some fundamental law of gravity.

"Hey," I say. The word is an exhale and her responding smile is all the oxygen I could ever need.

"Hey. Sorry I'm late," she says, then quickly skirts the fire to find a seat. "And, shoot, for interrupting." Even in the darkness, with the light of the fire flickering over her apologetic features as she settles into the chair next to Olena, her presence alone lowers the volume on the sharp static in my head.

Realizing I'm in the middle of my speech, I tear my gaze away and clear my throat, trying to focus on the words in front of me. But, as I scan the page, none of it feels right. With a resigned sigh, I fold the paper up and stuff it back in my pocket.

"I'm actually..." I scrub at the back of my neck. "Uh... I'd written this whole thing, but it's not..." My eyes reach Caroline's again. "I know what I wanna say."

She gives me an encouraging nod.

Just speak from the heart.

"Sobriety has been rough. Messy. Ugly, sometimes. They say *one day at a time* a lot in AA, but that makes it sound so simple. Linear." I shake my head. "But not every twenty-four hours is the same. Some days it's easier, and some days feel... fucking impossible."

Gus bobs his head, likely remembering all the *impossible* he's had to navigate with me lately.

"*Thank you* feels like a shitty way to cover it. Each of you has shown up for me in so many ways, big and small, to keep me on track, and I'm not exaggerating when I say I wouldn't be here for this—or maybe not at all—if it weren't for you. Gus, you've physically dragged me to the gym and forced me to stick to my routine. I think you'd probably rip my skull open to pour in the happy brain chemicals if you could, but you always seem to find a way to get them there, anyway, whether it's through lunges or, y'know, musical torture."

He laughs and points at me. "Not regretting calling you *Fuckwad*." When I smirk, he relaxes back into his seat, lifting his chin. "Just kidding. Love you, man."

"Olena, my fellow ADHD goblin." I jump down and jog the couple of steps closer to give her a quick fist bump, then return to the gazebo to continue. "You always make me feel seen. Plus, you make my brother happy, and that's pretty awesome."

Jude puts his arm around her and kisses her temple.

"Couldn't ask for a cooler future sister-in-law," I add. "And thank you for *not* baking my cake tonight."

"You're welcome," she says with a serious dip of her head.

"And Jude..." I meet my brother's eyes and my throat constricts. "Fuck, man. You've been through so much of my shit with me. I've probably given you thousands of reasons to walk away, but you never have. I dunno if you're a glutton for punishment or you're really *that* patient and forgiving, but uh..."—I swallow—"Mom and Dad would be so fucking proud of you."

His brow crumples and I can tell he's fighting to keep his shit together.

Olena squeezes tight to his side, welling up along with him.

"You've all done so much for me. And the honest truth is, it's still hard as shit sometimes. I had one of those days recently." A breeze picks up, the flames from the fire licking over to one side like reeds in a current. I can't tell if it's the wind or the memory of that night making me feel colder. "About two and a half weeks ago, I came very close to drinking."

Caroline's lips part, concern and understanding transforming her features. She must have guessed what I was grappling with over the phone, but the confirmation etches sadness into her features all the same.

"Like, glass-in-my-hand close," I add. My gaze trips between my brother and Olena, then Gus, catching the same sad expression on each of their faces. It's not disappointment. Not pity. Not resentment.

It's compassion. Empathy. Love.

"It's when you're at your lowest moment that those old habits really come for you, y'know? And, that night, I was in pain." I can't help but look at Caroline when I say it, still not quite believing she's here. "Unbearable pain."

She covers her mouth, her fingers trembling.

"More than anything, I just wanted it to stop."

The fire crackles, breaking the silence.

"But, instead of picking up that glass, I picked up the phone."

The twist of anguish in my girl's beautiful eyes is almost too much to bear.

"Caroline… This is gonna sound dramatic as fuck, but you reminded me I have a life worth living. A sober life. A healthy life. A life full of goodness and understanding and acceptance. You reminded me that I can do this. That I *have* done this and *am* doing this. That I owe it to myself to keep going. Even when it's hard, or messy, or it hurts to the point where I think I can't do it anymore."

Olena shifts closer to Caroline and grips her hand, both of them in tears.

"You reminded me that I'm loved. *Worthy* of love—not broken or hopeless." I have to pause for a second so I don't lose my composure entirely. "I'd say you saved me, but what you really did was remind me I had it in me to save myself."

Caroline rubs at her chest, her gaze briefly falling to her lap. When she lifts her eyes to meet mine again, the light flickers over her tear-streaked cheeks and I nearly break.

"I'm gonna keep going. Keep fighting. For you, so I can be the man you deserve." I nod to the others and add, "So I can be the brother and the friend you deserve too… But also, and most importantly, I'm gonna keep fighting for myself."

There's a tense silence for a beat and awkwardness threatens to creep in.

"Anyway, I guess that's my speech, so…"

I'm not sure who launches out of their chair first, but it's Olena who tackles me in a hug as I step down to meet her, followed by a tearful Gus who mutters muffled words into my shoulder—"fuck you for making me cry" and "proud of you" are all I catch.

I turn to Jude, almost unable to look him in the eye as my throat knots up again. He sniffs hard and yanks me into a hug so tight it practically cracks my spine. "Mom and Dad would be so proud of you, too, man." His voice breaks with emotion. "I know I fuckin' am. You did this."

I can't respond. Can't find the words to tell him what it means to me to hear him say that. Even if I could, I don't think I could speak right now if I tried.

When he finally lets go, I have to stop myself from diving straight for Caroline, burying my face in her hair, and telling her exactly what she means to me. She might have come tonight—and just having her in front of me again might be soothing the bruises left on my heart after the last month—but I need to tell her properly that I'm ready. That I want this. Want us. Want everything.

Her cheeks glisten in the firelight and I drift closer, almost involuntarily drawn toward her and powerless to resist. She's had me hooked like this since the first time I saw her.

"Oh, hey," Gus says behind me. "Wasn't I supposed to talk to you two about those, uh… the uh… *plants*?"

"The plants! Yes!" chirps Olena. "Almost forgot. Remember,

Jude? Gus wanted to talk to us... *inside*... about the whole... plant thing?"

"Riiiight, the plant thing. We better..." I glance over my shoulder as Jude gestures weakly toward the house. "We better go inside to discuss the very important... plants."

"Because of the landscaping," Olena awkwardly clarifies.

"Oh my God, just go already," I say, rolling my eyes at their ridiculous excuses.

They file inside, leaving me and Caroline alone beside the fire. When the sliding door to the kitchen snicks shut, it's like neither of us knows what to do.

"Oh, fuck, I wanna say so much right now," I say with a chuckle. "But I've talked my ass off already and—"

"Did you mean it?" Caroline asks in a rush, cutting me off. "The part about fighting for me?"

"God, yes." I nod, trying to stop the trembling in my chin.

"Miles..." Relief touches her expression, but there's still caution there.

I inhale to steady myself. "I wanna do this properly." My voice breaks just saying the words. "You and me. For real this time."

"But you said you weren't ready," she counters.

"I was scared I wasn't. But this last month... Losing you put me through hell. And I still did it." I fish the bronze chip from my pocket and hold it out to her. "I didn't drink."

When she takes it, our fingers brush, and even that small contact makes me want to haul her against me.

"Proof I can handle hard shit, right?"

She looks up and a tear slips down her cheek.

"Everything's easier with you, Caroline. Everything." Throat tightening, I wipe at my tears. "So, whaddaya say, fancy girl? You wanna get on this messy-ass ride with me?" Remembering the other reason for our separation, I add, "And fuck what your dad said. I'll figure something out with work and—"

She's kissing me before I finish my sentence and it's like coming up for air—like I can finally breathe again. Through her. With her. Because of her. Because of *us*. Every rattled, ragged part of me feels like it's sliding back into place, rough edges smoothed by having Caroline in my arms again.

We break the kiss and I bend to press my forehead to hers.

Her voice is soft when she speaks. "You don't need to worry about your job anymore."

I pull back. "What? You serious?"

"I told my dad off. Long overdue, but..." she trails off, lifting a shoulder.

"Holy shit. Are you okay?"

"Yeah. Maybe Adrian's right about my villain era." She looks down at my chest. "But I finally hit my toxicity limit, I guess. He's a real piece of work."

"I'm sorry." I hug her closer, resting my chin on the top of her head. "You deserve so much better."

"No, I'm the one who should be apologizing." She draws back and lifts her gaze, tears welling in her eyes again. "For how he treated you."

"He was a dick to us both. But you're his *daughter*. He shouldn't have—" I cut myself off and shake my head. "How did it feel?"

"Felt *great*, actually." There's a hint of guilt in her expression. "Hard, but great."

"So proud of you," I whisper, then kiss her again.

She hums a little sound of relief when our lips part. "God, I missed kissing you."

"Well, we'll have to make up for all those missed ones." I smirk, tucking a stray curl behind her ear. "But seriously, you sure about this? 'Cause I'm not gonna promise smooth sailing. I can't promise—"

"I know." She nods.

"I mean, being sober—*staying* sober—is something I'm gonna have to face every day for the rest of my life." I should probably shut up, but I need to be sure she knows what she's signing up for. "And I'm not asking you to save me or fix me, okay? I'm gonna keep working on myself. It's *my* job to keep getting better."

"Miles, I know." She takes my face in her chilled hands and lifts to kiss me. "And yes, I'm sure."

Something tight in my chest seems to release its grip. "I fucking love you."

"I fucking love you too." Slipping her fingers over my jaw, she arches a brow. "And, honestly? You had me at *messy-ass ride*."

I laugh and lift her off the ground, wrapping her legs around my hips.

"So, should I take that literally, or...?" she continues. Her grin is flirtatious, stoking that familiar heat deep inside me.

"Fuuuuck," I groan out. "I can't wait to get you alone. More alone than *this*, anyway." I kiss her again, reminding myself we can't get carried away out here. "We gotta finish that list of yours, right? And let's just say *this ass*"—I palm her through her jeans, squeezing hard—"is in for one hell of a messy ride."

Her burst of laughter masks the opening bars of the song, but we both go still when we finally hear the music coming from the porch.

"Is that...?" I screw up my face, then crane my neck to catch Gus slowly sliding his kitchen door shut, pumping his eyebrows.

"Oh, God," Caroline says, obviously recognizing the tune.

Then I place it. The muted trumpet part at the beginning.

Sweet Caroline.

"Bro!" I call out to him, setting Caroline on her feet again. "Turn it off!"

He motions to his ears through the glass, mouthing an exaggerated, "Can't hear you, sorry!"

Fucker.

I roll my eyes, though I don't think anything could wipe the dopey smile from my face.

Caroline and I share a resigned look, then break into laughter when we spot Olena making a nonplussed Mr. Lumps—wearing a lopsided little Santa hat and matching jacket—wave to us through the glass.

Caroline tugs me against her, grinning.

"Thought you hated this song."

"Oh, I do," she says, beaming up at me. "But, for some reason, I'm just really *fucking* happy right now."

I know the feeling.

She gasps, then pulls away. "I have something for you."

"What?" My brows quirk together as she retrieves a small gift bag from beside her camping chair.

"A sobriety present," she explains, holding it out to me. "Open it."

I dig out the item inside, making quick work of ripping back the tissue paper from the little framed pencil sketch.

"Baby, is this—?" But I don't even need to ask. It's our hands —inexplicably but unmistakably our hands. My pinkie hooked to hers in a promise. The promise I made to us both. To keep going, to keep fighting—and to stay sober. Already welling up again, I lift my eyes to my beautiful girl. "How did you...?"

"Ada did it for me." Caroline tucks herself under my arm as we gaze down at the drawing. "Hope it's okay." She scrunches her nose in a sheepish apology, peering up at me. "I had to show her the photo you sent me so she could get your hand right." Lifting up on her toes, she presses a gentle kiss to my cheek. As she brushes her chilled fingers along my stubble, she smirks. "Don't worry, though. She promised to take the knowledge of your sad-boy beard to the grave."

31

CAROLINE

I crouch beside the bucket of sand and roll up my coat sleeve, holding the lighter out over the roman candle Gus planted in the center—the whole thing looking like it's some kind of explosive birthday cake. "I've never done this before," I say, hesitating a bit. "How does it work? What do I do? And is this even legal?"

After having given us some time alone to talk—and cry and kiss and cry some more—the three worst actors in Lennox Valley declared their contrived plant conversation complete and came back outside to join us.

"Well," Gus drawls smoothly at my side, "you've come to the right guy with your questions. Basically, light stick, stick go boom."

"That your professional explanation, you fuckin' caveman?" Miles deadpans from over my shoulder.

"Hell no!" Gus says on a laugh. "But there isn't much more to it than that. You're gonna light it, then back up and let the magic happen."

"Right. Okay…"

"And don't worry," he adds. "The fire marshal hooked me up with a permit."

"A permit?" Miles echoes. "Fuck, man, we really *are* almost thirty." He crouches at my side, gently rubbing my back. "Want me to go first? Like, if you wanna watch one before you——?"

"No, I got it." I shoot him a brave smile. "Trying new things, right?"

"Attagirl." He kisses my temple. "Light it up."

I flick a flame to life and, when the fuse catches, hurry to back up a few steps, dragging Miles with me.

He pulls me in front of him and wraps his arms around my waist as we watch the shots whiz into the night sky.

We Are the Champions comes on as Gus steps up to light the next one.

"Seriously, man, have you got a song for everything?" Miles asks.

"Almost like it was planned," he retorts with a wink, then sings along in an obnoxious falsetto that has us all laughing—and Miles groaning. As Gus' roman candle fizzles out and he passes the lighter to Jude, tiny raindrops start to speckle our cheeks.

"Damn," Jude says, blinking up into the night. "Olena, we better do ours together before we get rained out." Tucking their coat collars around their necks, they huddle up and put their fire-works in the bucket side by side. It's not long before twin sparkling arcs zing upward, leaving fizzing crackles of smoke in their wake.

"Alright," Gus says when the pair are spent. "Guest of honor." He hands Miles the last one and sweeps an arm toward the launch bucket in invitation as the rain picks up. "But, uh, maybe be quick about it."

Shrugging against the rain, Miles heads over and makes fast work of lighting his.

"Happy one year, buddy," Gus says, giving him a good-natured slap on the shoulder as they both back up to watch the first shot launch.

Olena whoops as the little yellow fireball shoots skyward. "Aww, gold stars, Miles!"

Miles grins and squeezes me tightly to his side.

"Proud of you," I whisper, rising up to kiss his cheek.

He opens his mouth to respond, but a flash of lightning cuts him off, followed by rolling thunder and a downpour that feels like someone turned on a tap in the sky.

"Shit, that's our cue," Jude says.

With the rain hissing around us, we scramble to gather up all the chairs, blankets, and anything else that might not survive the downpour, quickly stashing everything under the shelter of the gazebo before making a break for the house. Gus hangs back to douse what's left of the bonfire, trailing us inside with an easy smile despite looking like he just walked through a lawn sprinkler.

I can see why he and Miles are close. They've got the same kind of energy—like they've both seen enough heavy stuff that they don't get hung up on the small things.

It's only when I go to hang up my wet jacket near the front door that my memory finally jogs. An enormous inflatable Jack Skellington bobs in the rain outside the living room window. Past the *Nightmare Before Christmas* display Gus has set up in his front yard, the entire street is decked out to the nines in over-the-top Christmas decorations.

"So, what's the deal with this street, anyway? Is it like this every year?" Arriving late and then getting swept up with Miles, it had completely slipped my mind to ask. After touring local care homes and making arrangements for Grandpa all day, including having an appointment with his lawyer which had run late, I'd had to get ready and drive here in a rush. On top of that, the novelty street sign had sent me on a confusing detour, taking me around the block and right back into the bottleneck of cars trying to get access to Westview Crescent—otherwise known as Candy Cane Lane.

"Yeah, it's tradition." Gus appears beside me at the window, ruffling his wet hair with a towel as we peer out at the steady stream of sightseeing traffic crawling in and out of the cul-de-sac. "If you buy a house here, it's part of the deal. Fun, right?" He grins, his features lit up with delight like he's an overgrown kid.

"Is that why you were late?" Miles circles his arms around my waist from behind—and it's like my whole body exhales. He kisses my cheek. "The weird Christmas explosion thing hold you up?"

"Partly." I nod.

"Hey, it's not weird, man," Gus says with a scoff. "It's awesome! It's Christmas! Best time of the year, hands down."

I twist around, catching Miles rolling his eyes like he's heard this from Gus a thousand times before.

"So you signed up for this?" I ask Gus, gesturing at the spectacle outside.

He laughs beside us. "Not exactly. This house belonged to my folks. They're the real Christmas keeners. Anyway, they downsized and passed the place to me and my ex." When I tilt my head, he adds, "Uh, long story. Just me here now, though."

"What's with that one?" I ask, noticing a less-than-stellar effort from the house directly across the street.

Gus follows my gaze, then grumbles, "Don't get me started. They've got a house sitter this year."

"Are we ready for dessert or what?" Olena calls from the kitchen, pulling our attention.

"Hell yes!" Miles drags me along with him, then stops short and lets out a resigned chuckle when he sees the cake.

I tuck myself into his side and read the loopy pink lettering. "*Sober but still a dumbass*" is scrawled above a cartoon unicorn.

"Wow, thanks, buddy," he calls over his shoulder at Gus, who's just crouched down to set up the fireplace.

Gus straightens and strolls over with a curious look on his face, then barks out a laugh. "Hey, man, wasn't my doing," he says, holding up his hands. "Jude's the one who ordered it." He squeezes Miles on the shoulder before turning back to his task.

Miles turns to Jude, pinning him with a long stare.

"Gotta keep you humble," is all Jude says, then scruffs up Miles' hair before taking a gentle jab to the ribs.

CAKE DECIMATED, we all sit around the crackling fireplace, sipping some kind of cranberry-pomegranate punch Olena concocted. Miles has his arm slung around me on the couch and there's something hypnotic about the way he brushes soft strokes on my arm with his thumb while we watch the flames dance.

"So, wait," I start, tilting my head at Gus, "you're a firefighter, but you lit a bonfire in your backyard, set off fireworks, and have a wood-burning fireplace? Isn't that, like, a paradox?"

"Yeah, should we report you somewhere?" Olena teases, draping her legs over Jude's lap and leaning back on the love seat's armrest. "Firefighters behaving badly, or something?"

"Nah, I love it," Gus says, stretching out on the recliner next to them. "You'd be surprised how many folks in the fire service love fire. I think when you know firsthand how powerful it is, there's a bit of a thrill in taming it."

Jude smirks. "Well, you *look* thrilled, man."

"I am! I am," Gus insists, then fails to fight off a yawn. "Thrilled for my best buddy here." He stretches forward to bump fists with Miles, then flops back into his seat. "He got his one-year chip, he got his girl back, it's almost Christmas... What's not to love?"

Jude watches his brother for a moment, then nods. "I'm happy for him too." Then, with a hint of a smile, Jude's eyes shift to mine. "Happy for them."

I squeeze tighter to Miles' side and try not to get too emotional. The quiet approval from Jude feels like a rare gift—one that I won't take for granted.

Gus' black cat lumbers into the living room, still wearing the jingle-bell collar and Santa vest from earlier.

"Hey, there's my buddy!" Miles jumps up from the couch to scoop the cat into his arms, then sinks back into the seat beside me, slouching low with the furball on his chest. "It's about time ol' Lumps joined the party."

"Lumps?" I let the cat sniff my hand, then give it a tentative scratch around the ears.

"Miles didn't tell you about Lumpy?" Gus asks. "Well, his real name's Coal, but nobody calls him that."

Miles makes a snuffled sound as Lumpy headbutts his nose.

"Aww, Lump of Coal. I get it," I say, snuggling back into Miles' side and helping myself to a few more strokes of the cat's silky black fur.

Already purring, Lumpy makes a half-turn and settles onto Miles' chest like it's the best seat in the house.

Miles quirks a brow my way. "He's basically my mental health mascot."

"But wait," I start, turning to Gus, "isn't a lump of coal a punishment? Miles here isn't looking terribly punished."

Quite the opposite; he's grinning.

"Nah, pretty sure he's suffering horribly," Olena deadpans. "He's way overloaded with cuteness."

"Aw, but this isn't even his cutest outfit," Miles says, glancing at me. "Speaking of which," he adds, lifting his chin at Gus, "did you get the new one?"

"The new one?" Gus asks, sounding equal parts weary and

amused as he sets his drink down on the coffee table. "As in *another one*? Dude, you gotta stop buying my cat ridiculous costumes."

"Fuck that!" Miles says before handing me the cat and pushing off the couch. He jogs to the front door and opens it, then lets out a victorious laugh. He shuts the door and strolls back inside, beaming as he tears open the package. "Thought it was coming today."

"By all means, open my mail," Gus deadpans.

"Hey, I bought the damn thing."

"Okay, I'm confused," I say, looking to Olena and Jude for an explanation as Lumpy settles onto my lap, still purring. "What's happening?"

"Someone entrusted Miles with a credit card," Jude explains with a smirk, then takes a sip of his drink.

"Fuck off," Miles says through a chuckle. "This is within my entertainment budget."

And, when he manages to wiggle the indulgent cat's paws and tail through the little plush getup, I know it's money well spent.

"Oh my God," I say. "He's the world's cutest dump truck. Or I should say, *Lump* truck!"

Miles lights up at the pun. "Lump truck? You're fucking perfect. C'mere." He presses a kiss to my forehead, squeezing me closer.

Looking amused, Gus reaches over to pat Lumpy's back. "Isn't this a little on the nose, though? Old Lumps already has a dump truck ass, dude."

Miles puts on a horrified face, covering Lumpy's ears. "Don't body-shame my chonky boy! There's nothing wrong with having a badonkadonk."

Gus holds up his hands. "Hey, I'm not arguing with that. You know I like big—"

Miles cuts him off, eyes wide. "Don't you fucking sing!"

32

MILES

We crash against the elevator wall and I shove my hands under Caroline's sweater, needing to feel her skin. The last of my restraint came apart some-where between the lobby and when the doors slid shut and we were finally, properly alone. I gave in, letting myself get lost in her —nearly taken out by each mind-melting stroke of her tongue. I'm practically panting with need as I grip her bare waist, my thumbs curling to tease and tug at the waistband of her jeans.

God, her skin... Yes.

"I've missed you so fucking much," I mumble between crushing kisses. "Missed how incredible you feel."

And, Jesus, has she always smelled this good?

"Me too." She drives her fingers under the waistband of my jeans and I moan—loud enough to snap her back to remembering where we are, I guess, because she pulls back slightly. "Miles..." she almost whimpers my name as she slips her hands back out from my pants.

I already hate the inch of space between our lips. After the last month, denying myself any longer feels torturous.

"We have to…" she trails off, her words lost to the flick of my thumbs over her nipples. Even through her bra, they feel hard and… needy.

Can nipples be needy? These ones sure are. As in, they need my mouth on them.

"We have to what?" I ask, sucking and licking her neck. "Don't say wait. 'Cause I can't wait another fucking second."

The door grinds open and she drags me toward my apartment door, laughing. "Come on."

"Fuck, I need you." I tug her back against me as we stumble along.

"You can have me," she teases, equally unable to tear herself away. "Just… not in the hallway."

"Oh," I deadpan, "fancy girl's got *standards*."

I don't know how we navigate from the hallway, through the door, and into my bedroom, but clothes and shoes form a scattered trail in our wake. We careen in a half-naked tangle until we topple onto my bed like desperate, fumbling teenagers.

"Take these off." Caroline shoves my already-unzipped jeans over my hips and I awkwardly roll to the side to tug them down, along with my boxer briefs. They're still around my calves when I crash back into her, and she laughs. "All the way off!"

"Fuck it," I mumble against her lips before tugging her panties to the side and driving two fingers into her perfect warmth. *Fuck*, she feels so good. Like home.

"Oh my God," she groans.

The way I'm working my fingers isn't gentle or slow, but I don't hear any complaints. And, when she spits into her palm and slips her hand between us to stroke my aching cock, I know we're not messing around here. It's been too long. We've been too starved of each other.

"Get on your back," she whispers before giving my shoulder a firm shove.

I pull my fingers out as I roll onto my back, then stare up in wonder at the confident girl tearing off her panties to climb over me. "Where'd this bossy attitude come from?"

"Figured out what I want." Brow arched, she guides me into position, still stroking with a gentle squeeze. "And what I want… is to ride you until I come."

Biting her lip, she whips her head around to my bedside table and leans over. But I guess she yanks the drawer open a bit too enthusiastically, because the entire thing comes flying out and she yelps as its contents spill onto the floor.

"No! Dang it!" Left holding nothing but the little empty drawer by the knob, she lets out a plaintive groan.

I lift up on my elbows and sigh when I clock the state of affairs on the floor—specifically, the box of condoms now well out of reach. I flop back on the bed with a tired sigh but can't quite resist gripping my shaft and slipping the tip through her wetness once more.

"Well, shoot…" She sets the drawer on top of the nightstand and moves over me, tilting her hips like she can't help it, but then catches herself and backs off with a pained sort of impatience. "I should get the…"

I squeeze her hip, my fingers digging into her skin. "My tests were clear."

Her eyes flit between the spilled box of condoms and my face, her brows pinching with need as I press the heated crown of my dick against her clit. "Um… same. I mean, I got tested after…" She makes a little gesture with her hand, obviously not wanting to get into the *why*. "And I've had an IUD for years. We could"—she swallows, then whimpers as I circle her clit—"go without, I guess?"

I tug her down firmly by the back of the neck so our lips are almost touching. "You sure?" I kiss her hard, hungry and desperate. "You want me to fuck you raw?"

But she's already working her hips to guide me inside her.

"Baby, *fuck...*" I lie back and hold her steady for a torturous beat. "Are you sure? Tell me."

"Yes, fuck me bare. God, *please.*" Her breaths skitter and catch as she sinks down, tilting and grinding as she takes me deeper. She's so ready, she doesn't have to lift her hips more than once before she takes it all on the next stroke.

"Shit, Caroline," I say, reaching up to pinch her perfect nipples.

She rocks her hips and I can't do anything but encourage her.

"Look at you."

She doesn't stop.

"You're so fucking sexy when you take what's yours. And you" —I pause, bucking up to meet her—"are fucking *taking it.* So well, honey."

A small, almost enamored smile touches her lips.

"What?"

"I dunno, I just like when you call me *honey.*"

"Yeah?" I lift a brow, slipping a hand between us to thumb her clit. "But I thought you weren't sweet."

"I'm not." She starts to bounce gently up and down, uninhibited and greedy for every stroke.

"No?"

"Maybe I used to be. But I'm done being sweet." She bounces harder. "Done being nice." Voice breaking, she adds, "And I'm done being good."

"Tell me what you are then." I sit up to crush her mouth to mine, working her clit faster as she grinds against me. "What are you, Caroline?" I lightly collar her throat, my grip gentle and reverent; I can't believe I got this lucky—that this incredible woman wants me as much as I want her. "Tell me what you are while you soak this cock."

Her movements become frenzied as she chases her release, but she doesn't slow down. "I'm... I'm..."

"You my bad girl?" I increase the pressure on her clit, speeding up, then draw her nipple into my mouth. "You my perfect little slut?" I murmur around her tight bud. "My desperate little whore?"

"Miles, I'm gonna..."

"God, I fucking love you like this." I pull my hand away only long enough to slap her ass, then get right back to work. "Say what you are, Caroline. Say it and come those pretty brains out for me."

Clenching around me, she can barely speak but manages to suck in a gasp as she starts to break. "I'm your..."

"Do it. Own it. Now, baby." She's fucking *everything* in this moment.

"I'm your dirty... little... slut..." She barely gets the words out before she's spiraling, keening, practically convulsing in the safety of my arms as a warm gush envelops the throbbing heat where our bodies are joined.

"That's my fucking girl," I bite out, then quickly lie back, lifting her hips slightly. Pounding upward hard and fast, I piston into her, my thrusts become more erratic. And, when I go over the edge into an almost frantic oblivion, I don't give a shit what the neighbors can hear. I moan loudly through my own release, spilling hot and deep inside her as she rides out the last waves of her pleasure.

As she slows and softens, I lower her, drawing her close to press my forehead to hers. Our chests heave and shudder as we settle in each other's arms, and I kiss her, loving how the involuntary twitches of my cock echo the faint clenches in her core.

"Shit," I say through a low chuckle, "I never got my pants all the way off."

Laughing, she glances over her shoulder at my jeans, still

bunched around my ankles. She turns back to me, grinning and sex-addled and perfect. "I love you." She kisses my cheek, then my temple.

"I love you too." I swallow. "Felt like I couldn't breathe without you."

Tears well in those beautiful eyes and she cradles my jaw. "God, I missed you. Missed *this*. *Us*."

I kiss her again, slow and searching.

"How do you do it?" she asks when our lips part, looking at me with wonder. "One minute you're dressing up cats in silly costumes and the next you're this... this *sex beast*."

"Sex *beast*?" I nose her cheek. "Thought my title was sex *sensei*."

She bites her lip. "Maybe you can be both."

"Well, what can I say... Guess I *contain multitudes*." I do an aggressive eyebrow waggle for good measure, selling the corny reference to the day we met.

"Oh, very clever." She rolls her eyes, then kisses me like she can't help it. "But seriously. You're everything. Everything I didn't know I wanted. Needed. And you were right, I had no idea what I was missing—and not just with sex."

"Neither did I."

Her gaze falls from mine, a delicate smile on her lips.

"Caroline, seriously, you..." I exhale hard, trying to steady my emotions, then brush the hair back from her cheek. "You make my brain quiet."

She looks up and runs her thumb over the cleft of my chin. "That's a good thing, right?"

"Best feeling in the world."

CAROLINE

I've always loved this painting; three little girls running through a Middle Eastern marketplace. They're young—that innocent, oblivious age before you develop any awareness of how others might perceive you. Before you start nipping away at those rougher edges, checking yourself to fit in. When you can run—laughing, heart hammering, limbs flailing—simply because it feels good.

That messy joy is beautiful.

The colorful contemporary piece by Faizal Baban used to hang above Grandpa's bed at the house. He said it was his favorite because the girls reminded him of me and my cousins when we were small. But his move into Lennox Seniors Lodge last week meant downsizing. When I suggested donating it to the art show, he'd been delighted. Ever the practical thinker, he simply wanted to find it a new, loving home.

I'd first proposed the charity art show back in October, but the real light-bulb moment had come when Sunny mentioned wanting to collaborate with a few smaller galleries in the city. Not only had I convinced her and Julian to invite a handful of the young local artists I've been watching to donate a piece, but we'd partnered with Found Family to promote its youth art programs. Pulling it off before Christmas was a real *teamwork-makes-the-dream-work* feat: Adrian had performed a miracle by finding a Seattle hotel with space for the event, Sunny and I had organized the artist contributions, and Ada had even persuaded some of the teens in her program to contribute pieces. It's been incredible to see how proud they are of their work.

Absentmindedly playing with my necklace, I move to inspect the next piece. Pen and ink over splotchy watercolor, it depicts a teenage boy with a ball cap on backward—sort of a bust viewed from behind. I lean in to read the tag; it's by one of the youth in Ada's group: Rolando Esposito, age fifteen. He's good. His hat reminds me a little of Miles.

I slowly drift over to the next painting, but I barely have time to take it in before Miles comes up behind me and slips a palm over my right hip, warming my skin through the fabric of my ruby shift dress. He dips down to kiss my cheek. "Hey."

"I was just thinking about you," I say, half turning toward him.

"Good." He draws in close, pressing against my back in a way that makes me close my eyes to drink in the sensation. I have to remind myself to focus on the art in front of us. It's a surrealist piece: a woman hovering above a collection of outstretched, claw-like hands. She's positioned in a deep backbend, and an explosion of color erupts from her abdomen and ripples outward. I peek at the small card on the wall. *"Jesse's Girl."*

"Oh, this is Ada's piece!" I say, grabbing the arm Miles has wrapped around my waist.

"Man, Ada's fucking killing it." Adrian's familiar voice comes from over my shoulder.

"Hey!" Stepping out of Miles' arms, I twist around to pull Adrian into a tight hug. "And seriously, yes, she's incredible."

"I had no idea how good she'd gotten."

The three of us turn back to admire Ada's work for another beat before Adrian breaks the silence. "Anyway, Care, I have fucking incredible news."

"What?" I ask, brightening as I turn to him again.

"Guess who just secured a substantial new donor?" He points both thumbs at his chest, then adds, "Well, for next year, anyway."

"What? Shut up!" I break out in a wide grin. "Who is it?"

"Uh, this older Lennox couple? Charles and Carol Faulkner. They run this bed-and-breakfast where my buddy, Kai, got married last summer. I guess their kids are grown and they wanted to do something for youth. That woman is *chatty*. Talked my ear off for ages. She *might* have been flirting with me."

I laugh. "You think everyone's flirting with you."

"Must be a relief," Miles says, then rushes to add, "The donation part, I mean."

"Seriously." Adrian's eyes widen and he nods. "Anyway, I gotta do the rounds. I left Casey with Marcus and Renee, and I wanna catch up with them."

"Yeah, yeah, go. Do your thing," I rush to say, then grab his arm. "Wait, Casey? As in big, sexy puppy Casey? I thought—"

"Yeah, well, things might have changed," Adrian says, with an almost coy little half shrug. "I'll tell you more later."

The moment Adrian leaves, Miles slips his arms around my waist again from behind. I turn my head and he noses my cheek. "Mmm, speaking of big sexy puppies…"

"Uh, should I be flattered?" When I lift a brow and nod, he smiles, then leans in close, dropping his voice to whisper in my ear. "Meet me in our room."

I straighten. "What? Right now?"

"Yeah, right now," he rumbles against my cheek.

"But won't people notice?" I say softly, looking around to make sure no one will overhear us.

"Not if we're quick about it."

I turn to gaze up at him, both stunned by his audacity and, admittedly, already planning my escape. Getting a hotel room for the night was definitely the right move—a silver lining of being on the outs with my parents, I guess.

"Unless you think they need you down here," he says. His focus drops to my mouth and he bends to kiss me.

"No, I don't think— I mean, everything's running pretty smoothly."

"Okay," he says. "You wanna try something from your list?"

Mind reeling, I can only nod.

Yes, please. Whatever it is, I'm in.

"That's my girl." His lips curl in approval. "I'll give you a ten-minute head start." With a wink, he walks away, all calm and collected while I'm left with my heart pounding so loud I'm sure the other patrons will hear it.

God, he looks good.

He may not be in a tuxedo this time, but that tailored charcoal suit I got him as an early Christmas present has been testing my restraint all night.

When I arrive in our room, the chair is already set up; Miles must have snuck up while I was helping Adrian get ready to open the show. There's a towel draped over the seat, along with two strips of silky fabric and a scrawled note.

I want you naked, ankles tied to the chair legs.
The safe word is aubergine.

A thrill courses through my center as I quickly shed my clothes, following orders. I'm grinning as I snug the bow over my left ankle, and I have to fight off a giggle by the time I'm done tying the one on the right. I straighten in my seat, biting my lip as I grapple with the heady, nervous arousal lighting up my entire body.

What is my life?

The door clicks open and my heart leaps.

Miles is already tugging off his tie when he slips inside the door, his eyes darkening the moment they lock on mine.

I shift back on the seat, swallowing my nerves as he stalks toward me.

When he closes the distance between us, he grips my jaw in one hand, towering over me as he jerks my face up.

With a gasp, I arch my back.

"Fuck. You're perfect." His gaze lingers on my lips another moment before he bends down and takes my mouth with his.

And I mean *takes it*. Devours it. It's drugging and deep; every stroke of his tongue, each scrape of his teeth, sends a swirling pulse of pleasure straight to my toes. I'll never get sick of being kissed like this. Consumed like this. I'm arching, swaying, bending, and begging for more, like if I meet him without backing down, I might have a hope in hell of holding onto some scrap of control—of not falling apart under him right here, right now.

But maybe I don't want to be in control anymore. Maybe I want to fall apart. *Need* to fall apart.

When he breaks away, his lids are hooded over dark, blown pupils. He straightens, backing away a couple steps, and the loss makes my core ache.

He shrugs off his suit jacket and tosses it on the bed, then starts to unbutton his shirt.

I swallow, heat creeping up my neck and cheeks as my fingers drift between my legs.

"Uh-uh." He shakes his head. "Not yet."

My brows twitch with need, but I stop, stroking my thighs instead.

"Such a good listener."

His gaze rakes over my body as one hand falls to his belt. A muscle in his jaw ticks as he eases the leather from the prong and flicks the buckle loose, the clink of metal strangely erotic. Then, without breaking eye contact, he pulls the length of it free in one swift, snapping tug.

Something inside me snaps along with it and my fingers find my center again.

"Ah, ah, ah," Miles cautions. "What did I say?"

I bite my lip and keep stroking my clit, my vision glazing over. "So make me stop."

"Bratty fucking girl. Arms behind your back." Belt in his grasp, Miles circles me like a cat stalking its prey then drops to his knees behind my chair. As he wraps my wrists together, I realize I'm trembling. He seems to notice, too, and kisses my shoulder. "You good?"

"Yes," I whisper. "Just nervous."

Nervous and wildly, inexplicably, uncontrollably turned on.

"It's okay to be nervous," he says quietly.

"I feel kind of... I dunno."

Silly? Vulnerable? Raw?

"Hey," he says, moving back in front of me. Hooking his finger under my chin, he lifts my face. "You might be tied up, but you're still running this show. You can tell me to stop anytime. *Anytime.* You understand?"

I nod, then remember his note.

"Why *aubergine*?" I ask, my voice soft.

He slowly rolls one shirtsleeve and the sight of those forearms flexing has my imagination spinning one filthy thought after the other. A hint of a dimple appears on his cheek and his shoulder lifts in a half shrug that's equally boyish and exceptionally sexy. "I dunno. Fancy word for my fancy girl, I guess."

"And because of the eggplant emoji, I assume?" I raise a brow.

Miles fakes shock and moves to roll up the other sleeve. "You know about the *eggplant emoji*?"

"Hey!" I let out a small, rueful laugh. "I know things."

"You know things, huh?" He unfastens his pants, and my mouth starts to water.

"Mm-hmm." A shiver slips down my spine and I squirm in the chair, unable to shift much with my ankles and wrists bound.

"What, baby?" His voice is a deep drawl. "You wanna move?"

Biting my lip, I nod.

"Well, you don't get to yet. Not before I play with you." He strokes my cheek. "Now, open that gorgeous mouth for me."

I drop my jaw, exhaling hard.

"Fuck," he barely whispers, dragging a thumb over my lower lip.

My tongue darts out to lick it, seemingly of its own volition.

"So pretty when you do what I say."

"Please," I beg as he pulls his underwear down, freeing his thick cock.

There's a gentle warning in his gaze as he tips up my chin. "Please what?" He waits until I lift my eyes. "Come on. Say it."

My core pulses at his commanding tone. "Please, sir."

"Better." Miles grazes his open palm over my curls, his brow pinching as if he's holding himself back. "God, I just wanna sink my fingers into your hair, but…" Instead, he holds my face in both hands, pressing the crown of his dick between my lips, his voice wavering with restraint as he says, "But it's so pretty. Wouldn't wanna mess it up—" He shudders out a moan as his thick warmth slowly fills my mouth. "Jesus, Caroline."

I whimper as he withdraws before sliding in again, once, twice, until he's slick and speeding up.

His grip tightens on my cheeks. "Fuck, you feel so good."

A heavy heat gathers in my core as I lick and suck—welcoming him, opening for him, letting him use my mouth like this. I tilt my chin slightly, experimenting with the angle. When he pushes deeper, it's more than I can bear and I jerk my knees together in a vain attempt at relief.

"You okay?" He pulls out to let me speak.

I nod, willing him closer. "More. Don't stop."

"Fucking hell." Slowly, he runs the tip of his cock around the outer edge of my lips.

I try to move to take him but he grabs my jaw, holding me still. "Greedy girl," he almost growls as he finishes the slow, teasing circle. "Gimme that tongue."

I stick it out and jolt with need when he slaps his hard shaft against it a few times, each strike sending a pulse of hot mayhem through my body. When he drives into my mouth once more, I arch and strain to get closer, taking each thrust deeper with a shaky moan that's only silenced by him filling my throat. I can't breathe, I can't speak, I can't make a sound—and the pleasure is exquisite.

He tenses, hips bucking faster. "Fuck, baby, I'm already close."

I tighten my lips around him, fighting uselessly to get my hands free, to touch him, to press my thighs together—*anything* to ease this ache.

"Don't swallow," he bites out between thrusts. "When I come, don't you fucking swallow."

My eyes fly up to his, but I manage a small nod, tilting my hips against the nothingness between my legs.

Faster, harder, he fucks my mouth until I hear that familiar catch in his throat, that stutter and gasp, then the silence before he breaks.

"Fffuuuuck!" he groans as he spills onto my tongue and I almost come with him—without even being touched.

I suck up every drop, struggling to hold it without swallowing; I want him inside me any way I can get him.

"Show me," he grits out as he withdraws. With one hand, he grasps my chin, tilting my head up. "Open up and show me."

I obey, entranced by his request and the way my core pulses from the act of compliance alone.

"Look at that," he drawls as he tugs my jaw down and pushes me back slightly. "Now let it out for me. Let it fall, honey."

His cum spills from my lips, its warmth dripping down my belly and over my pussy. I moan in some kind of sex-induced stupor, lost in this profoundly filthy act. I've never done anything like this before. Never wanted this kind of thing before. But, with Miles, I want to push against the edges—brush up against too much and flirt with too far, safe in the knowledge that he's got me.

"God, just look at this pretty little mess we made," Miles says, slipping his fingers through his release, painting my pussy with it as he lowers to his knees between my legs.

"Miles..." My voice falters when he cups his free hand behind my neck and leans in close.

"Caroline," he teases as he thumbs the wetness from my lower lip. Then, in the same moment, he crushes me in a kiss and drives his slick fingers deep inside my core.

The relief is intense and I cry out into his mouth, trembling as pleasure rocks through my entire body. When he pumps his fingers, I buck against my restraints, desperate to chase the sensation.

He breaks the kiss and tilts his head, a slow grin spreading over his features. "God, you're fucking feral for more, huh?"

"Please," I beg. Fighting the restraints once again, I try to move toward him. "Please."

He pulls his fingers out and glides them softly over my slick pussy. Too softly. "Please what, pretty girl?"

"Please, just..." I pant, the desperation growing intolerable. "I need to come."

He tuts. "Bad girl." His voice is like velvet as he flicks my clit, sending an arc of electric heat through my center that threatens to undo me. "You forgot how to ask."

I meet his gaze with a heady mixture of lust and resentment.

"You know it's 'please, *sir*'."

I swear, I'd keel over if I wasn't tied to this chair. I try again. "Please, sir." Pleasure rips through my body when he drives his fingers back inside me. "Oh, God!"

"Shhh..." Miles shakes his head, though I don't miss the sly smile as he clamps his free hand over my mouth. "Can't let anyone hear my little slut begging to come, can we?"

I'm shaking. I might actually fall apart.

"I can't—" I try to say, though my voice is muffled against his palm. Shuddering and frenzied, I try to stifle my moans as he rubs my clit with his thumb, working his fingers at some new, delicious angle.

"If you make too much noise," his voice is slow and liquid, "we'll have to stop."

The violent way I shake my head has him chuckling.

"No, huh?"

"Mm-mmm." My eyes are pleading when they meet his.

"Aw, my bratty whore just needs to come so bad."

I nod, desperation holding me in its grip.

"Alright, then," he says, adding another finger that makes my vision blur. "Here's what's gonna happen: you're gonna ride my hand until you come so hard you can't see straight."

"Mm-hmm." I nod again.

Already there.

"And you're gonna be nice and quiet."

Yes. Anything.

"Then you're gonna slip those panties back on," he adds, his gaze dropping to where his fingers curl delicious strokes against my inner walls, "over our little mess down here."

The visual floods my senses and I swallow.

Miles continues, dropping gentle kisses on my neck. "You're gonna get back in your pretty red dress and come downstairs with me." He sucks my earlobe and a shiver rocks me from head to toe. "And the only one who's gonna know what a *dirty, filthy slut* you've been..."—he pumps his fingers hard, and I moan against his palm—"... is me."

I'm suddenly desperate to do exactly that. To share this secret with him.

Carefully, he lifts his palm away from my mouth. "Can you do that for me?" Then, as if to test me, he pulls out to deliver a quick slap to my clit.

I gasp, barely stifling a cry, and try to hum through the pleasure instead.

"Attagirl," he praises, stroking my cheek with his free hand. He sinks his fingers back inside me and speeds up, drawing me closer and closer to unraveling.

My core tenses and my breaths catch and shudder, as if the air in my lungs is fighting to hold itself steady—my throat wrestling to contain every scream and moan I'm desperate to let out.

"That's it," Miles encourages, fucking me faster with his fingers as I tip over the edge. "Let go. Fall apart. Oh, *fuck*, you're doing so good for me, baby."

He crushes me in another deep, consuming kiss the moment my release slams into me. I cry into his mouth when he slips his fingers out and rubs them over my clit in fast circles, drawing me into more blissful, pulsing ecstasy.

As the tension in my body slackens, he breaks away and brings his fingers up to my lips.

In an addled daze, I hesitate.

"Clean it up."

My tongue responds as if of its own volition, lapping and

sucking at his fingers like they're my last meal, the echoes of my orgasm still tripping through my core.

"God, your tongue..." His jaw clenches. "Fuck. See how good we taste?"

I nod, confirming I've lost my ever-loving mind.

When he finally releases me from all the restraints, he takes my hand and pulls me up from the chair. It's an almost gentlemanly move, contrasting starkly with the way he just tied me up, fucked my mouth, and had me spit his cum onto my...

Jesus. Even the memory makes the heavy heat between my legs throb.

I'm still so out of it, I barely register him finding my discarded clothes and kneeling at my feet. The slight smirk on his face as he helps me step into my panties is almost more than I can bear. When he slowly slides them up, gently covering my swollen, slick center, I have to look away.

Too handsome. I might die—or come again—if I make direct eye contact.

I don't know how, but we go through the motions of cleaning up and getting dressed in a haze—the kind of satisfied, sleepy warmth that makes me wish we could skip the rest of the event and bask in this bliss together for hours.

"You sure you don't wanna call any of your old friends while we're in the city?" I ask as he shrugs on his suit jacket.

"I'm sure," he says as he buttons it. Closing the small distance between us, he tugs me closer by my waist. "Those friendships weren't what I thought they were. Feels like a past life, and not one I wanna dredge back up, honestly." He brushes a thumb over my cheek, then dips down to kiss me. "This right here is what I wanna focus on. My life with you."

Despite my reluctance to leave our little bubble, Miles coaxes me out the door. The wet, sticky heat between my legs stirs the embers of my arousal with each step I take, every shift of my hips reminding me of our dirty secret and his earnest promise of round two later tonight.

I soak up our last moments alone as the elevator whirs its way down to the main floor. Between the feeling of Miles' big, warm hands on my back and the way he murmurs that he loves me with his lips smushed against my forehead, it's hard to want anything but more of this. More of *him*.

Before I'm ready to face it, we step back into the fray of the bustling art show and make our way through the crowd.

Julian catches my eye and winds between the other patrons as he approaches. "Caroline."

"Julian," I say. "You remember Miles?"

"Right, yes." Julian gives Miles a tight smile. "Nice to see you again. And, uh, apologies if we got off on the wrong foot when you first came to the gallery."

"Oh, no, that's—" Miles glances my way, looking slightly awkward, before returning his gaze to the older man as they shake hands. "All good. Nice to see you too."

"Listen, Caroline," Julian starts, shifting his attention to me, "I wanted to say, you've done a wonderful job with the show tonight."

"Oh," I manage, trying to hide my surprise at the compliment, cutting my gaze to Miles when he squeezes my fingers. "Thank you. I mean, it's been a team effort, really."

"Well," he says, "I'll be eager to see your plans for the spring exhibition at the Gareth Mason."

A grin splits my face; I can't wait to show him what I've got up my sleeve—and introduce him to some unique new art. "Thank you, yes!" I finally manage, delighted and a bit thrown by the way he's come around.

"Julian! There you are!" Sunny's familiar voice comes from somewhere behind me and Miles. As we spin around, his elbow collides with the glass in her hand, sloshing its contents over the rim. Half the drink spills onto Sunny and the rest splats onto the floor.

"Shit, sorry," he says, wide-eyed. "I can, uh... I can get you another one."

"Oh, it's only water. I'll live." She waves him off.

A nearby volunteer snags a couple cocktail napkins and passes one to Sunny, who blots at her loose-fitting, flowy dress.

"Think we'll need a few more for the floor," Miles says, and the guy scurries off for reinforcements.

Sunny passes her glass to Julian, moving to pull off her many rings. "Caroline, darling, hold these for me, would you?"

"Oh! Uh, sure." I collect them in my palm and give her a moment to pat her hands dry.

The volunteer returns with some paper towels, and he and Miles crouch down to clean up the small puddle on the floor.

"Thank you," Sunny says. One by one, she plucks each ring from my palm, sliding them delicately over her fingers. "You know, I just hate that wet feeling under my rings and— oh!" The last ring slips from her grasp and falls to the floor, skittering a couple feet away.

"I got it!" Miles says. "Here."

It's only when the camera flash goes off that I realize how this looks; Miles is down on one knee, holding a ring toward us. Toward *me*.

In a stunned moment of slow-mo understanding, Miles glances down at the ring, then at me, then does a double take at the photographer.

Tripping through my own state of shock, it takes me a moment to process the recognition on his face. I turn toward the man with the camera, my jaw dropping.

Blond, curly hair. That newsboy cap.

The moaner's wide eyes flit between the two of us and he clutches his camera to his chest.

With resigned amusement, Miles drags himself up to his full height as the guy silently shuffles backward, then pivots on his heel and strides clear across the room without turning back.

"Well," Miles says to me, passing Sunny her ring. "That just happened."

"At least he kept his mouth shut this time?" I laugh and wrap my arms around his waist, lifting on tiptoe to kiss his cheek. "Should we track him down and explain?"

"Nah." He glances toward the moaner once more, then hugs me close, pressing a kiss to the top of my head. "I don't think he'll be brave enough to do anything with that photo. And, even if he did, worst-case scenario is, what? Someone spreads a rumor that we're happy?"

I gaze up into his blue eyes, my safe harbor, feeling like my heart might burst.

"Think we can handle that," he adds. "Right?"

I nod and lift up again to kiss him.

Because he's right. We can handle anything.

EPILOGUE
MILES

Eight months later

"My feet are killing me," Caroline sighs, picking her way toward her front door in bare feet, a pair of bright turquoise heels dangling from her finger-tips. She sweeps a stray curl from her eyes and glances over at me, her voice breathy when she adds, "But that was so much fun."

"Yeah." I reach for her hand when she wobbles, steadying her. "Still kinda bananas that my brother's married now."

Humming a soft sound of agreement, she digs out her keys, then seems to notice I'm hanging back. "You coming?" She throws me an expectant look over her shoulder as she unlocks the door.

"Yeah, in a sec." I stretch my neck. "Gonna stay out here for a few. Get some fresh air."

"Okay."

I cross the porch and pull her close for a kiss. "I won't be long."

"Good," she murmurs against my lips.

I jog down the steps as she disappears inside, then quickly check my phone. It's one in the morning. I'm beyond beat, but I can't resist a quiet moment alone, with only the burbling river as my acoustic backdrop. After all the loud music, talking, and shouting over the noise at Jude and Olena's wedding, my ears are almost ringing. With a deep inhale, I let nature's version of quiet wash over me. A bat skitters across the night sky somewhere to my left, and I can just make out the occasional hoot of an unseen owl across the river.

My nocturnal buddies.

I cast a glance back at the house. Caroline's huge bedroom window glows golden in the night and I catch sight of her moving through the room inside, her arms up as she shakes out her hair.

Stepping a few paces to my left, I position myself better to watch her.

Anywhere else in town, she'd have drawn the curtains for privacy, but, out here, she can brazenly undress in front of an open window without worrying about prying eyes. It's only me here, drinking in the sight of my girl as she slips out of her flowy yellow dress.

Fuck, she's beautiful.

It's been almost a year since we met, and I still can't help but stare at her every chance I get. It's been like this since that first morning at the gym.

Caroline disappears from view and I stuff my hands into my pockets, letting my gaze drop as I toe at the scattered gravel and dry pine needles at my feet. When my attention snags on a small pine cone, some obscure recess of my brain lights up.

I don't throw it hard—just enough to make contact with her window.

Nothing.

It doesn't take long to find another one, and I give it a bit more juice.

Caroline reappears wearing only her bra, panties, and an adorably confused frown. I've got no complaints about my view when she presses against the glass and shields her eyes to peer out into the night.

I wave when she spots me, then gesture for her to come join me outside.

She throws her arms out at her sides but turns from the window to grab her little silk robe. Moments later, the front door opens and she peeks out at me, tying the belt. "What's going on?" she calls over, slipping on a pair of sandals on the porch.

"Just c'mere."

"I was gonna get in the shower."

"We'll shower after." I hold out my hand as she comes down the steps to meet me.

She looks suspicious. "After what?"

I kiss her forehead, then draw back and start guiding her along with me toward the river's edge.

"Miles, I'm not dressed."

"Perfect." I'm already unbuttoning my shirt as we carefully make our way down the hill. "Because you've still never been skinny dipping. It's the last thing left on your fuck-it list, right?"

"What? No! What?" she stammers, snugging her robe tighter to her chest. "Now? Here?"

"No one's around; you live in the middle of nowhere!"

"I dunno," she says, scanning around us like someone might jump out of the bushes at one in the morning.

"The season's finally right." I can tell she's tempted. "The water will be warm enough now. C'mon." We stop at the river-bank and I tug off my dress shirt before draping it over a rock. I toe off my shoes and socks, and I'm busy emptying my pockets when I catch her staring at me, frozen. I laugh. "Get naked already!"

"That's..." Her gaze slips down my chest as I straighten.

I glance down, inspecting myself, before meeting her eyes again. "What?"

"That's not a bad look. Just dress pants and nothing else."

"Yeah?" I step closer, pulling her into my arms. Brushing my lips over her cheek, I whisper, "You know what this reminds me of?" I tuck my index finger under the strip of silk around her waist and tug it loose. "That night you came over to my place." Opening her robe, I make a little groaning sound and slide my palms around her bare waist. "Wearing just a coat over that sexy fucking lingerie."

"Oh my God," she sighs, letting her gaze drop. "Still can't believe I did that."

I press my lips to her forehead as I unhook her bra. "Well, *I'll* never fucking forget it."

She kisses my shoulder and peers around us one last time before letting me slip her robe and bra from her shoulders. Kicking off her sandals, she steps back and tugs down her panties, eyeing me with a warning glare. "If we get caught, I'm telling the police this was all your doing."

"We're not gonna get caught." I step out of my pants and underwear, chucking them onto our pile of clothes, then reach for her hand.

Walking backward, I wade into the water. The river feels incredible—warm enough to be comfortable, but cool enough to soothe.

Caroline steps in after me, shoulders shrugged to her ears, and sucks in a soft gasp when she gets deep enough for the water to hit more sensitive places. The current flows gently against our skin, taking with it all the salty, sticky sweat from dancing all night.

I sink under the water, scrubbing my dripping hair back from my forehead when I resurface. Reaching for Caroline, I ask, "You alright?"

She lets me drag her against me, dropping her arms around my neck with a satisfied little hum. "Yeah. It feels really nice, actually."

"See? You were missing out. This is good shit."

"*You* feel really nice too." She drags her fingers down my chest and her hands disappear under the water, trailing over my waist, then sliding around my hips to my ass.

I reach down to adjust my erection, pinning it between us with a smirk. "Ignore him. He saw your boobs in the moonlight and he's feeling romantic."

She laughs and brushes her lips over mine, loosely stroking me under the water. "Well, I wasn't planning on ignoring him."

I don't know whether it's a second wind, the whole naked-in-nature thing, or the fact that my beautiful girl is stroking my dick, but when I kiss her, it's like something primal inside me wakes up. My veins fill with a vital thrum and my cock pulses against her palm. I deepen the kiss, taking her face in both hands, and moan when she squeezes on the upstroke.

She pulls back and peers up at me, still working me in her fist. "Why are you looking at me like that?"

"Like what?" I let out a low hum of pleasure.

"Like you wanna, I dunno,"—she arches a brow—"howl at the moon and beat your chest and drag me back to your cave?"

"You got all that from a look?" And here I thought I was the one who had a good read on people.

She fakes a gasp. "You're not, like, a secret werewolf, are you? Or some time-traveling caveman?"

"Well," I say, nipping at her lower lip, "I do like the idea of dragging you back to my cave. Respectfully, of course."

Her fingers tighten around me. "Mmm, well, I'd respectfully be okay with that."

"But, seeing as I have no time machine... and no cave," I say, my voice wavering as I graze her tits with my knuckles, "I guess you're stuck with a modern guy with a shitty apartment."

"I'm *not* stuck with you." She tilts her head. "And your apartment isn't shitty."

"Um, yes, it is." I throw a pointed glance at her house on the hillside. "Compared to this place? C'mon, we both know you won the house lottery."

"I guess." Her features pinch with guilt.

Accepting the house has been tricky for her. George, for his part, is delighted to have helped her stay in the home she loves. He reminds her of this every weekend when we visit him between his chair yoga class and crossword club—dude is *living it up* in that care home—but I know Caroline sometimes worries it was too much. It's an incredibly generous gift.

"Anyway, like I said, I'm a modern guy." I smirk and pinch her nipples hard enough to make her gasp. "And this modern guy will happily howl at the moon then drag you back to *your* cave."

"Well, what if it was *our* cave?" She peers up at me, slowing her strokes.

"W-what?" I sputter and she stills.

Those crystal eyes look almost gray in the moonlight. "Move in with me."

"Hold on. What? Wait…"

"I have this huge house, and you're here all the time, anyway."

"Just…"—I swallow and pull her hands away—"stop touching my dick for a sec so I can think, here."

An amused patience dances in her expression, like she's used to my chaotic thought spirals by now.

"Are you sure?" When she nods, I rush to add, "I don't want this to be a convenience thing, like a practical shrug or some shit 'cause I'm here all the time." I slide my palms up her arms. "Baby, do you *want* to live with me? For real?"

"You're surprised?" She takes my face in her hands, brushing a thumb over the scar at the corner of my mouth. "I love you, Miles. Of course I want to live with you."

"Oh my God," I murmur before I scoop her up and spin us

around, peppering kisses all over her cheeks, her nose, her forehead. "I love you too. So *fucking much*."

Giggling, she wraps her legs around my waist and crushes her lips into mine.

When I draw back, I whoop, swiping at the water and sending a splash into the air beside us. "Shit, now I really *am* thinking about howling at the moon."

Her laughter is like beautiful music. "I take that as a yes?"

"Yes! Fuck yes!" I can't stop grinning.

"Good!" She wipes away a droplet of water running down my forehead.

I snag her hand and kiss her fingertips. "Man, I can't believe I got myself a sugar mama. Wha— Hey!" I protest when she whacks me, only squeezing her tighter, and drop my voice low. "Wait, was that not what you were offering?"

Caroline groans. "Immediate regret. I take it all back. Rescinded."

"Nah, no backsies." I squeeze her ass. "I'm your fancy boy now."

"Oh my God, *stop*," she says through laughter, which quickly escalates to shrieking giggles when I bite my lip and start doing goofy, haphazard hip thrusts.

"C'mon," I say, chuckling as I set her on her feet. "Let's go in." I lead her toward our pile of clothes on the riverbank, trying to sluice some of the water from my skin.

I drag my pants back over my wet legs, hating the sensation but too tired and too in love with my girl to give a shit.

She wants to live with me.

Caroline tugs on her robe and picks up her bra and panties to carry back.

"Hey, fancy girl?" I ask as I snatch up the rest of my stuff. I toss my shirt over my damp shoulder and tuck my phone and keys back into my pockets.

She looks up, squeezing a trickle of water from the ends of her hair. "Yeah?"

"You still up for trying new things?" Other than skinny dipping, we'd checked everything else off her fuck-it list months ago, along with a few unplanned side quests. These days, she's always game to try something new and I fucking love how brave she's become since we met—how open we can be together as we explore what she likes. Well, what we both like, really; I've had some firsts along the way too.

"At this time of night?" She slips on her sandals.

"Hey, I think all that dancing earned us both a sleep-in tomorrow." It's one of the few times I'll justify skipping my morning workout. I can already feel the muscle aches setting into all those little places the gym doesn't touch.

Do I need to start training the tops of my feet, somehow?

Quickly checking I've got the last of my things, I reach for Caroline's hand. "Unless you want me comatose when we go meet your mom for lunch."

"No," she says quickly, throwing me a wide-eyed look as we head for the house. "We need to be on our game for that."

Caroline and Valerie have been reconnecting lately. It's been slow and cautious, but promising. I think finding out her mom served her dad with divorce papers a couple months ago gave Caroline permission to start over, in a way.

Personally, I'm hoping Valerie takes that rat bastard for all he's worth.

"Anyway, what—" she starts, then fails to fight off a yawn. "What did you have in mind? For tonight?"

"Well..." I scoop her into my side as we walk up the hill, draping my arm around her shoulders. "Let's just say I hope you're ready to get fucked slow and cuddle-puddled hard."

"Mmm, sounds delicious." She bites her lip, then grabs my

chin and plants a kiss on my cheek. "But is that really new? Like, we've done that plenty of times before, haven't we?"

I stop walking and she turns to face me. "Not in *our* house, we haven't."

"Aww." With a melty little smile, she slips her arms around my waist. "*Our house.* I love it."

"But, like, if you wanna go *new* new, I mean..." I narrow my eyes, raising a brow. "You still got that glittery tentacle dildo?"

CAROLINE'S FUCK-IT LIST

~~Skinny dipping~~

~~Outdoor sex~~

~~Multiple orgasms~~ !!!

~~Using sex toys~~

~~Getting tied up~~

~~Spanking~~

~~Phone sex~~

~~Hair pulling~~

~~Exchanging nudes~~

~~Squirting?~~

~~Deep throat?~~

~~Blindfolded~~

~~Lingerie under a coat~~

ALSO BY HANNAH BRIXTON

Loved **Sweet Caroline**? Read more from the *Lennox Valley Chronicles*:

Book 1

Hey Jude

https://mybook.to/heyjude

Book 2

Jesse's Girl

https://mybook.to/jessesgirl

Book 4

Title TBA (pre-order now!)

https://mybook.to/LVC4

ACKNOWLEDGMENTS

I have so many beautiful humans to thank for their part in bringing *Sweet Caroline* from a fuzzy concept to a dreamy reality.

To Andrea Bugslag: Thank you for loving me through all my arm-waving, messy thoughts about my fictional friends. You always meet me where I'm at, are always so understanding about my chaos brain, and I love that you genuinely want to hear about my books over tea. This story—and Lennox Valley in general—wouldn't exist without you! I'm so lucky to have you in my life! Gold stars, friendo.

To Katie Van Brunt: Thank you for always making the time to put on the popcorn (or coffee) and listen to my rambly podcasts (voice memos) about everything from writing spicy scenes to our bunny/squirrel brains. Being your friend-from-afar has been such a joy over the last year-plus. I can't wait to squeeze you someday! (And yes, the butt stuff manifestation joke was an Easter egg just for you!)

To Miley Howard: Thank you for encouraging all my chaos in the best way and for lending your brain beans to workshop Miles and Caroline—especially their encounters with the infamous moaner! You're my soul sister and a gem, and I can't wait to hear what unhinged middle names you give to these characters.

To Cherry Keeley, Genesis Bird, and Laura-Elise Bishop: Thank you always for your friendship, your honesty, and your compassion for me and each other as we all navigate this messy author thing. We've all come a long way, and I'm so glad to be on this roller coaster with you three!

To Kari and Emily, my sensitivity readers: Thank you for trusting me to portray Miles' sobriety journey with care and for your input about the nuances of his recovery. Special shout-out to Kari for going above and beyond as a beta reader (and re-reader) and for laughing at that one extra joke I just had to add. Your love for Miles and Caroline was exactly what my heart needed, and I can't thank you enough!

To the rest of my beta reader team—Elsie, Nicole, Prerna, Riya, Katie, Heather, Sarah, Breanna, Cherry, Jess, Sophie, and Jessica: Thank you massively for all your help and support in talking through everything big and small about *Sweet Caroline*. I'm sorry for making most of you cry! (Y'know, in a sorry-not-sorry kind of way.)

To my Street Team: You are such a bunch of fabulous babes for volunteering your time to support me and hype up my work. Thank you for all the love, the screaming from the rooftops, and the chaotically unhinged discussions (looking at you, Kitty)!

To Laura at Hummingbird Editing: Thank you for helping me write and edit the dreaded blurb! Working with you was lovely!

To my fabulous editor, Myranda Bolstad: Thank you for all the warm encouragement and every "you got this" you sent me along the way. You're incredibly patient and flexible, and I am deeply grateful to be able to entrust my work to such capable hands. You're awesome!

To my husband: Thank you for bringing me coffee, for brainstorming with me, and for being my own personal handsome goofball. I couldn't have written this book (or any book) without you. I love you so fucking much!

To my kids: Thank you for being my tiny (okay, not so tiny anymore) cheerleaders! You are three incredibly kind and empa-

thetic people and you're so unapologetically yourselves. I love you all and I'm bonkers proud of you!

To my mom: Thank you for giving me the gift of words, for encouraging me to write, and for cheering me on! Love you!

Finally, to Sara Nicoll, for enduring the real moaner with me: Bet you never thought that bozo would end up in a romance novel, but life is weird like that. I love you, pal!

ABOUT THE BOOK

This story might be titled *Sweet Caroline* but, in my heart, it's Miles' book. In many ways, writing it felt like hanging out with an old friend. Since Miles originally showed up as a side character in my debut, *Hey Jude*, it feels like he and I go way back. There's so much of me in him, especially his sense of humor, his clumsy goofball moments, and the way his brain works. It was so much fun to explore ADHD from the male perspective in this book, and I loved getting to dive into Miles' head and tease out more of his personality—and his struggles.

In terms of the sobriety and mental health themes touched on, it was important to me to show that Miles saved himself, rather than depending on Caroline to rescue him. Because, as Caroline herself rightly said, love isn't enough; it doesn't fix or cure everything. True change has to come from within, and Miles had to grapple with his sobriety and his mental health in order to realize he could trust himself to fully show up for a relationship with her. His change and growth wasn't *for* Caroline, but *alongside* her.

Readers might notice Caroline didn't drink a drop of alcohol throughout this book. And her abstinence wasn't just to protect Miles in his sobriety; even before she learned he was a recovering alcoholic on the night of the fundraiser, she wasn't drinking. This was intentional. Given Pete was likely a high-functioning alcoholic himself, I wanted to show Caroline rejecting the toxic example her dad had set as a step on her journey to finding her own voice and finally standing up for herself. I loved how falling for Miles empowered her to be her authentic self, and how she needed him just as much as he needed her.

Getting to write Miles and Caroline their hard-won happily ever after was such a gift. I hope readers will see *Sweet Caroline* as a story of hope. Please know that, even when things feel fucking impossible—even through grief, addiction, family strife, shitty relationships, and/or mental illness—it can get better.

♡ Hannah Brixton

Note: If you struggle with alcohol dependence, please reach out for help. Alcoholics Anonymous (https://www.aa.org/) is one program of many that exist to support people who want to get and stay sober. If someone else's drinking has affected you, Al-Anon (https://al-anon.org/) is also a resource for mutual support. Finally, if you or someone you love is struggling with an acute mental health crisis, please reach out and get the help you need. Dial 9-8-8 anywhere in the US or Canada to access year-round crisis and suicide prevention support 24/7. Internationally, please visit Find a Helpline (https://findahelpline.com/).

ABOUT THE AUTHOR

Hannah Brixton lives with her husband, three children, and two cats on beautiful Vancouver Island in British Columbia, Canada. In her spare time, she loves to read, listen to podcasts, and sing along loudly to music that embarrasses her children.

Hannah Brixton's books are available on Amazon

Contact Hannah:
Email: hannah@hannahbrixton.com
Website: www.hannahbrixton.com

Subscribe to Hannah's Newsletter:
https://hannah-brixton-author.kit.com/f8158e2beb

Follow Hannah:
@hannah.brixton on **Instagram**
@hannah.brixton.author on **Tiktok**
@hannah.brixton.author on **Facebook**
@Hannah Brixton on **Goodreads**
@hannahbrixtonauthor on **Pinterest**

www.ingramcontent.com/pod-product-compliance
Lightning Source LLC
Chambersburg PA
CBHW061614210726
48287CB00001B/127